For the Love of Charley

Book Three In the Romance In the Yukon Series

By

Patty Schramm

©2021 by Patty Schramm

First publication 2021
Flashpoint Publications

ISBN 978-1-949096-28-6

Cover Design by AcornGraphics

Editors Verda Foster and Nann Dunne

Publisher's Note:

Acknowledgments

To my many beta readers; Sharon G. Clark, Brenda Adcock, Trinka
Kittle, Mary Hettel, Jeanine Hoffman; you all are the best. Especially
since some of you, Sharon and Bren, read this monster more than once. I
can't thank you all enough.

To Lori L. Lake for being my "third" editor, as always, thanks for your
help. I'm a better writer cause of you.

To Verda--thanks for making sure my timeline is accurate.

To Nann--thanks for fixing my commas. LOL.

But most especially I want to acknowledge my esteemed friend, Renee
Bess, who was my sensitivity reader. I can't thank you enough, but I'm
sure I can send you some goodies from my side of the Atlantic.
Seriously, I had a lot of things wrong and without your guidance I don't
think the book would have been any good.

Dedication

To Lori L. Lake. Mentor. Friend. Big Brother. Love you! p.s. Your head is bigger than mine!

Chapter One

Blood seeped under the partially open bathroom door.

Her skin was grey and mottled.

The shotgun lay across her torso.

Charley Townsend screamed, but there was no sound. She sat bolt upright in bed. Cold sweat covered her trembling body, the residual effects of the nightmare, more vivid than usual and hard to shake. She tried breathing techniques to calm the hammering of her heart. Her breaths slowed and her pulse eased to a normal beat.

She glanced at the clock. Ten past five in the morning. She'd managed almost three hours of restless sleep. Tossing the duvet off as she rose, she stripped out of her damp T-shirt and, dressed in her sleep shorts, hesitated at the door to the bathroom. She needed a shower, but couldn't make herself go in. Her eyes slammed closed against the barrage of images, as clear as they were ten years ago.

Red covered every surface.

The edges of her vision darkened when she opened her eyes. Her hands grasped the edge of the door frame to steady herself. A shower could wait.

She wandered into her kitchen and started up the coffee maker. In another three hours she would be at work. The job wouldn't help her escape the dream, but at least it would give her brain something else to focus on.

She leaned her tall, broad-shouldered body against the faux marble counter and let her gaze wander over the spartan room. Nothing like her place from years ago, which she'd decorated with lots of colorful appliances, including an orange microwave. Sometimes she missed that stupid microwave.

This kitchen was functional enough, though she spent very little time in it. The coffee maker finished up, and she poured a cup, letting the caffeine do the work of waking her up.

She didn't bother to look at the date on her calendar, well aware today was the eighteenth of April. For the last ten years, she'd had the same dream on this date and no amount of grief counseling kept it at bay. Like her brain was programmed to give her a stark reminder of why she was alone.

She put her empty coffee cup on the counter and headed for the bathroom.

One five-minute shower later, she stood in her bedroom and performed the same routine she'd done for the last fifteen years. She reached into her closet, pushed aside her Red Serge dress uniform, and grabbed the perfectly pressed Royal Canadian Mounted Police light-blue shirt and navy pants with the yellow stripe down the outside seam. She stood in front of the closet door mirror and dressed, careful to ensure each epaulet was straight, the collars perfect, her tie neat, her badge square and shiny, and her name tag level upon her breast pocket. She pulled on her socks and boots, zipped them up, and slipped on her navy-blue, wool pullover and adjusted the epaulets.

After unlocking a cabinet, she grabbed her gun belt, ensured her weapon was safely tucked into the holster, and put it on. Fully dressed, she donned her coat and hat and left the apartment. While the car warmed up, she scraped ice off the windows. That done, she got in her car and headed to work, carefully navigating the icy streets.

Whitehorse, with a population of about 25,000, was the capital and only city in the Yukon Territory. Spring might be in full bloom somewhere in the country, but here, the weather was still bloody cold. Charley shivered and wondered if anyone else in the city was up this early.

Her phone rang and she unclipped it from her belt, not surprised to see her mother's face on the screen. She steadied herself and answered. "Good morning, Mom."

"Hi, sweetheart. How you doing?"

"I'm wondering why I don't live someplace that isn't freezing in mid-April."

"Because you were born here. Now answer my question."

"I'm fine," Charley said as she switched to Bluetooth.

"Don't lie to your mother. You know I can always tell." Josie Townsend's rough voice held a bit of hesitation. "Honestly, Charlene. How are you?"

"I'm on my way to work, Mom. Can we maybe talk later?"

"Normally I would say yes, but something tells me this is the perfect time to talk. I have a feeling you didn't sleep. Right?"

Charley sighed. There was no getting out of this conversation. She did her best not to take her frustration out on Josie. "I had the dream again and woke up around five. I didn't bother going back to sleep, so I'm a little tired."

"Come over for dinner tonight, please. We're at the trailer at Gracie's Glory. Your dad's been working later since we've got more daylight, and he found a new cut to start on. But I made him promise to be at the trailer by six."

During the gold-mining season, her parents spent the summer working at Gracie's Glory. The mine was owned by their long-time friend, Harry Kato. The Katos were extended family for whom Charley was eternally grateful. Harry hired her parents many years ago to work the mine, thus giving them something to do in their retirement.

"I'll be there, Mom."

"Good. We both need to see you, sweetheart. We want to give you a hug and remind you how much we love you."

The sentiment almost brought tears to her eyes. How the hell did she get so lucky to be given such wonderful parents? "I love you, too, Mom. I'll be there. Promise."

"Good. See you then."

Charley clipped her phone onto her duty belt as she came to a stop at an intersection. She glanced in the rearview mirror and caught her reflection. Her skin was pale, and shadowy circles underscored her dark eyes. She ran a hand through her black, buzz-cut hair before going through the intersection and heading to the RCMP station.

****

Jada Deveraux glared at her reflection in the mirror. How dare she look tired? Maybe the *Black Lightning* marathon was a bad idea. But seriously, how could she not watch, or ogle, Nafessa Williams? The girl was hot with a capital H.

She'd never be as hot as Nafessa.

She didn't consider herself ugly. Her skin was smooth and her complexion a rich, dark brown. She kept her hair medium length, an inch or so above her shoulders and didn't bother with wigs or streaks or coloring or perms. She thought it looked fine. More than fine. To Jada, her hair was beautiful. Even if her mother was appalled by the way she wore it.

But she loved the long, curly, coiled look after she washed it. Her hair was full and soft and looked different on any given day. What's not to love? She fluffed her hair and stopped.

"No way," she whispered. A gray hair?

Right in the middle of her beautiful curls. She plucked the offending hair and dropped it into the wastebasket. Time permitting, she'd search for more.

She washed her hands and returned to the ER.

As a flight paramedic, she worked the emergency room when they weren't out on a call. Emergency flights didn't occur every day, and while some of her colleagues didn't enjoy the ER time, she did. Today they were flooded with patients, and the variety of issues presented a welcome challenge. But she'd still rather be flying to an emergency. She was a trauma junkie and had no problem admitting it.

Taking off in a helicopter to parts unknown and largely difficult to reach gave Jada an amazing rush. She could never be sure what problems lay ahead and always had to think on her feet. She lived for those moments when she knew she was saving a life in a way few others could ever do.

"Deveraux! I need a hand!" The very loud call came from bay eight, where Nurse Cranky Pants was dealing with an eight-year-old who required stitches to his left temple.

This would make the tenth time in the last hour Cranky Pants felt he needed her assistance. She knew full well he didn't, but Cranky Pants seemed to believe much of what he was assigned to do was beneath him.

She stepped into the room and squeezed past the boy's mother so she was on the opposite side of the bed from Cranky Pants. "You bellowed for me?"

Cranky Pants glared at her. "I need you to hold his head still so I can get the lidocaine in." He held a syringe a foot or so from the kid's head and the boy stared wide-eyed at it. Each time it got anywhere near him, he tossed his head back and forth. "See what I mean?"

Gently, Jada touched the boy's chin so he'd look at her. His sea-green eyes watered, but he managed to keep the tears from falling. "What's your name?"

"Tyler," he said, his voice soft and barely audible. She waited a moment as she tried and succeeded in connecting with him.

She kept her voice calm and soothing as she spoke to him. "Hey, Tyler, I'm Jada. Look, I know Nurse Cranky Pants here looks all big and mean and this needle probably looks gigantic, but none of that's true. Well, he is cranky."

Tyler giggled but stopped when Cranky Pants glared at him.

Jada got Tyler's attention again. "We need to give you stitches because you can't go around with an open cut and this one is going to need more than a bandage. But hey, you'll get a cool wound you can show off at school."

"I don't wanna." Tyler's voice wavered. "It's gonna hurt. My brother Tommy said it would be like getting poked in the eye with a sword."

Jada bit her lip to keep from laughing and noted Tyler's mom didn't seem surprised. "Tommy isn't a doctor, is he?"

"No."

"Is he a nurse?"

"No. He's ten."

"Ah, well then he probably doesn't actually know what it's going to be like. Unless he's had stitches before."

"Nuh uh. Tommy had my helmet so he's okay. Travis had stitches once though, but he was three and don't remember it."

Jada nodded sagely, maintaining eye contact with Tyler. "So let me tell you what it's really like. We're going to put some stuff on your cut to make it numb. You won't feel any pain when we do the stitches, but you'll feel it pull a little. Then you get a bandage and you go home. Job done."

"And I'll get a scar?"

"Probably."

"Cool."

Jada laughed then, as did Tyler's mom. She shared a quick glance with the woman. "So, we all set to do this then?"

Tyler shook his head. "I don't want him." Tyler pointed at Cranky Pants. "Will you do it?"

Jada gave him her most charming smile, and Tyler grinned back. "Of course I will. Give me a minute, okay?"

Tyler nodded and Jada scooted past his mother and pulled Cranky Pants into the hallway. He was a bit shorter than her and broke her grip on his arm once the door closed behind them. She stepped away so Tyler and his mom wouldn't hear her. "Do you do this shit on purpose?"

"What—"

"If you don't want to do the fucking stitches, come get me next time and I'll do it. Takes a lot less time, and the patients are better off. So fucking ask. And if you bellow for me again, I'm going to shove a box of gloves down your throat." She gingerly took the syringe from him and returned to the room, closing the door behind her.

Jada deposited the syringe into a sharps container and donned a pair of gloves. "So, Tyler, how'd you get this big old cut anyway?"

"My skateboard. I crashed on purpose because we were playing stuntman, but I didn't see a wall on the other side of the bushes. My sister, Theresa, was there, and she started crying because she's only five. Tommy laughed and Travis ran to get mom." He glanced sheepishly at his mother. "She was mad."

"I'm not mad," his mother said. She turned eyes the same color as Tyler's to Jada. The woman was probably in her mid-thirties, like Jada, but she looked much older. Jada often wondered if she looked older than her own thirty-two years. Finding a grey hair didn't exactly boost her confidence.

"See, she's not mad," Jada said.

"Oh yes she is." Tyler pointed at her. "She's got that look. I know that look. She gets it every time I do something bad. I'm gonna get grounded for sure."

"Not this time," his mother insisted. Her smile was kind, and the corners of her eyes crinkled a little, telling Jada she found this amusing. Not the usual parental response. "I'm Fran, by the way. And this little man here is exaggerating. The only thing I care about is that he's okay. A few stitches sort of comes with the job of raising rambunctious kids." Fran looked like she was about to laugh. "He was trying to keep up with his older brothers."

"Nothing wrong with that," Jada said. She turned to Tyler. "But sometimes older kids do dumb things. Like take your helmet so they don't get hurt, but you do. So maybe next time make sure you don't do the same dumb things, 'kay? And no more skateboarding without a helmet."

"Okay," Tyler mumbled. He kept his eye on Fran as if he wasn't convinced grounding wouldn't be in his future.

"The hard part's all done, Tyler."

"Huh?"

"I put some stuff on your cut so you won't feel the stitches. I wanted to glue the cut closed, but I can't, so I put some medicine on there. Did you feel me doing it?"

"Nope." Tyler's eyes widened in amazement. "I don't feel nothing."

"Good." She said to Fran, "Distractions always work. I used lidocaine cream to numb the area." Jada double-checked the suture kit then made quick work of sewing Tyler's wound closed with three precise stitches. She placed a gauze pad on it, taped it down, and removed her gloves. "All done."

"Wow. You're fast!"

Jada laughed. "Nah. You were a super good patient. You make it easy to do my job."

"Thank you," Fran said. "I was beginning to think we'd be here all day."

"No problem." Jada found a pamphlet about wound care and handed it to Fran. "With three boys, I doubt you need this, but take it anyway. I'll tell the charge nurse he's all done, and someone will be in here to discharge you."

Fran nudged Tyler. "What do you say?"

"Um, thanks?"

Jada gave him a fist bump and left the room. She was immediately greeted by Betty Ryan, the shift's charge nurse. "Hey, Betty."

"I was looking for you." Her hazel eyes narrowed at Jada.

"Let me guess, Cranky Pants?"

Despite her laughter, Betty said, "I wish you wouldn't call him that."

"Maybe he shouldn't live up to his name. Was he mad I kicked him out of the room or mad I told him off?"

"A little of both, but I handled it."

"Cool. And I did his job for him. Tyler's ready to go home."

"You're amazing with kids. Ever think of being a pediatric nurse?"

"Heh, no way," Jada said. "I live for adrenaline, remember? Flying off to exotic locations to save people. Doing awesome things with my mad medic skills."

"Exotic locations? Seriously?"

"More exotic than Ottawa."

"Less busy as well. But it's their loss and our gain."

"If you say so. Do me a favor and keep Cranky Pants off my ass. If you do, I'll try my best to call him by his real name."

"No you won't, but I'll see what I can do." Betty tucked a strand of long, blonde hair behind her ear and sighed dramtically. "I'll get Tyler out of here. Why don't you head to triage and give Ange a break?"

"Yes, boss." Jada saluted Betty and happily trundled off to the triage area.

****

Charley could hear the Andersons screaming at each other the moment she was out of her vehicle. She adjusted her duty belt, walked up the five rickety steps of the porch, and knocked on the door. At the same time, her backup, Corporal Elle Ferguson, pulled in next to her car. Elle was almost as tall as Charley, a bit rounder in the middle, with mousy brown hair floating around her shoulders in a curly mess. She stepped up next to Charley just as the front door opened.

Mrs. Anderson, her wrinkled face flushed, her rheumy eyes flashing anger, shoved the screen door open and nearly knocked Charley down. "'Bout time you showed up." She pointed behind her, toward the kitchen at the end of the long, dark hallway.

Charley'd been there so many times she practically had the layout memorized. "He in the kitchen?" she asked.

"Where else?" Mrs. Anderson answered. Charley could smell the alcohol on her breath. "He's in there screaming at me about having a boyfriend or some such bullshit. He's lost his damn mind, and I want him out of here!"

Charley nudged Elle. "Go check on him."

"Got it." She disappeared into the house.

Charley stepped inside and ushered Mrs. Anderson into the dingy living room. "What happened?"

"Stupid ass started screaming while I was watching TV. I didn't even know he was downstairs. I can't handle him no more. He's got to go."

"Dementia, right?"

"What the doctors say." Mrs. Anderson sat her heavy body into a well-used recliner. "I called our son, but he wasn't home. Left him a message on his voice mail thingy."

"Good." Charley heard a commotion in the kitchen and raised voices. "Stay here." She rushed down the hallway as Mr. Anderson came running toward the living room.

"I'm gonna kill her!" he screamed. He raised his hand over his head. He held something Charley couldn't quite make out in detail. She suspected it was a weapon.

"Stop!" She stuck out her right hand to slow his progress. The weapon suddenly came toward her in a sweeping arc. Reflexively, she raised her left hand to deflect it.

Seconds later, burning pain seared her hand. Elle grabbed Anderson from behind. She shoved him up against the wall and disarmed him quickly. Anderson stopped struggling and began crying hysterically.

Charley grabbed a butcher knife off the floor with her right hand and held it away from him. "Cuff him, Elle, then put him in your car."

"We arresting him, Charley?"

"Yeah, but he's got dementia, according to the missus." She glanced down at her hand. "Shit. I need something to stop the bleeding."

"I'll get the First-Aid kit," Elle said. "Hang on."

She carefully guided Anderson out of the house. Charley fumbled her way into the kitchen, grabbed a fistful of paper towels, and pressed them to her hand.

Elle returned and placed her First-Aid kit on the table. She looked at Charley's hand. "Uh, you need the hospital. I'll call an ambulance."

"No way." Charley pulled away from her, found a mostly clean towel hanging from the oven handle, and wrapped it around her hand. "I'll drive myself. You good to write this up?"

"You can't drive, Charley." Elle blocked her from heading down the hallway. "I'm not going to let you go. That towel's already soaked with blood. At least let me drive you there."

"No. You need to take care of Mr. Anderson. Get hold of their son and get his ass over here." She checked her hand again and headed for the bathroom. She changed out the towel for a larger one and joined Elle in the living room. "I'm going to the ER to get this checked out. Call me soon as you clear the scene."

Elle opened her mouth, but Charley glared at her until she closed it.

Charley tightened the towel and headed for her car.

****

Charley parked her patrol car near the emergency room entrance. She got out and slammed the door shut with her good hand, cradling her left as she stomped toward the entrance. The towel she'd wrapped it in was soaked in blood, and it seemed the madder she got the more blood pumped out.

Walking into the ER waiting area, Charley wished she'd accepted the ride. Dizziness set in and she wobbled a bit as she approached the triage desk. Her arm felt wet, and when she looked down, her vision blurred. Was that blood on the floor?

The woman seated there was unfamiliar to Charley, who knew nearly everyone in the emergency department. Her soft brown eyes looked up from the computer and held Charley's gaze for an impossibly long time.

"You okay?" she asked in a sweet, sultry voice. Or was Charley hallucinating? She couldn't tell because the woman looked a little fuzzy all of a sudden.

"Um, not sure, actually." Charley held up her hand. "I almost got stabbed."

"You almost got stabbed? You're bleeding a lot for *almost*." It sounded like a laugh was hidden in her sentence. The woman got up and walked around her desk to stand in front of Charley. They were nearly eye to eye, and it was a little disconcerting. At 6'2" Charley was usually taller than everyone else, especially women. "Let me see," the woman said.

Charley let her peel away the towel while her gaze somehow wandered to the woman's chest. She wore blue scrubs and nothing underneath them, giving Charley a nice view of the valley between her breasts. Her dark brown skin was soft and inviting, and Charley wondered what it'd be like to snuggle into the valley and go to sleep.

She blinked several times and brought her gaze up to the woman's face. She got blurry again, and her lips were moving, but Charley heard nothing but the buzzing in her ears.

"...get me a wheelchair," the woman said.

"What for? Someone hurt?" Charley asked.

"Yeah, Sarge. You."

Next thing Charley knew, she was being pushed through the ER and into one of the trauma bays. The fast ride made her nauseous. The taco she'd had for lunch threatened to come back and haunt her.

Someone helped Charley out of the wheelchair and onto a bed. She looked to her left and found the woman—what's her name—by her side. Charley searched for an ID, but she couldn't make out the name on the badge dangling from her neck. More voices joined the weird cacophony of sound. Charley laid her head back and stared at the very bright lights in the ceiling.

"Sarge, can you tell me what happened?"

Charley closed her eyes. "Who are you?" she asked.

"Jada. What happened?"

"Anderson happened. He had a butcher knife. Couldn't let him stab his wife, ya know?"

"Sure. Good work then."

Charley felt like she was floating. Someone pinched her right arm while someone else did something to her left. A third person—or was it the same person—put an oxygen mask over her face. Charley didn't mind, even if it brought this weird smell with it.

"...need an IV...blood loss..."

The words floated around her but didn't make any sense. Charley decided to let them go through her and gave up trying to decipher anything. Her eyes were already closed; sleep came easily.

Chapter Two

Jada worked fast. The sergeant lost a significant amount of blood on the way to the trauma bay, and she had no idea how much loss occurred before then. She removed the bloody towel to get a look at the wound while Betty got an IV going on the right arm. Someone else placed a non-rebreather oxygen mask over the sergeant's mouth and nose.

Most of the bleeding had stopped. A laceration about 15 centimeters in length started at the tip of her middle finger and ran the length of her palm to the edge of her wrist. Half a centimeter in width. For a second, she wondered where the person with the knife was.

"Talk to me."

Jada didn't need to look up to know Doctor Fabulous was standing near the foot of the bed. Okay, so that wasn't his name, but she swore the man showered and shaved after every patient and used enough glue in his hair she doubted a tornado could displace it. What was his real name again?

Betty answered for her. "Laceration from a knife and unknown amount of blood loss. Heart rate is 60, respirations 28, blood pressure 80 over 50. I've got one IV Normal Saline wide open. Pupils equal and reactive. She passed out as we got her into the trauma bay."

"The lac's not bleeding much now," Jada said. She'd cleaned up the hand enough to see most of the damage. "I think we need a surgical consult. Looks like it cut through the tendons and into the bone. Must have been one helluva sharp knife."

Doctor Fabulous leaned over Jada's shoulder. She held her breath to prevent inhaling his overly pungent cologne. "Let's get a quick X-ray and page Doctor Hughes. I talked to her an hour ago, so she's probably still here."

"On it," someone said from behind them.

"B/P is 88 over 60," Betty called out.

Jada finished cleaning the wound with antiseptic, careful not to incite more bleeding, then placed sterile bandage pads over it, held in place with gauze wrap.

The doctor said, "Get me a cross match in case we need a transfusion. Get another IV into her left arm, wide open. Did anyone come in with her?"

"Fool brought herself in here," Jada said, starting the second IV as ordered. "There's a trail of blood from the waiting room, and I wouldn't be surprised if she's lost a liter or more. No idea how long ago this happened. She came in with her hand covered in a blood-soaked towel."

The doctor grunted, his eyes on the monitor next to the bed. She could see the patient's oxygen level was at 98%. Her heart rate was up to 64 and her breathing slowed to 22 breaths per minute. Jada adjusted the flow of the IV fluid and watched as the blood pressure machine took another reading.

"100 over 60. Improving," Betty said.

"Continue to monitor her and let me know when Doctor Hughes gets down here." Doctor Fabulous left the trauma bay.

Betty removed her gloves and tossed them into a red container, which held all disposable bio hazard material. She gently touched the sergeant's forehead and frowned. "How the hell did you manage this, Charley? You're supposed to be Superwoman out there."

"You know her?" Jada asked.

"Yeah. Charley Townsend. We've known each other for years."

"Charley Townsend?" Jada bit back a smile. "As in?"

"Yes. As in the TV show *Charlie's Angels*. But don't say anything to her. She's sensitive about it."

"Seriously?" Jada raised an eyebrow and looked at Charley. "She's as big as an ox. Who'd be stupid enough to make fun of her?"

"Oh, you'd be surprised. She wasn't always so big and tough. Trust me."

"Okay."

Jada worked on removing Charley's blood-soaked clothes, with Betty's help. It took them some time, but eventually they had her cleaned up, in a hospital gown, and covered with a warmed-up blanket. Betty kept careful watch over their patient as

Jada adjusted the oxygen mask.

Jada did another check on Charley's vitals. "Blood pressure is 115 over 87. Her color's getting better, too." She took a moment to wipe blood from Charley's face. "Handsome woman," she said absently.

"Very," Betty said. "I've always had a bit of a crush on her."

"Aww, how sweet," Jada said with a goofy smile. "I bet you'd make a lovely couple."

"Don't you dare tell her." Betty blushed a little. "My husband would kick my ass, and Charley would avoid me forever. And I kinda like having her around."

"Your husband doesn't know you're bi?"

"Oh he knows. He's afraid Charley might steal me away. Probably right to be, too. She's one of the kindest people I've ever met. I'd like to smack the asshole who did this to her."

"She said something about being stabbed by Anderson when she came in."

"Old man Anderson?" Betty shook her head in wonder. "I can hardly believe he and his wife haven't killed each other yet."

"I think Sarge stopped it." Jada pointed to the injured hand. "And it looks like this might be her last call for a while."

A new voice came from the doorway of the trauma bay. "What?" A short, thin woman with long, red hair and pale skin stood there with a look of shock and fear on her face. Her gaze went to Charley and suddenly she was rushing forward and practically bowled over Jada to get to Charley's side. "What happened? Is she going to be okay?"

"She's going to be fine, Josie," Betty said, coming to their side of the bed. She placed her hand on Josie's shoulder. "She lost a lot of blood, but she's on the mend."

"Thanks, Betty," Josie said in a relieved tone. She avoided touching the injured hand and leaned across the bed to kiss Charley on the cheek. "And you wonder why I worry about you so much."

Jada gave Betty a questioning look, and Betty said, "She's Charley's mom."

Josie turned to the two women, tears in her eyes. "You sure she's going to be okay?"

Jada said, "Yes. Her vitals are getting better now we've

got some fluids going into her. We've called for a surgeon to come look at her hand."

"Is it bad?"

Jada didn't want to give Josie any false hope; she'd seen wounds similar to this one. If it went deep enough to damage tendons and nerves, it would be difficult to regain complete use of the hand. But she didn't dare tell Josie. Instead she gave her a reassuring smile and said, "She'll probably need surgery and rehab, but it's a guess."

"An educated one, though," Josie said.

"Yes."

Josie's gaze went back to Charley. "Of all the days for this to happen. What am I going to do with you, Charlene?"

Betty asked, "Can I call anyone for you?"

"No, my husband's on the way. I happened to be in town so I drove right here. Thanks."

"Sure. A tech will be by in a few minutes to take her to X-ray, but you can wait in here. The door will be open so you call out if you need anything." Jada pulled a chair over and offered it to Josie.

"Thanks," Josie said and took a seat as Jada and Betty left the room.

****

Charley first became aware of the incredibly bright lights above her head. They pierced her eyes and gave her the mother of all headaches. Then the sounds came and they confused her. Beeping, talking, typing on a computer. Where the hell was she?

She turned her head to the left to discover her mom staring at her, tear streaks on her face. She tried to reach out to her, but her left hand felt like it weighed a ton and she didn't have the strength to move it.

"Mom?"

"Hey there," Josie said. "How do you feel?"

"Like I got run over by a train. What happened?"

"You were on a call to the Andersons again. I don't know the details, but your hand got cut during a fight."

"My hand?" She tried to look at her hand, but it made her woozy to move. "How the hell did my hand get cut?"

"I don't know, sweetheart. But a surgeon was here a minute ago, and you're scheduled to have an operation today. She said it'd take an hour for the operating room to be ready."

"Surgery? What for?" Charley simply couldn't wrap her brain around any of this. "I don't have time for this. I need to get back to work."

"You've already been replaced at work. I talked to Elle about twenty minutes ago. She called Inspector Pike. You're on medical leave until further notice."

"Mom—"

"Charlene, your hand has been flayed open like a gutted fish. The surgeon says the knife sliced through a tendon and possibly the nerves, and they have to repair it immediately so you don't lose function in your hand. So it's either do what she tells you or lose your hand. Your choice."

Charley blinked as if it would somehow make the pieces of this bizarre puzzle fall into place. And they did. Very slowly. "Anderson was going after his wife with a butcher knife."

"Well, that explains the size of the cut, I guess."

"I didn't see the knife when I attempted to stop him from going after her. I had my hand out, and I tried to get it away from him. I don't remember it hurting. I saw Elle grab the old man. I think I drove myself here."

"Yes, you drove yourself here, and if I wasn't so worried about you, I'd slap you for doing something so dumb." Charley cringed the way she always did when her mom was mad. Like she was about to be grounded. "You're lucky you got here in one piece. You bled all over the place, and as soon as they got you into a bed, you passed out."

"I don't remember much after getting here. There was this nice nurse at the triage desk. I think she got me a wheelchair."

"Her name is Jada, she's a paramedic, and she's very nice. You'd like her. I think she's still on shift, so you might see her again before you head to surgery."

"Where's Dad?"

"He might not get here in time to see you, but I can call him if you'd like. He was at Gracie's Glory working the back end of the claim. You know how he is when he thinks he's found good gold."

"Yeah. I do." Charley was obviously disappointed. Few

people in her life ever mattered more to her than her parents—her father being the most important of all. Her emotions were all over the place while she sorted through everything. She needed him.

Josie touched her cheek, and Charley looked up at her. "I'll call him. He's got to be close by now. Last time he rang, he was over halfway."

"As long as he uses his Bluetooth. Don't let him be on the phone and drive at the same time."

Josie laughed softly. "Always a cop, aren't you?"

"A damn good one, I might add."

"You certainly are." Josie dug her cell phone out of her purse and soon had Charley's father on the line.

Charles "Charlie" Townsend had a gruff demeanor which belied his sweet nature. Despite the confusion it often caused, Charley was proud to be named after him. When his voice reached her ears, she felt like her world righted itself.

"How you doing, Charlene?"

"Lousy, but I'll be okay. No speeding."

"I'm not speeding."

"Yes you are, Dad. I know you."

He laughed and it made her smile. "You gonna give me a ticket?"

"I might. Be here when I come out of surgery, okay?"

"Of course I'll be there," he said. "Let me talk to your mother."

"I love you, Dad."

"I love you, too."

Josie took the phone back, spoke quietly for a few moments, and hung up. "Feel better?"

"I do." Charley smiled at her. "You never seem to mind I'm a daddy's girl. Why?"

"Kind of a weird time to ask, but I'll tell you this—I never minded you two being so close. I only ever want you to feel loved and happy. Besides, I'm not exactly chopped liver. Right?"

"Yuk. No, you're not. I love you, too."

"You better." Josie kissed her forehead.

"Did you call anyone else?" Charley asked. Her mother was often the town crier, and if Josie knew something, so did the rest of Whitehorse.

Josie hesitated. "Well, I got the call from Shirley at

dispatch and was on my way. I called your dad, and I called Harry to let him know what was going on. He said he'd tell Liv and Gracie."

"That's all? You didn't tell Mike?"

Josie gave her a sly grin. "Mike was with Shirley when the call came in. I told you he liked her."

"So everyone knows then? The important people?"

"Yes." Josie straightened the hospital gown where it rode up to Charley's neck. "Gracie wanted to come here, but I sent her a text to let her know you're okay. It's better she stay with Harry."

Charley tried to sit up, but she lacked the strength. Her mother must have read her thoughts when she said, "He's fine. Last night he had some trouble breathing, and Gracie stayed home to keep an eye on him. He's his normal ornery self."

"Shouldn't he be in the hospital? Mom, he's ninety-four."

"I know, but he's already seen his doctor. I promise you, he's fine."

"And a pain in the ass," Charley said with a smile.

Josie brushed her fingers through Charley's buzz cut. "You know I miss your beautiful, long hair."

"Sorry you didn't get the cute little girl you wanted, Mom."

"What? Oh don't you ever say such a thing again, Charlene Marie Townsend," Josie gently admonished her. "I got exactly what I wanted. A beautiful child to love. Now get some rest before you make me start crying. I'll let everyone know you're okay."

Elle entered the room, and Charley gave her a tired smile. "Anderson doing okay?"

"I released him into his son's custody. I'll get charges filed this afternoon." Elle stood on the opposite side of the bed from Josie. "More importantly, how are you really doing? And don't tell me you're okay."

"I don't know how I am. I'll live, so there's that. I need surgery to fix the damage, so who knows how long I'll be out."

"I'm sorry. I should have restrained him sooner. If I had, this wouldn't have happened."

"Don't go there, Elle." Charley held Elle's gaze. "What's done is done. No sense going over it a million times. You might have restrained him, and he might have dropped dead from a heart attack. You can't predict this stuff. Should you have restrained him? Maybe. Maybe not. Write up your report. I'm sure the inspector will pick it apart for us."

"I'm sure he will. But that doesn't make my guilt go away." Elle ran a hand through her unruly hair. Her amber eyes shone with remorse. "I need to get back to the office, but if you need anything, you call me. Got it?"

"Thanks."

Elle said her goodbyes and left.

"I always did like her," Josie said. Her hand squeezed Charley's. "Why haven't you two ever—"

"Mother, stop. Are you ever going to give up trying to set me up with someone?"

"No way." Josie laughed stoftly. "It's too much fun." She brushed her fingers against Charley's cheek. "Your eyes are drooping. Go to sleep. I'll be here when you wake up."

Charley's eyelids soon became too heavy to keep open.

****

"Jada, can you do me a favor?" Betty asked seconds before Jada was about to head for the locker room. Her shift ended an hour ago, and she was more than happy to get out of there. Cranky Pants was on her last nerve, despite Betty's interventions.

"Depends. What's in it for me?"

"Nothing, actually. Except maybe some quality time with a certain handsome Mountie who was brought in earlier."

Jada smirked. "Huh. Didn't notice."

"Which is why you pointed it out to me, you big liar. Anyway, I don't have any transporters available, and she needs a ride upstairs to surgery. Can you do this one last thing for me? Then I promise to forget you're here."

"You'd better forget. Once I leave this ER, you won't see me again for three days."

"Fair enough. Thanks." Betty waved as she headed into bay seven.

Jada avoided Cranky Pants and stepped into the trauma bay where she found Charley talking quietly to her mother. She was holding Charley's good hand, and a tiny pang of jealousy hit Jada. She'd never known such love from her own mother.

"I believe someone called for a taxi?" Jada asked, giving them her best smile.

Josie spoke first. "If you're taking her to surgery, then yes. We sure did." She tapped Charley on the shoulder. "This is the nurse who helped you out. Her name is Jada."

"I'm not a nurse, I'm a flight paramedic," Jada said. "But it's nice to officially meet you, Charley."

"You, too." Charley looked at Josie. "This is going to take awhile, Mom. Why don't you go get something to eat and wait for Dad? You can come up to the waiting room then."

"I'm going with you, Charlene."

Jada almost laughed at the expression on Charley's face when her mother called her Charlene. How adorable. Like a three-year-old who didn't get what she wanted. "You don't need to come with me, but you do need to eat. Please."

"She's right, Mrs. Townsend. Once I get her up there, they'll put her out and you won't be able to see her anyway. Might as well get some crappy cafeteria food while you can."

Josie's gaze went from Charley to Jada before finally agreeing. "Don't take any crap from her, okay?" she said to Jada.

"I won't, ma'am. I'm good at not taking crap."

"My name's Josie, not ma'am. You make me feel old."

Jada winked at her. "I never would have thought you were her mother if Betty hadn't told me when you first came in. I'd have guessed you as a younger sister."

Josie laughed and Charley made a weird groaning noise. Charley said, "I can't believe you said that. I'll never hear the end of it."

"Thank you, Jada." Josie looked quite proud of herself. She ran her fingers through her hair to put her fiery-red locks in order. "I think you just made my day."

"You're welcome." Jada wheeled Charley out of the room and headed for the elevator. Josie followed. "You don't look old enough to be her mother."

"You can stop sucking up now," Charley said.

Josie playfully slapped her shoulder. "Shut up. I like this woman." She leaned close and whispered in Charley's ear. Jada couldn't hear her, but the look on Charley's face was priceless.

Somewhere between shock and horror.

Before Charley replied, the elevator door opened and Jada pushed her in. She waved to Josie as the doors closed.

"Your mom's pretty nice."

"She can be."

Jada stole a view from her position at the head of the bed. Handsome was a good word to describe the woman lying before her. Thick, black hair in a buzz cut accented a round, light brown face. She didn't look anything like Josie, and Jada wondered if she favored her father. Dark eyes looked forward and Jada thought she detected some worry there.

"I still can't believe you managed to drive yourself here. I heard the call you were on was on the other side of the city."

"I've been told off a few times already, thanks. I don't know what I was thinking. Must have been the adrenaline. I guess I didn't realize I was hurt so bad." She lifted her bandaged hand a few centimeters off the bed. "It hurts like hell."

"You're going to be out of commission for a while."

"I figured," Charley grumbled.

The doors opened and Jada resumed their course.

"Look at it as a free vacation. The weather will be getting warmer in the next couple of weeks. Lots of stuff you can do with one hand."

"Such as?"

Jada bit off her first reply. The idea of what those long fingers of Charley's hand could do to her was sudden and exhilarating. And way too inappropriate. Right? She cleared her throat. "Hiking, for one. There are some amazing hiking trails here, and it's my mission to explore every one of them."

"You haven't been here long, have you? I know I haven't seen you before. I would have remembered you."

"Aw, is this your way of flirting with me, Sarge?"

Charley averted her gaze. "I know almost everyone here."

"I'll take it as a yes. You happened to catch me during one of my ER shifts. I've been here about eight months."

"I haven't had to come to the hospital in a while, and the last time I had a call with the helicopter was several months ago."

"Well, we haven't had a lot of calls since I got here either. Though I do remember one for an old man with a bad heart. He coded on us twice. Back in the fall, I think."

"Harry Kato? You were on the crew who flew him in?"

"In his nineties and lives in a cabin outside Blue River?"

"Yes. He's a family friend. You guys saved his life."

Jada shrugged off the compliment as she always did. "Part of the service. You know how it goes." She stopped to hit the button on the wall to open the door to the surgery ward. "Did he do okay?"

"He's living with his granddaughter and her wife. Doing fine last time I saw him. Surprised I didn't meet you then. I remember seeing the flight crew load him up."

"Well, you've met me now." Jada leaned a bit closer when they stopped at the nurse's station. "And now that you have, let's make it a point to meet again. Okay?"

Charley didn't reply, but Jada sure did enjoy it when her face glowed with embarrassment. She was so damn cute. She handed Charley's paperwork to the nurse and was off to the locker room, glad to have her shift end on such a nice note.

Chapter Three

Jada stepped into her studio apartment and dropped her backpack on the floor as she kicked the heavy, wooden door closed. She'd not seen the place in fourteen hours, and while it still didn't come close to feeling like home, it was a place to shower, eat, and sleep. Not necessarily in that order.

She removed her shoes and let them land somewhere between the kitchen area and the door. A pizza box from two nights ago—or was it three?—still adorned the table. She wasn't interested in penicillin and avoided it, moving on to the fridge. There she found two bottles of beer, a box of wine she was sure had nothing left in it, and various condiments, some of which probably needed to go.

It sucked living alone. She was terrible at keeping up with things like groceries, and if not for automatic payments coming out of her bank account, she'd be bad at paying bills, too. The place was little, maybe 700 square feet, but never as clean as it should be. Hence the outdated pizza box.

Jada shoved the offending food into the trash bin and dialed the same pizza joint to bring her a fresh one. And a two liter bottle of diet Coke. She could use the caffeine, and the pizza was big enough for breakfast leftovers. If she remembered to put them in the fridge.

She abandoned the foodless area and stripped out of her scrubs on the way to her sleeping spot. She pulled an oversized T-shirt from the chest of drawers along with an old pair of basketball shorts and plopped down on her couch/bed. She clicked on the TV and queued up last night's Blue Jays game.

Her bare feet landed on the rickety coffee table as she settled in to watch the game. Her pizza arrived during the second inning.

She dug money out of her wallet, tossed it back into her backpack, which now rested against the wall by the door, and let the pizza kid in. Same kid as always, not as tall as she was, but pencil thin with mid-length curly hair that was sometimes blue, sometimes green, but always in need of a good wash. He turned his pimply face to hers and smiled. Someday his smile would dazzle—once the braces were gone.

She handed him a twenty for a ten-dollar pizza. "Keep the change, Seth."

"Thanks, Jada!" He placed the soda and pizza on the kitchen table for her, waved, and was out the door in a flash.

Jada took the box and soda and put them on the coffee table, hit Play, and went back to the game. A base hit put a Jays runner in scoring position. She took a bite of pizza as he stretched his lead from second base and her phone rang.

She ignored it at first while the Yankees pitcher wasted energy keeping the runner close to second. After four attempts to get him out, the crowd started booing. The batter was nonplussed, and when the pitch finally came—and her phone rang—she nearly knocked over the pizza box as the ball soared over the outfield wall for a home run. Damn, she wished she was sitting in Rogers Centre to see this.

Those season ticket seats were right behind home plate where she could look over and see into the Jays dugout to watch them celebrating the homer. She'd laugh at their goofy antics and dances they did, listen to them cheering and making jokes, being a team. She loved that about baseball. Always a team effort, though sometimes one person stood out and did something spectacular. Kind of like her job. Always a team working to save someone's life, but once in a while, someone stood out and did something amazing.

That person used to be her.

That person used to sit in those season-ticket seats and enjoy the atmosphere and let all her troubles roll off her shoulders for the next two hours or so. The excitement would be enough to allow Jada to reset herself and get ready for the next shift or the next call, but never quite enough to get ready for the next hard knock life would throw at her.

She took a chug from the bottle of soda, almost laughing at the belch that came after drinking it too fast. Francine would have yelled at her for it. But Francine wasn't there. Hell, Francine had no idea where she was.

Her phone vibrated from its spot on the kitchen counter,

alerting Jada she had a voicemail. The inning ended with a strikeout, and during the commercial break, Jada got up to retrieve her phone.

She cussed the moment she saw who'd called. Then the phone rang again—the same person trying hard to get her attention. Few people had her new number, and they all knew if she didn't answer on the first try, it meant she was busy and would call back. Hence the invention of voicemail. Except Jada had to answer this call and dreaded it. This could only lead to trouble and more stress. But if she did nothing, the phone would keep ringing.

With another muttered curse, she tapped the Answer icon. "Hello, Mom."

"Jada Lee, where have you been? I've tried to call you several times today."

"I was working," she said, not bothering to remind her mother of the nature of her job. "What did you need?"

Liselle Deveraux's voice was shrill and cut through Jada like a knife. "Your sister quit her job today, and it's your fault!"

Jada never understood why it was always her fault. Everything. If her sister, Celeste, who was four years her junior, got into mischief, Jada was to blame. Celeste once threw a baseball through the kitchen window, and despite taking the blame, Jada got punished and lost her allowance until the window repairs were paid off. And she was grounded from playing baseball the entire summer.

Harsh punishment for the innocent actions of a ten-year-old who had been teaching her little sister how to throw a ball.

Jada shook off the memory and tried to keep up with Liselle's tirade. Something about Celeste's partner brought her back to the conversation. "Wait. Stop. What's Anton got to do with any of this?"

"Have you not heard a word I've said?" Liselle sighed dramatically. "He told her to do what she wants. He told her he doesn't care what kind of job she has or if she even has a job. They're not even legally married. Celeste has to protect herself, but she doesn't want to."

Jada tried to pick out the most important points. "Anton makes good money, Mom. They don't need a second income. If

Celeste wants to—"

"She's pregnant and she's going to end up dependent on him for the foreseeable future. What kind of life is that? What kind of example will it set for her child? She went to college for eight years to be a doctor. She's worked all of three years in her practice. How the hell does she even know if it's not the right job for her? Did I throw all my hard-earned money away on her education for nothing?"

Jada closed her eyes and wondered what would happen if she hung up on her mother. None of this was about Jada. She knew Celeste never wanted to be a doctor. She simply didn't have the passion for it. But their mother, a brilliant cardiovascular surgeon, determined at least one of her daughters would follow in her footsteps. General practice wasn't the direction she wanted Celeste to take, but at least she had MD behind her name. Unlike Jada.

Medical school was never an interest of Jada's. She opted to seek something more exciting. Early on, she discovered her love of adrenaline. She played all manner of sports and pushed herself physically as often as possible. After a few volunteer shifts with the local ambulance service, she found her calling. And nothing—or no one—would ever change her mind. The day she explained her career path to her mother was the last time she saw even a micro hint of affection from her.

Her mother was still ranting on the phone, and Jada decided to put a stop to it. Not like the chasm between her and Liselle could get any bigger. "Mom, stop. Celeste is a grown-ass woman capable of making her own decisions. Anton loves her and he'll take good care of her. She wants to enjoy being pregnant and spending time with her partner. It's a huge bonus he works from home. Why can't you be happy for them?"

"And again my words have fallen on deaf ears. I don't know why I bothered calling you."

Me either, Jada thought. She closed her eyes and bowed her head, knowing the worst was about to come and unable to disconnect the call and stop it.

"You never once appreciated the work I did to bring you two up in a nice home, in a good neighborhood. I worked hard for the career I have. I would never throw it away—especially not because I got pregnant. I did surgery almost up until the time I went into labor with each of you. Your father understood how important having a career is. Especially for a black woman. What would I have done if I didn't have my career when he died? What would have happened to us? Do you think I could have sent either of you to private schools if I was on welfare?"

"Dad left us a bundle of money. We would have been fine. And how did this conversation become about you? And by the way, I'm fine, thanks. I'm settled into my new apartment and enjoying the laid-back life here in Whitehorse. We had an interesting trauma today, but I'm sure you're too busy losing your shit about Celeste to hear the details. When you think you can give a fuck about me, feel free to call me back. Otherwise, don't bother."

Jada tapped the End icon before her mother had a chance to respond. She almost threw the phone across the room, but she liked this one and didn't want to break it. She'd broken enough phones in the last two years.

The stupid thing rang before she could do anything with it. This time her sister's number popped up, and she answered immediately. "You okay?" she asked, knowing the answer already.

"No," Celeste cried into the phone. She was four months pregnant, and her hormones had kicked in, full tilt. She cried at the drop of a hat. Literally. When she dropped her hat on the way out of the house two days ago, she cried and blubbered a voicemail to Jada over it. Pregnancy, in Jada's opinion, should be avoided at all costs.

"She's a bitch. You know this."

"But she's not wrong," Celeste wailed. "What if something happens to Anton? Then what? How would I live?"

"Celeste, your hormones are getting the best of you. Take a deep breath and seriously think about this. You're an intelligent woman. Just because you're leaving the practice doesn't mean you can't ever be a doctor again. An excellent doctor I might add."

Celeste sniffled and blew her nose.

Jada closed the lid on her pizza, no longer interested in eating. Family drama always ruined her appetite.

"You think it's the hormones?" Celeste asked.

"Completely. Trust me. Mom will get over this

eventually. Probably when you have the baby and hand it to her for the first time. And you know damn well if, God forbid, anything happened to Anton I'd take care of you. I'd even move back to Ottawa."

Celeste was unusually quiet for a few moments. "You'd move back here? After everything that happened?"

"In a heartbeat. For you. Only for you, baby sister."

"Wow. I mean, I knew, but to hear you say it means so much to me, Jay."

She heard the tears starting up again when Celeste sniffled. "Hold on there. I sense another wave of hormones coming. Is Anton home?"

"He's in his office. I didn't want to interrupt. He's trying to code something to make it stop doing a thing which prevents something from happening."

Jada shook her head and laughed. "Well that's very specific. And to think you're an educated woman."

"Ha-ha," Celeste said, a hint of humor now in her voice. "I can give you the pathophysiology of leukemia if you'd like."

"Can it wait until I finish watching the ball game? It might help me go to sleep."

"You're an ass."

"I am, but you love me, so you're an ass lover."

"Jay, is it possible you might never grow up?"

"I believe it is." Jada felt the weight lift from her shoulders a little as she heard the tension leave her sister's voice. "And I think you're going to be a great mom."

"I love that you think so. I hate to say this since it's only been eight months, but I wish you were here. I miss you and could use a hug."

Jada's grip tightened on the phone. "I know. Right now I'm wondering why the hell I chose the ass-end of nowhere to start over."

"Because it was the right thing to do. You and I both know you needed as much physical distance from here as you could get without moving to Russia."

"I know." Jada sighed softly. "It was the right choice, sis. I mean, this place is so laid back and slow—I had a twelve-hour shift last week, and we never so much as turned a blade. We spent it checking stock, cleaning the helicopter, the helipad then I finally went into the ER to find something to do. I ended up in fast track doing stitches, treating drunks, casting broken bones and I loved it. Even when I'm bored, I'm happier now."

"What about all the trauma junkie stuff? Don't you miss it?"

Jada didn't hesitate in her answer. She'd thought about this topic since she moved to Whitehorse. "I don't miss having adrenaline rushes coming at me so much I don't come down from them for days. It's like addicts being on a high for so long they lose track of themselves. I don't want that anymore. I want to know I'm making a difference. Saving lives and helping people. Even if it's holding the basin while they puke."

"Ick. You know how I feel about it."

"You're a doctor and about to become a mother. I think you need to get better at dealing with people blowing chunks." Jada grinned at the groan Celeste made. She loved teasing her about this one peculiar issue. "And with a baby coming soon, you'd best get used to it."

"I'm going to make Anton deal with all of it. Momma don't do sick."

"That will change soon enough. You're going to be cleaning it up from now until that child leaves your house."

"I know I said love you, but I might have to take it back."

"Nope." Jada was full-on grinning now. "No take backs. You love me. Deal with it."

"If I was there, I'd probably hit you right now."

"Damn. From hugs to slugs in like five minutes. That's got to be a record, sis."

She finally got a soft laugh from Celeste and Jada relaxed. Celeste said, "Promise me you'll come see me for my birthday."

"I'll be there. Even if I have to steal the helicopter for a ride. Okay?"

"Sure. Look, Anton just came out of his office. I can tell by the look on his face he fixed the something, and I'm pretty sure he heard me yelling and crying. I better let him know what happened."

"Get a hug from him and pretend it's me. I love you, little sister. Call me whenever you need to talk. And I'm serious right now—I will be on the first flight home if you need me. Got it?"

"I got it. Love you. Bye."

Celeste hung up and Jada stared at the darkened phone. She hadn't been home a full hour yet, and her emotions had run the gamut. Her gaze landed on the TV where she'd paused the game. The pitcher, a rookie they'd brought up this season from the minors, was into his windup and looked like a ballet dancer, with his leg higher than his head.

Jada wondered if maybe he'd been pressured into a sports career when all he wanted was to be a dancer.

All Celeste ever wanted to do was get married and have kids. She didn't want a career or a job more difficult than serving someone their lunch. Celeste had no drive, and it made their mother crazy. Anyone with an A personality had a hard time understanding someone who wasn't interested in a career. For some, like Celeste, you got a job to make money and pay bills—to survive. That's it. No other reason for it.

Liselle and Jada had one major thing in common. They both had a calling and thrived on the work, ethics, skills, and determination it took to succeed in their chosen fields. Celeste was Mensa level intelligent, but she saw no interest in applying anywhere, except to teach her kids to read.

Jada loved her for being strong enough to do what she felt was best for her family, their mother be damned.

Jada pressed Play on the remote and watched the balletic movement of the Jays pitcher as he threw the first strike of the third inning. She grabbed another piece of pizza and tucked in for the rest of the afternoon.

Chapter Four

Charley fumbled with the TV remote, not quite able to make her right hand do what she wanted it to. If she couldn't operate the remote, how the hell was she going to get herself dressed and undressed when she left the hospital?

Her left arm felt like a club was attached to it instead of a hand. A splint kept her middle finger straight and the bandaging around the rest of the hand, going past her wrist, guaranteed she wouldn't be able to use it for anything more than waving at someone. Except she didn't have the strength to lift it.

She fingered the remote again, but nothing worked. She was ready to toss the damn thing across the room when a gentle hand covered hers.

"Easy, Charley. It's just a remote." Grace Templeton smiled sweetly at her as she sat beside Charley's bed. Her long, silky, black hair was tied into her usual ponytail, and her nearly black eyes shone with sympathy. "It sucks to be left-handed right now, but you'll get better."

"At least you're right-handed, so when you had surgery on your left arm you were still able to do stuff."

Grace's eyes clouded over for a moment, and Charley immediately realized her mistake by the expression of sorrow on Grace's face. "Shit. I'm sorry, Gracie. That was insensitive. I should have thought before I said something."

"It's fine. It's normal to talk about it."

"But still hurtful," Charley said. She couldn't believe she'd mentioned the injury Grace received at the hands of her abusive ex-wife. What a stupid thing to do. "Maybe it's all the pain meds they're giving me. Makes me say stupid things."

"It's not stupid." Grace gave her a half smile. The normally light-brown skin of her face paled. "And you're right. It was easier for me to do things like getting dressed and going to the toilet." At Charley's expression, Grace laughed. "Yes, you'll have trouble with the most basic things. And no, I won't help wipe your butt." She reached for Charley's good hand and gave it a squeeze. "But I'll be around to help you with other stuff."

"I thought you'd be working the mine. Mom's already decided she has to move in with me. She thinks I'm an invalid."

"You kinda will be for a few days until you get the gist of how to do things. I'm going to take some time off to help you out and run some interference between you and Josie. I know how she can be."

"You don't—"

"When I got hurt, you flew to Seattle to stay with me for two weeks so Matt and Sherry could take a break. I was driving my brother crazy, and you saved us from having a huge fight." Grace bent over and kissed Charley's forehead. "We're family. It's what we do, right?"

"Right. Thanks, Gracie."

"Thank me after I get your mother to go back to work."

"Are you talking about me?"

With her usual perfect timing, Josie strode into the room. She looked from Grace to Charley, waiting for an answer.

Grace said, "We were and it's all secret stuff."

"And why am I surprised?" Josie sat on the edge of the bed, next to Charley's legs. "Did you tell her how stubborn you're being?"

"Stubborn about what, exactly?" Grace asked.

"Not coming home. She's making me stay in that teeny tiny apartment of hers."

"It's not teeny tiny, and I'm not making you do anything. As if that would be possible. You don't need to stay with me, Mom. I'll be fine. Besides, Gracie just told me she's taking some time off work to come over and help me out."

Josie gave Grace a gentle pat on the arm. "I heard you hired four new guys to work the mine. One of them covering for you then?"

"Not really," Grace said. "We need help with the new cut, and I wanted to give you and Charlie a break. You two work way too much, especially your husband. No sense overdoing it. I told him this morning he's got these new guys to boss around and he's not allowed any more late nights. He's worse than the two of you combined."

"He is. I'll try to get him to listen. No promises." Josie

rested her hand on Charley's leg. "I was at your apartment with Elle. She made sure your gun is locked in the safe for you. I did your laundry and stocked the fridge and I was appalled to find it nearly empty. Did I not teach you to cook?"

"You did," Charley said, feeling rather sheepish at the admonishing look Josie gave her. "But I don't have time. It's easier to get a sandwich at the store or go to the drive thru."

Josie released a very dramatic sigh and Charley almost laughed. "You're impossible sometimes. But this imposed vacation is going to do you some good. There's more to life than the Royal Canadian Mounted Police."

Charley resisted the urge to roll her eyes. "And?"

Josie squeezed Charley's calf. "You could always go back to singing. You used to love it. You have a beautiful voice."

"No thanks," Charley muttered, already dreading where this conversation was going. Such talks always ended in the same place. "Mom, let's not do this right now, okay? It's bad enough I can't use my hand. Don't try to fix me."

"I will always try to fix you, Charlene. It's my job as your mother."

Grace cleared her throat and brought Charley's attention to her. "Josie, let's take baby steps here, okay? We'll get Charley home tomorrow and settled in. She needs rest first and foremost, as well as tips on using her right hand for things she's not used to doing. That's going to take up a lot of energy. Trust me."

Josie stood up. "Okay. I need to run a few more errands before tomorrow. I'll be here in the morning, Charlene. Don't you dare try to leave here without me."

"Yes, Mother." This time Charley did roll her eyes, and she received a playful tap on her leg from Josie. "I'll see you later."

Grace laughed softly when Josie left. "So, that went well."

"She's going to make my life hell. I love her, but it's going to suck."

"Nah. I'm good at running interference. Once we get you through the first week or so, she'll back off. Hey, I got an idea. How about we plan to take the boat out for a weekend? Soon as you feel up to it."

"Define 'we'."

"Me, Liv, Terry, Sara, Mike—anyone you want to invite. If we get too many people, we can rent a pontoon boat. It's already getting warmer. Might even be warm enough to swim."

"You're worse than my mom, you know that?"

"I'm your friend, Charley. You know that?"

Charley bit her lower lip. She didn't want to admit an outing with a few friends sounded like fun. Even if it included her doofus cousin, Mike. She'd kept mostly to herself for the last several years. Her parents practically had to drag her along to the occasional bonfire or cookout. She couldn't remember the last time she'd been out on the lake.

"Your brain must hurt right now," Grace said.

"Ha-ha." But Charley grinned at her, hoping to sound genuine as she spoke. "Let's keep the guest list short, okay? I can't handle too many people, especially if they're going to be all full of sympathy for my stupid hand. I don't need it."

"Short list. Got it. Boat fun first weekend you're feeling up to it. Awesome. I'll take care of arrangements." Grace kissed her again and got up. "You're not going to regret this, Charley. You're going to have a good time."

"If you say so."

"I know so. Trust me on this."

"I do." Charley trusted very few people, but Grace was one she always counted on. She was one of Charley's closest friends in the world, and while they didn't see each other often or talk more than a few times a month, they'd never once lost that openness with each other. Grace was the only person who knew the full story of Raina. Not even Charley's parents had all the details.

"Tell me what you're thinking," Grace said, her expression serious.

"You're a good friend."

"Of course I am. You've put up with me since we were kids."

"Because I had a crush on you." Charley smiled at the shock on her face. "I'm serious. I was always too chicken shit to do anything about it."

"You're a sweetheart, Charley." She bent and gave her a kiss on the cheek. "But you're too much like a sister for us to have worked out. Though I'm still holding out hope you'll find someone."

"Don't. Romance isn't something I'm interested in." Charley glanced down at her hand. "Right now I'm more worried about my career."

"Why? I thought the surgeon said you should make a full recovery."

"He did, but you know they aren't always right. What if there're complications? What if my physical therapy doesn't work?"

"What if the moon really is made of green cheese?"

Charley narrowed her gaze at Grace. "Not funny."

"It'll be fine. I know you. You'll work hard at whatever they tell you to do, and your hand will be good as new in a few months. Yes, it will suck that you're off work. Yes, you're going to be bored out of your mind, but we'll find other stuff for you to do. I got your back, Charley. Just like you had mine after Carly nearly killed me."

Charley took Grace's hand. "Did you expect me to stay here? Of course I got the first flight possible. Too bad Carly was already in jail. I might have enjoyed a few moments with her alone."

"You're worse than Liv."

"We want to keep you safe."

"I know, but seriously, stop it. Carly doesn't even know where I am. And if she did find me, I think my dear wife would be more than happy to deal with her."

"And I'd make sure Liv didn't get arrested for it." Charley winked at Grace, who knew full well Charley would never circumvent the law. Not even for family.

"Speaking of Liv, if I'm late she's going to freak out. We have a very important appointment today."

"Oh? Is it *the* appointment?"

"Yup. The fertility doctor's office is downstairs, and Liv's been worried about this all week. I can't convince her it'll be okay."

"Go hold her hand. I'll see you tomorrow evening. I'll text you when we get to my apartment. Tell Liv I said to butch it up. You might not get pregnant on the first try."

"I know." Grace sighed dramatically and released Charley's hand. "So until tomorrow. In the meantime, you get some rest and try not to break anything."

"I'll do my best. Thanks, Gracie. Sorry if I'm being an ass about this."

"It's fine. You're allowed to be angry."

Charley gazed at her hand, feeling doubt creep into her brain. Being a Mountie was the only thing she'd ever wanted to do or knew how to do. It meant everything to her, and she wasn't ready to give it up yet. Not even close. Thirty-six was hardly old.

"Stop it," Grace gently said. "You'll be fine."

"Hope so." Charley gave her a lame smile. Grace shook her head a little and left the room.

Charley gripped the remote and went back to attempting to watch TV.

****

Liv Templeton greeted Grace as she came out of the hospital elevator. "How's Charley doing?"

Grace gave Liv an easy smile and took her hand, surprised by how cold it was. "She's better than you, apparently. Why are you so nervous? It's only a consultation."

"I know." Liv tightened her grip on Grace's hand. "We haven't decided which of us is going first and then we have to find the right sperm donor and what if we can't agree on who to use—"

Grace shut her up with a kiss, sliding her fingers into Liv's unruly, blonde locks and pulling her closer, letting the moment heat just a little. She leaned back and laughed at the way Liv's mouth remained puckered. "You were saying?"

"Um, I forgot?" Liv sucked in her bottom lip. "Sorry. I'm so freaked out."

"Really? Hadn't noticed." Grace tugged her arm and herded Liv toward the doctor's office.

"I want to ask Matthew," Liv said.

Her comment came out of nowhere, and Grace had no clue what she meant. "Ask him about what?"

Liv pulled Grace to a stop a few meters from the waiting area. "I want to ask him to be my sperm donor. I want to go first. If we use my egg and your twin brother's sperm—it'll be the closest we can come to having a kid who's ours. One who resembles both of us. And maybe, if you want to have a kid, then we ask David to use his sperm because he looks more like me than my brother Timothy does."

The vulnerability in Liv's eyes was astonishing and kept Grace from answering her right away. Liv meant every word she'd just spewed and clearly spent some time thinking about. Not that her reasoning wasn't sound or the ideas didn't have merit—the weird thing was very simply Grace had been thinking along the same lines.

Her face broke into a slow smile, and she kissed Liv again, this time letting things positively smolder between them. "I love you."

"I love you, too, but it doesn't answer my question. Or does it? I'm kinda confused right now."

"It so answers your question because I was thinking the same thing. We're lucky enough to have brothers, and I mean, why not? I know Matthew would do it, but are you sure about David?"

"No clue about David, but I'm willing to ask him." Liv twined their fingers together as they continued to the waiting area. "This is the one thing that's been freaking me out the most. I don't want to use some stranger's DNA to make our child. Even if our brothers decline, please let's ask men we know first."

"Deal." Grace kissed her again, and they took seats in the tiny waiting area. "You want to go first?"

"Why not? Besides, it'll be a little easier on me. I'm not the one climbing rock walls and mountains and stuff."

"You climb with me sometimes."

"That's different. It's not my job."

"It doesn't have to be my job either," Grace said. She gazed down at their linked hands and sighed. "I mean, I love teaching others to climb, but I don't quite have the passion for it I once did. I think it faded after I had to stop doing it for so long." She flexed her left arm and winced at the ever-present ache.

"You want to work at the mine more? I mean, you're already running Gracie's Glory. Do you need to spend more time there? Am I missing something?"

"You're not missing anything. I guess I am a little. Sometimes I miss my job in the army. If I were still in, I'd be in the Middle East translating and making a difference. I mean, I didn't have a job where I was generally put in danger, but I felt like I did something important. It's hard to translate one language to another and still get the nuances right, and I was good at it."

"You never told me this before," Liv said quietly, turning so they faced each other. "Honey, you do whatever you want to do. I don't care. You know I can support us. If you want to do something as a volunteer, you go do it. Okay? Tell me what I need to do."

"Nothing. You don't need to do anything." She sighed and leaned against Liv for a moment, enjoying the fresh scent of her. "I'm going to quit at Rock World. That's step one. I've already offered to be an on-call translator for the local RCMP. Charley helped me set it up. I was thinking of doing the same with social services. I've gotten pretty good at Arabic and French, even if I'm self-taught. I'm sure I'd be useful."

"You're practically fluent in French now. You'll be more than useful. I'm sure of it."

"Thanks, but you're biased. I'll offer my skills and see what they say."

"They'll say yes." Liv kissed her softly. "So, did you want to go first?"

"Thanks for finally asking," Grace said with a laugh. "But no. I want to see you all pregnant and glowing."

"Pregnant and glowing?" Liv raised a questioning eyebrow. "You think I'll glow?"

"I know you will." Grace tapped her on the thigh as their names were called out. "You'll be a beautiful pregnant woman. Wait and see."

****

"Time to break you out of here, Charlene." Charles Townsend's voice boomed in the small hospital room.

Charley's face broke into a big grin, as it did anytime she saw her dad. "Hey, Dad. I thought Mom was coming to get me."

He pushed a wheelchair next to her bed. "She's at your place getting it ready, whatever that means."

"It means I won't know where anything is when I get home," she said, and pointedly looked at the wheelchair. "You know I hurt my hand, not my legs, right?"

"The nurse said it's hospital policy you get wheeled out.

Now get in this thing so we can blow this joint."

"Blow this joint? You're a gangster now?"

Charles shrugged. "I watched a couple movies last weekend. Your mother threatened to lock me in the trailer if I didn't take some time off work so I picked some of my favorite movies to re-watch."

"Uh-huh. And you chose the ones you know she hates? Like *The Godfather*, for example?"

She settled into the chair, cradling her arm in its new sling. Charles leaned closer to whisper, even though no one was in the room with them. "I might have."

"You're a shit, Dad." Charlie laughed as he wheeled her out of the room and into an elevator as if they were being chased. "You in a hurry?"

"Yep. If we get moving then we can spare some time for lunch. I told your mother it might take awhile to get you signed out and stuff."

"It usually does. So how come we're out of here so fast?"

The elevator door opened and he all but ran outside to his truck. "Well, I got connections, see?" His very bad gangster impression made Charley laugh. "And a little gold goes a long way."

"Oh you did not just tell me you bribed someone!"

"Well, one tiny nugget in a sealed container for his daughter's show-and-tell next week. I'd been promising to get it to him, and we never met up until now."

"You mean Ned? My nurse?"

"Yep. So he got the doc to sign you out first thing this morning so I can take you to Marge's for some real food."

Charley couldn't have erased the smile on her face if she'd wanted to. "I love you," she said as she got into his truck. He closed the door for her and winked at her before returning the wheelchair.

He was back in a flash, and they were off to Marge's Diner.

They fell into a comfortable silence on the drive to the tiny town of Blue River, a good forty-five minutes from the hospital. Charley knew damn well her father's excuse about hospital paperwork wouldn't stand up against her mother's inquisition. But it didn't matter. Being with Charles was fun, and she took any and every opportunity to spend alone time with him.

She glanced at him as he drove, taking in his strong profile. Morning stubble adorned his rounded chin and cheeks adding a rugged look to his otherwise soft features. His hair was more grey than black and at the moment needed a trim. No doubt he'd kept too busy to let Josie get her clippers out. Charles preferred his hair long. Not "hippie" long as he would say, but he liked it to touch his shoulders.

Laugh lines crinkled along the edges of his eyes, and when he turned to meet her gaze, he was grinning. "I got something on my face?" he asked with one eyebrow arched.

"Nope. Thinking about how old you look."

"Not the compliment I was fishing for," he said wryly and returned his gaze to the road. "But I'm like your grandpa. I'm looking older than my age already. He was right. Have kids and they'll make you old real quick."

"Ha," Charley blurted out. "You only have one kid, and I never gave you any trouble, you big liar."

"You're giving me trouble right now."

"Not the point. You earned those grey hairs all by yourself."

Charles made a grunting noise. "Wait until you start getting them, young lady. You won't be a bit happy."

"I probably won't get grey until I'm in my seventies. My hair's too black, and I keep it short enough you won't be able to tell anyway."

He raised an eyebrow again. "You think your First Nation blood is going to keep you from getting old?"

"Not keep me from getting old. Keep me from *looking* old. Kathy Jenkins is sixty-four and look at her. You'd never know it with her hair still black as night. She said I'd be the same way. It's in my DNA." She gave him her most brilliant smile and stuck her tongue out. "So there."

"You did not get such an attitude from me," he grumbled, despite the grin on his face.

It felt good to laugh with him, Charley thought. They didn't spend enough time together, both of them driven to work all hours. Charles because he loved it. Charley because she had to.

Marge's finally came into view. The idea of a 50s diner in

the middle of the Yukon was kinda crazy, but Marge's pulled it off. Had done so for many years now. Most of Blue River still looked like an 1800s mining town. But not Marge's. The place resembled one of those metallic campers, and the second Charley and Charles walked in, they were overwhelmed with the amazing aroma of home-cooked food. The inside was designed to look exactly like a diner from the 50s, complete with chrome trimmings and red vinyl seats.

Charley was about to sit at the bar when she noticed someone waving at her. She froze when she recognized her mother. Immediately, she turned to her dad. "You set this up, didn't you?" She pointed a finger at him, shaking it a little.

"Seriously, I did not. But she texted me when I was taking the wheelchair back into the hospital. It said, and I quote, 'You're both busted. See you at Marge's.' You know we can't hide things from that woman."

"That woman looks way too pleased with herself right now," Charley said. She moved past her dad and hugged her mom with one arm. "Fancy meeting you here."

"Uh-huh. He tried to bribe your early release and didn't think I'd find out about it. Except Ned called me because your father didn't answer his phone and he had a question."

"Must've been in a dead spot," Charles muttered and pulled out a chair for Charley then settled beside his wife. He gave her a quick peck on the cheek. "What'd he want?"

"Another nugget. He forgot to get one for his wife, too."

"Does she need one for show-and-tell," Charles asked with a laugh. Josie's look told him she did. "Seriously?"

"You didn't know Amy's a teacher? She needs it for a geology lesson." Josie sighed. "Never mind. Get another one so he can pass it off to her. You owe him big time. But if you ever do something like this again—and I'm sure you will—you might want to make sure they don't tell me anything."

Charley shook her head. "Dad, you suck as a criminal. Maybe you're watching the wrong movies. Try *Ocean's 11*. Or better yet, *Ocean's 8*. Might give you some insight into how women think."

"Won't help him," Josie said, now perusing the menu. "He'd be too busy drooling over Sandra Bullock."

"Me, too. Guess I know where I get it."

Josie glanced at Charley over the top of her menu. "We certainly do. All your bad habits come from him. Everything else is from me."

Charles rolled his eyes and picked up his menu. Charley took a moment to watch her parents now interacting over what to eat and if they wanted to share parts or all of a meal, wheeling and dealing what to order as they always did. She loved how close they were and how they never, not even in the hardest of times, argued or fought with each other. They may not agree all the time, but they always found a middle ground.

Biology didn't bind her to these special people, but love sure as hell did. It was one of the reasons she didn't care who her DNA donors, as she called them, were. Kathy Jenkins had worked for the *Ta'an Kwäch'än* Council for twenty years. She'd offered many times to find Charley's family. Thing was, Charley already had a family.

Chapter Five

Cappuccino, as Jada was happy to tell anyone within earshot, was essential to life itself. She could go hours without food. Days without sleep. But to do so without cappuccino? The sweet taste of steamed milk and added bonus of cinnamon combined with expresso was as close to perfection as possible. And Jada couldn't wait to get her hands on the hot, steamy goodness. Especially on a cool morning such as today.

The problem was in order to get cappuccino with the amazing ingredients needed to send adrenaline into her veins, she had to stand in the longest line ever. She folded her arms over her chest and blew out an impatient breath.

Her gaze followed the people behind the mahogany counter. Neither of the twenty-somethings seemed in any kind of hurry to fulfill their orders. Like they had all day to brew coffee and hand it out as they saw fit. Three people stood between Jada and her chance to order, and she started to fidget. She needed her fix. Scratch that. She needed to buy a cappuccino machine in order to make the stuff at home in the morning instead of standing in this maddening line from hell. She shouldn't have left hers with Francine.

She glanced at her watch, even though she had nowhere to be. She was on the last of her three days off and really, really wanted to start out with her drink of choice. Her brain froze when she heard one of the kids behind the counter, the counter she was now two people away from, call out, "Sorry folks. The machine is down."

"How does that even happen?" someone behind Jada asked.

"Seriously? I've been in line for, like, ten minutes," the blonde teenage girl in front of Jada said. "Can't you, like, fix it or something?"

"No," the so-called barista replied. He went back to taking orders for anything but a delectable, caffeinated, milk-spiked drink.

Jada cursed quietly and left the stupid place. She stood on the sidewalk and checked out the restaurants and other businesses around her. She was a block from the National Bank of Whitehorse, which she could see from where she stood. It had a small café type restaurant next to it, but she doubted they sold anything more than black coffee with cream and sugar. The idea gave her the willies.

Eight months in this small city, and she still wasn't familiar enough with the layout. She never got lost and mostly stuck close to the hospital or her apartment. But today she needed to venture farther out. She needed her cappuccino, and she needed it now. She couldn't exactly spend time exploring the city without it.

That's when she spotted her salvation. Or rather, a possible tour guide. Jada spotted Charley heading into the bank, striding with the purpose only a cop had. She nearly jogged the block distance and got to the front door as Charley was coming back out.

"Hi there," Jada greeted her with a big, toothy smile. "Fancy meeting you here."

Charley wrinkled her brow as if she wasn't sure who Jada was. Maybe she didn't remember her at all.

Jada saved her from embarrassment. She pointed to Charley's bandaged hand. "I'm the paramedic who saved your life last week. I'm glad to see you up and about, though I'd have thought you'd still be resting."

Dark eyes studied her with a hint of a sparkle. Charley was amused. A good sign. Charley said, "Thanks for the save." She nodded in Jada's direction. "I'm currently on a bid for freedom from my mother. She's in my apartment making everything a certain way so I don't need my left hand. She won't leave until she's sure I can get by without her. By the time she's done, I won't know where anything is. I had to make a break for it and check on something here at the bank." Charley pulled her cell phone from her pocket with her right hand. "She's already texted me five times."

"Kinda sucks. But hey, at least she's there helping you. That's good, right?"

"It is." Charley sighed dramatically. "I love her, but she's making me crazy and I've only been home two days."

"Well, I have a sure-fire cure for this." Jada leaned forward, nearly eye to eye with Charley. "Cappuccino."

"Cappuccino?"

"Of course. It cures everything. But I can't find any. Damn place over there broke their machine. I feel like I'll die if I don't get some soon. Got any suggestions? I mean, you've got to know every nook and cranny in this city, right?"

"I do, indeed." Charley cradled her injured hand as she considered Jada's question. "Two blocks north of here is a tiny bakery. Mostly frequented by locals in the area, but she's got amazing donuts. Like Michelin Star quality donuts. And she's famous for her coffee, so I imagine she's got the machine you're looking for."

"Sarge, I will love you forever if you take me to this amazing place with the magic machine."

"My name's Charley, and I'd be happy to show you where it is. I need to text my mom so she doesn't send search and rescue after me." Charley fumbled with the phone in her good hand for a few seconds, unable to figure out how to hold it and type at the same time.

Jada took pity on her. "Give me the phone." She held out her hand. "Tell me what to tell her, and I'll do it for you."

"I can do it," Charley said. She cradled the phone on her bandaged left hand and tried to type the message with her index finger on the right hand. The phone kept slipping and finally Jada grabbed it from her. "Hey! Give it back."

"No." Jada typed a text and returned the phone. "Now, for next time, learn to use the talk-to-type function. Much easier when your hands are busy."

"Thanks," Charley mumbled and stowed the phone in her pocket. "So, you want to go to CoffeeNut with me?"

"CoffeeNut?"

"Yeah. The place with the killer donuts." Charley pointed down the street, but it didn't mean much to Jada. "It's over there. C'mon. Least I can do since you already told my mom we were going for a cappuccino, which she won't believe since I hate those froufrou drinks."

"Froufrou?" Jada said, one eyebrow lifted in shock. "We need to sit down and have a serious discussion about the important things in life. Starting with how cappuccino is not froufrou and just how vital it is to society."

Charley laughed softly. "You're serious about your coffee."

"It's not coffee. It's cappuccino, you Philistine."

"Wow, okay. I surrender." Charley laughed outright, and it soothed Jada in a way she never expected. The laugh was genuine and it lit Charley's face. Jada wanted nothing more than to make it happen again. Often. She liked the expression on Charley's face. The joy caused by something as simple as making light of Jada's obsession with cappuccino.

"You're kinda easy. I thought a tough girl like you would have fought a little harder."

"I'm careful how I pick my fights. I want to win." Charley winked at her, and for a moment, Jada saw the twinkle in her eyes again. It didn't last long, and it saddened Jada to see it leave so fast.

She shook the unexpected feeling away and concentrated on the beautiful eyes staring back at her. "A smart woman always knows when to fight and when to walk away. She knows how to win and when it's best to lose."

"She does indeed."

They walked a few more minutes, and Charley stopped in front of a stand-alone building with plate-glass windows along the entire front of it. You could see everything going on inside. Booths covered in deep-green vinyl lined the window area. Tables for four sat scattered through the rest of the open space. Each chair had a green seat.

Jada stopped to examine the image on the front window of the café: A coffee cup with steam coming out the top silhouetted in white against the plain window. The name "CoffeeNut" was displayed in the center of the cup, with various nuts spilling out of the top.

Jada moved past the interesting image and into the most heavenly place on earth. The smell alone would make her want to move in and live there forever. She could almost taste the cappuccino from the aroma. Caramel drifted across her alert senses, followed by a host of other tantalizing flavors. How would she ever choose just one?

"Hey, Charley!" A pretty blonde woman called out from behind the counter.

Charley's face lit up as she stepped closer to the woman. "Stefi, how's it going?"

"Better than it's going for you. Didn't they teach you at that fancy RCMP academy how to handle a knife. Like, by using the *handle*?"

"Funny."

"Well, at least you finally get to take some time off. Sorry your hand is messed up, but I'm glad you get a chance to rest."

"I don't want to rest. I want to fight crime."

Stefi rolled her eyes and said, "Whatever. You looking for a donut? I made a batch of coconut cream ones. Wanna try?"

"Coconut cream?" Jada asked.

Stefi looked a little surprised. Her gaze went to Jada, but she spoke to Charley. "Are you going to continue to be rude and not introduce me to your friend?" She lifted an eyebrow when she emphasized the word friend.

"Stefi, this is Jada. Jada, Stefi. Okay?"

Jada bumped Charley out of the way with her hip and extended her hand to Stefi. "This is the best-smelling place I've been to in years. And I can practically taste the caramel macchiato I know you're going to make to perfection for me."

Stefi's grip was strong, but Jada found her hand to be smaller than expected.

"I thought you wanted a cappuccino," Charley said.

"I changed my mind. I'm a woman. It's what we do."

"I like her," Stefi said, pointing to Jada. "You should keep her. I'm going to make a drink for you and get you both a coconut cream donut. You'll love them. I promise."

Jada watched in fascination as Stefi moved with precision behind the counter. She began making her drink and Jada realized Stefi's arms were short and kind of stubby. Her fingers weren't very long, and while she did everything with complete confidence and efficiency, Jada had to take a moment to be amazed. Stefi must have been standing on a platform because Jada now realized Stefi wasn't much more than four feet tall.

Her light-blue eyes held a hint of grey in them, and as she worked, she occasionally used her hand to tuck golden strands of her straight hair behind her left ear. She hummed a tune Jada couldn't quite make out, and in just a few minutes had Jada's beloved caffeinated drink ready for her.

Jada had never met anyone like Stefi and was completely in awe of her. "Thanks," she said and took a drink. The taste was perfect, and she mirrored the smile on Stefi's face. "This is amazing. If you're available, I might want to marry you."

Stefi laughed heartily and handed them each a donut before she rang up their order. She held out a hand to Charley for payment. "I'm serious. You need to keep her."

"She's not mine to keep, Stefi." Charley sounded a tiny bit miffed while she paid. "You've got it all wrong."

"No way." Stefi grinned at Jada. "I know what I see. Now go have a seat and enjoy the donuts. Send your friends here. Next month I'm going to make Oreo cookie donuts. It'll be like an orgasm in your mouth. Trust me."

Charley shook her head and carried their donuts to a table in the corner. "Never mind Stefi."

"I like her." Jada sipped her drink and watched as Charley very carefully tested the donut. "And?"

"Mmm. I didn't think it'd taste very good, but this is great. I mean, it's not a taste I'd expect for a donut, but she sure has this one down. The coconut is a nice surprise. I didn't think I'd like it."

Jada wholeheartedly agreed and ate her donut in three bites. It felt good in her empty stomach, followed, of course, by the rest of her sugary, caffeinated goodness. "Thanks for showing me this place. I'd have never found it and would have suffered without my froufrou drink."

"You're welcome. You should take more time to explore the city. There's a lot more to Whitehorse than most people expect."

"Exactly my plans for today. Wander around and see what kind of trouble I can get into. Wanna come with?"

Charley sucked in her bottom lip and the action created a pleasant sensation in Jada's belly. What she wouldn't give to be the one to suck on that lip right now. Take hold of her gorgeous face, run her fingers along soft, brown skin and kiss her into next week.

"...go home."

Jada snapped back to the here and now, realizing she'd not heard a word Charley said. "So you need to get back home?" She guessed.

"I do. I don't want Mom to worry, and she doesn't know where I am."

"I understand. Moms are important people. You need to hang on to her as long as you can." Jada cleared her throat. "If you bring up the icon for your text messages, you'll find a little microphone in the corner where you would type. Tap it and speak your message, and it'll type it for you. Make sure you speak clearly because it can send some crazy shit if you don't pay attention."

"Cool." Charley immediately tried it out by telling her mom she was on the way home from CoffeeNut. But the text message said Comma Hut instead. Jada giggled.

"See what I mean?" she said.

"Well, she'll get the idea." Charley got up and put their paper plates and napkins in the recycle bins.

"Thanks again for showing me this place." Jada waved to Stefi on her way out. "I might have a new friend and a new place to fuel myself in the mornings."

"Happy to help. Have fun exploring."

"Um, hang on." Jada touched Charley's arm long enough to get her attention, then she let go as if it were made of fire. The sensation she got from touching Charley was unlike anything she'd ever felt before. Not at all unpleasant. "You're on injury leave at the moment, and I'm off again on Friday if you're up for it, how about you give me a tour of the city? I mean, you know everything and everyone, right?"

"Well, not everyone and everything, but most people and most things. But why do you want me? I bet if you go back into CoffeeNut, Stefi would shut down the place and show you around."

"You think she's into me?"

"I know she is."

"Sister, you're blind. She's nice and friendly, but she wasn't into me at all. Besides, even if she was, I wouldn't go out with her."

"Why the hell not?" Charley was suddenly on the offensive, and Jada wanted to backtrack to figure out why, but Charley steamed right ahead. "She's a great person, lots of fun, and good-looking to boot. You got something against people who aren't as tall as you or me?"

"Whoa! When did this become about her height? I'm not into her, you dumbass. I'm into you."

Charley blinked at her so much Jada wondered if she were trying to talk to her in Morse Code. "Me?"

"Yes. When I finally had a chance to look at you in the ER, you woke up and I realized there might be someone in there I'd like to get to know. So, when you get your head out of your ass, you come find me." Jada pulled Charley's phone from her pocket, typed in her number and handed it back. "Call me."

Jada left Charley on the sidewalk, mouth hanging open like she was catching flies for a living. But she had a very strong feeling Charley Townsend was going to call her. Maybe not today, but soon.

****

An hour later, instead of going back to her apartment, Charley walked into the RCMP station. She needed a distraction to take her mind off Jada. Her phone felt warm in her pocket, like it begged her to use it and call Jada right now. Charley fought against wanting to call her, go out with her, and spend more time looking into her amazingly warm, rich-brown eyes. Beautiful didn't describe her well enough. Charley could hardly take her eyes off Jada's long legs, perfect ass, and deep, dark skin. She shivered at the memory of Jada's hand brushing against hers.

She wanted to shut the feelings down immediately.

Work was her number one stopgap when she didn't want to feel or remember. So, she sent a message to her mom to say she was stopping by the station.

When she arrived, Inspector Pike was in front of the reception desk talking to someone Charley didn't recognize. The man was in jeans and a green T-shirt and animated as he spoke. She waited for him to finish and was a little surprised by the stern look Pike sent her way when he realized she stood there. Like a teacher about to scold a student.

Pike crossed his arms over his chest and sighed. "Townsend, do you not understand the meaning of injury leave?"

"Inspector, I thought I'd come by—"

"Stop right there. While I appreciate your dedication, you are not going to do any work for the next several weeks. You just had surgery, and I'm not about to let you re-injure yourself. Even if you're only here to do paperwork, which would be interesting to see you try with your right hand."

Charley wanted to stomp her foot like a petulant child. It didn't feel right not spending time at the station. It's where she usually ended up on her off time. It's where she felt alive. And it's how she occupied her brain. Kept it away from stuff like Raina. Or Jada. Right now, all she wanted to do was head to the canteen and see who might be hanging about. Was it too much to ask?

She met Pike's gaze and realized he looked upon her with genuine compassion. "I get it, Townsend. I do. Just a couple of days away from work, and you're jonesing to get back to it. Except you can't. I promise once you start doing some physical therapy, and your therapist says your hand is strong enough, I'll try to find you some kind of light duty. Maybe come in once a week and shuffle paperwork or something. But right now you need to go home and rest. Do nothing with your hand until your therapist tells you it's okay. Hell, at least wait until the stitches are out before you come back here." Pike put his hand on Charley's shoulder and gently turned her toward the door. "Want me to give you a lift home?"

Charley was numb. Everything he said made perfect sense, and a reasonable person would be okay going home and doing nothing. But she didn't feel like a reasonable person. It didn't feel reasonable that she was in this situation. Doctor Hughes said the surgery went well. But it didn't mean Charley'd be able to use her hand again, did it? She was lost, and this station was the only place she ever felt stable. Like it centered her somehow. Was her anchor.

Pike watched her with a curious expression on his face. Before he spoke, Charley said, "Sure. I'm kinda tired from walking. I'd love a ride home."

He gave her a brief smile. They went out the front door and down the steps to the parking lot. Once inside his car, Pike said, "I got a call from your mother about half an hour ago." He started the car and let it warm up a moment before pulling out of his parking space. "She told me you'd be stopping by. Charley, I mean it when I say I get you want to be back at work so bad it hurts. I've been there. But you have to rest. Your body needs to heal, and if you aren't careful, you might not get back to the job. It's lucky your trigger finger wasn't the one cut open."

Charley looked down at the bulky bandages. Yes, she was lucky there. If her trigger finger had been damaged, it would be game over for her career. Her physical therapist said as much. But in order to shoot her weapon, she needed to grip it properly. It was unclear how long it would be for her to regain the use of not only her middle finger, but most of her hand. Gripping was going to be the hardest thing to retrain her hand to do.

She glanced at Pike as he drove. He was one of those guys who kept climbing the ranks. She was surprised he'd stayed at inspector. He was a good guy, though, and she looked up to him. When he was in full dress uniform, he was the poster boy for the RCMP. Handsome, perfectly cut hair, muscular build, and perfect posture when he rode his horse; Pike made everyone else look like slobs.

She briefly wondered if she'd be able to ride a horse again.

"I'm sorry if I'm being a pain," she said.

Pike didn't speak right away. He pulled into her apartment complex and parked the car, leaving the engine running. "You're a good Mountie, Townsend. Never forget that. This injury is going to be fine. I know you'll work on it as hard as you work on anything else. Don't overdo it, and focus on getting back to work." He reached into the chest pocket of his shirt and handed her a business card. "I had to spend four months off duty when I injured my knee in a foot pursuit years ago. I thought I'd go insane, and let's just say my wife had to take a vacation to get away from me for a while." He gave her a weak smile. "Call this psychologist. She's amazing and will know exactly what to say to help you along. Trust me. You'll feel better if you do."

"Thank you, Inspector." Charley placed the card in her back pocket. "Can I ask you something?"

"Of course."

"Why were you at the station today? You don't come out here often. Seems a little odd you'd be here."

"With you off, we're short an officer. While we wait for a temporary transfer to come in from Vancouver, I decided to take your place. Gives me an excuse to get back on the road and be with my officers. Plus, I had this feeling you'd be hard to keep away from the station. I'll be here for the next two weeks, and I'm going to make sure you stay away for a while." He gave her a friendly pat on the shoulder. "Take this time and relax. Talk to Debra. You won't regret it."

"Debra?"

"On the card I gave you. Now get out of my vehicle. I need to head over to the Andersons. The mister is due in court next week, and I want to be sure he understands he has to show up. I don't know if anyone told you, but we got a report Mr. Anderson has dementia. It explains all the violent outbursts he's had for the last few years. Their grandson's getting him into a facility where he can be taken care of. That's who I was talking to when you came in. I guess the grandson is going to move in with Mrs. Anderson to take care of her."

"Good to know." Charley opened the door and stepped out of the car. "Thanks, Inspector."

"You got it. I'll be in touch."

Charley closed the door and watched him leave, then she pulled the business card from her back pocket. Debra was a psychologist with an office across the city from Charley's apartment. She didn't think she was ready to see a psychologist again but kept the card anyway. It would probably help, but inevitably the conversation would turn to Raina and Charley simply wasn't ready.

Chapter Six

Grace glanced at the clock on the microwave. It wasn't quite five, so she had a bit more time before Liv would be home. Home. It still felt a little weird and exciting to think they finally lived under the same roof. The ring on her left hand made her smile. She'd never expected to get married again, but this time it was right. She knew, deep down, she and Liv would be spending the rest of their lives together.

And with any luck, Liv would soon be carrying their first child.

Her smile never faded as she got things ready for dinner. Grace enjoyed the chance to cook for her family. *Ojiichan* certainly enjoyed her meals, and he looked better for the healthier eating she provided for him. He was a man of many talents, cooking not being one of them. At ninety-four, *Ojiichan* was still going strong.

He could be a grumpy, stubborn old man, but she loved her grandfather dearly and wouldn't trade a minute of their time together for anything in the world.

She finished peeling the potatoes and smiled when she heard Harry close the door to his tiny apartment, which was an extension of the first-floor guest room of their two-story home. They'd added on to it, making use of the half-acre backyard, and now Harry had his own bathroom, bedroom, and seating area. He made good use of the kitchen whenever he wanted, happy to microwave his food when Grace wasn't around.

"Did you sense dinner is being prepared?" she asked him when he joined her in the kitchen.

"Yes, but it will not be done for a while. I have come looking for a snack."

"Apples are in a basket on the table."

"Ha. I want a cookie," Harry said, sliding past her to get to the cookie tin.

"You'll spoil your dinner."

"I will not."

"You will, too." Grace slapped his hand away when he tried to open the tin. "*Ojiichan,* you're worse than a child."

"You wish I was like a child. Wait until you have one. Then you will see how easy it is to get along with me." Harry successfully dodged her next hand slap and got to the tin. He opened it and popped a peanut butter cookie into his mouth. He kept a second one in his hand and backed away from Grace. His dark eyes were full of merriment. His smile made the corners of his eyes crinkle a little. He wasn't as tall as Grace's 5'6", but he always stood ramrod straight. Probably from spending thirty plus years in the army. He held the second cookie in his now arthritic hand and shook it at her. "You are worse than your *obachaan.* She never let me snack before dinner."

"She was a smart woman who looked out for your health. Why do you think you got to be so old? It was all her doing," Grace said, shaking a finger back at him. "If she were here, she probably wouldn't even buy those cookies for you. I'm going to have a talk with Olivia about it."

"Don't you dare," he said, munching on his second cookie. "Liv is my buddy. She likes buying things for me. Especially cookies."

"Because they happen to be her favorite, too."

"Which is why I like her." Harry gave her his most charming smile, winked, and left the kitchen.

Grace sighed. Even though she thought his antics were adorable, she had a tendency to worry. His heart attack last summer still weighed heavily on her mind. She wanted him to live another ten years and thought he was totally capable of it, but the odds weren't in his favor. A couple of cookies wouldn't matter in the long run.

She put the potatoes into her Instant Pot and set about getting the rest of her ingredients for stew added in. She was washing the carrots when she heard a knock at the door. Grace wiped her hands dry and answered it without thinking to look out the window to see who it might be. Had she done so, she'd be on the phone calling the police.

Standing on the porch, the evening sun highlighting her pale, blonde hair, was Carly Osbourne. Like a nightmare come true, Grace's ex-wife was less than a foot away from her. Carly smiled and took a step inside.

Grace froze in place. She couldn't stop Carly from walking past her and closing the door once she was in. The King County prosecutor's office in Washington told her Carly was released from jail three weeks ago, her sentence being shortened due to a lack of space in the jail and time served or something.

It didn't matter. She was there, in front of Grace, as calm and cool as ever. Her smile was almost kind, and when she spoke, it was like nothing bad had ever passed between them.

"You look good, Grace."

"Why—what are you doing here? How'd you find me?"

"Not happy to see me?" Carly closed the distance between them. She lifted her hand and caressed Grace's cheek.

Grace flinched at the touch but didn't move away. Her body refused to follow any directions from her brain. She opened her mouth to speak, but nothing came out.

"I still love you." Carly's voice was soft, sensual. "I never once stopped thinking about you these last few years." Her fingers traced the jagged scar along the side of Grace's face. Grace remained still, recalling the slam of the bat against her head that nearly took her life. "I'm sorry for what I did," Carly said.

"You've said that before."

"And I meant it every time." Carly leaned her head to the side as if she were trying to decide something. Her eyes were cold, steely, and they never left Grace's. "I came to bring you back with me."

"What the hell?" Grace was surprised by the forcefulness of her own voice. "I don't want anything to do with you."

"I make you happy, Grace. I'm the one who can give you what you want. What you need." Carly's face was inches from hers, and Grace trembled with fear.

She wanted to run. She needed to get the hell away from her.

The sound of a vehicle entering the long driveway pulled Grace's attention from Carly. It had to be Liv. For an instant, Grace was terrified. Would Carly try to hurt Liv? What about *Ojiichan*? She'd momentarily forgotten he was there as well.

Her thoughts must have been obvious as Carly backed away. "I'll be back, Gracie. I promise you." And then she was gone.

When the front door opened again, Grace nearly screamed.

Liv had a confused expression on her face and dropped the bag she was carrying onto the counter. "Hey, what's going on? Who was that woman?"

Grace was still shaking and fell into Liv's embrace. She forced the tears back while Liv held her. "It was Carly."

"Carly? Carly Osbourne?" Liv asked.

"Yes."

She felt Liv tense, like she was about to go after her. Grace tightened her hold on Liv. "What the fuck was she doing here? How did she find us? Did you call the police? Did she hurt you?"

"I don't know and no. I—I didn't do anything. I stood here in shock." She looked up into Liv's face, a mix of compassion and anger reflecting back at her. "Don't go after her." Grace knew she was reading Liv correctly when Liv wouldn't meet her eyes. "I need you here."

"I won't go anywhere," Liv said and gently released her. She looked out the front window then pulled her cell phone from her pocket. "I'm calling the police. I don't see her now, but I did see a dark-blue Ford something or other parked on the street. Maybe that was her car."

Grace's body finally obeyed her commands. She made her way to the living room and collapsed onto the couch. Harry came out of his apartment. He joined her and waited for Grace to start talking.

Grace listened to Liv tell the police what happened, then she turned to Harry. She said, "Carly was just here. She found me and said she came to bring me home. She means to come back for me."

Harry took Grace's hand in his and wrapped his gnarled fingers around hers. "We won't let it happen, Gracie Lee. You'll be fine. The police will find Carly."

"They're on the way. Probably about ten minutes or so." Liv joined them. She knelt in front of Grace and rested her hands on Grace's knees. "He's right. We'll make sure she doesn't come back here." She met Grace's gaze. "If she does, she'll be the one in the hospital."

"Don't," Grace said, even though she wanted Liv to follow up on her threat. It wouldn't do any good, though, and Liv would end up in trouble. "Stay away from her if you see her. Promise me."

"No." Liv leaned forward and kissed her. "I'd break it. Just like I'll break her if I see her. It was hard enough not to go chasing her just now. At least I know what she looks like."

"Don't argue with her, Gracie Lee. It will do you no good," Harry said. "It is best we allow the police to handle this, Olivia, if possible. Can you agree?"

"Of course," Liv said. "For now."

Grace rested against the back of the couch, relieved about the safety of her family surrounding her.

A few minutes later, Charley entered the house, not bothering to knock. Grace tried her best to smile, but she knew it didn't come close to reaching her eyes. Charley still had her hand in a sling but strode up to them with such authority it surprised Grace. She'd never seen this side of Charley before.

"You're sure it was her?"

"Of course she's sure," Liv said, getting to her feet. "You think she wouldn't know her own ex-wife?"

Before Charley replied, Grace said, "Yes. I'm sure. She walked right in here, Charley. Said she'd come back for me."

"There's a unit looking for the car Liv described, but right now there's not a lot we can do unless she assaulted or threatened you."

"She damn near killed her three years ago, Charley! Doesn't that count for something?"

Harry stood and put his hand on Liv's shoulder. The effect was instantaneous and she calmed down. "Charlene knows the law, Olivia. We must have cause to have her arrested. I suggest we get Gracie Lee to the courthouse right now. She can file for a peace bond. Then, if Carly returns, the police can act. Right Charlene?"

Charley nodded, her expression stoic as she continued to look upon Grace. "Why don't you go get that done now. Head to the station and have them write it up for you. You'll have to testify before a judge tomorrow. A peace bond will protect you for a year, so that's more than enough time for us to find her and get her out of our country." She offered her good hand to Grace and helped her up. "I had no idea she was out, Gracie. Did you?"

"I did, but I didn't think she'd ever find me here. I mean,

the house is under my married name and so is my driver's license, both the Canadian one and the one for the US. Who back in Seattle even knows where I live?"

"We'll figure it out later. Go. I'll see if she has a probation officer or not."

Grace nodded numbly and took Liv's hand. "C'mon. You need to drive me."

"Of course." Liv kissed her tenderly on the cheek and walked Grace to her truck. Once in it, she turned to Grace before starting the engine. "I'm sorry, Gracie. I know my protective streak freaks you out sometimes. I didn't mean to. I can't stand to think about you being hurt."

"I understand," Grace said and placed a hand over Liv's. "I love that about you. But I know Carly better than anyone, and I know what she's capable of." Almost unconsciously, she twisted her left arm so the scar was more visible. "I couldn't bear the thought of her doing this to you. All the bravado in the world won't convince me she can't or wouldn't hurt you, Olivia."

"I'm sorry," Liv said quietly and started the truck. "After we get this protection order, let's see a lawyer. Maybe there's something else we can do."

"Sounds like a plan."

Liv squeezed her hand and kept a tight grip on it as they made their way to the city courthouse. Grace stared out the passenger window and fought her tears. She'd cried enough over Carly and all the damage she'd brought to Grace's life. She'd be damned if she'd spill another tear.

****

They found no trace of Carly or the blue Ford. Charley suspected she'd left the city. She might be staying in Blue River, and Elle would be going there tomorrow to look around, but Charley didn't hold out much hope of finding Carly.

All the years Carly beat on Grace, she'd managed to skirt the law. Even when Charley intervened and tried to get Grace away from her, Carly was a step ahead of them. There were no bruises on Grace's skin, so no evidence to prove abuse. It'd be Grace's word against Carly's, and Grace wasn't strong enough to up and leave her. Not then.

Two months later, Grace was in intensive care and Charley often wondered if it was because she'd failed to be more forceful and yank Grace away from her, or had Carly retaliated because Grace was on the brink of leaving her. It didn't matter so much anymore, but it was one of those memories Charley wouldn't forget.

Like Raina.

Charley stepped off the porch of Liv and Grace's home and approached the police unit as it pulled into the driveway. Quentin Sommerfield was in the passenger seat and Inspector Pike was driving. She steeled herself for the ass-chewing Pike was going to give her.

"Hi, guys." Charley stood at the passenger side of the car and gave details about what happened between Grace and Carly. "Liv and Grace are heading to the courthouse to get a protection order against Carly Osbourne. Shouldn't be difficult since she nearly killed Grace a few years ago."

"You're kidding," Sommerfield said.

"Nope. Grace was in a coma for three days." She leaned down to see Pike watching her, his face a mask. Yep. She was going to get an ass-chewing for being involved in this. Probably later though. "I know I jumped your call, but you know I don't live far away, and Gracie's family to me. I needed to make sure she was okay." Charley gave them a description of Carly and the vehicle she was in.

"Understood," Pike said. "We're going to patrol the neighborhood for a while. Text Sommerfield when the protection order is in place."

"Yes, sir."

"And Townsend?" Pike leaned across Sommerfield, his eyes like lasers zeroing in on her. "Injury leave. No responding to calls. I don't care who's involved. Got me?"

"I do, sir." Charley felt a flush of heat come over her face at the embarrassment of being called out in front of one of her officers. "I don't guarantee it won't happen again."

"I didn't expect you would." He settled back against his seat and drove off.

Charley sighed. She wasn't entirely sure what would happen if she responded to another call at Gracie's house, but ultimately she didn't care. She couldn't keep Carly away from her in Seattle, but this was her city. She'd be damned if Carly was going to hurt anyone here.

Charley couldn't go to the station. If she showed up, Pike would be called and she'd get kicked out in no time. Instead she headed to her apartment. She had a couple of ideas about how to handle the Carly situation and needed time to think them through.

She should have expected to see her mother there when she walked in. Josie stood in the middle of the living area, hands on her hips, and ready to lay into Charley. Her face was nearly as red as her hair. Charley held up her hand, palm facing forward, to stop her.

"If it wasn't Gracie, I wouldn't have gone. But as soon as I heard the address, I had to get over there. You can't honestly expect me to stay here when I know something's going on. Do you?"

"Actually, I do. Gracie has Liv and Harry. If she called for the police, there's a good reason, and you know perfectly well they can handle things. I'd love it if you'd turn your police scanner off. I swear you're looking for an excuse to avoid this place. And me."

Charley noted the hurt in Josie's voice and immediately pulled her into a tight embrace. "That's not true and you know it. The last part, anyway. I love how you're looking out for me and all. But honestly, I can't just sit here when someone I care about might need my help."

Josie stepped back and looked up at Charley with watery eyes. "I'm worried about you. You've been here, in this apartment, for almost nine years, and there isn't a single personal item to be seen. No pictures. Nothing colorful. Not a single piece of mail to show you exist. I never realized how bad it was until I came here to help you. Is this why you never asked me or Dad to come visit you? Because you've never made this your home?"

"Maybe." The sadness in Josie's eyes hurt her, and Charlie looked away. She made it a point to go to the kitchen. "You want some coffee?"

"No. I want you to talk to me."

"It's not so simple, Mom. I don't feel like I belong here."

Josie was quiet while Charley brewed the coffee. She spoke again as they sat at the kitchen table. "You said that when you left for the RCMP Academy. You never felt like you fit in and wanted to go off to other places. Find adventure. See new things."

"It wasn't a slight against you. Or even this city. I was young and needed to do other things."

"Which is how you ended up in Prince Edward Island."

"You liked visiting me there." Charley smiled wryly.

"I did, but it wasn't the same as having you home. You're my only child, Charlene. I missed you. Sometimes I miss you even more now, and your apartment is twenty minutes from our house."

"I'm sorry." Charley stared at her coffee like it held all the answers in the world. "When I met Raina, things changed for me. I wanted so much more out of life—so much more with her."

"She was good for you," Josie said, her voice wavering as she spoke. "I miss her."

"Me, too." Charley cleared her throat in hopes of not crying. It didn't work. "Look, I don't know if I'll ever feel like I have a real home again. This place is where I keep my stuff, eat, and sleep. Nothing more. I don't want anything else."

"Come back home, then. Your dad's talked about remodeling the basement. Maybe we should make it your apartment. It's bigger than this tiny place, and you'll have all the privacy you want, but still be at home. We can go shopping for some colorful kitchen items. Maybe even find you another orange microwave. It'd be fun."

Charley gave her mother a warm smile, and understood she was, again, trying very hard to protect her. "I'll think on it, but honestly, Mom, I'm not sure it's the way to go. I know you want me as close as I can get. The problem is I don't know what I need." She gestured around the room. "Maybe this is all I need. Maybe it's what I get to live with forever. I don't know. Hell, I don't even know if I'll still have my career once this stupid hand is healed up. Right now isn't the time for me to be moving or changing things."

"I think right now is exactly the time for change, sweetheart." Josie reached across the table and gently stroked Charley's uninjured hand. "This is helping you reset your priorities while forcing you to come out of hiding. You've tucked into work for so long you don't know what the outside world is like. When was the last time you went out and had fun?"

Charley shrugged, even though she knew exactly when it happened. "Couple years ago," she admitted.

"When your dad guilted you into going out on a pontoon boat with us for the weekend. Four years ago," Josie corrected "You were relaxed and fun and enjoyed the entire time we were out there. But as soon as we got back, you were off to work and you never took time off again. Why not?"

The questions, as usual, were going right into the heart of the matter. How her mother could do so was beyond Charley's understanding. Must be some kind of mom superpower. "I felt guilty." She finally met Josie's concerned gaze, letting go of some of her sadness as she did. "Who was I to be out there having a good time when Raina was gone? She's never going to be out on the boat with us again. She's never going to head off to Cancun for a vacation, or go on a cruise, or skiing, or hiking, or any number of things we used to do. Ever. And the worst part is I don't know why. What was so wrong with our life? Why would she feel the need to kill herself? What did I miss? I'm a cop. I'm trained to deal with these situations. Why couldn't I fix my own wife?"

"Because you know as well as anyone else Raina hid it from all of us," Josie said. "Some people are able to hide every symptom and every thought until they've decided this is it. This is the day I'm going to take my own life. I hate how we'll never truly know why she did it. Maybe it was stress from work. Maybe it was how her parents disowned her for being gay. Maybe it was that she was unable to cope with the day-to-day stresses life brings us all.

"None of it makes her a bad person, honey. She was broken. If you were a psychologist, you probably wouldn't have figured it out. She was always loving with you, always up and ready to face the day's challenges."

"But it was all a lie. And I can't even talk to her about it. So who am I to go out and have fun?"

"Honestly, I think it's what she'd want for you. She took her own life, and in doing so, took her problems with her and away from you. Like she was saving you. Have you ever thought of that? Maybe she was doing it to allow you to move on and have a happy life. Maybe she was trying to protect you."

"No way." Charley got up, feeling a strong urge to run

away. "How did her suicide save me?"

"I don't know. Maybe she was at her breaking point, and if she broke down then she might be a burden to you."

"You almost sound like you know why she did it." Charley hadn't meant to sound accusatory.

Josie recoiled at her words. "What? I don't know why she did it. But your dad and I went to counseling, too. Raina never left so much as a good-bye note. No journal to go back and read. It wasn't a time when everyone was on social media, and even her cell phone didn't have anything in the photos or texts to indicate she wanted to kill herself. It's not unheard of for a person to hide depression so well. And you were focused on your career. If she became a burden to you, what would it mean to you in the long run? Raina knew damn well how much being a Mountie meant to you."

Charley shook her head even though everything Josie said made sense. Too much sense, actually. The impulse to leave overwhelmed her. "I need to take a walk," she said.

Josie stood and caught her arm before Charley got to the door. "Honey, I'm sorry. I didn't mean to hurt you, but I think it's time you faced the situation head on instead of ignoring it."

"I'm not ignoring it, Mom. I see it every day when I wake up and take a shower. She's dead and I'm not and I have to live with it for the rest of my life. Being a Mountie is all I ever wanted, but maybe I should have wanted Raina more. Maybe if I had, she'd still be here."

She heard her mother's horrified gasp as she walked out the door, careful not to slam it behind her.

Chapter Seven

Grace couldn't move.

Couldn't scream.

Her arms dangled at her sides as though they weren't hers.

A hand grabbed hers and she tried to pull back.

The hand was strong, the grip like iron, and there was nothing she could do…

Grace sat up in bed and looked around the room, trying to discern what had just happened. Liv was next to her, holding her hand and talking, but Grace didn't understand her words. Something about a nightmare maybe?

Liv's fingers gently brushed against Grace's cheek, and she turned to stare at Liv. Her brain wasn't processing things correctly.

"What happened?" she asked.

Liv cupped her face in her hand, and Grace wished the light was on so she could see Liv's expression. "You had a dream. You were mewling like a hurt cat and thrashing around. I had to grab your hand to keep you from going off the bed."

"I'm—I'm sorry." She looked down at their joined hands and released the tight hold she had on Liv. "I don't remember."

"Probably good you don't." Liv kissed her lips softly, then turned on her bedside lamp. "You okay now?"

"I think so. I feel shaky. Like whatever was going on in my head is still happening. It's weird. I can't describe it."

"You don't have to. Tell me what I can do to help you."

Grace leaned against Liv and felt her arms encircle her. "Hold me for a while."

"No problem," Liv said, her breath tickling the side of Grace's neck. Liv rubbed her back, nearly putting Grace back to sleep. "I love you," she said.

"I love you, too." Grace leaned back a bit and saw the worry etched on Liv's face. "Did I startle you?"

"Oh yes. Totally. It felt like forever before you woke up. I was about to call for help."

"Honey, it was only a dream. A bad one, but a dream. I'm fine."

"It was because of Carly, wasn't it?"

Sometimes, Grace hated how direct Liv was. She supposed the dream did have something to do with Carly. It'd been a long time since she'd had any nightmares, and it made sense she'd have one now, after seeing Carly in their home.

"Probably. I don't remember."

"I'm going to talk to Charley tomorrow. There's got to be more they can do about her."

"They have to find her first."

"I'd like to find that bitch—"

Grace put her hand on Liv's chest and felt the rapid rise and fall of it. "Calm down, honey. She's not worth getting worked up over."

"I know, but I have so much hatred for her I can't stand it."

"So do I. I'm sort of thinking maybe it's good she's here, because I can talk to her face-to-face."

"What?" Liv sat up and stared at her. "There's no way in hell I'm going to let you."

"There's no way in hell you can stop me," Grace countered. She moved away from Liv and got out of bed. "I've been thinking about this all evening. I need closure. I never got that, Olivia. I want to talk to Carly. Just me and her. I need to find out why she did what she did. I guess I need some kind of reasoning or answer for it."

"She did it because she's a mean bitch. She was trying to control you, and when she couldn't do it with her words, she decided to use her fists." Liv also got out of bed and stood in front of Grace, hands on her hips. "There are times when I want to know every detail of everything the bitch did to you, but I don't think I can handle knowing all of it. How anyone would willingly beat someone with as kind a heart as yours is unfathomable. It turns my stomach, and I feel this intense anger over it. Gracie, I'm not sure I want you in a room with her, alone or not."

"It's for me to handle, Olivia. I appreciate how you feel,

but ultimately it's about me. It's about how I feel and what I need to do. Carly did more than beat me, but you don't know everything and you're right. I'm not sure you can handle hearing it. There were times—" Grace stopped. She wasn't sure this was the time to tell Liv about her most dangerous, inner thoughts. Thoughts she hadn't had in years but still haunted her. Thoughts about how the only way to stop Carly would be to end her own life.

"Please, Gracie, don't do this. It might be a moot point since we don't even know if she'll be back or not, but I can't let you get hurt."

Grace curled her arms around Liv's waist and held her close. "You can't always protect me, Olivia. I love how you want to, and I love you being here for me. I wish this was easier."

"Me, too." Grace heard the tears in Liv's voice as she continued. "I want to wipe the floor with the bitch's face."

"I know. Violence won't solve anything. You'll feel better for a minute, but imagine how you'll feel when you're done. It's not who you are, Olivia. Even if it's how you want to show your anger, it's not worth it. It never is."

"I promise to do my best, okay?"

"Okay." Grace kissed the bare shoulder under her cheek. "I'm not sure I can go back to bed."

"Me either. Let's get something to drink. Maybe we can finish the box set of *Downton Abbey*. Whatcha say?"

"I say an English costume drama sounds like a fine distraction." Grace kissed Liv gently and wiped her tear-stained face with her thumb. "You set up the DVDs, and I'll get us something to snack on."

"Deal."

****

Charley was in line at CoffeeNut the next morning when her phone rang. She let it go to voicemail as she stepped up to the counter. Stefi greeted her with her usual bright, sunny smile, and Charley gave her one in return. Depression didn't come easily around someone so positive all the time. "Hi, handsome," Stefi said, handing her a cup of ordinary, black coffee. "How are you?"

"Same." Charley tossed a five on the counter, knowing

Stefi would keep the change as always. The extra attention was worth paying double for her coffee.

"Your face smiles, but your eyes don't."

Charley shook her head. "How do you do that? Have you been talking to my mom?"

"I'm observant. It's what makes my business successful. People like it when you know their moods and know what coffee to get them accordingly. Also when they need the added bonus of something sweet to eat."

"Uh-huh. What you're saying is you're nosy and you use it to your full advantage."

Stefi narrowed her eyes at Charley, then stuck her tongue out. Her manicured fingers tucked a lock of blonde hair beneath her white ball hat. The hat had the CoffeeNut logo on the front of it. "You're no fun. Have a seat and I'll join you in a minute."

"Sure." Charley hadn't intended to stay, but as she didn't have anything to do, figured it couldn't hurt. She took her phone out of her pocket, saw the number, and groaned. Her dad. No doubt he'd found time to catch up to her after her row with her mom last night. She tapped the Redial icon and waited.

"Charlene, I'm only going to say this once, so listen up. I did not raise you to treat people the way you treated your mother last night. I want you to come over to the house tonight and apologize to her. She's trying to look out for you." He paused for effect. She knew he wasn't done. "It's taken us a long time to decide to talk to you about Raina. We've been patient with you, especially after you moved back to Whitehorse. I told your mother we needed to let you grieve and work through things in your own time. Well, time is up, Charlene. I want you to get back into counseling. You're done working until you're too exhausted to sleep. If it means I have to talk with your inspector, I'll do it."

He stopped speaking and Charley paused before answering. She stared out the window, watching people walk by, wondering if their lives were as complicated as hers suddenly was. A week ago, she had things figured out. She had her routine, and she didn't have to think about anything she didn't want to. But all this free time was messing with her ordered world. Worst of all, her dad was right. But she didn't want to admit it.

"I'll be by tonight to apologize to Mom. I shouldn't have left like that. I honestly didn't know what to say to her or how to handle what she was saying to me."

"I can accept your apology, but I can't accept you disrespecting her. It hurts more than anything you said to her. Do you understand?"

She knew he was hurt as well, and perhaps that revelation was hardest to swallow. Charley hung her head in shame, even though he couldn't see her. She felt a pressure on her arm and turned to find Stefi's kind face watching her.

"I'm sorry, Dad. Honestly. I'll be over tonight for dinner. We'll talk then."

"I love you, Charlene."

"I love you, too." She hit the End icon and dropped her phone onto the table.

Stefi quietly sat across from her and waited.

"I got mad at my mom last night and stomped out of my apartment, almost slamming the door behind me." She stared at her phone, unable to look at her friend, knowing she'd see compassion there. "It was horrible of me, and Mom didn't deserve it."

"What made you do it?"

"The truth hurt."

"Always does. But I've never known you to fight with your parents. You're so tight with them."

"It wasn't a fight, but her words hit me hard."

Stefi didn't speak until Charley looked up at her. Of course, compassion was written all over Stefi's face. "Moms know all the right places to hit. It's what they do. You can't fault her. She must have had some reason to be worried about you. Is it because of your hand?"

"Partly. Mostly because I work all the time. I like it that way. I don't want or need free time."

"Why not?"

"Because then I end up thinking about stuff I'd rather shove into the past where it belongs."

"Ah. Never a good plan, my friend. Never." Stefi spun Charley's phone around so it was facing her and started typing on it. After a moment, she handed it back. "Her name is Debra. Call her. She's a friend of mine from university, and she's a counselor. She started her practice here a few months ago. You'll like her. She doesn't take shit from anyone, and she's very straightforward."

Stefi got up as more customers came in. She put her hand

on Charley's arm as she passed her. "And she's an expert on PTSD."

"How—"

Stefi waved off her question and got back to work behind the counter.

Charley stared at the phone, disbelieving. This was the same person Pike told her to call.

She took a sip of her coffee, got up to leave, and nearly collided with Jada.

"Hey!" Jada smiled at her and didn't move out of her personal space. "I was coming over to say hello. Where you rushing off to?"

"Um, no place." Charley took a step back, thrown off balance by Jada's sudden presence. "I want to get home so I can work on a project of sorts."

"A project?" Jada glanced down at Charley's injured hand. "You need help with it?"

"Not that kind of project." Charley shifted from one foot to the other, a weird nervousness settling over her. "My friend Gracie's ex-wife showed up at her house unexpectedly. She's here to cause trouble, and I want to find something on her to get her ass sent back to America."

"Sounds serious," Jada said. She seemed hesitant to leave. "Well, I guess I better let you get to it."

"Yeah, it's important. She nearly killed Gracie a few years ago, and I don't want her to get the chance to do it again."

"I'm sorry." Jada stepped aside to let Charley pass her. "Hope you find what you need then."

"Me, too." Charley wanted to leave, but her feet were glued to the floor. What was it about this woman that made her act so weird? "Um, are you out for the day? Or on your way to work?"

"Heading to work. I've got a split shift and needed to get perked up with caffeine before it starts."

"Jada," Stefi called out from the counter, holding a reusable mug in her hand.

"Ah, that's me."

"So it is." Charley followed her to the counter. Jada paid for her coffee, and they walked out together. Charley fell into step beside her. "Mind if I walk with you? I could use the exercise."

Jada looked her over and chuckled. "You don't look like you need any exercise. Seem perfectly fit to me."

"It's an illusion. I have to work hard to keep fit, and right now I'm not doing anything. Most of the stuff I do at the gym I need two hands for. Even the leg machines require both hands to adjust the settings."

"Ah, a problem I'm not used to hearing. Someone who's upset about not going to the gym." She gave Charley a sideways glance. "I'd say your gym routine has done well for you. Honestly, you look like you could run a marathon and pick up a car if you needed to."

Her remark earned a laugh from Charley. "I hate running."

"I thought you athletic types were into all kinds of sports and stuff."

"No. I was athletic in school. Since I became a Mountie, I like to work out so I'm strong. I'm a woman in a man's field, and I've always had to be stronger than them to prove myself. And I need to be strong enough to take down a man in a fight because, believe me, they always go after the female officer figuring we're an easier target than the males."

"I didn't realize Whitehorse is so rough."

"It's not, but we have our moments. All places do. Even towns like Blue River. Takes all kinds, and you never know what someone's like when they're drunk or high. And we've certainly got our share of bars here."

"I noticed," Jada said with a wink and a grin. "I found Pot O'Gold is the best spot on a Saturday night. Lots of lesbians to be found."

"It's been our spot for as long as I can remember. The women owners have been here more than twenty years, and they know their clientele well enough to keep some things the same and change with the times as they need to. Marion especially has a great head for business."

"You do know everyone around here, don't you? Betty said you did."

Charley said, "Most, I guess. I grew up here, so I probably went to school with them or their kids or their parents. And my dad is from here. We're also related to a good number of people in the area. Plus, if I didn't already know them, I've probably met them responding to calls."

"Do you ever forget someone's name?"

"Never. Kind of a weird thing I have. I don't forget addresses either. Or calls I've been on."

"You have a photographic memory or something?"

"Hardly. As my mother recently pointed out, I live for my job. It's my whole world." Charley finished the last of her coffee as they paused at an intersection, waiting for the light to change. "Do you? Remember all your patients?"

"No. I try to forget them. Too much damage to keep in my brain. I love my job, but I have a life outside the hospital."

The light turned green, and they crossed the street that would eventually take them to the hospital. Charley asked, "What do you like to do? Besides hunt down the perfect cappuccino."

"Well, cappuccino is very important, you know?" Jada grinned and laughed softly. "What do I like to do? I'm crazy about baseball, and when I lived closer, I never missed a Blue Jays game. Had season tickets."

"Season tickets? It's just baseball. Now hockey…"

"First, it's never *just* baseball." Jada held up her finger for emphasis. "Second, it's baseball. I never miss a game. I've gone for the last four years to Clearwater, Florida, to catch them in spring training. March to November—it's all about baseball."

"Wow. Okay. Noted."

"Good. Apart from baseball I like to be outside. That's one reason why I enjoy being a flight medic. Not always stuck in the ER, though I do enjoy working there, too. After I've had a run of long shifts, I like to take off for a hike, or maybe go skiing, though I'm not very good at it."

"You don't have to be good to like skiing. As long as you wear a helmet."

"I do wear a helmet, actually. Too many head traumas for me not to. Anyway, what do you do for fun?"

Charley paused. What had she done last for fun? Sadly, she realized she hadn't done much of anything. "Watch hockey. I used to do a lot outdoors, but I haven't for a while now. Going to the gym is fun."

"Boring." Jada yawned and bumped shoulders with her. "You need to get out more."

"So I've been told."

"By who?"

"My mother."

Jada had an unreadable expression on her face, and Charley wondered what just changed. "You get along with your mother?"

"Usually. We had some words last night, and I apologized, but she didn't mean to upset me. She's doing her usual worrying thing."

Jada mumbled something then paused as they reached the hospital entrance. "So, you've got my number, and you still haven't called. Should I be insulted?"

"No. I'm not very good at this sort of thing."

"What sort of thing? Using your phone?" Jada's genuine smile was back, and Charley found she liked it.

"Ha-ha. I meant calling someone for—you know—like a date or something."

"You wanna go on a date?" Jada was teasing her now, and Charley knew it. It felt good.

"Now that you ask, sure. I'd like to."

"When and where?"

"I'll call you." Charley winked at her.

"You sure you know how?" Jada said through soft laughter.

"I'll find the instructions. Once I've figured it out, you'll be the first to know."

"You read instructions?" Jada was at the door now, walking backwards. They smiled at each other before she slipped inside the hospital.

Charley spun in the opposite direction and started walking. A warm, silly feeling washed over her. She couldn't recall the last time she'd felt playful with anyone other than family. Weird how Jada brought it out in her so easily.

Then it hit her. She'd agreed to go on a date with Jada. What the hell was she thinking? She didn't date anymore. And even if she did, what would they do? Where would they go?

Charley had a sudden urge to slap herself in the forehead.

****

For the past two days, Grace spent most of her time

looking over her shoulder. She never saw Carly, but plenty of small, blue cars popped out at her. She'd had little sleep, and Liv made her crazy by never leaving her alone. After what amounted to a very short fight, Grace left the TNT office and went to the pub. She called her favorite lunch buddy on the way over and now sat across from Sara Hyatt, Liv's best friend. She recounted, in detail, the nightmares she'd been experiencing.

"I haven't had bad dreams since I started sleeping with Liv," Grace said. "Like her presence was enough to keep them away."

"And now it's not?"

"No. The other night was the worst one I've ever had, and I scared the crap out of her. She's ready to hunt Carly down, and I honestly, don't think I could stop her if she were to see Carly on the street." Grace ran her finger along the edge of her glass of iced tea and sighed. "I don't know if I'd want to stop her."

"Well, sounds pretty normal to me, Gracie. After what Carly did, no one would blame you for wanting Liv to knock the shit out of her."

"Yeah, but as soon as I think it, I feel guilty. Like I'd be just like her if I let Liv loose on her. Liv, I'm quite sure, would put Carly in the hospital for a long time."

"She'd deserve everything she got. Don't for one second put yourself in the same category as Carly. You're nothing like her."

"Oh, um, bad timing?"

Grace looked to her left. Charley stood at their table, a glass of cola in her hand. "Nope." Grace pointed to an empty seat. "Join us for lunch. You can even join our bitch session. We have one every Wednesday, but I decided we needed one on Friday—today."

"Any specific bitch this session is about?" Charley settled in her seat.

Sara looked at Grace for a moment. "Gracie was telling me about having more nightmares since Carly showed up. We were discussing the merits of letting Liv beat the shit out of her."

"No merits there," Charley said. "Always a bad idea. Let the law take care of her."

"They did," Grace said, leaning back in her chair. She felt out of sorts, and her feelings went from anger to sadness to frustration in a matter of seconds. "Seattle locked her up but not long enough. They let her go, and there's nothing I can do to get her back in jail or back to Seattle."

Charley held up her hand to slow Grace's tirade. "I did look into her being released in Seattle. I couldn't sleep the last couple of days, so I've been working on this. And it's true she wasn't put on probation or parole. Early release for good behavior plus they were running out of room. She's a violent offender, but it was her first conviction and she managed to convince the parole board to let her go. I guess she worked hard in jail. Was a model prisoner and all. Anyway, doesn't matter. She's out. But—" Charley smirked and met Grace's curious gaze as she continued. "She shouldn't have gotten into the country to begin with. She's got a felony record, and that's a clear no-no when crossing the border. As a matter of fact, I'm sure she can't get in. It's too soon after her release, and there's a helluva lot of hoops she'd need to go through to get permission to come here. I can't see her being able to do any of it. No, she got in here illegally."

"So this is how we send her back then? Literally?" Grace asked. Her stomach clenched at the possibility they would be rid of her for good.

"There's an All Points Bulletin out on her right now. I talked to Inspector Pike, and he's going to contact border patrol to see how she got in. Once we find her, she'll go to jail and it won't be long before they kick her ass back over the border."

Grace, in her enthusiasm, nearly knocked Charley off her chair when she jumped up to hug her. She gave her the tightest embrace. "I love you, Charley!"

"I know, I know. I'm loveable, but I can't breathe." Charley laughed when Grace released her. "Happy I can help." She held up her injured hand. "This might not work, but at least I managed to find a way to get rid of her. I wish I could go looking for her right now."

"I can't thank you enough," Grace said. She grabbed her phone and immediately sent a text to Liv, giving her the basic information about Carly. "Let me buy you lunch."

"I never turn down free food." Charley waved to Izzy, who took her order from across the pub. "So, any other gossip?"

"Wait, did you say gossip?" Sara feigned being shocked. "I do not believe Charley Townsend is wanting to gossip with us simple town folk."

"Hardy har har." Charley tossed a tiny ice chip at her, missing since it was her right hand she was using. "I'm bored. I figured out what to do about Carly, and I need something to occupy my time."

Sara glanced over at Izzy, who was industriously cleaning the bar. "I'll start you off with this tidbit. First, Bren got notices yesterday that Angel plead guilty to assault with a motor vehicle. We should know her sentence next week, but the prosecutor thinks she'll get five years minimum."

"Good," Charley said. "And the next tidbit?"

"Izzy and Bren finally made the decision to give things a try between them. They're officially dating."

Charley couldn't help grinning. "Awesome. Those two deserve it after all they've been through. I saw Bren the other day, and she's using a cane now instead of crutches. Said the last surgery went well, but she's going to see a specialist in a few months. There's at least one more surgery needed to put things right."

"She's a strong young woman," Grace said. "She and Izzy make an adorable couple. I'm glad to hear things are going good for them. Guess it takes something tragic for some people to come together."

"Sometimes," Sara said, giving Izzy a little wave. "Sometimes not." She now sported an evil little grin, and Grace knew she was about to spew out more gossip. She didn't know if she should be worried or excited.

"I know exactly how you can occupy your time, Charley."

Charley raised an eyebrow but didn't comment.

Sara released an overly dramatic sigh. "Jada Deveraux. She seems like a good choice to spend time with."

"How do you know Jada?" Charley asked, not meeting Sara's gaze. Or looking at Grace for that matter. Even when Izzy delivered her food, Charley made eye contact with the table.

"Hang on," Grace said, trying hard and failing to get Charley to look at her. "You like this woman. Don't you?"

Charley said nothing.

"Ha!" Sara was way too proud of herself. "I was right. And I know her because she comes in here sometimes. We met a few weeks ago when Terry and I came for Karaoke."

"I don't have a thing for her," Charley mumbled.

"Thou doth protest too much, methinks," Sara commented and made kissing faces at Charley. "I saw you two walking around the other day. You'd been to CoffeeNut, because Jada had her hands around an oversized cup from there. You were heading toward the river."

"Must have been after we met up. She wanted a tour of the city, but I didn't have time. We split up not long after you saw us. I haven't called her back yet."

"You didn't have time?" Grace asked. "Exactly what are you doing that's so important it can't wait a few hours. You're not working, remember?"

"I was working. I needed to get home so I could find a way to get rid of Carly."

"That didn't take you days or weeks. I know you, Charlene. You were done in an hour, max."

Charley's eyes remained fixed on the tabletop, as if it held the answer to all life's problems. "Forty minutes, to be exact, once I figured out what I needed to do. Not the point."

"Then what is?"

"Fine. I have a thing for her. But it's bad timing. I'm not 100% and I can't go getting involved with someone while I'm like this. It wouldn't be fair to her. Or me."

"That's a new one," Grace said. She took a few bites of her burger and waited for Charley to elaborate, but she didn't. "You haven't made time for anyone in years. Over a decade. You need to, Charley. There's no reason you can't let someone else in. Not everyone is like Raina. Trust me."

"I get it. I do." Charley shrugged in a helpless manner. "I'm not ready."

"You can't keep saying that," Sara said. "We don't want to see you spend the rest of your life alone."

Charley took a deep breath and slowly let it out. "I appreciate what you're trying to do, but it's not going to work. I'd just as soon stay single."

"I think she'll change your mind," Sara said in her most confident tone. "I've seen how she looks at you. She's into you, my friend."

"Then she'll be very disappointed." Charley took a sip of her cola and stopped once she'd swallowed. The glass remained close to her mouth, stopped in midmotion.

Sara and Grace followed her gaze to the front door. There stood Jada. She removed her bright-yellow, winter coat and hung it near the door. When she spotted Charley, her face lit up and she made a beeline to their table. Sara elbowed Charley.

"Here we go."

Charley didn't bother to admonish her, her gaze still locked with Jada's.

"Hey, gals," Jada said cheerfully when she arrived at Charley's side. "How are things?"

"Great," Grace replied. She gave Charley a kick to the shin to break her out of the spell she'd come under.

"Hey, Jada," Charley finally said, still staring at her.

Grace laughed and held out her hand. "I'm Grace Templeton, and I guess you've met Sara. We're friends of tall, dark, and silent over here. But apparently she forgot we're here."

Jada smiled and Grace found her expression super friendly. "She sucks at introductions. Been there, done that. Anyway, it's nice to meet you. Mind if I join you?"

"Sit down." Sara indicated the fourth chair at their table that happened to be next to Charley. "We just got our food, but feel free to order. Grace and I were having our weekly bitch session when Charley crashed in on us. We don't mind if you join in, too."

"Cool. I love bitch sessions. Any particular bitch today?"

Grace gazed at Charley and realized Charley only had eyes for Jada. Her stiff, cranky demeanor from a few moments ago was gone the moment Jada showed up. Charley now sported a smile that reached her eyes. It warmed Grace's heart.

Sara ordered a beer and turned her attention to Jada. "Oh there's lots to bitch about, and I've also got a ton of gossip. What do you want first?"

"Gossip. Always gossip. It's what makes the world go 'round. And since I'm new here, I need all the gossip I can get."

Sara laughed and tapped Charley with the back of her hand. "You need to keep this one. I like her."

Before Charley had a chance to respond, Sara and Jada were off discussing the latest gossip while Grace smiled and looked on, happy to watch all this play out in front of her. It helped her forget her own troubles and enjoy the moment with her friends.

****

Liv was waiting for Grace when she stepped out of the pub an hour later. Jada and Sara were already gone, leaving Charley to walk out with Grace. The moment they were outside, Liv embraced Charley. Charley wasn't normally a hugging type person, and the expression of shock on her face gave Grace the giggles.

"Um, what's this for?" Charley asked as she moved back from Liv.

"For figuring out how to get rid of the bitch. I owe you one."

"No, you don't," Charley said. "It's my job. At least for the moment. Keep your eyes out for her and don't engage. Got me? Call 9-1-1. Let the police sort it out."

It looked to Grace like Liv might balk, but she finally said, "Okay. Unless she starts something. I won't guarantee not to finish it."

"Fair enough. I need to get home before Mom decides to call out the Mounties to come find me. See you two later." Charley waved as she walked in the direction of her apartment building.

Grace linked arms with Liv, and they started toward Liv's office. "What did you do after I escaped the office?"

"I needed to get some paperwork done on an order for a new trommel out at the Big Dive mine. Dave already got the repairs started over the weekend to try to get their wash plant up and running this week. I told him not to worry about paperwork, just get them fixed up. I hate this part of the business. I want to be out there working on the wash plant with Dave." Liv made the most adorable pouty face.

Grace pulled her to a stop and kissed her pouty lips, giving her a gentle nip as she did. The expression on Liv's face changed immediately. Grace said, "I might have some kind of solution for you. If you think you'd be up for it."

"Honey, I'm always up for anything you want." Liv waggled her eyebrows, and Grace laughed at her antics.

"Not exactly what I had in mind, though maybe later. Anyway, I've been running the admin side of things for *Ojiichan* for the last year, and it's still pretty interesting to me. A new challenge, I guess. And since I need a job I can up and leave when I'm needed for translation services, how about I come work with you? I can do the paperwork for Gracie's Glory anywhere. I can take over some of your paperwork. You'd be freed up to go get dirty with your brother and enjoy being out of the office."

Liv's face softened and a crooked grin appeared. "I don't think I can possibly love you more than I do right now. Are you serious? You want to do admin for both TNT and Gracie's Glory? Seems like a lot of work to me, and I went to school for it."

"Yes, but I need something new, and this is staring me in the face. And, if you get pregnant, you're going to be stuck in the office. Might as well get in some time playing at the mines and in the garage while you can. I mean, you can still do a lot of stuff while pregnant, but you might not fit into some of those places like you do now."

"Like crawling inside a trommel?"

"For instance."

"I'm loving it. Want to get started now?"

Grace laughed at Liv's enthusiasm as they started toward the office again. "Totally. Under one condition."

"Name it."

"I get my own office space. Your desk always looks like a tornado hit it. I need somewhere tidy and organized."

Liv tried to look affronted but failed. "I'm tidy."

"Your office is, yes. Your desk, no."

"I know exactly where everything is."

"Uh-huh. Not the point. I need to know where things are, and besides, you suck at sharing space."

"Hey! I made room for you in my house when we first started seeing each other."

"Olivia, half a drawer in a chest of seven drawers isn't making room. You still hog most of the bathroom, and if I hadn't brought my own chest of drawers, my clothes would be in boxes along the wall. You need your space. Seriously. So keep your messy desktop and give me a spot to work out of. It's not like there aren't three other offices not being used."

"One of them is Dave's."

"I haven't seen your brother set foot in his office once in all the time I've been here."

"Fine. You can have his. Not like he'll notice it anyway. It's the one next to mine, so we can share the lounge area." Liv slowed enough to kiss Grace's temple. "Does this mean I have to stock the fridge at the office now?"

"It does. I'll be making us lunch most days, so get ready to eat healthy. You're going to need it when you're pregnant."

"Hmm. Maybe I don't want to go first then," Liv said, her tone light as she was clearly joking.

"Too late. Matthew's already agreed to donate the sperm, and we're set up now with the doctor for later this month to inseminate. You're stuck, honey. No backing out now."

"Hey, since you'll be working at the same place as me, how about we convert the lounge into a nursery? Then we don't have to pay for a babysitter, and we'll be able to see the baby all day long."

Grace shook her head at how fast Liv changed topics. But this was one she happened to love talking about. "We could match it to the one in the house. That would be cute. You sure Dave won't mind us taking over the place?"

"Hell no. It'll confirm he isn't going to have to start working behind a desk. At least not yet. Like you said, we've got more than enough room in the old house. We'd have more if I ever get Dave to move out and get a place of his own."

"Won't happen until he meets the right woman, Liv. You know this. Why would he move out? He's lived there rent free since he was five years old. And who can blame him? It's a beautiful old house."

"He's lazy that way. So unless I get him married off, we're stuck with him. Anyway, soon as we get there we can dive into some stuff. I've got a lot of accounting for the workshop that needs sorting. If you can get it moving in the right direction, I'll feel like I can breathe easier and maybe go help Dave with the trommel repair."

"Accounting. Got it." Grace tightened her hold on Liv's arm. "It's all so romantic." She released a dramatic sigh and laughed at Liv's chuckle. "Anyway, it gets me out and about. And hey, we can maybe take turns getting out of the office. You can help Dave, and I can head to Gracie's Glory. I'm sure I can convince Charlie to let me help out. I miss it, too."

"Deal." Liv suddenly stopped, jerking Grace off her stride.

"What—" Grace followed Liv's stare. A blue car was parked across the street from the offices of TNT. The old Victorian home was in a cul de sac so there was little reason for anyone who didn't live there to be in the area. Someone visiting the office would park in the designated lot next to the house.

Grace felt Liv tense, so she held onto her. "We don't know if it's her. There are a lot of blue cars in the city."

"It's empty, which means she may be anywhere. Maybe hiding near the office. We should head back to our house, call the police on the way."

Grace gently tugged Liv toward TNT. "No. She doesn't get to direct our lives, Olivia. We're going to the office and that's final. If she's there, we'll call 9-1-1 like Charley said to do."

"I don't want to take the chance, Gracie."

"It's a moot point now anyway." Grace pointed to the car. A man in his mid-60s, wearing a T-shirt and jeans a size too small for his pot belly, got into the car and drove away. "It's not her. Let's get to the office and start work like normal people, okay?"

"We need to make a plan in case we do see her."

They started walking again. Grace said, "What plan? We call 9-1-1. Period."

"And while we're waiting? What do we do if she confronts us? I want to promise I won't hurt her, but there's a chance I'll renege on it."

"Don't make a promise you can't keep. Besides, you might not get the chance. Next time I see her, I'll be ready." Grace paused at the front door to face Liv. She cupped the side of her face with the palm of her hand. "Maybe I'll be the one to knock her down. I won't let her paralyze me again, Olivia. Next time, if there is a next time, Carly isn't going to get the best of me."

A slow grin made its way across Liv's face. "You'll flip her onto her back the way you did to me that one time I startled you?"

"And then some. Carly won't know what hit her until it's too late."

Chapter Eight

Charley stared at the business card for a long time before finally dialing the number. She was rewarded with an immediate answer.

"This is Debra."

"Uh, hi, Debra. My name is Charley Townsend. Inspector Pike told me to give you a call."

"Oh, hello, Charley," the cheery voice responded. "I'm glad you called. And your timing is perfect. I have the afternoon free."

"Good." Charley didn't have a clue what to say next. It wasn't like she'd never been to counseling, but the last time was years ago. She honestly thought she was past the need for such services.

Debra was quiet, as if waiting her out.

Charley said, "I guess I need to make an appointment."

"You need to or you want to?"

Charley sighed. "I've been told to by two different people. I don't honestly want to."

"Inspector Pike didn't make it mandatory or he'd have told me." Debra's voice sounded soft and kind. Charley felt an immediate connection with her. "It's your choice, Charley. This isn't something you should feel forced into."

"It's—I've done this all before. I don't understand why I need to do it again."

"Can you be more specific?"

Charley hesitated, not sure how much she wanted to reveal about herself, even though she felt safe to spill it all. "My wife killed herself ten years ago. I spent over a year in counseling."

"I'm glad to hear you sought help afterward. So it went well for you? The counseling?"

"It did. Helped me get myself back together enough to go to work again. Though it took a whole year before I got back."

"So you stayed with counseling until you felt it was

enough and then stopped?"

The question wasn't an accusation, but Charley understood the impact of it. She thought about it a moment. She had indeed stopped when she felt she'd had enough. Not when she'd been told she was ready to face things on her own. Was this her main issue now? Had she left counseling too soon?

"Don't over think the question," Debra said gently. "It's not meant as anything more than it is."

"I guess I did quit too soon. I don't think I was ready, but I wanted to get back to work. It's all I have."

"Are you sure?"

"You ask hard questions."

Debra laughed softly. "It's my job."

"You're good at it," Charley said. "I think I should make an appointment. I need it. I—I'm not handling this so well. I mean, my family's great, and I have some good friends who want to help. I've been getting calls or text messages every day from the guys at the station. Especially from my friend, Elle, who was on the call with me when I got injured. But it's not enough."

"Want to come in today?"

"Seriously?" Charley asked, now aware of the crushing grip she had on her phone. She eased up on her hold. "What time?"

"Depends on how soon you can get over here."

Charley hardly believed her ears. "It's such late notice."

"If I wasn't sure, I wouldn't offer you the time. Come to my office. I'll be here waiting. The address is on my card."

Charley glanced at the card. The address was close to the RCMP station. "Got it. See you soon."

"I'll be here." Debra disconnected and a smile crept across Charley's face. She sent a quick thank-you text to Stefi, let Grace know she'd be busy for a while, and left. She felt better, knowing she was taking her first right step in forever.

****

Charley knocked on the plain, white, door and waited. It opened and she was greeted by a slightly overweight woman in her fifties, her dark-brown hair swept into a loose bun at the base of her neck. She reached a hand forward, and Charley shook it, surprised by the strength she found there.

"Hi, Charley. Come on in." Debra waved a hand toward the office and let Charley pass her. She closed the door and took a seat, once Charley settled on a bright-green sofa with soft, yellow pillows. Debra sat on a wing-backed chair situated catty-corner from her. "Would you like something to drink?"

"Water, please."

"Sure thing." Debra reached behind her into a small refrigerator and handed Charley a bottle of water.

Charley took a long drink, happy to wet her suddenly dry throat. "Thanks."

"You're welcome." Debra crossed her legs at the ankle and placed a thick notebook on her lap, pen at the ready. "I understand from Inspector Pike you were injured on a recent call." She glanced at Charley's hand. "How's it going?"

The fingers of her left hand tingled, and Charley flexed them a little. "It's going slow. I've had one surgery and hope I won't need another one. The doctor won't be sure for a few more weeks, when the swelling's gone. I can move my fingers a little, and with any luck, I'll be allowed to start physical therapy after my next appointment with her."

"And you're left-handed?"

Charley nodded. "My friend Gracie helped me figure out how to do things with my right hand."

"But you're worried."

"I am." Charley looked into her honest gaze. "I can't shoot a gun if I can't get my fingers to work properly."

"What about your family?"

"What about them?" Charley asked, her frustration mounting. "I love them and they've been there to help me through all this—my mom especially. But my job is my vocation. You know what I mean?"

"I do, but it isn't all you have, Charley. Not if you've got a loving family."

"I don't know how to explain it to you, Debra. My job is so important to me. It's all I've ever wanted to do with my life, and I don't know what the hell I'm going to do if I can't work."

Debra abandoned her pen and paper and leaned forward. "I hear you. Being a Mountie is important to you. I work with a lot of Mounties, and I realize how dedicated you all are to the job.

But I think this goes beyond your injury. You told me your wife committed suicide."

Charley felt the urge to be anywhere else. She wanted to jump up and run away.

"I get the idea this is still very fresh in your mind," Debra continued. "You don't have to talk about it now, but I think it will be something we'll discuss later."

"I don't know if I can," Charley said.

"It's okay." Debra gave her a kind smile again. "We'll figure things out as we go along. This isn't a race. There's no timeline. We will take as long as it takes."

The tears came as a surprise, and Charley wiped them from her cheeks with the tissue Debra handed her. "Raina never left a note. I said goodbye to her in the morning and came home in the evening to find her dead."

Debra placed a hand on Charley's knee and caught her gaze when she looked up. "The first step is always the hardest. Now, let's get started."

****

Jada wandered into the Pot O'Gold around seven Thursday evening. She had just gotten off her shift in the ER and needed a break. This pub was becoming her favorite place to be. For reasons she still refused to acknowledge, her tiny apartment didn't feel like home. Nothing much about Whitehorse felt like home, and she didn't know how to fix it.

Case in point was the phone call she got from her mother the previous day. After their last conversation about Celeste, Jada didn't expect to hear from Liselle so soon. She expected at least two weeks for the storm to die down. But she was so very, very wrong there. Her last comment to Liselle fueled the fire as if Jada had sprayed it with gasoline.

"I'll have you know," Liselle said without even a cursory hello, "I give a damn what happens to you girls. I realize you don't believe me, and I can't change your mind, but I refuse to stand idly by while Celeste throws her life away. She's an intelligent woman and needs to be able to support herself. I brought you two up to be independent women without the need to rely on any man. Or woman."

"I realize that, Mom, and it's exactly what Celeste is doing. She's being independent. She's making a choice all on her own. Anton has nothing to do with it, though he is supporting her no matter what. If she wants to work up until she goes into labor, he'd be all for it. He respects her."

"Oh, and I don't?"

"You said it. Not me."

"It's implied," Liselle said with a sigh. "You think I don't know you, Jada, but I do. And I tried hard to stop you from making mistakes. Had you listened to me, you'd still be here in Ottawa and not hiding in the wilderness."

Jada paced the confines of her apartment, her restless energy ready to explode from within. "Mom, you don't know the first thing about me. You have no idea what was going on in my personal life, and you sure as hell didn't give a damn to know what was going on in my professional life."

"I told you to stay away from that woman from day one. I knew enough about her to see what she would do to you. But you're just like your father. Too blind to see what's in front of your face. That bitch—"

"Was my mistake. Not yours. You want me and Celeste to be independent, but you can't stop trying to control us. You never could. Probably what drove Daddy to an early grave."

The comment was out of her mouth before Jada had a chance to rethink it. But it was in the universe now, and while it wasn't the smartest thing to say, it was the truth. Her mother's constant need to be in control was never easy on her father. Daniel tried so hard to be a cushion between Jada and Liselle; so much so, she was sure it led to his heart failure. He was never a strong man, always had a weak heart, and the stress was probably too much.

"Your father had a 100% blockage in his aortic arch. That caused his death. Not me and not anyone else. He refused to watch his diet, refused to exercise, and eventually it's what killed him. How dare you say it was my fault."

"And we're back to it being about you," Jada said. Why was she arguing with her mother. It'd be more useful to slam her head into a brick wall. "I don't want to talk about this anymore. Accept that Celeste is doing what she wants, or don't. I don't care anymore." She disconnected the call, laid the cell phone on the kitchen table, and left her apartment.

The call was an hour ago, and while it felt freeing not to have her cell phone with her, it also felt weird. Like Jada was missing a piece of her hand. She glanced at her hand as the bouncy server came to her table. Her spiky hair was green and orange today. Last week it was some weird combination of blue and purple.

"What can I get ya?" she asked, not hiding the fact she was checking Jada out.

"What's the lunch special?"

"Chili."

"Sounds good. Add in a pint of whatever you have on tap."

"You got it." She flounced to the bar, and Jada remembered her name was Izzy. It suited her.

"Lucky you're not working today," someone spoke from behind her. Jada twisted in her seat to see Charley standing there.

"I was a couple hours ago. Why? Something interesting happen?"

"Unless you call a two-car accident with seven injuries interesting. Couple trauma cases flown in from Highway 1 near Ibex Valley. Took an hour to extricate them. The others got transported by ambulance and police units. Had to get an extra RCMP car out there to get the littlest one brought in. No room for his car seat."

"Wow. Guess I left right on time then. Nothing like sorting out a bunch of people from one crash. I'm good here." She pointed to the empty seat across from her. "Wanna join me?"

Charley hesitated and looked around as if she were meeting someone. "You sure?"

"I wouldn't have asked if I wasn't."

"Okay. I guess so." She settled into the seat and waved at Izzy. "My usual," she said.

Izzy nodded and eventually brought over Jada's beer and a cola for Charley. "You're not on duty. I imagine it's allowed if you want to drink."

"I don't drink."

"Ever?"

"Nope."

"Not even to celebrate something? Like New Year's Eve?"

Charley took a sip of her cola, her gaze on the table. "No. Not even then."

"Wow. I don't think I've ever met anyone who never drinks. Have you even tried it?"

"Oh yeah. I used to get a beer after work or on the weekends, days off, maybe at a barbecue. But not anymore."

"You sound sad." Jada watched as Charley's eyes closed for an instant. "I'm sorry if it's a touchy subject. My mouth runs away with itself sometimes, and it lands me in trouble. A lot."

"I can believe it." Charley looked up and tried to offer Jada a smile. It didn't quite land the way it should, and Jada's heart broke. "It's no big deal, really. I made that decision years ago when a close friend of mine was in an abusive relationship. Her wife would get drunk and beat her."

"Please tell me she's away from this woman and she's okay now."

Charley gave her a wry smile. "She is. She lives here now and is happily married. She doesn't drink anymore, and I sort of stopped in support of her. I don't miss it one bit."

"Does it bother you if I drink?" Jada felt the need to be more sensitive now she'd put her foot in it. "I can switch to a soda."

"You drink what you want. Seriously, it doesn't bother me."

"Got it. Any other secrets you got hiding in there? I'd rather not make an ass of myself again."

A new smile crossed Charley's features, and this time Jada saw it was genuine. "I've got lots of secrets. Guess you'll have to figure them out. What fun would it be if I told them all to you at one time. Not like you don't have any of your own. Right?"

"Well, there is that," Jada conceded. She liked this new side of Charley. She was more fun, and if she wasn't mistaken, the woman was actually starting to relax. "Speaking of secrets, I've found the best way to let them out is on a long walk in nature."

"A walk in nature. Like a hike in the mountains?"

"Exactly. I'm long overdue for some time with nature. I found this place called Miles Canyon. Sounds fun. How about you come join me on a hike? We can walk and talk secrets tomorrow morning," Jada said.

"I know the area well. What time?"

Jada gave her a wide grin as she said, "6:30. I like to start as the sun's rising. It'll be kinda cold, but I guarantee you'll heat up as we go."

Charley choked on her drink. Jada wasn't sure if the bug-eyed look on her face was from the choking or Jada's comment, but either way, she loved the startled look in Charley's eyes.

After a few moments, Charley finally said, "I'll be there. 6:30 sharp."

"Don't be so militant, Sarge. 6:30-ish is good. Not like there's a fine if you're late."

"I'm never late."

"Maybe you should be. Just once. You might find it's more fun than being on time."

Charley raised one eyebrow but said nothing, the expression on her face was enough to make Jada laugh. Jada glanced at Charley's hand. "You okay to drive? Should I pick you up?"

"Nah. I have an automatic, so driving one-handed isn't a problem. Just took me time to get used to it."

"Cool." Jada took a sip of her drink and forced back the comment about doing things one-handed.

This was going to be a fun weekend. She took another draw on her beer and felt her stress and all thoughts of her mother fade away. More days like this one, and she might actually enjoy her new life in the wilderness. Provided the woman across from her let loose some of her own secrets. Jada had a feeling she'd enjoy getting to know Charley Townsend.

****

The sun was still creeping over the horizon when Charley met up with Jada in the parking area at Miles Canyon on Friday morning. A brisk nine degrees centigrade, but she'd worn a sweatshirt over her T-shirt. Once they started walking, Charley would warm up fast. She double-checked her backpack. Two bottles of water and five power bars would be enough for the morning's walk. She'd already planned their route and hoped Jada would enjoy it.

Charley spent most of the previous evening looking forward to this. She liked spending time with Jada, and doing so appeased her mother. Jada was her new friend and exactly what Josie'd been pushing her to do. Make new friends. So here she was. Waiting for her new friend to arrive.

Five minutes late, Jada pulled up beside Charley's truck and parked. She wore orange spandex shorts, tan hiking shoes with thick, white socks, and a white, spandex shirt. For a moment, all Charley did was stare at how the form-fitting clothes molded to Jada's body. Every curve was perfectly outlined, and when Charley's gaze got to her ass she had to blink and look away. Wow. She wanted to touch her incredibly firm butt in the worst way.

Charley swallowed the lump in her throat and forced her gaze to the canyon below them. "You ready to get moving?" Her voice wavered a little and she hoped Jada didn't notice.

"Yep. Got my backpack filled with water and a couple granola bars. I had two donuts and coffee for breakfast, but it won't last. How about you?"

"I didn't have breakfast, but I've got power bars and water. And I've got a route I think you'll enjoy."

"Cool." Jada put a slim fanny pack on. It had enough room for her cell phone and nothing else. She tucked the phone inside, zipped it up, and slipped on the backpack. "Ready. Lead the way."

"You got it." Charley first took Jada down to the old suspension bridge that hung over the Yukon River where it flowed through Miles Canyon. Made primarily of wood, at one time it was painted white. The paint flaked off in places where people walked across it.

The sun was finally making its presence known, and as it rose in the sky, the rays bounced off the clear water below them. They took a moment to look out over the river from the bridge. Jada snapped a couple of pictures with her phone then put it away. "It's beautiful here."

They leaned on the rail for a few moments. Charley watched Jada instead of the view before them, deciding the beauty of the moment was right next to her. She'd honestly thought any urge to be with another woman was long ago buried.

Jada, with her beautiful, shoulder-length curls tucked

under a Toronto Blue Jays baseball hat, her dark eyes fixed on the horizon, captivated Charley like no one ever had. Charley almost reached out to touch the smooth skin along her delicate jawline. Instead she clenched her hand into a fist and looked away.

"Let's keep going. Lots more for you to see," she said.

She pushed off the rail and continued across the bridge and onto a trail through the woods. Pine trees mostly grew there and created a dense forest. The path led them pretty deep into the forest, but Charley knew exactly where they were. She'd traipsed these parts as a kid and told Jada as much as they walked along, listening to the birds calling out as they passed them.

Jada said, "It's an amazing place to grow up. I had no idea how wild it is up here. I mean, I'm a city kid at heart. It's where I thrive. I like hearing cars and buses and trains and people, but this is heaven. We haven't seen a single human since we started walking."

"We probably won't either. Not until we head back. We might see some tourists by the suspension bridge, but they don't usually go very far into the woods."

"So any dangers I should look out for?"

Charley laughed while picking her way over a fallen log. "Watch where you walk, so you don't trip on something. Most anything around here is going to run and hide when it sees us."

"Yeah? Like what?"

"Deer, elk, foxes." Charley looked over her shoulder at Jada, whose expression was neutral. "Why? You scared now?"

"Hardly. Just want to be prepared."

"Like a Girl Scout?"

Now Jada laughed and the sound made Charley smile. It rolled over her like a warm wave of water. "No way. My mom didn't want me wasting my time. She didn't see any point in it. She wanted me home studying so I'd get straight A's in school. I did take piano lessons. She thought that would make me more cultured."

"Piano? You any good?"

"No. I hated my teacher as much as I hated the lessons. Mom gave up on me when I turned fourteen."

"What happened when you turned fourteen?"

"I turned gay. At least that's how she tells it. You can't convince her I was born gay and figured it out when my hormones woke up. I had this huge crush on a girl in my class. We kissed one day after school, and for the next two years, she was my girlfriend. My mom hit the roof. If not for my dad, she'd have kicked me out of the house."

Charley was quiet now. She recalled how Raina's parents had kicked her out of their home and left their fifteen-year-old daughter on the streets to fend for herself. If not for the local police, she'd have probably ended up on drugs and dead before she was twenty. Charley heard Jada's voice and tried to tune back in to what she was saying.

"Dad was amazing. He was my rock. Mom eventually sort of got over the gay thing when she realized I was interested in working in the medical field. My mom's a cardio-thoracic surgeon—one of the best in the country. She sort of expected my sister and me to follow in her footsteps."

"And you're a medic who works on a helicopter. Not exactly what she wanted, I take it?"

"Not even close. I did a tour with the local ambulance company before I started university. I fell in love with it and became a paramedic instead of a surgeon. After I graduated college and was a certified paramedic, I got a job in an emergency room and worked my way up. I was head flight medic before I moved out here."

"Wow. Where was this?"

"Ottawa. Born and bred."

"Again, wow. Must have been pretty exciting. They're always busy. I did a tour there after I finished the academy."

"We were. It was a constant thing. Rare to have a shift where you didn't have a flight, and if you didn't, you worked in the ER, which was always hopping with stuff to do. I loved it."

"But you're here." Charley stopped so Jada could catch up. She tried to get hold of her gaze, but Jada was looking up as if to find something in the trees. "Is this a topic I should drop?"

"No. I mean, kinda. I guess. Things went south in Ottawa, so I had to move on. I got a referral from our medical director who heard they were starting a medical helicopter here, and that's how I got the job. She worked out here as a resident years ago so had a few connections. She knew I needed to get away from Ottawa. I didn't want to leave, but it was for the best." She looked at her shoes as she scuffed the dirt on the trail.

Charley felt the anxiety surrounding Jada and had a strong

urge to take her in her arms and tell her everything would be okay. She actually started toward her but stopped and wondered what the hell had gotten into her. They barely knew each other. Hugging as a greeting or salutation might be okay, but the kind to give comfort wasn't. No matter how much her heart ached to do so.

"What a massive change. How are you adjusting?"

"I'm okay. Got a couple of gals at work I like to hang out with now and again, when our schedules let us. One guy at work's a total asshole, but otherwise, it's all good. I'm not totally settled here yet. I've never lived outside Ottawa."

"I've lived in several places. I moved around when I first joined the RCMP. But none of those places compare to here. I mean, it's not the only spot in the country with forests and amazing views, but there's something about this area that makes me smile."

"I like it when you smile," Jada said as their eyes met.

Something very warm settled in Charley's stomach as she soaked in the new connection she had with Jada. It was scary as hell, but she enjoyed the moment before breaking contact to point behind her. "Let me show you the best part. Okay?"

"Right." Jada followed as Charley continued along the trail.

After an hour, they found it. Charley stopped at the edge of a cliff that loomed about twelve meters above the Yukon River. Across the river was a tiny beach and another cliff with animal trails leading to the water from the forest above. The water was sparkling blue. The air smelled clean and fresh and was filled with the sounds of nature. Birds flew around them. Most called out danger signals; some trilled their morning songs. A soft breeze rustled through the trees and brought more scents with it. Charley closed her eyes and took it all in, a reminder of why she chose to never leave the Yukon again.

"It's beautiful," Jada said, her voice quiet as if she were afraid to disturb someone. "Do you come here a lot?"

"Not as much as I'd like." Charley removed her backpack and sat near the edge of the cliff, close enough to see the other side of the river, without being so close she fell. "It's a great place to feel like your problems aren't so significant when compared to the rest of the world. Puts things into perspective."

"It certainly does." Jada joined her and sat so they were shoulder to shoulder. She pointed at the beach on the other side of the river. "Are those animal tracks?"

"Probably elk. I've seen a few come to the river to get a drink."

"Wow." She got out her phone, took some pictures and put it back. "Pictures can't show this place off, can they?"

"Nope. I soak it all in, keep it in my head for when I need it later. It's why I'll spend most of the day here when I do come out this way. And if you'll notice, there's no cell signal. So no one can find us."

Jada leaned back on her hands and squinted up at Charley. "Nice spot to hide in."

"Yep."

They fell into a comfortable silence. After a while, Charley lay on her back, letting the sun warm her face. It wasn't long before she had her sweatshirt off and stuffed into her backpack.

Jada eventually lay beside her, closing her eyes against the sun. "I lost a patient at a massive car crash. It wasn't my fault, but the media picked up the story and it became my fault he died. It's why I'm not in Ottawa anymore."

Charley wanted to ask for details, but she understood Jada needed to talk at her own pace. Give the information she felt comfortable letting go of.

"It's a long story for another time, but my nurse-partner started this hate-filled online campaign against me. She blamed me for the patient's death. Even though nothing any of us could do would have saved him."

"How bad was it?"

"Horrible. Francine—my girlfriend—left me. I almost couldn't handle it. I had to take a leave of absence from work." She took a shaky breath, and again Charley had to tamp down the instinct to pull Jada into her arms. "I never went back. I lost my dream job. Sure, I'm still a flight medic and nothing can change that. But I wanted to be a flight medic in Ottawa. Saving lives is all I ever wanted to do."

"You do that now," Charley murmured and gently touched Jada's hand. "We're not as busy, but you're still needed here."

Jada twined their fingers together. Energy soared through

their tiny connection and surprised Charley. Her brain knew this woman was someone special, but her heart needed to accept it as well. As usual, her heart was the first part to close off.

"You're a good, new, friend, Charley Townsend." Jada gave her hand a squeeze, released it, and sat up. "Wanna have lunch with me? We can trade energy bars for granola bars."

"Depends," Charley said, also sitting up. "Do your granola bars have honey in them?"

"Is there another flavor?"

Charley grinned. "A woman after my own heart." Her eyes widened a little at the remark, and she was sure Jada's did as well before she looked away and into her backpack. Charley got handed a granola bar with honey and gave away an energy bar.

They touched the bars together and Jada said, *"Bon appétit."*

****

The walk back to their cars was quiet and Jada enjoyed it. She'd opened up about her past to Charley and still reeled from it. She had a hard time talking about the incident in Ottawa. Few people knew all the details. So why was it so easy to spill everything to Charley? What was it about this woman that made her want to open up to her?

Must be a cop thing. They were trained to talk to people, right? Or maybe it was those puppy dog eyes of hers, brown like the earth and always looking on her with affection. Might even be because the woman was sexy as hell and Jada would love to run her fingers through Charley's short, black hair and snuggle against her strong chest.

Jada's gaze wandered down Charley's body. She stumbled and slammed into Charley, tried to catch herself by grabbing Charley's backpack, and ended up taking them both down. In the end, Jada was flat on her back with Charley half-sitting, half-lying across her lap.

The fall stunned her for a moment, but as her eyes focused, she was staring at Charley's sparkling eyes as laughter bubbled up between them. Jada felt compelled to pull Charley toward her and kiss the laughter away, but she got tugged to her feet instead. "Shit. Sorry about that," she said. "I wasn't watching where I was going."

Charley adjusted her backpack and tightened the straps. "It's okay. Didn't hurt me a bit. Landing was kinda soft, ya know?"

"You're welcome. I can't say my landing was soft, and I think you shoved my stomach into my back when you toppled onto me."

"Hey, not my fault." Charley laughed again and pointed an accusing finger at Jada. "You pulled me down. Not like I had any control in the matter. You're stronger than you look."

"Thanks, I think." Jada brushed off dirt and grass from her butt and around the back of her legs. "I think my ass is bruised."

Charley quirked an eyebrow at her, her laughter now faded into a very cheeky grin. "Want me to check?"

"Sure." Jada stared her down, loving the challenge in her eyes and the electricity that suddenly hummed between them. She'd love for Charley to do more than check her ass for bruises. It wouldn't suck at all. Charley's grip was gentle when she pulled Jada to her feet with her right hand. What would her hands feel like on other parts of her body? Soft? Warm? Would they make Jada scream her name?

The challenge didn't last long because Charley looked away after a few seconds. Jada was instantly disappointed. "Too soon?" she asked, hoping to get the levity of their mood back.

"Maybe a little," Charley said and started along the trail again.

Half an hour later, they were standing alongside Jada's car. She tried to lean against it, but her ass was well and truly bruised. Driving home was not going to be fun. "I had a great time today."

"Me, too." Charley looked anywhere but at Jada. God, it felt like they were school girls on their first date.

"I didn't expect this to be all awkward when we got done. I meant it when I said I had a good time. And I'd like to do it again with you. Or something else. Whatever."

"I think I'd like that, too," Charley said. "I got a lot of time right now. I can show you around the city some more. Hit the spots tourists don't know about."

"Sounds great. Promise you'll call me, okay? Don't ghost me after this." Jada was half-joking, but it worried her she'd never hear from Charley after today. There was something special about her, and Jada needed to explore this thing between them. And she badly wanted to kiss her.

"I won't. If I say I'll call, I mean it. I don't break my promises. Besides, I did promise you a date." Charley met her gaze then, and Jada saw the seriousness behind her comment. "Maybe tomorrow for lunch? I'd go today, but I've got an appointment with the hand surgeon and then I have to report to my mother. It's going to take up the rest of the day."

"I understand." Jada opened the driver's side door of her car. "Take care, Charley. I'll talk to you soon."

"Bye." Charley gave her a little wave as Jada pulled out of the small parking lot.

She glanced in the rearview mirror. Charley stood there watching her go. For some reason, the image made her sad, and again she had the instinct to go wrap her arms around Charley and hold her tight.

But it also might be for her own good because she needed someone to hold her and Charley would sure be a great choice. One problem—they were friends. Jada had precious few real friends, and this was one time she wasn't going to let her libido ruin things.

Chapter Nine

Charley curled up on her couch and watched Grace vacuum her living room. Even though it was Saturday and she should have been at home with Liv and Harry, Grace was here cleaning up for her. Charley hated to rely on so many people, but she was thankful to have them in her life. She got another text from Elle and spent a few minutes responding to her, typing carefully with her right thumb. She still didn't have that talk-to-text thing down, but she was good at typing with one digit.

The vacuum stopped. She looked up and Grace was staring at her, a question in her eyes. Charley smiled in response.

"You're very quiet today," Grace said as she put the vacuum away.

"Not much to say, I guess. Besides, I was answering a text."

"Uh-huh." Grace ducked into the kitchen, returned with a couple of sodas, and handed one to Charley. "Who from? I heard you had a date yesterday." She settled on the opposite end of the couch and faced Charley.

"What?" Charley knew her face betrayed her, showing how embarrassed she was. She couldn't look at Grace. Instead she stared at her can of soda. "Where'd you hear that?"

"Where do you think? You know as soon as your mother hears something the whole city is informed. Right? She called me after she left here yesterday. Said you were glowing."

"Glowing? I do not glow. Only pregnant women glow."

"Not true. I've seen this look on your face before."

Charley looked up into Grace's teasing smile. "When?"

"When Jada showed up at the pub when you were talking to me and Sara. Or any time you mention Jada, which is a lot, I might add."

"I don't talk about her a lot." Charley paused. "Do I?"

"Totally," Grace said with a laugh. "Josie told me you

chatted about your hike for half an hour. I've never known you to be so excited about anything not related to the RCMP. And the look on your face right now is adorable."

"Adorable?"

"Yep." She stretched her leg out and gently kicked Charley's thigh. "You're totally into Jada."

Charley so wanted to deny it. But she simply couldn't look at Grace and outright lie and that's what it would be. A lie. Because she was into Jada, no matter how much she wished otherwise. Her silence was answer enough for Grace.

"I'm glad, Charley. Honestly. You need someone in your life."

"I don't. I'm fine as I am."

"What a load of bullshit," a deep voice said.

They both turned toward the front door where Charles stood watching them. How the hell did he always do that? Charley never heard him come in. He had this weird knack of being quiet, like a burglar. She wondered if he secretly practiced sneaking up on people.

"Hi to you, too, Dad." Charley pointed to her recliner. "Have a seat. What brings you here? Shouldn't you be doing something with Mom today?"

"Stop deflecting, Charlene." Charles sat down, popped the leg rest of the recliner out, and got comfortable. "Who's Jada and why haven't I heard about her before now?"

Charley sighed and kicked Grace when she started laughing. "She's the paramedic who was working the ER the day I got my hand cut. And how long were you listening to us talking anyway?"

"Deflecting again," Charles said. "I got an earful from your mom this morning about some date you went on. I decided to come hear about it myself. You know how your mother exaggerates."

"I do." Charley took a sip of her soda and put the can on the coffee table. She stared at it until the colors all blended together. "Her name's Jada and I like her. We're friends and nothing more."

"Why?" Charles asked in a soft voice. "If you like her, what's the problem? Is she straight? Does she not like you back?"

Charley recalled their near kiss and knew she was

blushing. Again. Dammit. "Oh, she's not straight."

"What's the problem?"

Charley glanced at Grace who was being very observant and intentionally silent. She looked amused and Charley glared at her. "Dad, do we need to get into this?"

"If you have to ask, then yes. I guess we do," he said. "For one thing, I don't like hearing you say things like you're fine as you are. You haven't been fine in years. If this woman makes you smile, then take a chance and go out with her again. You're young. Enjoy the time you've got."

"You're hardheaded," Charley said. Her dad grinned at her, knowing he'd won this round. She wasn't in the mood to argue with him. Or to tell him the truth of the matter. She was attracted to Jada and terrified it could go somewhere. They had an amazing connection, and Charley had a hard time wrapping her head around it. She didn't think taking the relationship further was a good idea. She was sure to screw it up. Certain she'd do something to make Jada not want to be with her. Leave her like Raina did.

"Hey." Grace's gentle voice brought her back to the conversation. "I'm going to head home to check on *Ojiichan*. You okay?"

Charley nodded. "Thanks for cleaning the place for me." She raised her injured hand. "I owe you."

"Like hell you do." Grace kissed her on the temple and slapped Charles' booted feet as she passed him. "Talk some sense into her if you can."

"Don't have that much time," he muttered. Once Grace was gone, Charles put his feet down and rested his arms on his knees. He waited until Charley looked at him before he spoke again. "I love you. You know this. It's why I worry about you."

"I'm fine, Dad. I promise. I've been on my own for ten years. I don't need someone else in my life. Not like a partner or girlfriend. It's too complicated."

"Sweetheart, life is complicated. But going through it alone? I never wanted that for you. I get it's hard. You loved Raina. But she's been gone a long time now, and you need to move on. You've got such a big heart—I don't want you to feel like you can't share it with someone."

Charley stared at her dad. Never in her life had he spoken

to her like this. He was a sweet and gentle man for sure, but she'd never had such a heartfelt talk with him. She didn't know how to respond.

Charles said, "It's okay. I know we don't do the sensitive chats much. I sort of raised you to be my buddy more than I raised you to be my daughter. But I honestly can't stand the idea of you being alone. You're like me. We're not built to be by ourselves. We need someone with us."

"Would you move on if Mom died?" she asked, not entirely sure where the question came from.

"Eventually."

"How long? A year? Five years?"

"Honey, there's no time limit on these things. But I think, for you, ten years is long enough. And whether you believe it or not, your mom and I agree Raina wouldn't want you to be alone."

"I love you, Dad," Charley said. Her right hand clenched and unclenched as she digested his words. "But it's not your call to make."

"No. It's not. But what kind of parents would we be if we didn't care about you enough to encourage you to move on? To live your life to the fullest?"

Charley got up and knelt beside his chair. She put her right hand on his arm and kissed him on the cheek. "I couldn't have picked better parents than you guys. I love you dearly, even if you bug the crap out of me sometimes."

Charles laughed and touched her cheek with his calloused hand. She leaned into the gesture. "Best kid ever."

"I know. So now that you've got all the sappy junk out of the way, why don't you take me to lunch? Mom left me a dozen frozen meals, but I'm in the mood for something else. Burgers maybe? When we're done, you can drive me to my doctor's appointment."

"Chauffer duty. Got it. Burgers so unhealthy you about have a heart attack looking at them?"

Charley stood, laughing. "Exactly."

"Done." Charles also got up and engulfed her in a bear hug. "C'mon kid. Let's go."

****

"Clear!" Jada triple-checked no one was touching the patient or the bed and pressed the button to shock him. 360 joules of electricity slammed into his chest, aimed at restarting his heart. She checked for a pulse and found none. "No pulse," she called out.

"How long has he been down?" Doctor Jansen asked.

"Forty-five minutes," Betty replied as she resumed compressions.

Doctor Jansen looked over the chart another nurse was using to annotate what they did. "We've done four rounds of ACLS," he said as much to himself as anyone else. "Cardiac history plus his age…"

Jada looked down at the man on the bed. He was mostly bald, with a tiny streak of white hair over the ears and around to the back of his head. His mouth was covered by the device that kept the endotracheal tube in place. His chest rose and fell each time the nurse squeezed the attached bag.

His stomach was bloated and his skin grey and clammy. She knew what the doctor was getting at and patiently waited for him to call a stop to their efforts. No matter what medications they gave or how many compressions or how much oxygen they supplied, this man was gone. He was eighty-three and apparently ready to leave.

Doctor Jansen, who was probably in his late twenties, put his hands behind his back and stepped away from the table. He glanced at the over-sized clock on the wall. "Let's call it. Any objections?"

No one spoke. They stopped what they were doing, clearly in concert with the doctor's plan. "Okay," he said. "Time of death is 1850. Betty, can you get someone to escort the family to the quiet room? I'll be in to speak to them shortly."

"Yes, Doctor." Betty got down from the portable step she'd stood on to do compressions, rolled her shoulders, and left the room, disposing of her gloves as she did.

Jada sighed, took one last look at their patient, and followed the others out. She sat behind the nurse's desk to help chart their work and started when the door to trauma bay one was closed. They wouldn't do anything with the man's body until Doctor Jansen spoke to either his family doctor or the Chief Coroner of Whitehorse. Once one of them agreed with Doctor

Jansen's assessment, they'd clean the man up and get him ready to be transported to a funeral home. She hoped they wouldn't have to do an autopsy. She hated the family going in to see a loved one who wasn't cleaned up from all the medical procedures done during a code. It was ugly and traumatizing.

Betty bumped shoulders with her as she sat beside her. "That's one of the longest codes I've been on. Young doctors tend to take a while to call it, but forty-five minutes? With his history, it should have been more like twenty. He was living on borrowed time. I remember when he came in a month ago. He had a blockage in the aortic arch."

"The widow maker," Jada mumbled, recalling the day her father died.

"Yep. I know it sounds bad, but I'm glad he was old. Hopefully he lived a good life."

"Hope so. Better to do a code on an old guy than a kid."

"Amen." Betty ducked her head to get started on the paperwork. Always an extra ton of it when there was a code.

Jada finished hers and handed it over to Betty. "Mind if I take a break?"

"Sure. I'll be right behind you. There're cookies on the table if you want some."

"Uh, have you met me?" Jada asked as she backed away from the nurse's station. "I won't even ask what kind because it doesn't matter. I'm on my way to go eat them, so you best hurry or they'll be gone."

"Better not be!" Betty yelled after her.

Jada smiled and stopped at the soda machine in the waiting room to get a diet cola before heading toward their break room. She'd turned from the machine when a scream sent shivers down her spine.

Doctor Jansen was speaking to the man's family. Jada took a deep breath and held it as she hurried past the room he'd gathered them in. She released her breath once she gained some distance and no longer heard the sobs from the bereaved loved ones. A part of the job she didn't simply dislike, she didn't want to deal with it. Not in her wheelhouse. The few times she'd had to tell family members their loved one was dead—those times were burned into her memory.

She made it into the break room about the time Betty did

and joined her at the table. Jada dug right into the cookies, allowing the double chocolate goodness to do its work and soothe her. "These are heavenly. Did you make them?"

"No way. Who's got time to bake? I bought them at CoffeeNut this morning. These things are like crack, and I can't stop eating them. Ever. I could eat them all day long and not care if I gained a hundred pounds."

"I see what you mean. Takes all the bad shit of the day and tosses it away, right?"

"Sometimes." Betty's gaze rested on Jada's hands, which were systematically tearing a cookie apart. "Did the cookie piss you off?"

"Huh?" She looked down, half-aware of what she was doing. Why rip apart a cookie? "I have no idea," she said as much to herself as Betty. "I guess I have a lot on my mind."

"Wanna get some things off your mind?" Betty leaned back in her chair. "I'm not Dear Abby, but I can listen. It's been a shitty shift, and I don't blame you if you need to talk about it. Or anything else."

"Thanks, Betty. I guess—it's not the shift. Well, not completely. I mean, when I got my soda, I heard this scream come from the quiet room. Then I heard the family sobbing, and it hit me hard. My dad died from a blockage in the aortic arch."

"I'm sorry. You need to take off early you can. We're good here."

"Maybe. I just didn't expect it." She took a sip of her soda and another bite of cookie. "You know what I want?"

"Tell me."

"I want to go home and cuddle with someone on the couch and watch a sappy, romantic movie then go to bed. And I don't mean I need sex—though it would be a nice bonus. I need someone to hold me while I go to sleep."

"I hear you. Seriously. It's all I want most days when I go home."

"Do you get it?"

Betty said, "Sometimes. Depends on if my husband's home or if he's had a shitty day, too. We always cuddle in bed though. Kind of have this pact we made years ago that we'd always go to bed together and snuggle. It's our thing I guess."

"You're damn lucky."

"I suppose. You'll find someone to cuddle. Maybe it'll even be some handsome Mountie."

Jada nearly spit her soda out. "Are you talking about Charley?"

"Are you dating another Mountie?"

"We're not dating."

"Uh-huh." Betty leaned back, her hazel eyes alight with mischief. "She's taken you around the city, then you spent an entire morning hiking in one of the most romantic places we have, and you've been texting her most of today. What do you call it?"

"Being friends."

"Yeah. I don't text with my friends like you two do. Like you can't be away from her for a minute."

Jada removed her phone from her pocket as another text came in. She didn't bother to hide the fact it was from Charley. "Fine. Maybe I like her. A lot. But it doesn't mean we're dating. She's more gun shy than I am, Betty."

Betty smiled knowingly and patted Jada on the arm. "You reply to the text you got and enjoy yourself. Maybe get some takeout and surprise her with dinner. You're shift's almost over. You never know what might come of it."

"We'd be closer friends?"

"Yes. Closer. Definitely closer."

Jada stuck her tongue out at Betty then replied to Charley, who was texting about the weather. Jada hadn't noticed it was raining but was sure glad she had her umbrella. After a few more texts, Charley stopped replying. The idea of going to her house to surprise her with dinner was very appealing to Jada.

****

Charley stood at her window and watched the rain. Huge drops splatted against the window, and she blinked like they were going to hit her. She leaned her forehead against the cool glass.

There'd been a lot of rain this year, and she was tired of it. Ordinarily she didn't mind, but it was depressing. When she worked, she never paid much attention to the weather. Her coat protected her well enough, and she was usually so focused on the job it never mattered if it were hot, cold, wet...

But work was something she wouldn't be doing anytime

soon. Three more months—minimum—her doctor said today. No less than three months before she would be back to work and then only light duty. Administrative crap. Might be longer before she'd have the strength to hold her weapon and fire it.

She wanted to slam her stupid hand against the window. Not being able to hold her weapon was like telling a painter she couldn't hold a brush. It felt like she'd lost an extension of herself. Her weapon was a piece of her. A marksman and range instructor—would she ever be competent enough to continue teaching? Would she be competent enough to keep her job?

The surgeon was very specific about do's and don'ts she'd have to get used to. And he was very careful to avoid the question of whether or not Charley would return to work.

Inspector Pike, as promised, set up a desk job for her once she was cleared by her physical therapist to work. But it fell flat in the end. Charley wasn't sure she'd want to be at the station and feel completely useless every time a call came in. Bad enough she couldn't keep from listening to the police scanner.

Then there were her parents. She loved them dearly, but her mom was getting in the way and her dad was calling or texting two or three times a day. She was fine. But they refused to believe her. Grace ran some interference for her with the parents, but even she was concerned about Charley's wellbeing.

Maybe they were right to keep checking on her. Some days, like today, Charley wanted to be done. Curl up in her bed, under the duvet, and never come back out.

And that's when a picture of Raina popped into her head.

Long, silky, brown hair flowing in a summer breeze. Her face lightly tanned from being on the lake for the weekend. Her bathing suit damp from their swim. Her misty green eyes full of mischief and love. She took Charley's hand and led her to the water where they spent time being alone together and loving each other.

But her memory, as always, flashed to Raina taking her own life.

Tears flowed down her face while Charley recalled finding Raina on the floor. She had a twelve-hour shift and came home tired and ready to lounge around with her wife. Raina promised her a warm meal and fun movie already in the DVD waiting for her. That's what she'd said in her text three hours before Charley got off duty.

It would have been about the time Raina killed herself.

Charley pulled away from the window and tried her best to shut down the images. They did her no good. Didn't matter why Raina killed herself. She was dead and Charley could do nothing about it.

Charley managed to shy away from any hint of a relationship with a woman. Any woman. Until Jada stepped into her life. Like a breath of fresh air or the lifeline to a drowning woman, Jada occupied a lot of her thinking time. And she did a lot of thinking now. She also did a helluva lot of texting. It was hard to believe she'd sent two dozen texts to Jada over the course of the late afternoon and evening.

Someone rang her doorbell and Charley shook off her thoughts and answered it with a polite smile. Which turned into a big stupid grin when she saw Jada standing there. She had a pink umbrella and held a reusable bag filled with a divine smell. Her smile mirrored Charley's.

"I got food. Thought maybe you could use some."

"Always." Charley stepped aside to let her in then took the umbrella and left it by the door inside her apartment. "Whatcha got?"

"I got a variety because I wasn't sure what you'd like. I know most everyone likes Chinese, so I sort of got one of everything." She went to the kitchen table and started unloading her bag. "The only thing I didn't get was drinks. I wasn't sure what you'd like."

Charley leaned on the door frame to the kitchen and watched Jada work. "Water is fine with me. I don't mind. But what made you do all this? And how did you find my apartment? I never told you where I live."

Jada stopped halfway to putting a paper container of fried rice on the table. "I begged Betty to tell me where you live, and she finally gave in. After more than a little teasing about it. And I'm doing this because I want to. Thought it might be nice to spend some time with you. I figured you might be lonely, but I don't have to stay. I guess I should have asked if this is a bad time."

"It's not, it's—not many people randomly show up at my door to give me dinner."

"Good. I don't like to be like other people. This is a first and you'll love it." Jada pointed to a chair. "Have a seat and let me get this all organized. Do you like Chinese?"

"I love it, actually. Pretty much anything is good with me."

"And this is why I like you. You're easy."

Charley gave her a grin. "I'm easy, huh?"

"Well, maybe not so easy." Jada sat across from her. Obsidian eyes held Charley's gaze for the longest time. Like Jada sat there and saw right into Charley's core. It gave her goose bumps, but in a nice way. Right along with this weird fluttering in her stomach. She hoped she'd be able to eat the delicious food in front of her.

Jada dug into her food, using the wooden chopsticks instead of the plastic fork. Her long, slender fingers gripped the sticks with practiced ease, and Charley had a sudden vision of what those fingers would be like on her heated skin.

She squirmed in her seat and tried very hard to look away from Jada.

But she was busted. "You're totally checking me out."

"Was not. Simply admiring your skill with the chopsticks. I'm not much good with them. Got to go with the fork."

"I bet you have skills in other places though, right, Sarge?"

Charley squeezed her legs closed as a very uncomfortable feeling came over her. The kitchen was hot, and she wanted to run away and hide.

"You're adorable," Jada said, still picking through her food. "And your dinner is getting cold."

"I—I don't—okay." Charley didn't have enough words to make a sentence. Where the hell was her mind going? Sure, she liked Jada a lot, but damn. Did she need to practically undress her when she saw her? Fantasize about her beautiful fingers and luscious lips waiting to be kissed? Charley needed a cold shower.

"I'm sorry if I made you uncomfortable," Jada said. She stopped eating and looked at Charley with concern. "Are you okay?"

"I'm—I'm fine." Charley cleared her throat and took a few bites of her food. "I don't have any excuses. I was sort of daydreaming when you showed up."

"Oh? Nice daydreams?"

Charley shook her head and pushed the containers away. Her appetite was well and truly gone. "Nightmares mostly."

Jada reached across the table and gently laid her hand over Charley's. "You don't have to talk about it, but if you want to, I'm right here. Okay? We don't know each other well, but I'd like to think we're friends. Right?"

"Right. Of course we're friends." Charley turned her hand over so she was holding Jada's. "Sometimes I get these thoughts and pictures in my head, and it's hard to get rid of them."

"Do they come to you when you see something in particular? Smell something? Hear something?"

"Sometimes it's when it rains like this—like on that day."

"Sounds like PTSD. You get a trigger, and boom, you're back in the memory." Jada tightened her grip on Charley's hand. "You look like you need to talk about it."

"I do, but it's hard." Charley ignored the tears as they fell again. "I mean, I'm a cop. I should be able to handle this, but when it's your wife whom you love dearly it changes things."

Jada abandoned her dinner and moved her chair to be next to Charley. She placed an arm around her shoulder and with the other she wiped away Charley's tears. "Start from the beginning. Tell me everything."

"I've only told one person *everything*."

"I bet I know who." Jada handed her a box of tissues and stood to make them some coffee. "Gracie. Am I right?"

"Yeah. How'd you guess?"

"You two seem pretty close, and I can see she gets you."

"She's like a sister to me, even though we hardly see each other. We went three years without a visit, back when she was with the bitch, Carly. She's on the other side of the city now, and we still have trouble finding time to get together. Text messages and phone calls are nice, but nothing beats the real thing. I've seen more of her in the last few days than I have in months."

"I get it." Jada kissed Charley on the temple. "It's good you have someone like Gracie, but I'm here if you need a shoulder to lean on."

"Thanks. I did counseling and stuff." Charley sighed. Deep down, she wanted to tell Jada everything, but she couldn't summon the courage. How could Charley tell Jada the last woman to love her killed herself? After a few moments she said, "I was married once. But she died ten years ago."

"Oh wow. I'm so sorry. What happened?" Jada rested her hand on Charley's forearm.

For a second, Charley almost pulled away from her touch. She didn't feel as though she deserved the compassion. "It doesn't matter. She's dead. I can't do anything to bring Raina back."

"Were you married long?"

"Five years, almost to the day."

Jada was quiet for a while, never letting go of Charley's arm or moving away from her. Jada's presence soothed Charley. "There's nothing I can say to make you feel better, but know I'm your friend, okay? You can trust me."

"Thanks." Charley patted her hand and carefully pulled away, instantly missing Jada's touch.

Jada scooted back to where her dinner lay ready to be consumed. She picked up the chopsticks and pointed them at Charley. "I think you need a change of venue."

"A what?"

"A change of venue. You need to take a trip with me. Just two friends exploring a new place together."

"A trip with you? And where would we go?"

"New York City. I've always wanted to go there for Pride."

"New York City? Seriously? You do know we have Pride here, too."

"We have it in Ottawa, but no one does it like New Yorkers."

Charley hesitated. It seemed like such a huge step. A trip together sounded fun, but she wasn't sure she should do it.

"This is supposed to be spontaneous. Stop over thinking it. Say yes. I promise you it'll be a blast."

"I—um, it's sort of like a date then?"

Jada laughed and the sound melted Charley's heart. "It's totally a date. You and me having a good time. Getting to know each other and exploring someplace awesome. Say you'll do it."

"I'll do it." Charley could scarcely believe she was going for this spontaneous idea. It was completely out of character. "I'm not good at planning trips."

"All you need is the plane ticket and your passport. I already did everything else." Jada kissed her cheek softly. "I got this, honey."

Charley didn't linger on the endearment Jada used, but she certainly wanted to explore the comment. Or slip of the tongue. Either way, she was thoroughly enjoying the impromptu late-night dinner, even if her appetite waned before she got started.

"Hey, I'm sorry I didn't eat very much. It all still looks so very good."

"It's okay. Makes for great leftovers. Hey, how about we find a movie to watch, and maybe you'll be hungry when it's over."

"Sounds like a plan." Charley bumped hips with Jada on her way out of the kitchen and smiled at the contact. "Do you like action movies?"

"Be more specific."

"Marvel, DC, X-men."

"You've won my heart, Sarge." Jada joined her in the living room. "Tell me how many times you've seen *Wonder Woman*."

"Um, six or seven."

Jada sighed dramatically and plopped onto the couch. "Yep. I'm in love."

Charley laughed nervously, pleased they had this much in common. "I've got all the movies on my iTunes. Got a preference?"

"*Wonder Woman*." Jada grinned.

Charley matched it. "You got it." She retrieved her iPad, turned on the TV and found the movie. Charley chose to sit on the opposite end of the couch, popped up the recliner portion, and stretched her legs out. As the movie began, Jada settled next to Charley. Their bodies touched along their lengths, and her legs rested next to Charley's.

For the first time in forever, Charley enjoyed the feel of someone in her personal space. She leaned back, put the iPad on the end table, and turned her attention, mostly, to the movie.

****

Hours later, Jada awoke curled around Charley's body. The TV was still on, the screen projecting the movie poster for

Wonder Woman. She could reach the remote to turn it off, but it meant letting go of Charley and she didn't want to.

Charley's body was surprisingly soft and pliant, and Jada wanted to hang on for dear life. Her head was tucked under Charlie's chin, and with one hand she massaged the muscled planes of Charley's abdomen. So strong and solid under her fingertips. The touch gave her a thrill, and she wanted to keep it up. But she knew she shouldn't and pulled her hand away.

"Why'd you stop?" Charley asked, her voice husky.

"I didn't want to wake you up."

"I kinda like it," she said. The other eye opened, and Charley moved a little to connect with Jada's gaze. "I don't mind you touching me."

"I sort of figured, since I'm draped over you like a blanket."

"I like it." Charley held her gaze and lifted her head so their faces were centimeters apart. "I like you, Jada. A lot."

"I like you, too," Jada whispered right as Charley's lips captured hers. The kiss was light at first then took a pleasant turn as they explored each other. Charley's arms wrapped around Jada and held her closer, her good hand running through Jada's hair. It sent shivers along her body when Charley's fingers tenderly combed her thick curls.

Jada lifted her head to give Charley more access as she trailed kisses along her neck, to her shoulder, and back again. She closed her eyes to enjoy the sensation she hadn't realized she'd been longing for. Charley's touch was like magic, and she wanted it to go on forever.

Charley's kisses left a fiery path along Jada's skin. When she reached the valley between her breasts, Charley stopped. She pulled back a little, her eyes alight with passion as she held Jada's gaze. "This is going to sound so very old fashioned."

Jada cupped Charley's face in the palm of one hand and stared into those sweet, brown eyes. "Tell me."

"I'm attracted to you. I think it's obvious."

Jada giggled. "Yeah. Pretty much."

"But I—the thing is, I don't mind kissing and touching, but I can't go any further."

Jada stared at her, trying to figure out what Charley was talking about. The question must have been written on her face.

"I don't want to have sex until I'm married."

"Really?" Jada asked.

"Really." Charley gently disentangled herself and got up, leaving Jada stretched out on the couch. "It's important to me and hard as hell to explain. It's something I've had in my head since I was a kid. I don't want to sleep with someone I'm not married to. Raina was my first, and we didn't make love until our honeymoon."

"Wow." Jada got up as well and moved to stand in front of Charley, who was avoiding her gaze. "You're serious, aren't you?"

"I am. If this is a game changer—well, it's okay. I thought I should tell you now before we, well, you know."

"Have sex?" Jada smiled at the hint of a blush on Charley's cheeks. "Do you know how adorable you are when you blush?"

Charley opened her mouth to speak and closed it again. She still wouldn't look at Jada.

"Baby, I'm okay with this. I won't push you into anything you're not ready for or want to do. I like you and I'm attracted to you, too. It might not be easy sometimes, but I'll respect your wishes." Jada waited patiently as Charley processed her words.

Charley's expression went from terrified to confused to sad. Jada couldn't stand it any longer and pulled her into a warm embrace. She lightly kissed Charley on the lips. "It's okay. I promise you."

"You sure? It's—I don't know if I ca—"

"Shh." Jada pressed her lips to Charley's again, lingering as long as she dared. "Look, it's been a long, hard day for me. And it wasn't overly pleasant for you, either. I don't want to mess up whatever this is between us. But there is something I'd love for you to do, if you're up for it."

There was a hint of doubt in those eyes before she asked, "What?"

"I don't have to work tomorrow, and I was wondering if you'd sleep with me. Literally. I want someone to hold me tonight. I'm not asking for anything else. I want someone to make me feel better. More secure." She didn't dare say the other word in her head.

Loved.

"Done." Charley gently untangled herself from Jada. "I'll get you one of my old T-shirts to wear. Sound good?"

"It does." Jada allowed Charley to take her hand and lead her to the bedroom at the end of the short hall. She found a T-shirt and gave it to Jada and left while she got changed. Ten minutes later, they were lying in Charley's bed, beneath the duvet.

"What do you need me to do?" Charley asked with a slight tremble in her voice.

God, she's cute when she's nervous, Jada thought. "Get comfy and I'll curl up to you. Okay?"

"Sure."

Jada curled into Charley's side, tucked one arm against her midriff and the other securely around Charley's stomach.

Charley slid her right arm out from under Jada and wrapped it around her. She felt awkward at first, but they eventually settled into the embrace like they'd been lovers for years.

Jada kissed Charley on the cheek and rested her head on Charley's shoulder. "G'nite."

Chapter Ten

The smell of fresh coffee combined with fried bacon roused Jada from the most peaceful sleep she'd had in forever. She stretched and tossed the duvet aside to get out of bed. Charley's bed. Jada remembered the safety of those strong arms holding her and sighed in the most dreamy way. So weird that they only *slept* together. Okay, she wasn't a slut or anything, but her attraction to Charley charged the room whenever they got close to each other. She knew Charley felt it, too, and it didn't take much imagination to know what she wanted to do with her.

The connection they had was strong. So was their budding friendship, and Jada didn't want to mess it up. It's how she convinced herself sex could wait. She made a promise, and she'd stick to it. She wasn't about to make the same mistake with Charley she'd made with Francine.

She wandered into the bathroom to pee and clean up a bit. Francine wasn't like Charley at all. Francine was wild, beautiful, loud mouthed, and opinionated. She was also a talented trauma surgeon and the most unfortunate relationship Jada ever had the displeasure of being involved in.

Had it not been for a friend at work, Jada never would have crossed paths with Francine. Worse yet was how Liselle constantly told her Francine was bad news. She'd been right, but Jada was loath to acknowledge it.

She left the bathroom and padded into the kitchen. She took a seat at the table and watched Charley put together an omelet. "If my omelet has peppers in it, I might be inclined to propose to you."

Charley's laughter was soft and melodic and made Jada smile. Charley said, "It does have peppers and onions and cheese and bacon. Anything else I can do for you?"

"Oh the places your question is taking me."

"You have a dirty mind."

"Uh, so do you if you got my reference." Jada's eyes fixed

on Charley's when she turned around. She had to look away at their intensity and now noticed Charley wore a T-shirt and boxer shorts with some kind of logo on them. "Hey, is that Iron Man on your undies?"

"They aren't undies, they're boxers. And yes. It's Iron Man." Charley turned so she saw the full view of the character from the Marvel movies. "I have a pair of Wonder Woman ones in my dresser."

"Oh, I wish I could see those. Maybe get a picture. I need my phone."

"No way. No pictures of me in my boxers." Charley finished the omelet and put half on a plate and set it in front of Jada. "I don't want me half-naked all over the Internet."

"What makes you think I'd post it somewhere? Besides, I don't do social media. Not anymore." Jada ducked her head to avoid whatever look Charley was giving her and started eating her breakfast. "Damn. This is good."

"Why don't you do social media?" Charley asked once she'd sat down across from Jada. "I have a Facebook page. Don't use it much, but it's there."

Jada was uncomfortable with the topic. "I don't like it. Too invasive."

"Well, I'll give you that. And it's a time-sucker, but it can be kinda fun sometimes."

"I guess," Jada said. One look at the openness of Charley's face and Jada realized she needed to share part of herself, as Charley had done the night before. Jada put her fork down and leaned back from the table. "If you look up my name, you'll find out why I avoid social media. Most of the shit is still out there because nothing is ever truly gone from the Internet, even though I tried like hell to get rid of it."

"Can I ask what it was about?"

"You know you've got your cop voice going right now, don't you?" Jada tried to laugh, but failed. It sounded more like a snort. "I know cops, and right now you sound like one."

"I don't mean to. I seriously want to know, but if you're not ready to talk about it, it's okay." Those doe eyes watched Jada with deep concern. "Should I change the subject now?"

Jada so wanted her to do just that. Yet something told her she needed to give her all the details of the incident two years ago. The info was burned into her brain, but not like a PTSD thing. More like a reminder of who she could and couldn't trust in this world. Francine being the top person on her list.

Her hands shook a little as she took a deep breath to speak—right when the front door opened and Josie walked in. All three women stared open mouthed at each other for what felt to Jada like minutes, but surely was only seconds.

Charley was the first to recover from the shock of this surprise visitor. "Mom, what are you doing here?"

"I came to take you to your follow-up appointment with the doctor."

"It's in three hours." Charley looked to Jada like she was trying very hard to hold her temper in check. "Can you give us a couple of minutes?"

Josie didn't look like she knew what to do, exactly, so she wandered into the living room and sat on the couch.

Charley pushed her breakfast away and whispered, "I'm sorry. I had no idea she'd be this early. I thought we'd have time to talk."

There was a double meaning to her words, and Jada realized she wished the same. "It's fine. I promise. We'll make time to talk again. Okay?"

Charley nodded and Jada stood up. "Are you leaving?" Charley asked.

"I'm going to get dressed so I'm not parading in front of your mother in my undies. I'll be back in a minute." She leaned down and kissed Charley on the temple before going to the bedroom and closing the door.

****

Charley joined her mother on the couch. Josie was playing with her phone, but Charley understood she wasn't actually looking at it. "It's okay, Mom. I promise. You surprised us is all."

Josie's face was beet red. "You probably should text me if you're going to have someone over here, Charlene. I don't want to disturb you." She smiled up at her. "I'm so very happy you've found someone like Jada. I like her."

"It's not what you think, Mom. Seriously. We fell asleep watching a movie, and she stayed the night."

Josie's expression was skeptical. "Oh? You're both in your panties. Do you always wear only your panties when you have company?"

"Only when we sleep together." Charley found her mom's shocked expression funny and couldn't help laughing. "Honestly, we slept together. Literally slept. I don't know what's going on between us, and it's scaring the hell out of me. I'm not sure I can even do this."

"I don't think you get to choose these things, Charlene. They sneak up and hit you in the face." Josie now looked behind Charley, as the door to the bedroom opened. "I kind of think that's what's happening right now."

"Mom." Charley wanted to sound menacing, but the amused look on Josie's face took any force out of her words. "You're impossible."

"I know."

Jada stood in front of them, a sheepish grin on her face. "Hi, Josie. Nice to see you again. Sorry it was a little weird."

"I'm used to weird." She pointed to Charley. "She's my kid."

"So I've heard," Jada said. She shoved her hands into the pockets of her jeans. "And I probably should head out."

"Don't leave on my account. Besides, you two didn't finish your breakfast."

"The omelets are cold now, Mom."

"Then it's a good thing I brought donuts. A dozen of those crazy flavors you like from CoffeeNut."

Charley's mood brightened instantly at the thought of sugar for breakfast. She looked to Jada who was smiling like she'd won the lotto. "I think we can handle donuts. Let me get the table cleaned off. You want coffee, Mom?"

"You have to ask?" Josie carried the box of donuts to the table while Jada set out a few plates and napkins.

Charley observed them working in silence and, for the first time in years, thought she could get used to such a sight. If her dad were there, it would be perfect. And it scared the hell out of her.

****

Two days later, Charley was alone in her apartment. The details of the dream she'd had last night were fuzzy, but kissing Jada definitely took center stage. Better than a nightmare.

Her phone rang, and she turned from the window and crossed to the coffee table where her cell phone lay. She picked it up, unsurprised to find Grace's smiling face on the caller ID. "Hey, Gracie."

"*Dänch'á Éh ma?*" Grace asked.

Charley smiled at Grace's use of Standard Southern Tutchone. She replied, "I'm well, thanks. How are you guys?"

"You're no fun. You're supposed to speak back to me in Southern Tutchone. How will I learn it if you aren't speaking it with me? I need practice."

"Gracie, the last thing you need is to practice any language."

"Ha. You didn't hear me on our honeymoon butchering French all over France. Liv didn't have a clue, but I can tell you I got some seriously weird looks. Especially the couple of times I picked up on a few dialect words and didn't use them wrong, but used them on the wrong people."

"But you never got lost, and you figured out what you needed, right?"

"I showed up Liv." Grace laughed. "How's it going with you? Do you need anything? I'm sure you're bored to death by now."

"I am. Just standing here looking out the window. Mom left enough food to feed an army, so I don't have to go anywhere if I don't want to."

"How are things with Jada?"

"There aren't any things with Jada. We're friends." The last part Grace chorused with Charley, and while a little annoying, it did make her laugh. "You're an ass."

"I am, but I can tell you're interested in her. It's nice to see. I can't recall you being interested in anyone since Raina. Want to talk about it?"

"Oh, now I'm sure my mother has something to do with this little conversation." Charley returned to her window and stared out at the clear blue sky. "She told you Jada stayed the night, didn't she?"

"Uh, no. That's news. Seriously? She stayed the night?"

Grace's surprise was genuine, and Charley wanted to slap herself in the forehead. "No gossip from my mother? Honestly?"

"Honestly. But now you have to tell me what happened."

Charley related all the details, including the truly awesome kissing. She ended it with saying, "So here's the thing. I like her. A lot. What do I do with that? I haven't felt attracted to anyone in a decade, and I'm not even sure I want to be. I'm happy with my life as it is."

"No, you're not."

"Excuse me?"

"I said you're not happy." Grace sighed. "Okay, you're content, I guess. You spend more time at work than you do anywhere else. You only slept at your apartment until now, and if it wasn't for your injury, we would go weeks or months without ever talking. Is your life happy, Charley?"

Charley didn't want to acknowledge the truth in Grace's words. But what else was she supposed to do? If she stopped, there'd be time to think. Like right now. "I'm afraid to get attached to her. What if I find out I like her and things go wrong? Or something happens to her? Or I screw it up and we hurt each other? I don't know how to deal with this kind of stuff, Gracie. Maybe I'm one of those people who are supposed to live by themselves, you know? Never get married or have a family."

"Whoa, stop right there. I realize there's no timeline for these things, but Raina died ten years ago, Charley. You have to let yourself move on at some point. You can't keep your head stuck in the sand forever. And it's bullshit about living alone. You're a wonderful person and deserve someone to love you."

"You're biased."

"I am. You're right. I know you better than anyone, and I know how much you deserve to have a family. Don't let Raina ruin you. If you never take a chance, you'll never know love again. And it would break my heart."

Charley was quiet for a few moments, not sure how to respond. She wasn't sure she agreed with Grace. In order for her to have a family, Charley would have to let her guard down. Let someone into her heart, like she did with Raina.

For a moment, she was taken back to the day Raina died. The person she was sure would always be there, would be parent to her children, took her own life and left Charley to pick up the pieces. And not one single person in their lives understood why Raina did it. How could Charley ever trust someone again? She didn't think she would survive losing someone again. She'd barely survived losing Raina.

"Stop it," Grace said, her voice gentle in Charley's ear. "Don't use Raina as your guide to women. You can't compare Jada or anyone else to her."

"How do you know what I was thinking about?"

"It's a gift. Besides, even over the phone you're easy for me to read. And it's not a great big leap to realize why you're afraid to engage with Jada. You've closed yourself off to everyone but your family and even me at times. You can't go on like this, Charley. You have to open up to someone sometime. Why not let it be Jada? You know you like her and you're attracted to her. Why not give her a chance?"

"I don't know where to start, provided I've got the guts to give it a go."

"Well, that's the easy part. You don't do anything. Get to know her and if she's interested—as the kissing indicates—then she'll come to you. Accept her friendship first. Work on other things as you go. Don't try to plan it out or work on some kind of strategy. Take a deep breath, let it out, and accept your friendship might grow into something more."

"It's not so easy." Charley tried hard to keep the whining out of her voice.

"I know, my friend. I can hear it in your voice. But I'm telling you not to be fearful. Do yourself a favor and let things happen. Hang out with her and don't be afraid to open up. I'm not suggesting you spill your whole life story at once."

"I could always use another friend, right?"

"Exactly. Friends first. That's always the best way. If more happens, great. If not, so what? You've got a new pal to hang around with. You never know what's going to happen in life, so take every opportunity you get and run with it."

Charley considered it for a few moments and eventually nodded, even though Grace couldn't see her. "Fine. I'll try. You'd make a great counselor, Gracie."

"It's not my thing. Languages are my passion and organizing money is my superpower. So I guess I need to get back to work going over all the financial files for TNT. Keeps my mind busy and my ideas from wandering freely. I so need a lock on my brain. But before I go, we're having a bonfire at the mine on Saturday. Bring Jada so we can get to know her better. It'll be fun."

"I'll ask and if she's available we'll come."

"I want you there no matter what," Grace said, her voice taking on a playful sternness. But Charley understood Grace was serious.

"Fine."

"Good. Call me if you need anything. You hear?"

"Yes, ma'am," Charley muttered and hung up. She stared at her phone for a good long time before bringing up Jada's number. It rang a few times, and Charley expected it'd go to voicemail. She was preparing her message when Jada's breathless voice answered.

"Hey, Sarge! Sorry, I was in the shower. Just got back from a very long shift."

"No problem." Charley paused, unsure what to say.

"So, what's up?"

"Nothing much."

"Uh-huh. Wanna try again?"

Charley grinned. Did all women have the ability to read her? Even over the phone? "There's a bonfire at Gracie's Glory Saturday night. Wanna go?"

"Saturday night? Let me check my schedule." A longish moment passed before Jada came back to the call. "I'm off shift at three in the afternoon. What time did you want to go?"

"Um, probably around then. It's a two-hour drive up there. It's out past Blue River."

"I don't know where that is," Jada said. "Doesn't matter. I'm up for it. So what is Gracie's Glory, exactly? And who's putting on this bonfire?"

"It's a gold mine owned by Gracie's grandpa, Harry. It's the one my parents have worked at for years. Not a huge operation, but it supports itself and they make decent money doing it. The crew up there is a lot of fun. It's more like a family than anything else. Maybe you'll get to meet Harry if he's up to it. I think you'd like to see him after you saved his life."

"Oh right. The cardiac arrest. Hard to forget those calls. I'd love to see how he's doing, miracle of modern medicine that he is. Do I need to bring anything?"

"Nope. Come to my apartment when you're ready and we'll head out."

"Okay. I'm all set then. Now I've had a shower I'm going to bed for a while. My ten-hour shift turned into fifteen hours. Call me later?"

"I will. Bye for now." Charley heard Jada say bye and disconnected the call. Her gaze went back to the outside world. The flutter in her stomach was now a consistent feeling whenever she spoke to Jada. Somehow, she didn't mind a bit.

****

Jada walked into work with a very satisfied smile on her face. The previous night, as she was getting settled into bed, Charley called her. At first, she worried something was wrong, but it turned out Charley simply wanted to talk. Their first real talk since she'd spent the night more than a week ago.

"I guess I need a friendly voice," Charley said.

"Should I come over? Are you okay?"

There was a short pause. "No. It's late. But if we can stay on the phone until we get sleepy, that'd be great. Sort of like being in the same space, ya know?"

"But with a safe distance between us?" Jada asked. She recognized Charley needed space. Jada so wanted to talk about the sweet kisses they'd shared. She hoped it wasn't a one-off. They were definitely worth repeating.

"I guess so," Charley finally said. "I'm sorry if it seems rude. Sometimes it's easier to open up on the phone than in person."

"Because you can't see who you're talking to. Takes away the fear of looking into someone's eyes and thinking you're being judged."

"You sound like the voice of experience."

"A little. With my mom. I can tell her to go fuck herself when we're on the phone, but in person, no way. She's got this steely gaze, and it makes me freeze up. Like suddenly I'm ten again and getting grounded for something Celeste did. I can't stand up to her in person very well."

"Do you do that a lot? Stand up to her?"

"I didn't so much when I was a kid. But when I came out to her it sort of got the ball rolling. I decided I wasn't going to follow the path she had laid out for me. I would do my own thing. My dad was all for it, but he was such a sweet man. He always encouraged us to be independent. Mom wants that for us, too, but only if we're doing things the way she thinks they should be done. It's infuriating."

"My mom always encouraged me. When I told her I wanted to be a Mountie, she's the one who found out all the requirements. She got me signed up for track, and Dad took me to all my events. I couldn't have asked for better people to raise me."

"Can I ask you something personal?"

Charley paused before she said, "Depends. I mean, I might say I have no tattoos, but until you see me naked, you wouldn't know for sure."

If Jada had been drinking she'd have spewed it all over the place. As it was, she nearly choked as she squeaked out a laugh. "Whoa. Not where I was going, but okay. I might have to do a strip search one of these days."

"Keep dreaming," Charley said with a chuckle. "What's your question?"

"Are you adopted? I met your mom, of course, and I remember seeing a picture of you and a guy I assumed is your dad when I was at your place. You look nothing like either of them."

"Did the height gave it away? I'm three inches taller than Dad. Or was it how my skin is a lot darker than theirs?"

There was a hint of teasing and Jada smiled. "All of the above. I guess I notice these things. I've always been observant, which comes in handy considering my job. So are you First Nation then?"

"I am. I have no way of knowing what clan, though."

"You don't know your birth parents?"

"I was abandoned at the hospital. The Townsends were listed as emergency foster parents, and the night they brought me home, according to Mom, they fell in love with me and decided they'd adopt me if possible. Four months later, I was legally their kid."

"No one ever found your parents? Or the person who left you at the hospital?"

"Never. The police had a few leads, but nothing panned out. And this was, of course, long before CCTV was on every street corner. I was left in the waiting room in the middle of the night. I guess whoever put me there figured I'd be safe. Anyway, I never pursued it."

"Why not? I'd want to know everything about my family. What if you need medical records? Like does cancer run in the family or heart disease or diabetes? Those kinds of things."

"None of that matters. If I get sick, I get sick. Everyone has the genetics to get cancer or heart disease or diabetes. Honestly, Jada, I don't give a shit about the people who didn't want me. I have a friend who found them through a DNA sample I gave her, but I asked her not to tell me about them."

"I probably shouldn't keep going on like this, but don't you wonder about your history?"

"Sure. Kathy, my friend who works for the *Ta'an Kwäch'än* Council, has taught me a lot about our heritage. Being First Nation is the only thing they were pretty sure about me when I was found. The blanket I was wrapped in was very distinctive. Mom and Dad felt it was important I know my ancestry, so Dad found Kathy. She's been teaching me things my whole life. She's like an adopted auntie and I love her.

"I know it's weird, but I don't need to know anything about those people. For me, they don't exist. Josie and Charles Townsend are my parents. That means I get all the cousins from their siblings, my aunts and uncles, and all the drama of being part of a large, extended family." Charley paused in her story. "And I love all of it. I've never felt like an outsider, even if I'm way taller than most of them, and my brown skin stands out in pictures. No one cares. I'm family."

"That's wonderful. What an amazing group of people to belong to. I have aunts and uncles I haven't seen since I was a little kid. Dad died when I was twenty and Celeste was sixteen. Mom stopped making it a point to take us to see his family. I guess it was part of her grief process. I don't know. Anyway, I'm a little jealous. But I admit my curiosity is piqued over your bio parents."

"Mine isn't. Case closed. But I'm still involved in the community. Kathy told me I'm Tutchone, Wolf Clan. When I was about five, she started teaching me to speak Southern Tutchone. I go to events at the cultural center, where I'm also a volunteer."

"Sounds like I should meet this Kathy person."

"I can take you on a tour of the cultural center sometime next week if you'd like. We have a small, but amazing museum."

She heard Charley yawn. "Am I putting you to sleep?"

Charley's laugh was soft, and Jada had a strong urge to cuddle her. "I'm worn out now. Which is what I needed. I have an early physio appointment so I should try to sleep. Thanks for talking to me."

"Of course. It's what friends do, right?"

"Right. So you'll come to the center?"

"I'm off Tuesday, so it's a date," Jada said.

"Look forward to it. G'nite, friend."

"G'nite." Jada disconnected and put her phone on the nightstand. She burrowed under the duvet and stared into her dark room. Her brain was whirring, and there was no way she'd get to sleep now.

Four hours later, she entered the locker room by rote. She put her backpack away, grabbed her stethoscope and reusable coffee container, and headed for the kitchenette. She smelled fresh brew and went right for it. Her container filled, she turned to leave and ran right into Nurse Cranky Pants—Peter Tremblay. If not for the fact she'd just tightened the container lid, he'd have hot coffee down his front.

"Watch it!" he yelled and shoved past her.

Jada narrowed her gaze and shoved back. "I didn't do anything, you dickhead. I suggest you watch where the hell you're walking."

Peter opened his mouth to speak, but nothing came out. His gaze went to the door and Jada followed it. Betty came right at him and ignored Jada all together.

"You listen to me and you listen good." She pointed at him, now about ten centimeters from his face. "I will not have your attitude in my ER. You got me? If you don't want to work here, I will make it happen for you. As of right now, you're off shift. Come in tomorrow and sign off on your three-day suspension."

"What the fuck?" For a moment, Jada thought Peter was going to hit Betty. She intentionally stood to Betty's left. "I do my job. My attitude, as you call it, is fine. You've got it out for me. Always have. I'm better than you."

"In your dreams. I've forgotten more about nursing than you'll ever know. But that's not the point. You had my patient in tears, and that is unacceptable behavior. Three days might help your attitude."

"You can't suspend me without a union hearing."

Betty said, "Yes, I can. You'll get a hearing, and if the arbiter thinks it wasn't a just suspension, you'll get your pay back. I'm the nursing supervisor, Peter. You're suspended. Period. I want to see you tomorrow morning to sign the paperwork. Don't make me get Security to get you out of here."

Peter's face paled and Jada barely kept from smiling. His tone sounded threatening. "You wouldn't dare."

"Try me." Betty moved a tiny bit closer.

Peter hesitated. He took a step back, maneuvered around Betty, and left without further comment.

"Wow." Jada leaned against the counter and watched Betty pace the small area. "What happened?"

Betty ran a hand over her face and turned to Jada with sad eyes. "We have a psych patient in bay ten. I gave her care to Peter when the medics brought her in. She threatened suicide but didn't actively do anything we're aware of. When he came out, I heard her sobbing. One of the medics was near the bay and heard Peter saying if she was going to kill herself she should have just done it and saved everyone the aggravation of dealing with her.

"I had to calm the medic down because he wanted to kick Peter's ass. They spent half an hour at this woman's house settling her down before transporting her here. And the transport was from out past Blue River so this medic got to know her pretty well. Anyway, he came to me, I went to the patient, and she corroborated what happened. I assigned her a new nurse and told Peter to come in here and wait for me."

"Good call. No wonder he shoved me out of the way. I knew he was pissed off."

"He shoved you?" Betty asked.

"Yep. I shoved back though. I don't get paid enough to deal with Nurse Cranky Pants' attitude." She smiled at Betty. "That's your job."

"Gee thanks. But if you want to write something up about the incident, I can add it to my report. I want him gone, Jada. He went too far this time."

"I agree and I'll write it up for you today." Jada gave her arm a squeeze. "Seriously, you're the best supervisor I've ever worked with."

"Thanks. Look, I'll be awhile getting paperwork together on Peter, but would you like to get a drink after work?"

"I'd love to, but I sorta have a date."

That got a smile from Betty. "With a handsome Mountie?"

"Yep. There's a bonfire tonight and we're going. We have another date on Tuesday." She leaned closer to whisper, "Let's just say things heated up last week, and I think I might be breaking through her giant wall."

"How heated up?"

Jada felt her cheeks warm. "Kissing. Lots of very hot, sexy kissing. Nothing more. Well, we did sleep together, but nothing happened. And you know, it was one of the best nights I've had in my life."

"You sound like you've got it bad for her."

"I kinda do," Jada said. It felt nice to say it aloud. "But she's the most skittish woman I've ever met."

"She's got good reasons to be. Give her time. And speaking of time, I got patients to get back to. Raincheck on the drink?"

"Totally."

****

Charley stood back and watched Jada interacting with Harry and Grace. Harry wasn't as energetic as usual, but he insisted on coming anyway. The bonfires were always a pleasant time and wouldn't be the same without him. What made Charley smile was how Jada was flirting with him. And it wasn't fake flirting. She was genuine in her adoration for Harry. The amused look on his face was priceless.

"I like her," Liv said from behind Charley. "And if you're not careful, Harry's going to steal her away from you."

"She's not mine to steal, Liv."

"Hmm. Might want to tell her that."

Charley caught Jada's gaze, and her stomach did flip flops again. She wanted to look away, but she couldn't. For a few seconds, they were the only two people in the world. But someone spoke to Jada and she looked away. Charley was sad the moment was over.

"Nope. She's not yours at all," Liv said with a laugh before moving on to join Grace and Harry.

Charley would have ignored Liv, but she was right. There was something between her and Jada, and they needed to talk about it very soon.

"What are you over thinking about right now?" This time it was her mom.

Charley's shoulders slumped, and she gave her mom a sideways glare. "How do you do that?"

"I'm your mother. Now answer the question." Josie took a drink from her beer and followed Charley's gaze to Jada. "Ah. Never mind. I see what you're over thinking." She reached up and gave Charley a light slap to the back of her head. "Stop it."

"You're mean," Charley said. "I should report you for child abuse."

"You keep up this over thinking nonsense, and you'll get more of the same. And it's not child abuse. You're not a child. If any abuse is happening here, it's to me."

"Oh? How do you figure? You hit me. Not the other way around."

"You're breaking my heart, and it's worse than a slap to the head." Josie leaned back and looked Charley right in the eyes. "You take the last step, and enjoy that beautiful woman over there. Who, by the way, hasn't taken her eyes off you all evening."

"I need to talk to her about this thing we've got going on," Charley said, finally giving in to her mother's need for more details. "Everyone seems to see it well enough, but I don't know where it's going. We have to talk, but I don't know how to start."

"You don't start it at all. Let your relationship grow organically. Don't try to help it. Don't think about it. Don't talk it over. Let it happen." Josie tapped Charley on the chest. "This is all the guidance you need. Trust me, okay? I know what I'm talking about."

"You act like you've got all this experience," Charley said. "I know better. Dad's your one and only."

"Exactly. And that, my child, makes me an expert." She

bumped hips with Charley and laughed. "Speaking of your father, I see him talking to your girlfriend. He might even be flirting. I suggest you get over there and save her from his dumb jokes."

"I like his jokes."

"You would." Josie finished her beer and turned to leave. "I mean it, Charlene. Get over there and spend time with her instead of standing here staring at her and thinking about shit you can't control."

Charley wanted to respond, but Josie gave her a gentle shove toward Jada and walked away.

Charley sighed and took the hint. She joined the group, which now included her cousin, Mike. She arrived as her dad was about to tell a joke.

"Hi," Jada said, interrupting Charles. "About time you came over here." She patted the crate she was seated on and scooted to the edge. "Join me?"

Charley didn't reply but settled beside Jada. The people around them became weirdly quiet, and it was awkward. She looked at them as Jada scooted close enough their bodies were touching. She tried to glare at her family, but from the smiles on their faces, it didn't work one bit.

Charles cleared his throat. "Okay, so like I was saying. It was a dark and stormy night..."

Charley let her dad's voice float over her while she enjoyed the feel of Jada pressed up against her. Her brain immediately started wondering if this was the right thing to do, but her heart overruled it. She enjoyed it so much, she used her free arm to pull Jada closer. The cold was biting and while they both wore coats, Charley felt the need to help Jada stay warm. At least it's what she told herself.

Jada looked at her and smiled when Charley settled an arm around her. Jada's eyes conveyed something so special Charley found it almost impossible to look away.

"They're getting the fire going now," Grace said, getting Charley's attention. "*Ojiichan*, would you like to move closer to it?"

"Yes. But I cannot stay much longer. I'm sorry, Gracie. I am getting tired."

"It's no problem," Grace said. She squatted beside his wheelchair and held his gnarled hand in hers. Charley felt a moment of sadness. Grace was so close to Harry, and Charley was sure she realized how precious every moment with him was.

Harry squeezed her hand and said, "Thank you, Gracie Lee."

"Of course." Grace spoke to him softly, in Japanese, then wheeled him closer to the fire that was now about a meter high. By the end of the night, it would be three times higher. Mike and Liv followed quietly behind them.

Charley waited until they were gone, before she spoke. "I'm surprised he came out here tonight."

"Same here, but I'm glad." Her dad's voice cracked a bit, and she wondered if he was crying. She couldn't see his face very well in the twilight. "But he's lived a long life. And I'm not going to start missing him before he's even gone."

He got to his feet. "Jada, it's been a pleasure chatting with you. I need to find my wife and make sure she's okay and not drinking too many beers. Which would be three. She's a lightweight." He saluted them with the beer bottle in his hand and wandered off.

"He's a very cool guy, your dad," Jada said.

Charley noticed she held a soda in her hand and was glad for it. "He is. He's a lot of fun to be around."

"Your mom's pretty nice, too. A little tipsy already, but nice."

"Yeah, she is a lightweight. But they stay in their trailer here during the summer, so it's fine. They can walk a few meters and be home. Mike loves doing the fire part, and he'll stay awake until it dies down enough to be snuffed out with dirt. That'll be hours from now."

"He's pretty shy, isn't he? Your cousin, Mike. I couldn't get more than a few words out of him."

"Shy and awkward around girls in particular. Mom told me he has a girlfriend, but I'll have to see proof before I believe it. He's a good guy, and I think he'd be a good catch for the right woman. Poor guy keeps ending up with women who take advantage of him."

"Women suck." Jada tipped her can of soda up to finish it off. Her belch was loud, and both of them giggled. "Sorry. Happens every time I drink soda."

"It's fine. I'm not bothered by that kind of stuff."

"What does bother you? Anything? I mean, so far you've been like the most patient, accepting person I've ever met. There must be something that gets under your skin. Pisses you off."

Charley said, "Not much. Well, if I see someone hurting someone else, I get upset and try to stop it."

"Like with Gracie's ex-wife?"

"Exactly. It's why I'm a Mountie. I can't stand to see someone hurt. I want to stop bad people from doing bad things to good people. I want to protect the innocent and save everyone I can. I know it sounds corny and lofty, but it's how I feel."

"I get it. I feel the same about my job. But do you ever get so pissed off you lose your temper?"

"Never. I've never been so mad I hit someone or screamed at them. I've had to yell sometimes to be heard over other people, but not in anger. I guess no one's ever pushed me enough for me to get that pissed off."

"Wow. You are an amazing woman, Charley." Jada got up and moved so she stood between Charley's legs. Her cold hands cupped Charley's face. "I could fall in love with you."

"I don't think you'd—"

"Shh. Don't think." Jada's lips caressed Charley's.

Charley closed her eyes and melted into Jada's kiss. She put her arms around Jada as their kiss heated up. A warm sensation floated along Charley's body. She got to her feet, never losing contact with Jada.

Charley felt the need to be in control of things. Her hands slid to Jada's ass and held her in place as their tongues danced together. If they hadn't been in the open, with people meters away from them, Charley realized she might be inclined to make a mistake. No doubt she wanted Jada. Wanted her badly. She was on the edge of losing control and stopped. She put a few centimeters of distance between them., Her breath came in short bursts, and her heart beat wildly in her chest.

If they'd gone on for a few more minutes—if they'd been in her apartment and near the bed—Charley shook the thought away. She wasn't going to. She'd made a promise to herself years ago, and she intended to keep it.

Jada's eyes stayed closed while her breathing slowed. When she looked at Charley, it was with a mixture of passion and amusement. It confused Charley.

"I'm sorry," Charley said. "I thought it best to stop now—you know?"

"Oh sure. I told you before I won't push you to have sex, but you keep kissing me like that, and it's going to get hard to stop. I mean, like, nearly impossible. Shit. I've never been with anyone who lit my fire quite like you do." Jada leaned forward and gave her a soft kiss on the lips. "I don't mind one bit."

"Good to know." Charley hugged Jada again, and when they parted, she offered her good hand to her. "Want to go see the fire?"

"Baby, I'm already on fire, but if it's where you wanna go, I'm with you." Jada took the offered hand and said, "Lead on."

The fire was going well now, and when they reached the edge, Charley stood behind Jada and wrapped her arms around her. Jada leaned into her and covered Charley's arms with her own. Charley rested her chin on Jada's shoulder. She knew her family and friends were watchful of her, but she suddenly didn't care. She actually took her mother's advice and decided to live in the moment, and right now the moment was perfect. And if she thought too much about it, she'd shatter it into a million pieces.

She closed her eyes, absorbed the peace around her, and allowed happiness to settle in. Even if for this one night.

Chapter Eleven

"It's beautiful," Jada said softly, reverently examining a display at the *Kwanlin Dün* Cultural Centre. "The craftsmanship is amazing." Jada stood before the bust of a First Nation man, with the tip of an eagle's wing at the top of his head, like the eagle was touching him as it flew past. The material used was a shiny white. The only color came from the beads on a string of feathers attached to his head, above his ear. His long hair hung down to the bottom of the figure, which ended on a white base.

"Made from moose antlers," Charley said.

"Seriously?" Jada looked for the display description and read it. "Wow. This is amazing."

"It's one of my favorites."

Jada took a few pictures with her phone and slid it back into her pocket.

"How long have you been volunteering here?" Jada asked as they moved on to another display. This one held clothing made of moose hide and decorated with colorful beads and feathers. The tiny dress looked like it belonged to a child.

"I've been volunteering most of my life at one place or another, except the years I was posted away from here with the RCMP. This museum is pretty new, and I was excited to be here to help get it up and running. The idea of holding some of these items on display in my hands was amazing. Like I felt my history through the fabric or the wood."

Jada smiled at the light in Charley's eyes as she spoke. "It's a great place. Thanks for taking me here."

"Sure." Charley directed her along the hallway and stopped at a photo of two women.

It was black and white and they were dressed in traditional clothing. The caption read, "Two Spirits circa 1910."

"Two Spirits?" Jada asked.

Charley smiled. "We put this up for Pride Month. Those two women are married."

"Seriously? That's like over a hundred years ago."

"Two Spirits is a term we use instead of saying gay or lesbian or whatever. Two Spirits can be a feminine man, masculine woman, woman who loves other women, etc. In our history, a Two Spirit woman could be a warrior, but she also would do cooking and cleaning. We were often visionaries, healers, medicine people and respected as important parts of our community. It wasn't until the Europeans came here that we started thinking otherwise. Eventually, it was outlawed as it was in their society. But it's changed now, mostly. Having this display is a huge step in the right direction."

"So in your culture you're a special person?"

"I guess so."

"It's so cool." Jada linked arms with her, and when their eyes met, she smiled brightly at Charley. "I didn't need a display to tell me. I already know how special you are."

"You, my friend, are bli—"

Jada shut her up with a heated kiss and let it go on for as long as Charley allowed it. Which, to Jada's surprise, was a long time. When they parted, their gazes locked and Jada was so very sure she saw her feelings reflected in those beautiful eyes. The words were on the tip of her tongue, but she couldn't quite form them aloud. It would be so easy to fall in love with Charley.

Charley broke contact and took Jada's hand. "I'm hungry. How about I treat you to lunch?"

"I never turn down food."

"Food it is."

Jada let Charley lead her out of the museum. Would the fluttering in her belly stop long enough to eat? She kinda liked the feeling and increased her grip on Charley's hand a little, relishing the contact.

****

Liv took Grace's hand as they walked into the pub. It was Friday night and still early enough to be able to get a table and enjoy something to eat before the place was packed. They waved at Izzy, who was at her usual post behind the bar, and joined Terry and Sara at a booth. Terry had her coal-black hair pulled into a ponytail and was dressed in tan slacks and a royal-blue golf shirt that accented her eyes and almost matched the blue of the frame on her glasses. Grace thought they made a cute couple and hid her grin when she noticed them staring into each other's eyes.

Grace slid into the booth, followed by Liv.

"I thought you two were staying home tonight," Sara said. She was across from Grace, and the music wasn't yet so loud they couldn't hear each other.

"*Ojiichan* basically kicked us out. Said it'd be good to go have some fun. He's doing his usual worrywart thing. We went to the bonfire last weekend, and I thought it might be good enough, but he was insistent."

"He's right." Sara leaned forward and caught Grace's gaze with her own. "Have you seen her recently?"

"No. At least I don't think I have, but I get this feeling I'm being watched all the time. Must be my imagination."

"Or the psycho bitch stalking you," Liv said.

Grace put a calming hand on Liv's thigh but didn't respond to her.

"*Ojiichan* told us he saw a small, blue car drive pass the house several times yesterday," Grace said. "He was on the porch swing, but he couldn't quite make out the license plate number. I made sure we locked the doors before we left tonight and asked him not to open up for anyone he didn't know. You should have seen the look he gave me."

"Harry must have been pissed off," Sara said. "I mean, he's a retired Army Colonel. I'm sure he can take care of himself, Gracie."

"He's ninety-four and has a bad heart. I don't want to take any chances." Grace gave Sara a tight smile. "But he said the same thing. I'm sure I'm overreacting about this, too."

Liv slid a beer mug in front of Grace. "Just this once, have a few drinks and try to relax. I'm sure Harry will call if anything happens. It's not like we're far away. And I want you to have some fun. Maybe dance with me when the next slow song starts up." Liv leaned against her shoulder and kissed Grace on the cheek.

Grace took a sip of her beer and tried hard to enjoy the taste and relax. "I'm not sure I'm up for it. Maybe you and Terry ought to have the first dance." She winked at Sara. "I think you make a lovely couple."

Terry nearly choked on the nacho she was munching, and Liv outright laughed. She looked sideways at Grace. "You think so?"

"Oh yeah. Don't you agree, Sara?"

Sara held her hands up in a gesture of surrender. "Don't get me involved in this."

"Hey! You're supposed to defend me," Terry said.

"Not this time, babe. You're on your own."

Terry huffed and slid out of the booth and held her hand out to Liv. "This song's slow enough. Shall we?"

"We shall." Liv dramatically turned away from Grace and allowed Terry to lead her to the dance floor, leaving Grace and Sara in a fit of giggles.

"That feels good." Grace watched Terry and Liv try to figure out who was leading the dance. "And they do look cute together."

"They do," Sara said. "But since we're alone..."

"I'm scared. I know Carly's out there, and she's watching me and waiting. I know on some level I need to talk to her and find some closure, but at the same time, I'm terrified of her. When I saw her—Sara I couldn't move. I couldn't speak. Couldn't call for help. Harry was in the next room, and she stood there in our house!"

"I know. But I'm with Liv on this one. You and her alone is not a good idea. Maybe—and I mean maybe—if you got someone to mediate for you it'd be okay. Maybe someone from the community center would help you out. What about the woman who runs your therapy group?"

"Christine might help, but I have no way of contacting Carly. It's like a weird waiting game. You never know when or if she'll show up. I got a protection order, but it's hard to enforce it if the police can't find her and she doesn't come around."

Sara reached across the table and took hold of Grace's hand. "I get you want closure, but, honey, it's not worth it. She's not worth it. You've moved on. You and Liv are trying to start a family, and you need to focus on that. Promise me if you see her and you're alone you'll walk away or call for help."

"Sara—"

"Promise me. Please."

Grace hesitated. If she didn't respond, Sara would tell Liv

and it would end up with them in a fight. She didn't want that to happen, so she chose to placate Sara. For now. "Fine. Now, can we please change the subject?"

"Of course," Sara said, but her expression told Grace she wasn't done with the topic. She released Grace's hand and turned toward the dance floor. "Oh shit!"

"What?" Grace followed her gaze and her jaw dropped at the sight.

Terry and Liv were now in the center of the small dance floor. The song had changed to a more upbeat one, and they were dirty dancing with each other, gyrating and rubbing against one another as if they were ready to have sex right then and there. It'd drawn quite a crowd and most of the onlookers formed a semicircle around the two, giving them plenty of room to maneuver.

Liv's movements sent pleasant tingles through Grace, and she instantly wanted to trade places with Terry.

All thoughts of Carly were gone.

Sara must have had a similar thought because she got up and deliberately got between Terry and Liv. She had her hand on Terry's chest and didn't say a word, but she noted a sly smile on Terry's face before they started kissing.

Liv backed away and slunk to the booth. She slid in beside Grace, breathing heavy. A sheen of sweat formed on her brow, and she wiped it away with a napkin.

Their gazes connected and Grace knew exactly what Liv was thinking. She leaned forward, took Liv's bottom lip between her teeth, and gave a gentle tug. "Did you have fun out there?"

"Hmm. We did. Did you have fun watching us?" Liv nipped Grace's nose. "I saw Sara's face. Never seen her turn that shade of red before."

"You two are incorrigible."

"It was your idea for us to dance together." Liv's lips were so close to Grace's she felt Liv's breath as she spoke. Liv's hand rubbed along Grace's inner thigh in a slow, teasing, motion. "Maybe next time you can dance with me."

"Maybe. Depends. What's my incentive?"

"I can show you." Liv slid her tongue around the edge of Grace's ear, sending jolts of pleasure that caused a hitch in Grace's breathing. "Want me to go on?"

"I kinda want to go home," Grace said. She kissed Liv firmly on the mouth. "We might have lost Terry and Sara." She looked back at the dance area and lost sight of them. "I think they left."

"Nah. Terry said something about the ladies room and a fantasy of Sara's. I didn't let her give me details, just helped her play it out a bit. I guess her aim was to make Sara a little jealous."

"She wasn't jealous at all, but I'm very sure she was plenty worked up," Grace said with a light laugh. "We won't see them for a while then." She leaned back in the booth and straightened her shirt. "You hungry?"

"Is that a double entendre?"

"Wow. Such a big word for you. And French even."

"Ha-ha. And yes. I'm hungry." She kissed Grace softly, letting her lips linger for a moment. "Hungry for both."

"Well, let's feed the tummy first. We'll feed the other parts later."

"Promise?"

"Yes."

****

Pot O'Gold wasn't as crowded as Jada expected. She and Betty easily found a spot at the bar and settled in. The adorable bartender with the colorful hair greeted them with an easy smile. She pointed to Jada first. "Whatever's on tap." Then she pointed to Betty. "Jack and Coke."

"You're good," Jada said. "What's your name again?"

"Izzy and this is why I work the bar." She left to get their orders.

"Tell me about what happened with Peter," Betty said. "He's the reason we're here, after all. I don't think I've seen you so pissed off before."

"Pissed isn't the word for it." Jada felt the anger fairly seeping from her veins. "There's some shit I can ignore. He's always bossy and thinks he's my superior because he's a nurse. I've dealt with it before, but he crossed a line today. I want to fucking hate him, but hate means I'd have to give a shit enough to have that emotion toward him and I don't want to."

Betty remained silent and kept her gaze on Jada.

"He used the n-word today."

"What? When? Why didn't you come to me right away? I'd have kicked his ass out of the ER right then."

"We were slammed and needed him, even if he is a mediocre nurse. And there legitimately wasn't time. You know, I've had this feeling for a while now that my skin color was the reason he treats me like shit. Like I'm not good enough to be stuck to the bottom of his fucking shoe. And honestly, I don't give a damn. I know I'm better than him, and that's enough for me. He isn't important in my world, ya know? As long as he stays away from me, I'm good. But this—this was too much."

"Tell me what happened."

Jada let out a deep breath. "I was working with a cardiac patient who came in by ambulance. I needed to get an EKG and had an issue with the machine. You know the one that's been acting up?" At Betty's nod, she continued. "I didn't say anything to anyone. I went to the next bay and got another machine and did what I needed to do.

"Apparently, Peter brought a patient into the same bay right after I did this. I guess he used the bay last and expected the machine to still be there. When it wasn't, he stomped out and came looking for it. I told him where it was. He called me a stupid nigger and took off to go get it.

"I must have stared after him for a good ten seconds. I didn't say a word to him, and no one was around to even hear it, so it's my word against his. When those ten seconds were up, I wanted to beat the holy fuck out of him. He's got no right to call me or anyone else that."

Betty's stone-faced expression turned to anger. "What did you do?"

"I took a break because I had to get the hell out of there before I did something stupid. I know I have to write up a complaint, and I will, but my hands were shaking too much to do it." She glanced at her hands and realized they were shaking now. "I can take a lot of abuse, Betty. I get it from time to time from patients, but this—this I can't take."

"And you don't have to. You get it in writing, and I'll make sure something's done. After his last suspension, which we still haven't gone to mediation about, I have a feeling this one will end up in him being fired. We have a zero tolerance policy, and I'll make sure he feels its full effect." Betty laid a hand on Jada's arm. "I'm sorry this happened to you. I can't imagine how you feel right now."

"No, you can't. I doubt anything close to this type of shit has ever happened to you. Trust me, you never get used to it. Since Trump got elected, all the racists feel like they got free rein and that didn't stop at our border. It was awful in Ottawa, despite what the politicians keep saying. They've got programs and plans and shit, but so little of it actually trickles down into the real world. In my world, we live in fear. Fear the cop behind us might be one of the bad ones. Fear the guy watching us as we walk across the street might be a racist looking for someone to beat up. Add in that I'm gay, and it's like I attract all these crazy-ass people like a magnet."

"I got your back on this one, my friend. I wish I could fix the other stuff, but if one person can do one thing, then this is it. I'll take care of it. But you have to promise me something," Betty said. "You promise me if this happens again, at work or otherwise, you tell me immediately. I want to make sure I'm there for you. You do not deserve this. No one does."

"Thanks, Betty." Jada leaned forward and gave her a quick hug. Her hands still shook, but a little less now. It helped to get it all out in the open, but the residual effects would not go away anytime soon.

Izzy, her timing perfect, arrived with their drinks. "Let me know if you ladies need anything else." She winked at Jada and turned away.

Jada tried to smile but knew she fell short. "She's cute."

"And she knows it. Don't divert." Betty took a sip of her drink. "Are you okay?"

Jada shook her head. "No. It sounds silly, but I need a cuddle."

"It's not silly, and I bet I know where you can get one." Betty smiled at the questioning look Jada gave her. "I imagine Charley would be nice to cuddle up to."

"I believe you're correct."

Betty slapped a twenty on the bar, took one last swallow, and set the glass down. "Come on." She tugged Jada off the stool, waved to Izzy, and started for the entrance. "I'm going home, and you're going to see a very handsome, sexy Mountie about some quality cuddle time."

"You're the pushiest broad I've ever met," Jada said, even though she was smiling.

"Why thank you. That's the nicest thing you've ever said to me."

Jada rolled her eyes as Betty's cab pulled up to the curb. "I'll talk to you tomorrow."

Betty got into the cab and waved as Jada, hoping to get rid of her buzz by walking, started toward Charley's apartment. She pulled her phone out of her backpack and sent a text.

****

Sara and Terry left the pub an hour earlier than Grace and Liv, who fully understood why they wanted to take off. Grace was pretty sure Liv wanted to go home, too, but once she got into a game of pool with Izzy, Liv was no longer in a hurry. Her competitive streak was in full blossom, and by midnight, it was three out of five games for the win. Izzy was up by two.

Grace crossed her arms over her chest and leaned against the wall to watch game three. She enjoyed the way Liv looked when she was concentrating on her next move. The way she rested her lean body against the table when she stretched herself out to make a difficult shot. The room was certainly heating up, and Grace was sure the two beers she'd had weren't helping one bit. Alcohol had that effect on her, and right then she'd have jumped Liv's bones if they were home and alone.

But a small crowd stood around the pool table, chatting and having fun watching the two women. Liv's shirt rode up to expose her abdomen when she made a difficult shot. The sight made Grace ache to touch her.

"I bet my money on the kid with the green hair," a familiar voice said from beside her.

Grace opened her mouth to speak, but when she realized who the woman was, speech failed her. Carly, one hand wrapped around a bottle of beer, leaned against the wall next to Grace. She was intensely watching the pool game. Grace felt her blood run cold as her legs refused to obey her command to move.

"Kid's pretty good, but that wife of yours is holding her

own. More or less. She looks kinda hot in those tight jeans."

"What—what the hell do you want?"

Carly never took her eyes off Liv. "I already told you, Gracie. I'm not leaving until you agree to come with me."

"It won't happen. You're delusional."

"No, I'm determined. There's a big difference." Carly put her now empty beer bottle on a nearby table. "Oh look. I've been spotted. Here comes the big bad-ass now."

"You fucking bitch!" Liv threw down the cue stick and hurled herself at Carly. She grabbed her shirt with both hands and yanked her away from Grace. She held Carly close to her face, her eyes wild with anger. "I'm going to fucking kill you!"

"No!" Grace's legs finally moved and took her to Liv's side. Carly hadn't moved or tried to get away, and Grace suddenly realized her intent. "She wants you to hit her, Liv. Let her go. Please. It's not worth it."

"It's totally worth it." Liv released one hand to form a fist. She cocked her arm back to strike Carly, but Grace grabbed hold of her. She was stronger than Liv and used it to her advantage. She threw Liv off balance enough to make her let go of Carly.

Carly smiled at Grace. "You're good. I didn't expect you to stop her. I thought you'd want her to kick my ass."

"I'm going to do more than—" Liv started, but Grace stepped between them, her back to Liv.

"I'm going to call the police. Your ass is going to jail."

"Already called them." Harriet, the owner of the bar, was suddenly there, wooden baseball bat at the ready. She steadily tapped it against the palm of one hand.

Carly didn't seem fazed. She turned on her heel and walked out of the pub. Harriet followed her and Grace hoped the police would arrive in time to catch her. Carly didn't seem to care if they showed up or not. She had to know she'd be arrested on sight.

Grace didn't move from her spot in front of Liv until Harriet returned. She still held the baseball bat, and for a long moment, Grace stared at it. She fought hard against the memories.

Harriet asked, "You two okay?"

Liv pressed against Grace and slid her arms around her waist. "We're good. Sorry. She's Grace's ex."

Harriet nodded in understanding and put a gentle hand on Grace's arm. "She took off in a blue car. Why don't you two head on home?"

"We need to tell the police she tried to start a fight with Liv," Grace said.

Harriet lowered the bat, her eyes filled with sympathy. "I'll tell them everything. Go home."

"Thanks," Liv said. "Soon as I settle up the tab we'll take off."

"Later." Harriet gave them a little push toward the door. "I'll go out there with you to make sure the bitch isn't hanging around. You get Gracie home."

"Deal," Liv said and followed her out.

Carly was nowhere to be found, and it left Liv and Grace in peace to call a cab.

Twenty minutes later, they walked into the house, Grace still too stunned for words. A wonderful, fun evening turned into a nightmare so fast it was hard to wrap her mind around. How was it Carly knew where they were?

What if she'd gotten hold of Harriet's bat? Would she have used it against Liv? Or maybe Grace? So many horrible dreams remained around the pain of the aluminum bat hitting her again and again. Grace's stomach heaved and she ran to the bathroom.

She was barely aware of Liv's presence as she knelt in front of the toilet and emptied her guts. Spasms in her abdomen spread pain with each choking retch.

Liv's hand moved in soothing circles along her back. Liv passed her a cool, wet cloth, and she used it to wipe her face and mouth. The taste of beer and junk food made her want to throw up more, but nothing was left in her stomach.

She flushed the toilet and fell back against the wall, her knees bent and her arms hugging her legs. She rested her head on her arm.

"You okay now?" Liv asked softly.

"Maybe. I think I'm done throwing up for now."

"Good. Let me help you get cleaned up and into bed. Okay?"

Grace nodded and Liv pulled her to her feet. Once she was dressed in her undies and a T-shirt, teeth brushed and face scrubbed clean, she climbed into their bed. A few moments later, Liv lay behind her and tenderly wrapped Grace in her arms. She placed little kisses along Grace's bare neck.

"I love you, Gracie Lee."

"I love you, too, Olivia."

"I'm sorry about how I acted at the pub. It's just when I saw her standing next to you, and the look of panic on your face—I snapped. If you hadn't stopped me, I'd have started beating on her."

"I know." Grace patted the strong hands that rested against her stomach. "That's what got me moving. I had to stop you. I got the feeling it's what she wanted you to do."

"Why would she want me to hit her?"

"Maybe to get you in trouble. Or maybe to make me see she's the victim. She's done that before. Made herself out to be a victim and me the cause of her pain. Ironic, huh?"

"Psychotic is more like it," Liv grumbled. "I've yelled and screamed at people more times than I can count and felt myself physically so angry I could have beaten someone up. But I've never actually had my hands on another person like that. I've hit people in self-defense before, though."

"You've never been the aggressor," Grace said. "It's okay. You were protecting me. I get it, but I was terrified for a minute—terrified of you."

"What? But you stopped me. You got right in between us and made me stop."

"Yeah. I know." Grace rolled over so she was facing Liv. Her eyes had adjusted to the darkness enough to see the outline of Liv's face. She placed her palm against Liv's cheek. "But you might be pregnant. We've had our first insemination, and if you were to lose the child before we even knew it was there we'd both be devastated."

"I want to protect you, Gracie. I promised you I'd never let anyone hurt you again."

"We told Charley we'd call 9-1-1 if we saw her. Did you have to jump her?"

"I did. For you."

"I don't accept that, Olivia. I don't want you to do that for me. Not ever. Not unless I'm in the middle of a fistfight. And, trust me, I can handle myself."

"Oh, I know how well you can handle yourself, Gracie Lee. I've been on the receiving end. For a few seconds tonight, I thought you were going to slam me to the floor."

"Instead I chose restraint. It's why, despite being afraid of her, I got between you and Carly tonight. Fighting her, with fists or words, isn't going to change anything. I don't know how to make her leave us alone, but I know you hitting her would make things worse. She probably goaded you to make you throw the first punch and get arrested."

Liv moved her head slightly and kissed Grace's palm. When she did, Grace felt the wetness of her tears.

"I'm sorry. I seriously saw red when I realized who was standing next to you. The look on your face—I'm sorry."

"You're forgiven." Grace wiped the tears from Liv's cheeks and pulled her in for a sweet kiss on the lips. "Promise me you'll not do that again. Please."

"I can't. I've always had a hair-trigger temper. But I'll promise to try to choose my battles more wisely. And not to lay hands on Carly unless she comes after you—or me. If she touches you, I can't promise I won't react."

"Be careful." Grace touched foreheads with Liv and closed her eyes. She took a deep breath and let it out slowly. "You were so sexy dancing with Terry tonight."

"Whoa. Major topic change there."

"I need to move on to something else," Grace said. "And you being sexy is definitely something I'd rather be thinking about."

"You sure you're up for it?"

"I was while you were shooting pool." Grace lifted Liv's T-shirt and touched her flat abdomen. "I saw a little of your stomach when you were leaning across the table. Like a bit of teasing, even if you weren't aware of it."

"Had I known, I'd have made sure the shirt came up even more."

"No way," Grace said, kissing her chin, then her nose, and settling on her mouth. "I don't like to share."

"You shared me with Terry."

Grace laughed. "Hardly. She was using you to get at Sara. That's not sharing, and besides, I didn't think you two would get out there and dance."

"Me either, but I saw the look on Terry's face and thought what the hell? Might be fun. But let me tell you, she's one bossy butch. Wouldn't let me lead for a second."

"Yeah, we saw you two out there fighting about it. It was adorable."

"It was fun," Liv conceded. "But not as much fun as dancing with you. If Izzy hadn't goaded me into playing pool, we'd have been here hours ago." Liv slid her hands under Grace's T-shirt and slowly worked it up and over her head. "But we're here now. Might as well make use of this comfy bed."

Grace smiled. She slipped Liv's T-shirt off and pressed soft kisses along the edge of her naked breast. "Might as well."

****

Charley stared at the text from Jada. She was on her way over for a cuddle. Charley paused her movie and wondered if she should make some coffee or if Jada was hungry. She sent a reply text, but heard nothing else. That was twenty minutes ago.

Why the hell was she so nervous to see Jada? Maybe because she still had trouble accepting how she felt when Jada kissed her. How her heart rate sped up at the thought of touching Jada, holding her, being with her. She'd never felt this way before.

Not even with Raina, who she'd loved with all her heart. But Jada was so different. Was she serious about the cuddles? Charley wouldn't say no if she was.

A knock at the door startled her. She quickly answered and let Jada into her apartment. Jada dropped her ever-present backpack beside the door and was in Charley's arms in record time. She rested her head against Charley's shoulder and held her tightly.

"Wow, you weren't kidding. You really did want a cuddle."

"Sometimes I need someone to hold me and remind me it's okay to have a bad day. My dad used to say a hug a day is the healthiest thing anyone can have. I miss him and I miss getting hugs every day."

Charley held her closer and breathed in the scent that was all Jada, a heady mix of orange and lavender. "You can have a hug whenever you want one. Okay?"

"Deal." Jada sighed, let Charley go, and stepped a few feet away. "Thanks. I feel much better." She reached for her backpack, but Charley stopped her. "What?"

"That's it? You seriously only came here for a hug?"

"I kinda did. I didn't want to intrude too much on your evening."

"I started watching *Avengers: End Game* a little while ago. Stay and watch it with me."

"I'm grubby from work, and I don't have a change of clothes." Jada looked down at her scrubs. "Maybe another night?"

Charley wasn't sure why, but she felt it important that Jada stay. "I have a shower, and we already know you'll fit into one of my T-shirts. I can wash your scrubs, and if you want, you can go home when the movie's over."

Jada gave her a slow grin. "You want me to stay?"

"What kind of girlfriend would I be if I didn't?" Charley took Jada's hand in hers. She twined her fingers with Jada's long, thin ones and pulled her a little in the direction of the bedroom. "Take a shower. Or put on one of my T-shirts. Whatever. If you're hungry, I can fix you something to eat."

"I—I don't know what to say."

"You don't need to say anything. I can tell by the look in your eyes it was a difficult shift. Besides, if you were so desperate for a hug to come all the way over here, the least I can do is try to lighten your mood. Not like I didn't enjoy the hug for myself."

Jada laughed and shook her head. "This is why I like you. I'll take you up on the shower, and I'd be fine with pizza and soda. Diet please."

"Toppings?"

"Anything except anchovies. I mean seriously, fish on pizza? What kinda shit is that?"

"So shower, pizza, and Avengers. Right?"

Jada released Charley's hand and gently touched her cheek with the tips of her fingers. "Sounds like a perfect night. Be right back."

Jada's touch left a tingling sensation in Charley's stomach, and it took a moment to fade. So many images came to her involving those delicate fingers. She knew there was strength in them, felt it when they held hands. But when Jada's eyes met hers, Charley was reduced to a puddle of wants and needs. She wanted Jada—needed to feel her in places Charley tried hard to forget existed. Jada opened all those old, closed-off areas with ease. Not even Raina had been able to do that.

Her memories of Raina stopped her thoughts as quickly as a bucket of ice over her head. She made the call for pizza and was seated on the couch when Jada came back in, dressed in Charley's Wonder Woman T-shirt. Her dark-brown skin glowed from the shower, and she looked tired, but refreshed. Jada sat next to Charley and rested her head on Charley's shoulder.

"You have no idea how much better I feel."

Charley looked down at the T-shirt that reached mid-thigh on Jada. It didn't take much to realize she wasn't wearing a bra. The shirt was loose but also white, and Charley clearly saw Jada's nipples pressing against the fabric. She had to drink half a bottle of water to wet her dry throat.

"I'm happy to be of service," she finally said. "Pizza should be here in about ten minutes. Feel like telling me what's wrong?"

"I got brown skin."

"Um, I know. It's hard not to notice." Charley gently touched her cheek and felt her tremble. She put her arm around Jada and said, "Tell me."

"You remember the bastard nurse I work with, right?"

"Peter. You call him Nurse Cranky Pants."

"Yeah. More like Nurse Dick Head." Jada sighed. "He called me a nigger."

"Give me his last name."

"Why?" Jada looked up at her. "What for?"

"So I can find him and have a very long, involved talk with him. One that needs to be done in private right before I report his ass to the hospital's board of trustees."

"Calm down, Sarge." Jada put a hand over Charley's fast-beating heart. "I'm going to write him up first thing tomorrow. I told Betty everything. I was going to do it tonight, but I was so angry and upset my hands wouldn't stop shaking. He did it right in the middle of the ER."

"Did anyone else hear him?"

"No. At least I don't think so."

Charley pulled her closer, wrapped her arms around her, and held her for a long time. She wanted to protect Jada. And kick this Peter guy's ass. "I still want his last name. I know Betty will make sure he's disciplined, but that's not enough. I want the board to know what's going on. We got enough to deal with when it's the public. We don't need this kind of shit from our coworkers."

"But it still happens. I had it in Ottawa, too."

"I had it at the RCMP academy when some white punk called me a squaw because I beat his time on the obstacle course. He said I was only there because they had to meet some kind of minority quota. My first reaction was to cry." Charley closed her eyes against the memory of his angry words and how they ripped at her heart. Her chest hurt as she continued. "One minute I was full of adrenaline and pride from having a good run, getting congrats from some of my classmates, and the next I'm in tears because this one asshole goes off on me for no reason whatsoever. Before anyone did or said anything, I ran off to my room.

"I must have been there a good half hour before one of the instructors came looking for me. She kept apologizing and said they'd given him a misconduct write-up. She told me to get myself together and rejoin the class."

"That's it?" Jada pulled back enough to look at Charley directly. "Go back to class?"

"Pretty much. He was there, too. Kept glaring at me the rest of the day. Some of the guys started calling me a crybaby. The two other women in the class sort of stayed away from me. I heard one of them say I made women look bad by crying. I had a group of guys I got along with, and they stuck by me, had my back. But it was hard, you know? For the rest of the course, I kept wondering if I got in on my own merit or if he was right and I was meeting some minority quota.

"Women make up about 15% of the force now, but it was a lot less then. And the number of First Nation officers is lower. Around 8%. So I had it rough from two sides."

"You had every right in the world to cry, honey. You know that, don't you?"

Charley nodded. "I do now. Back then—I called my dad and asked him to come get me. It took him an hour to convince me to stay. Me—the kid that dreamed of nothing more than being a Mountie her whole life. He came to the depot in Saskatchewan a week later to talk to my instructors. Nothing ever came of it. The cadet graduated with the rest of us. Far as I know he's still a Mountie and works somewhere along the east coast."

"That's such bullshit. He should have been kicked out."

"Today he would be. Stuff's changed."

"Doesn't feel like it has."

"I know. It still hurts to talk about it. Sometimes I get looks when I respond to calls. I've been here a long time, so it's not as bad as it was, but I can feel it. You know what I mean? The micro aggressions people have."

"Oh yeah. Like they won't walk too close to you on the sidewalk, or they make it a point not to make eye contact with you."

"Exactly. I saw an elderly lady stumble and reached out to help her, but she pulled away when she saw my face. Almost fell doing it. She scowled at me and mumbled something about damn, fucking Indians and walked off."

Jada snuggled closer. "I hear you. I had a patient who needed an IV, but he wouldn't let me touch him. Like my blackness was going to rub off on him or something. I had to get someone else to take care of him. It's all so crazy, and no matter how much I try to push it off, at the end of the day it's hurtful. I could get angry and yell and scream, but what good would it do?"

"It wouldn't change a thing."

The doorbell rang. Charley gave Jada a kiss on the cheek and got up to answer it. She paid the delivery person, put the pizza on the kitchen table, and got them each a plate. Jada joined her, grabbed a couple of slices and her soda, and they returned to the couch.

They ate in silence for a while before Charley said, "I'm here for you, Jada. I feel like I should say it out loud."

"Ditto, Sarge. Thanks for letting me talk about it. I'll be even better once we finish eating and you let me cuddle up to you to watch the movie."

Charley grinned. "I think I'll feel better, too. But why wait?" She held up her left arm, and Jada moved next to her, their bodies touching again. Charley lowered her arm across Jada's shoulders and used her right hand to continue eating. "You can hit the Play button on the remote anytime you're ready."

Jada picked it up and started the movie. "You're not allowed to make fun of me when Stark dies. I cry every time."

"Me, too."

Chapter Twelve

Grace woke earlier than usual. The other half of the bed was empty. She saw light under the bathroom door but didn't hear any movement. The clock read 4:56 a.m. She waited another ten minutes before getting up and going to check on Liv. She knocked softly at the door. "Hey. You okay in there?"

There was a quiet sniffle before Liv answered, "No."

Grace opened the door. "What's wrong, honey?" Liv was seated on the toilet, and tears streamed down her cheeks. "Are you hurt? What happened?" Grace knelt before her and rested her hands on Liv's knees.

"I—I took it and it's negative." She unclenched her fist and held out a pregnancy test. Instead of a plus sign she saw a minus sign.

Grace gently took it from her and tossed it into the trashcan. "Honey, it's only been two weeks. You have to give it more time."

"The doctor said we could know as soon as eight days after insemination."

"He said we *might* know. It's not a guarantee, and you know those tests might not be completely accurate. We need to sit back and relax. It'll happen." Grace took Liv's hands and pressed her lips to them. "The doctor also told you it might take more than one try. It's fairly normal to have to do the procedure more than once. You have to give your body time."

"But I was ovulating and everything. This sucks."

Grace gave her a tired smile. "I know. Come back to bed and let me hold you. We both need some sleep. You especially. You're not going to get pregnant by worrying and being up late at night—or early in the morning." Grace stood and pulled Liv to her feet. She wrapped her in a tight embrace. "I love you. We'll make this happen, okay? Be patient."

"Heh. You know I can't." Liv let go of Grace to blow her nose and wash her face. Once done she followed her back to bed.

Grace waited for Liv to settle. She curled up to her, put her arm around Liv's waist, and rested her head on Liv's shoulder. "We've got an appointment next Monday. If you want, I can push it forward. See if we can get in sooner."

"No. I'll wait," Liv said with a sigh. "Or at least I'll try."

"I'll move the appointment." Grace placed a kiss on her shoulder. "Go to sleep, baby."

"I love you."

Grace held her closer. She wished she could make the pregnancy happen sooner if for no other reason than to give her wife peace of mind. She shut her eyes and said, "I love you, too."

****

Jada sat on the floor and leaned her back against the bed. The Blue Jays game was on, and at the moment, they were losing to the Astros. She wasn't a fair-weather fan, but with a score of 10 to 3, she was quickly losing interest. She picked up her mail from the previous day and sorted through the bits that required her attention. Beneath the pile was a tablet.

It lay on the coffee table, unused. It mocked Jada from the unopened box. Celeste was sweet to send it to her. Their weekly talks weren't enough, and while Jada could go back to Ottawa to see her, she'd rather not. So Celeste sent her this nice new tablet in order to video chat.

Jada wasn't opposed to that, but she didn't think Celeste realized how far removed she'd kept herself from the online world by not having a computer and not bothering to load any apps on her cell phone. She'd actually gone to the trouble of removing as many apps as possible. Her phone made calls, texts, and took pictures. She kept the mail app and ignored the app that would access the Internet.

Celeste knew about the articles and posts on social media and was Jada's stalwart defender through it all. And of course, when it was proven Jada did nothing wrong, it barely garnered an article in the local paper. The news was boring by then, and most of the excitement had blown over. More interesting things happened now, but like she'd told Charley, stuff on the Internet stays there forever.

The tablet was sent a month ago and was still in the box.

She ached to get it out and see what havoc awaited her, if any. Like some rubbernecker passing a horrific car crash, she simply had to look.

Twenty minutes later, she was into her social media account and scrolling through her feed. Most of it was filled with monotonous pics of pets or food or vacations. After almost half an hour, she was ready to give up, satisfied she was no longer a sensation.

Of course that's when she found it. A single link, but one kept alive by Nancy, as if she meant to rub salt into the wound. And Jada didn't understand why. She'd done nothing wrong. None of them had.

She shut down the tablet and put it back on the coffee table. How mad would Celeste be if Jada told her it'd been broken? Jada sat back on the couch and closed her eyes, counting to ten to calm herself. It didn't work. She needed to take a long walk to burn off the bad energy, but it was well past midnight and she didn't think it was a good idea. Just because Whitehorse was a small city didn't mean it was without crime.

She paced her apartment, unsure what she should do. Maybe go for a drive? But where? In forty minutes she'd be all through the city. And she wasn't familiar enough with the highways to take off on either of those. Her gaze kept going back to the stupid tablet until she finally shoved it into a cabinet in the kitchen to keep it out of sight.

A faint ping sounded, and at first she thought it was the tablet. But it was turned off. The ping came again, and she realized it was her cell phone. She dug it out of her backpack, surprised to see Charley's name next to a text. She rarely sent messages this late and probably thought Jada was at work. Maybe she was also having trouble sleeping.

Instead of replying, Jada called her.

"Hey, I didn't wake you up, did I?" Charley asked.

"Nope. I was pondering ways to break a tablet and make it look like an accident."

Charley didn't answer immediately, and Jada imagined her confused expression. "Maybe I shouldn't get involved. It sounds like it borders on the criminal."

"Oh no. This would be done out of righteous indignation. Remember how I told you I don't do social media anymore?"

"I do."

"Well, I did social media tonight."

"I take it this did not go well for you?"

Jada huffed. "What an understatement."

"Want to talk about it?"

"Yes, but only if I can come to your apartment. It's not something I want to say over the phone."

"Come on over."

"Thanks." Jada hung up, grabbed her keys, and left.

Charley answered the door, wearing a T-shirt, boxers, and a kind smile. Jada stared at the boxers and laughed at the image of Wonder Woman. "Love that T-shirt. Never thought I'd meet someone crazier about superheroes than me."

"Who doesn't love superheroes?"

"Right?" Jada asked as she walked in. Charley pointed to the sofa and they sat down. "Last time I saw the Wonder Woman movie, we sort of forgot to finish it."

Charley said, "All those women in battle gear can have that effect on people. Oh, I should have asked. Do you want something to drink?"

"Hard liquor?" Jada asked, half-joking.

"Nope. Coffee I can make or there's soda in the fridge."

"It's okay. I'm fine." Jada found the frayed edge of her jeans shorts very fascinating and spent some time picking at it. Her hand shook as she did.

"You're not fine or you wouldn't be here." Charley placed her hand over Jada's, stilling her fingers. "Talk to me."

"I told you you'd find out something awful about me if you searched my name on the Internet. Did you?"

"Nope. No need to. Anything I need to know about you you'll tell me."

"You're very sweet." Jada took a deep breath and exhaled slowly to help get her nerves together. "A year and a half ago there was a bad crash on Highway 417 outside Ottawa. Two cars hit head-on, and the impact was so hard it knocked them twenty meters apart."

She had to look away from Charley for a moment, disturbed by the kindness in her eyes. It wasn't until then that Jada realized how hard it was to recount what happened. Charley squeezed her hand gently. "Hey, you don't have to go into detail if you don't want to, okay?"

"I think I need to. I've never talked about it to anyone." Jada scooted closer to Charley and leaned against her, feeling her strength. "I never met anyone I thought I could tell it to."

Charley kissed her softly on the lips. "Go on."

Jada cleared her throat and recalled one of the hardest days of her life.

As their helicopter flew over the scene, Jada took note of the damage to both cars. A paramedic was giving them details over the radio about the patient he thought needed them the most. She recognized the voice of her pal Sean, who she'd gone to paramedic school with. He was one of the best, and she trusted his judgement.

Her nurse partner, Nancy, looked impassive as their helicopter landed in the middle of the two lanes going west. Once the pilot gave the all clear, both women grabbed equipment bags and exited the craft. Jada kept low until she was clear of the still-turning rotors and zeroed in on Sean's bulky figure standing near one of the cars.

Her gaze took in the amount of damage in seconds. The entire front end of the car was accordioned, and the driver's side airbag was deployed. The smell from the mixture of gasoline and antifreeze assaulted her nose as she got closer. Sean's uniform, a navy-blue golf shirt, sported dark stains she assumed were blood.

"Hey, Jada, Nancy," he said and started for the passenger side of the car. Jada took note of the driver, who had no rescuers working on him. His head was at a slightly odd angle, and she gave Sean a quizzical look. Sean said, "DOA."

"The passenger has the broken femur?" she asked.

"Yes. And the way he's pinned, it's going to take awhile to get him out of there." He pointed at the extrication team coming into view as they rounded the side of the car. "Dashboard has him trapped, but his left leg is deformed and I'm concerned as soon as we get him loose he's going to lose a lot of blood."

"Good call." Jada put her equipment bag down and looked for Nancy, but she didn't immediately see her. She crawled into the backseat of the vehicle, where another paramedic was leaning between the bucket seats to secure an IV she'd just gotten into the passenger's arm.

Jada didn't remember her name, but the paramedic nodded at her when she climbed in. "B/P is 110 over 50 and pulse is 134. He's conscious, Glasgow of 15, and his pulse ox without O2 was 90%. I've got a C-Collar on him, and Sean's got a traction splint ready when we get him out. There's no obvious bleeding, but I can't get to his right leg."

Jada looked over the young man's shoulders and saw the leg was pinned above the knee. There wasn't an airbag, or it didn't deploy on the passenger's side.

"How's my uncle?" the man asked. He tried to look at the driver, but the paramedic made sure he didn't move his head. "Is he okay?"

"Don't move," she said.

Nancy's voice was very loud suddenly. "Get me an IV going and my airway bag!" Jada had to look around to figure out where she was. Hands reached into the driver's side and she realized it was Nancy.

To the paramedic, Jada said, "I thought he was DOA." She tried to keep her voice low.

The woman nodded, confusion etched across her face. "Broken neck. Crushed trachea. Can't intubate him. We tried and called it."

"Gotcha. I'll be right back." Jada got out of the car and went to Nancy's side. "Hey, he's DOA."

Nancy glared at her. "You a doctor now?"

"No, but his broken neck would indicate an injury not compatible with life. Trachea's crushed. No way to get an airway. I need you on the passenger. He's going to crash soon as they get him freed."

"I got a patient and I'm going to work the code."

"Nancy, that's bullshit." Jada urged her to step back from the car. "He's dead. Now get over to the passenger side and help us out. This guy we can save."

"Who made you God?"

Jada barely believed she was hearing this from someone she always thought was a rational, professional rescuer. They all understood some injuries were incompatible with life. The protocols clearly designated when to declare someone dead and move on to help those still alive. Especially at an incident with multiple casualties.

They were wasting valuable time, and both turned when Sean approached.

"We're ready to pull the dashboard back," he said. "I told you the driver is DOA and the rest of our team is working on the three still entrapped in the other car. We've got two ambulances down there, but this is the guy who needs you. Can we get on with it, please?"

Sean was much more diplomatic than Jada. Nancy glared at them both, clearly stuck between a rock and a hard place. It wasn't that Jada didn't understand the difficulty of the situation.

"I can't run a code by myself," Nancy said. She jabbed her finger into Jada's chest. "This one is on you. I'll make sure of it in my report."

"Whatever." Jada left Nancy and returned to her patient.

Charley said, "I can't imagine having to make that call. I've seen it happen a few times."

Jada's hands were shaking, and she nearly wept when Charley gently gripped them. "It's the worst. You always end up second-guessing yourself. Wondering if there wasn't something you could've done. But Nancy, she was losing her shit over it. She tried twice to get an airway in and failed before finally helping us out.

"Our patient crashed when we extricated him, but we managed to get him stable and on to the hospital where the trauma team took over. In the end, we saved his life. That's all that matters, you know?"

"I do. It's why we're in the business. But I don't get what your partner was doing. Was she new or something?"

"Far from it." Jada leaned into Charley and rested her head on Charley's shoulder. "She'd been a trauma nurse for almost twenty years, the last ten or so with the helicopter. She's seen more shit than you and me combined. I thought she was rock solid. But some calls throw you off your game. I guess that's what happened to her."

Charley kissed the top of her head. "Tell me what she did."

"She made a separate report from mine and refused to sign the one I'd done. She told our medical director—going over our supervisor's head—that I declared the patient dead and refused to help her work on him, when she was sure if she'd had help we might have been able to do something for him. Which, as any first responder will tell you, was bullshit. There was nothing we could do. We're good but we can't fix dead.

"So I got called in and had to review my report, which corresponded with Sean's report. Our medical director said it was all good with her and was more concerned with whether or not we needed a debriefing than anything else. The EMS responders had one set up, so I went. I sure as hell needed to talk about it. Nancy got a reprimand for not following protocol and found someone to switch teams with her. I thought it was all over with."

Charley was quiet as Jada sorted her thoughts. "Two days after the incident, I got a call from the local paper. The reporter wanted to talk about the crash, but I declined. We're not supposed to talk to the press. I referred him to my boss. He never did. It took the fucker all of four hours to write his fake news article and post it online. It made it to my social media feed in no time."

"So Nancy called them?"

"I'm sure of it, but I can't prove it. He wouldn't reveal his source, but who else would tell him we let a guy die. Correction, I let a guy die because I'm a shit paramedic and made sure all my paramedic friends sided with me. There's never a mention of the fact the on-scene crew already accepted he was dead and moved on to another patient. No mention of the fact our protocol is clear—if the patient has an injury or injuries not compatible with life, you don't work on the patient. A crushed trachea from a broken neck qualifies. We couldn't do anything for him."

Charley released her hands and wrapped Jade in a warm, comforting embrace. "Did anyone come to your defense?"

"Sure, but the damage was done. The news vultures found out where I lived and camped out on my street. I couldn't go home. I tried to go to Francine, but she wouldn't let me near her. She refused to say if she believed me or not, but she didn't want to risk being associated with me and ruining her reputation in the medical community. Even though she knew what our protocols were for this type of incident." Jada felt the old anger welling up again. "How's that for someone who's supposed to fucking love you?"

"She didn't love you, Jada. Someone who loves you opens their door and takes care of you without a second thought for themselves." Charley pulled back a little and kissed her softly on the lips. "You're better off without her."

Their gaze held and Jada felt a flutter in her stomach. It'd be so easy to fall in love with this kind-hearted woman. How had she gotten so lucky as to find someone like Charley Townsend? She hardly believed she deserved her. "Thanks," she finally said. "Celeste took me in the minute I called her. No one knew where she lived, and I was able to stay there while I was on leave. The media found someone else to harass after a few weeks, but the damage was done. Even if my coworkers were behind me and my boss had my back, it was still awful. People on the street recognized me because my picture was in the paper, on the news, and all over social media.

"Worst part for me is I couldn't do anything. I tried but wasn't able to prove it was Nancy who went to the media. My boss believed me, but without proof, what could she do? Sean and his partner filed a complaint, and Nancy was suspended, eventually, for trying to run a code on the patient when it was clear he was dead. Too little too late. Damage done."

"You try to get the posts taken down?"

"No. I have no idea how. Shit's on the Internet forever, ya know?"

Charley gave her a half grin. "Not always. There are ways to get posts removed. I teach Internet and social media safety to kids and adults. And since I've nothing to do right now, how about you let me work on it for you?"

Jada mirrored her adorable grin. "Seriously?"

"Of course. What kind of girlfriend would I be if I didn't help you? I'm a Mountie, you know. It's what I do."

"You are the best girlfriend ever, Sarge." Jada hugged her tighter and choked back her sudden tears. "I think the shit with Peter got to me because of what happened with Nancy. I should get respect from my coworkers, ya know?"

"I do." Charley kissed the top of her head. "I called one of the hospital board members yesterday. Told him about Peter. He promised to look into it."

"Damn, baby. You do know everyone." Jada smiled up at her. It felt good to have someone on her side for once.

Charley said, "I sort of know him because he's my uncle. Don't tell anyone, okay?"

"You are the sweetest person I've ever met." Jada placed their connected hands over Charley's chest. "And you've got a heart of gold."

"Well, my parents are miners and I was born here." Charley laughed softly and Jada enjoyed the sound of it. "I like you, Jada, and I want to help you."

Jada cuddled as close to Charley as possible, enjoying the feel of their bodies pressing together. "You're doing it. You being here, letting me talk it out—I feel better than I have in a long time."

"You only have to ask and I'm here for you."

"I'd like to stay the night. I need to be with you right now. Like we did before. Sleeping together. Is that okay?"

"Of course." Charley kissed her gently. "Anything else I can do?"

"Order me a pizza? I'm hungry after all this talking."

"Pizza? You do realize there are other things to eat besides pizza, right?"

Jada laughed and it felt amazing. "I love pizza. I crave pizza. Please feed me pizza."

Charley laughed and grabbed her phone. "Fine, weirdo. Pizza it is."

Chapter Thirteen

Charley spent the better part of two weeks contacting social media outlets about the posts regarding Jada. She'd been mostly successful and gotten it pulled from three of four major companies. The fourth was being a pain, requiring more paperwork that she had to get from Jada's old boss in Ottawa. It felt nice to feel needed. But now she was in wait mode and bored out of her mind.

Elle called earlier to check on her. Charley asked if she wanted to go to a movie or something, but Elle picked up an extra shift and didn't get off duty until past midnight. Betty was equally busy at the emergency room. Liv and Gracie would be at their office by now.

Charley glanced at the clock, noting it was a bit past nine a.m.

She flexed the fingers of her left hand, but they didn't move much, and she considered driving the two hours to Gracie's Glory. But what would she do once she got there? Watch her parents work? Bug the hell out of her cousin, Mike? Not that it didn't sound like fun to mess with Mike a little. She wasn't sure she wanted to go alone.

Out of nowhere, Jada came to mind. Every time they touched it was like Charley's skin was on fire. She couldn't get enough of her and knew Jada felt it, too. She saw it in her eyes, felt it in her kisses. It caused an internal struggle for Charley, one she'd not thought about for years. Sex meant something to her; something deep. She wasn't willing to make such a connection with just anyone. When or if she was with Jada it would be to make love to her. To let her know she held Charley's heart.

For Charley, sex meant forever. It was a gift for the person who would be by her side the rest of her life. A gift she'd given Raina and no one else. She now wondered if she would ever be able to give it to Jada. It would mean they'd be married, and that caused a whole new sense of anxiety for Charley.

And it brought memories of Raina to the forefront. She didn't mean to, but she ended up comparing her to Jada.

Raina was a lot like Jada. Fun to be around, easy to talk to, and nothing they didn't share. Or so Charley thought. Raina kept a vital piece of information from Charley, and it was something she had a hard time forgiving. Would Jada do the same?

She loved Raina. Still did. That never seemed to change, even after a full decade. But forgive her?

Her gaze went to the bathroom, and she had to close her eyes against the onslaught of memories.

Blood.

Screams.

Tears.

She grabbed a jacket, left the apartment, and took several deep breaths of the cool morning air. She stopped alongside her truck and waited for her erratic heartbeat to return to normal.

What brought this on?

She closed her eyes again, this time conjuring an image of Jada. She pictured how her sweet smile filled her face and caused the corners of her eyes to crinkle. Her sweet laughter filled Charley's ears, and soon she was lost in new memories. Of an embrace that made her feel wanted. Of a night shared together, knowing, deep down, it was something she'd longed for.

Her cell phone was in her hand when she opened her eyes again, and without hesitation, she called Jada.

A few seconds later, she was rewarded with the smooth sound of Jada's voice. "Hey, Sarge. Good morning."

"Morning. I hope it's not too early for you."

"Nah. I was awake, just hadn't bothered to get out of bed yet."

"Good. Maybe I can give you some incentive. If you're off today."

Charley heard rustling noises before Jada said, "Oh? Do tell. I could use incentive."

Charley said, "I need to get out of my apartment. Go for a hike with me. I'll pack the food. You bring the beverages. There's this amazing spot I'd like to take you to. Tonight it's supposed to be clear skies. You'll love it."

"I think you had me at the food portion, but hiking is

good, too." Jada laughed softly. "What kind of beverages?"

"You can have beer if you want. I prefer water. It's a long hike to the place I'm talking about."

Jada hesitated and Charley heard her moving around. "Well, if it's a long hike, why don't we stay the night? I haven't camped in years, but I think I still have my sleeping bag and pup tent."

"I hadn't thought of that." Charley headed to her storage unit across from the parking lot. "I have camping gear. I've gone out with Gracie and Liv a few times. I'll bring the tent, you bring your own sleeping bag, and we'll make it a nice adventure. What do you say?"

"I'd say I love you, but it's too soon." Jada laughed at her own joke. "You're going to have room for food and camping stuff? Are you sure I don't need to bring more?"

"Positive." Charley got her gear out. "This is going to be amazing. Come over to my apartment, and we'll leave from here. In about an hour?"

"I'll be there." Jada hung up and Charley got back to work putting her gear together, for once not thinking about anything more than the adventure in front of her.

****

For the first hour or so, Jada and Charley hiked in silence. It was the comfortable kind where you don't feel pressured to speak. Jada lifted her face skyward and took in the streams of sunlight that filtered through the trees. She hadn't felt this free in years. Like all the stresses of the world were gone and it was her and Charley and nothing else mattered.

She let her gaze fall to Charley, much as she'd done through most of their hike. Strong legs carried Charley up an incline as if it were a normal set of stairs. She never breathed heavy from exertion and walked with a confidence few people had. Jada only felt confident when she was working.

Jada knew she was a damn good medic, and while not perfect, still performed well and saved lives. That was, after all, her job. Her calling.

She shook her head slightly, pushing thoughts of work out of the way. She wanted to be fully here, in this beautiful place, spending time with someone who had already worked her way into Jada's heart.

"What do you think?" Charley asked.

Shit. "I didn't hear the question."

Charley paused and half-turned to Jada. "I asked if you'd like to stop for lunch? There's a good spot at the top of this rise. We can set up camp there. It's as good a place as any to see the stars."

"Sure. I never turn down food, remember?"

Charley gave her an appraising once-over and smiled in a way that told Jada she liked what she saw. "Where the hell do you put it all? I know of one other person who can live on junk food. Sara Hyatt. If I ate like either of you, I wouldn't be able to fit into my pants in a week."

Jada chuckled. "I doubt that. Not the way you like to work out. And I don't know where the food goes." She came alongside her and bumped hips with Charley. "Good metabolism I guess. Anyway, you said you'd feed me, and I didn't walk a hundred kilometers for nothing."

"You didn't walk a hundred kilometers. More like four."

"Whatever. Feed me."

Charley raised one eyebrow, and the gesture caused Jada to giggle. "What if you don't like what I brought?"

"Is it edible?"

"Yes."

"Then I'll like it." Jada gave her a playful shove, and Charley started walking again.

Less than ten minutes later, they were at the top of the incline. A beautiful field surrounded by pine trees awaited them. Jada dropped her backpack and wandered around the area. She watched the ground for small critters and listened to the birds call out warnings as she strode along.

"It'll be perfect for tonight." Charley was working on putting up their tent, but she had trouble with her left hand.

"Let me help you." Jada gently took the equipment from her. "You get the food out, and I'll take care of this. Deal?"

Charley said, "It's just a tent. I can put it together."

"Yep. I'm sure you can, but I'm going to do it instead. You need to rest your hand. I saw you holding it close to your side an hour ago. It's bothering you and there's no sense in you hurting yourself when I'm perfectly capable of doing this." She demonstrated by setting the tent up in under ten minutes.

"You're a stubborn woman," Charley said.

"Heh. Takes one to know one. Food? I'm working hard here and need sustenance."

"One track mind, too," Charley muttered.

"Two tracks. We'll discuss the second one later."

Charley stiffened but didn't turn around, and Jada wondered if her teasing had gone too far. When Charley didn't move, she was sure she'd stepped in it big time. Dammit. "Sarge, I'm sorry—I was playing with you."

Charley's shoulders sagged a little. "It's okay. It's not about you. I promise." She opened a compartment on her backpack and removed two plastic containers. "I made pasta salad for lunch. Something a bit different for dinner, but you'll have to wait." She put the plastic containers on a nearby log and stowed her backpack in the tent.

Charley faced Jada and handed her a set of plastic utensils. "Don't lose these. It'll be hard to eat dinner without them."

Jada accepted the knife and spork, never letting herself lose eye contact with Charley. Those sweet eyes had lost some of their sparkle, and Jada so wanted to see it come back. She took a chance and gently cupped Charley's cheek in one hand. "I'm sorry. I don't mean to upset you."

Charley placed her hand over Jada's and gave her a smile. "You're forgiven. Seriously. I want to tell you—but it's hard."

"You can tell me anything."

"Thanks. I—you and me. I like it. I like it a lot, but it's scary as hell, too."

"Tell me about it." Jada slowly removed her hand and wrapped it around Charley's. "Let's see where things lead us, okay? We can talk or not talk. I want to be with you. Whatever happens, happens. Deal?"

"Deal. Let's eat then. I want to show you around before it gets dark. This place is amazing."

"I believe you." Jada gave her hand a tug and urged Charley to sit with her on the log. They each held a plastic container. "I like pasta salad. What kind of dressing did you use?" Jada asked as she took her first bite. The salad almost bit back and she loved it, closing her eyes to savor the experience. "Wow. You are an amazing cook."

"You should tell my mother. She acts like I can't feed myself because there's never much food in the fridge."

"Why not? Don't you cook for yourself?"

"I use zesty Italian dressing, to answer your question, and no, I don't often cook for myself. But sometimes I will cook up something, like when I'm off work. If I want to, I get exactly what I need and make enough for one meal. I never cook more than I need and very rarely have leftovers. If I do, I take them to the station for lunch or breakfast the next shift."

"Wow. This is great. And it's just a salad. I'd love to taste some of your real cooking."

"You're in luck. I'm going to do some real cooking later."

Jada looked all around them, not seeing a place for the fire; assuming they were even allowed to have a campfire. "Um, how? You going to heat it up with your hands?"

"I have a gas burner in my backpack."

"Holy shit. You got a kitchen sink in that thing, too? It's like Mary Poppins's carpetbag. Or Hermione's little purse in the last book. What else you going to pull out?"

"Don't you think it's weird to mention Mary Poppins and Hermione at the same time?"

"Nope. Both wonderful, beautiful, strong women. Did you know the woman who plays Hermione in the West End show in London is black?"

"She is?"

"Yep. There was quite an uproar about it since in the movies Hermione is this adorable white girl. But J.K. Rowling only ever wrote that she had frizzy hair, never her skin color, so who the hell knows what she looks like? I love that she's a black woman in the play. That's awesome."

"Have you seen it? 'Harry Potter and the Cursed Child?'"

"I have not."

"How very sad," Charley said around bites of her food. "You seem like a huge Harry Potter fan."

"Totally. I want to go to the amusement park in Florida, and I want to see the exhibit they have in London and go to the play. Hell it's more awesome than the Marvel stuff."

"No way," Charley said, the playful sparkle back in her

eyes. "You can't say anything is better than Marvel. I mean, Captain Marvel for one is incredible. I like Potter, but seriously?"

"Seriously. I grew up with the Potterverse and I love it. I've read each book at least five times, and I can't tell you how many times I've seen the movies. Francine hated Potter. Hell, she even hated the Marvel and DC movies."

Charley shook her head in sympathy. "How did you manage to live with this woman? She was so clearly wrong for you."

Jada caught Charley's gaze and held very still for the longest time. Her body tingled as they connected in a way she'd never connected with anyone in her life. She was thrilled and scared all at once. "You're right," she said, speaking softly. "She was terrible for me, but I never acknowledged it. Even when my friends and family told me to get away from her, I stayed. I don't know. I guess I was in love with the idea of being in love."

Charley placed her hand on Jada's bare knee and gave it a soft squeeze. "You deserve more, Jada. Much more."

For a moment—just a moment—Jada thought Charley would kiss her. She welcomed the idea and waited, watching those light-brown lips come ever so closer to her. But Charley pulled back before they touched, and Jada felt a pang of disappointment in her chest. She wanted to grab hold of the woman and kiss her until they both ran out of breath. Kiss her the way she knew Charley deserved to be kissed.

The look in her eyes, though, held Jada back. Something was wrong, and it was quite clear Charley wasn't ready to talk about it. She'd leave it for now, but like any wound, without proper care it would fester and get worse. Jada hoped Charley would come to her before that happened.

****

A few hours later, Jada spoke softly as she stared up in the clear night sky, "This is amazing. I've never seen so many stars in my life. Is that the Big Dipper?"

"It is. I love coming here. It's so peaceful," Charley said. They lay side by side in the grass, their hands lightly touching.

Jada moved her little finger and hooked it around Charley's. She half expected Charley to pull away and was elated when she didn't. After a few more quiet moments, Jada twined her fingers with Charley's. "Dinner was nice. Thanks."

"It wasn't a big deal," Charley said.

"It totally was. Those steaks were amazing, and I don't even pretend to know how you managed to get them so nice and tender. And I've never had corn on the cob cooked like that before."

"You've never cooked corn while it was still in the husk?"

"I don't cook. And I don't know anyone who ever did that. Then again, I don't generally go to cookouts. Not my thing. It was a big deal I went to your bonfire thingy."

"Why not? They can be a lot of fun. Horseshoes, cornhole, baseball, soccer. There's always something to do."

Jada leaned up on her elbow and gazed at Charley's face. The moonlight glanced off her smooth features, and she noticed the smile there. "I like doing stuff outside, and I love baseball, but cornhole? Seriously?"

"Hell yeah." Charley raised up on her elbow, her face centimeters from Jada's. "Cornhole sounds like the most ridiculous game you've ever heard of, but it's a lot of fun. I used to play in a league years ago. Me and a Mountie buddy of mine were quite the team."

"I bet you were." Jada carefully reached forward to touch the side of Charley's face. "Have I told you how beautiful you are, Charlene Townsend?"

Charley shook her head slightly. "You're nuts. I'm not beautiful."

"You're so wrong there, baby. So very, very wrong." Jada moved so their foreheads were touching. "Believe me. When you smile, the world is a better place. You're kind, considerate, and have a beautiful soul. And you mean a lot to me, Charley Townsend."

Charley moved back and Jada caught the tears on her cheeks. "Don't. I—don't."

"Don't what? Care about you?"

"Yeah. That."

"Why not?" Jada sat up, but kept her gaze on Charley. She wanted to wipe the tears away, but didn't think it was a good idea. "What's wrong? What aren't you telling me?"

"A lot. There's so much. I'm not worth it. Okay?"

"Oh hell no. It's so not okay. You're worth everything I

have to offer, and a helluva lot more. I'm not asking you to be the love of my life here, but I am asking you to let me in a little. I want to know you better. I want to be with you every free minute I've got."

"I don't think I can, Jada." Charley stood abruptly and walked a few paces away. "I want to, but I can't."

"You're going to have to be a little more specific." Jada tried hard to hold back her frustration, but dammit! She still wanted to grab the woman and kiss her senseless. Prove to her it was okay to like each other.

"I was wrong. I'm not girlfriend material. I'll mess things up, and then we won't be friends anymore and I like having you as my friend."

Charley looked like a wounded child, her face full of pain when she looked at Jada.

Jada stood and pulled Charley into her embrace. "Bullshit. It takes two people to mess up a relationship. I've had enough of them to know. But you will never mess up our friendship." She held her tighter, smiling when Charley returned the gesture. "I won't let you."

"It'll happen. It's why I have so few friends. Gracie and I grew up together, and she's like my sister, so I have her but that's about it. I have a good family and know a lot of people, but no close friends."

"I like you."

"I know." Charley sighed. "I like you, too." She rested her chin on Jada's shoulder. "I don't know how to do this. Seriously. I don't feel like I'm worth anyone's time."

"What happened to you?" Jada asked softly, not expecting an answer. When Charley spoke, the defeat in her voice almost caused Jada to cry.

"Raina."

That one name held a lot of baggage and more than a few questions for Jada. But she felt now wasn't the time to press on. Even though she was sure she'd stumbled upon the thing Charley wasn't ready to trust her with, yet.

"I'm sorry, baby. I wish you could see yourself the way I see you." She kissed Charley's temple and slowly released her. "Maybe you will, someday."

"You're looking at me through rose-tinted glasses."

Jada touched her own face and gave Charley a sly smile. "I don't wear glasses, dumbass. So I guess you think my eyes don't work."

Charley shoved her playfully. "You know what I mean."

"Weirdly, I do."

"Thanks."

"For what?" Jada asked, watching Charley stare at the ground.

"For being you. For coming up here with me."

"Not exactly a hardship. And I got to see the stars more clearly than ever before. I'm going to have to get Celeste and her husband up here. They'd love it."

"Not your mom?"

Jada thought about it for a moment. Had she ever known her mother to be excited about something so simple and natural? Or anything at all? She didn't even seem excited when Celeste graduated near the top of her class from med school. Then again, Liselle was probably disappointed Celeste wasn't valedictorian.

"My mom's not the outdoor type. I'm not sure she'd come to a place like this. Celeste and Anton would be all for it, though. They're adventurous."

"My mom's the reason I like the outdoors," Charley said. Her gaze turned to the stars again. "She used to bring me on weekend camping trips in the summer. She called it our girl time. My dad took me to all my track meets and mom took me camping. I think it was their way of sharing me."

"Sounds like they did a good job of it. Did they ever think of adopting more kids?"

"They did, but the agencies cost too much and even though they fostered a few kids while I was growing up, the kids always ended up with another family or were sent back to their own family. None of them were adoptable. And being a foster family was the least expensive route for them. My folks have never made a ton of money. We've always been happy with enough to get by."

"My mom makes a shit load," Jada said. "She's top of her field. My dad was also a surgeon, but he didn't specialize so didn't make as much as she does. When he died, the insurance money went into trust funds for me and Celeste. She's still got hers. I used most of mine to buy a house and a new car. Mom was pissed."

"Why? Did she want you to save it?"

"Oh yes. She was going to pay my way through college and said I should keep the money as part of my retirement. Let it sit in the bank and collect interest, yadda yadda. But I knew my dad would be fine with whatever I chose to do. So I bought a house and got a nice car the minute I turned twenty-five. Mom thinks I'm going to spend it all and be poor when I'm old. Hell, I don't think about it because I make enough money to support myself. The house I bought had two bedrooms and a nice little yard. I made a profit when I sold it. I have no idea what my mother thinks I'm going to spend it on."

"Partying? Were you ever a party girl?"

"Nope. I went to the clubs when I was younger, but I'm not into it so much anymore. I like the Pot O'Gold, though. It's nice and laid back. Not like the bouncy, noisy clubs I used to go to in Ottawa. I drink some, but I never saw the appeal in getting drunk. Maybe it's my job. I became a paramedic when I was nineteen."

"You see enough drunks you never want to be one, right?"

"Exactly. Some of my coworkers would disagree, so I usually ended up the designated driver. I never minded, though. It was fun."

"What made it stop being fun?" Charley asked.

"Francine. I was with her for five years. She slowly sucked the fun out of a lot of stuff for me. I didn't do the clubs anymore after I met her. We'd go for a drink now and again, but she's a snob and most of the bars I liked were beneath her. So I stopped going. I wanted to make her happy." Jada huffed. "Stupid move on my part. I should have left her much sooner."

"Why didn't you?"

"In yet another stupid move, I stayed with her because my mom hated her. I think I was pushing the rebellious shit a little too far. I gave up trying to please my mom when I became a paramedic and earned her eternal disappointment." Jada took a long look at Charley, though she couldn't see much of her features in the darkness. "But I think, eventually, that might change. I wouldn't mind doing stuff to please someone else—if that someone else was really special to me."

Charley didn't reply and Jada wondered if she'd gone too

far again. She had a hard time not expressing how she felt. All the warm, fuzzy emotions Charley evoked bubbled to the surface, and she felt all goofy and romantic. And now that she'd acknowledged it, Jada realized she was actually happy. The smile on her face, for once, felt very comfortable.

She took Charley's hand. "Okay, enough mushy crap. I'm kinda tired. Want to turn in for the night? Rest up so we can take our time tomorrow?"

"Sure." Charley let Jada lead her into the tent, where she lit a small lantern to give them daylight brightness.

"Damn. You didn't tell me you brought the sun in here."

"I keep it in the truck for emergencies. Thought it'd be nice to have. I don't usually need one, but I figured you might."

"Thanks. It's handy to see what the hell I'm doing." Jada unzipped her sleeping bag. Once her boots were off and put to the side, she crawled in and shivered. "I should have brought another sweatshirt. Didn't realize it'd get this cold."

"Um, we could, uh, put our sleeping bags together. Body heat will warm you right up."

Jada grinned, unable to help herself. "Are you saying you want to sleep with me again?"

"What can I say?" Charley unzipped her bag and started connecting it to Jada's. "I'm insatiable that way."

Jada barked a laugh. "I can't believe you said that!"

"What? I can joke."

"You sure have a lot of surprises in you."

Charley removed her boots, snuggled up against Jada, and closed up their sleeping bag. She turned off the light once they were settled. "Maybe—maybe someday you'll find out how many."

Jada put an arm around Charley's waist and rested her head against Charley's chest, finding the position comfortable and natural. She sighed, thinking about Charley's comment. "That's my grand plan. I want to find out all about you." She squeezed Charley's waist and kissed the small patch of bare skin beneath Charley's shirt collar. "I have a feeling it's going to be an eventful journey."

"I hope you're up for it."

"Are you?"

Jada felt Charley shrug. "We'll see." She kissed the top of

Jada's head. "G'nite."

"Nite." Jada closed her eyes and fell into a peaceful sleep.

****

"New York City?" Josie said, looking at Charley like she had two heads. They were seated at Charley's kitchen table, having breakfast a couple of days after Charley's camping trip with Jada. "Are you sure it's a good idea?"

Truth was, Charley hadn't been able to stop thinking about Jada's offer. It would get her away from Whitehorse for a while and maybe take her mind off things. Problem was, she'd be with Jada the whole time. Not that it was a problem, per se, but it would be hard not to think about her when she was right in front of Charley's nose. Or sleeping beside her in the hotel room. She suspected Jada would get a king-size bed.

And how Charley loved to sleep with Jada. It was cozy and comfortable and natural. Jada fit perfectly into her arms, and when they slept, they slept. She'd never been so well rested in all her life. How was it possible?

Was it such a good idea to be alone with her? Even for a week? Charley was wildly attracted to Jada, but she wasn't ready to take that step. Because that step would have to involve marriage, and there was no way she'd do it again. Was there?

"Charlene?" Josie touched her arm and brought Charley out of her reverie. "What's going on in your beautiful head?"

"All the reasons I should, and the ones I shouldn't, go on this trip." Charley sighed and pushed away the remains of her breakfast. Her stomach was now rejecting food. "She's special, Mom. We're friends and we're getting to be very close and what's worse is I'm attracted to her."

"How is it a bad thing, honey?" Josie smiled gently at her. "You've not had those kinds of feelings in years. Is that the problem?"

"Yes. Probably. I don't feel like I'm worth it, Mom. I care about Jada, and I don't want to do something to hurt her. I'm afraid I'll make another mistake, and things will go wrong and—"

"Wait. Another mistake? What was your first one? Did you guys have a fight already?"

"No. Well, not a fight. We did have a pretty heavy talk

while we were camping. I tried to tell her about Raina, but I chickened out. I didn't want to scare her off."

"I don't think it would happen, and if it does, then she's not good enough for you." Josie stood and cleared the table.

"She's too good for me, Mom."

"I doubt that." Josie placed the dishes in the sink. She returned to the table and sat next to Charley. "No one is ever going to be good enough for my daughter."

"You have to say that. You're my mom."

Josie laughed. "I love you. That's why I say it. And I'm sure you'll tell her about Raina when the time is right. But you didn't answer my question. What mistake are you talking about?"

"Raina."

"I don't understand."

"Mom—didn't you ever wonder if she killed herself because of something I did?"

"Never."

"But what if she did? Maybe I did something to caused her to kill herself. I could have said something, done something to upset her enough—"

"Stop. I don't ever want you to say any of this nonsense again, Charlene." Josie's eyes darkened with barely contained anger. Something Charley wasn't used to seeing. "You did nothing wrong. Period. The point is Raina killed herself. She made a choice and also chose to not tell anyone why she was doing it. We can't go back and analyze every moment of our time with her. We can't. You can't. You loved her to the best of your ability. And I honestly believe she loved you as much."

"Then why isn't she here? Why did she leave me?" Charley fought hard against the tears, but to no avail. This discussion, while more infrequent in recent years, always caused a torrent of emotions. "You say the same thing every time I bring this up, but you don't know it to be true, Mom. No one does. I've talked about this to enough counselors, including my new one, Debra, and I still can't resolve it in my head. How can someone love you and then take their own life? I want to be so pissed off at her, but when I try, I end up blaming myself. She left me."

"She did. She left you and you have every right to be pissed off. I know I am sometimes. Sometimes I see a picture of you two together and I miss her. I loved her like she was my own daughter. I loved her because she made you so very happy. Charlene, it might have been her own parents. Raina might have been upset by a phone call you don't know about. Or maybe she saw them in the city. Or maybe they paid her a visit. You know how awful they were to her.

"But, honey, it doesn't matter. It doesn't. She's dead. By her own hand or from an accident or illness—it doesn't matter. She's gone and you're still here. You're young and have a lot of years ahead of you." Josie scooted closer and took Charley's hands into hers. "I've tried very hard not to be too pushy, and I know sometimes I am, but dammit, Charlene, you have to move on. If you like Jada so much, then you go to New York with her. You enjoy your time together. Enjoy being young together. Trust me, youth is fleeting and you'll be old before you know it."

Charley gave her a half smile. "You're hardly old, Mom."

"I didn't mean me." Josie winked at her. "I meant your father."

"Of course you did."

"I'm serious though. Go to New York. Enjoy yourself. And if you find your feelings for Jada grow stronger, then let them. It's not illegal to have a good time."

"I know. I've never felt like this before. Not even when I first met Raina. It's all so new and different and scary."

"None of this is bad. It tells me there might be something very special about Jada."

"There is."

"Then you are hereby ordered to go on this trip. And when you get back, bring her to the house for dinner. I need to know more about this woman."

"What woman?"

They both looked up as Charles entered the apartment. Josie was the first one to speak. "Sit down and let your daughter tell you about Jada and their upcoming trip to New York City. I'll get you something to eat while you get caught up."

"New York City?" Charles sat down opposite Charley and tilted his head to the side. "When are you going to New York? And why am I always the last one to know?"

"I didn't tell you because there's not much to tell." Charley swatted at Josie when she walked behind her. "My mother has a big mouth."

"Well, you won't find me disagreeing," her dad said. "But if there's a trip to New York, then I'd say there's lots to talk about." He leaned his elbows on the table and held her gaze. "Spill."

****

"So is it true Charley's going to New York with Jada?" Liv asked. She zoomed around the slowpoke car in front of her.

Grace smiled. "How'd you hear?"

"The lesbian community in Whitehorse isn't as big as it seems, you know?" She gave Grace her trademark crooked grin. "I saw Sara at the bank yesterday. She heard it from Terry who heard it from Izzy."

Grace joined in her laughter. "I should have known. I found out this morning in a text. She was worried her mom would spread the word somehow, and I'd hear it from someone else. They made their plans to do this a few days ago and leave next week. It's so unlike Charley to be spontaneous, but I'm happy for her. It's been a long time coming."

"That's for sure." Liv pulled into the hospital parking lot and reached for Grace's hand. "This is going to sound corny as hell, but I've got a good feeling about today."

Grace squeezed her hand and gazed at her profile. She badly wanted to feel good about it, too. Today was their second try with insemination. "I'm glad, honey. But I worry you might get your hopes up. I don't want you hurt because it doesn't work. Remember, the doctor said it might take a few more tries."

"I know. And I got it in the back of my mind, I promise. It's—I don't know. I feel different this time."

"Let's hope you're feeling more fertile." Grace leaned across the console and kissed her on the cheek. "C'mon, honey. Let's go get pregnant."

Liv laughed heartily, got out of the truck, and hurried to Grace's side. She caught her up in a tight hug. "I love you."

"I love you, too. Now let's head inside."

****

Two hours later, Liv and Grace were seated at Marge's in

Blue River for lunch. Grace had her dessert first, as usual. This time it was a fresh slice of apple pie. "Mmm. This is heaven."

Liv chuckled. "I thought I was the one who's supposed to eat stuff like that."

"You can eat all you want, baby." Grace fed her a bit of her pie and smiled at Liv's groan. "But you know I have dessert first here. It's tradition. Besides, there's going to be plenty of time for you to start getting cravings and eating ice cream and pickles."

Liv nearly choked on her soda. "Seriously? Disgusting."

"My mom ate them the whole time she was pregnant with us. Dad got used to it after a while, but there's something to be said about the sweet and sour taste."

"Oh no. Tell me you don't!"

"I have and I love it. I don't do it much because, well, Carly hated it. I haven't eaten the combination in years. But I did hear babies grow up to either love or hate the stuff their mom craves while pregnant. For me and Matthew it was the ice cream and pickles. We love it."

"Well, if you want it, I'll buy it for you. Just don't ask me to try it out, ok?"

"Deal. Just like I'll buy whatever weird things you crave." Grace finished her pie and set the plate and fork aside. "I can't wait to see what you want. Maybe it'll be Pop-Tarts and sardines."

"Eww!" Liv gave her a little kick under the table. "You're mean. I hate sardines."

"Yeah and my mom hated pickles. Still does, actually, but not when she was pregnant with us."

The waitress arrived with their orders, and Liv held up the pickle for her hamburger and dropped it on Grace's plate. "I'd tell you to save it for later, but you already had dessert."

Grace narrowed her gaze at Liv as she picked up the pickle and ate it. "Smart-ass."

"Part of my charm."

"Part of something," Grace mumbled and moved her leg to avoid the little kick that came her way. "I need to go to the restroom. Be right back." She slid out of the booth and mussed Liv's hair as she passed by.

The ladies' room was painted white with red highlights

that matched the red of the vinyl seats in the front of the restaurant. The 50s music was easier to hear in the small room, and Grace sang along to a familiar tune. She finished up quickly and was washing her hands when she heard the door open and close. She paid no attention to the woman who entered, but when she turned to leave, she wished she had.

Carly stood directly in front of her, blue eyes flashing anger as she blocked Grace's exit.

"What—what the hell are you doing here?"

"Public restroom. I can be here if I want," Carly said.

Grace stepped to the right, and Carly matched her movement. "You need to get out of my way."

"No, I don't. You need to listen to me." Carly pressed her hand against Grace's chest and shoved her against the sink basin.

Grace wanted to react. She wanted to take the hand on her chest and twist it until she heard the bones break. But something stopped her. Maybe the look in Carly's eyes or the feel of her touch. she couldn't be sure.

Memories surfaced and she felt the sting of Carly's open palm slap against her cheek, the bite of her nails when she gripped her upper arms, the glassy look in her eyes after she'd been drinking.

"You should leave, Carly," Grace said with as much calm as she could muster. "I have a restraining order against you, and we know you're here illegally. Soon as they catch you—"

"They'll what? Send me back to jail? I survived over three years there. I'm sure I can take a few more, and it'll be worth it. But I'd rather you come back with me to Seattle. I don't see why we can't make this easier."

"I told you I'm not going back. I don't want you in my life. Didn't the divorce make that clear?"

Carly pinned her to the basin with her body and placed her hands on either side of Grace. Their faces nearly touched. "Your brother filed the paperwork, not you. How do I know he didn't force you to sign it? He always hated me and tried to break us up. Your parents, too. Far as I'm concerned, they made you do it." She pressed her cheek against Grace's and whispered in her ear, "Maybe we should have a quickie before you go back to the bitch. Remind you of exactly what you're missing."

Grace's body trembled, but her voice remained steady.

"You touch me and you'll be the one with a broken arm."

Carly laughed. "You won't touch me, sweetie. You tried. Didn't turn out so well for you."

Grace closed her eyes against the sudden vision. She'd punched Carly in the face and knocked her to the ground. When she got up—the look in her eyes was hard to forget. Murderous was the best word to describe it. Grace remembered nothing else before waking up hours later with a bloody face and broken arm.

She shook the memory and pushed against Carly, displacing her enough to get out of her reach. "I won't let you do it again, Carly. I never deserved what you did to me. No one does. I loved you and you turned that against me. It's taken me a long time to get on with my life, but I have. And you can't do anything about it."

"You're wrong," Carly said. "And if she wasn't out there waiting, I'd make sure you understand. You promised me forever, Grace. I aim to make sure you fulfill your promise." Carly calmly turned and started for the door. She tossed one more comment over her shoulder before she left. "I won't take no for an answer."

Grace waited until the door closed before collapsing to the floor. She bent her legs, wrapped her arms around them, rested her forehead on her knees, and cried.

When the door opened again, she heard Liv's voice call out to her. "Gracie? You okay?"

"No," she responded, not looking up when she sensed Liv kneel beside her.

"Baby, what's wrong? Are you sick?" Liv placed a gentle hand on Grace's back. "Tell me what you need."

"I need you to hold me and promise not to leave me."

"What? Of course I'll never leave you." Liv pulled Grace against her. She'd misunderstood Grace's meaning. "Tell me what's got you so upset."

"Carly. She was just here." She proceeded to tell Liv exactly what happened.

Liv's hold loosened a little, but then she tightened it again and kissed the top of Grace's head. "I won't go. But we need to call the police. Remember what we promised?"

"I do, but she's long gone." Grace sniffled. "She was waiting for me. I tried not to let her get to me, but she did. Everything she said—when she touched me—I had flashbacks."

"She touched you?" Liv asked, and Grace knew she had a very tenuous hold on her emotions. "Did she hurt you?"

"Physically? No." Grace used the back of her hand to wipe the moisture from her cheeks. "Carly's smart. Her words hurt me more than her fists."

Liv gently helped Grace to her feet. "I'm going to call the police. I want them here before we leave. I don't want to take a chance she's out there waiting for us. I might not be able to keep my promise to you."

Grace met her worried gaze and touched Liv's abdomen. "You have to. We can't take a chance on you getting hurt. If she's out there—don't do anything. Please?"

Liv was clearly fighting with her instincts and gave a curt nod. "Let's go sit down. We can get fresh food and make the call. It'll take awhile for them to get here anyway."

"I don't think I can eat."

"You don't have to. I'll take care of you." Liv slipped her arm around Grace's waist as they left the restroom. She swept her gaze around the restaurant and spent a few seconds looking out the window before going to their table. "I'm proud of you," she said once they were seated. This time they were side by side in the booth.

"For what? I let her run all over me in there."

"No. You stood there and took what she dished out and didn't react to it. That's what you did. And you told her off. Do I wish you'd have slugged her? Totally. But it's okay you didn't. You might have hurt your hand."

Grace released a little laugh. "I doubt it. The only thing that would have been hurt was her face." She leaned closer and kissed Liv on the lips. "Make the call. I want to go home."

"Consider it done."

Chapter Fourteen

Preparing for the trip to New York City was easy enough for Charley. Jada insisted she knew exactly where they should stay and took over making their plans. As it was her idea, she tried to pay for everything, but Charley wouldn't let her go that far. Two weeks after their camping trip, they were on their way to the States.

Eighteen hours and two layovers later, they landed at LaGuardia airport. Charley yawned as she followed Jada into the Immigration Hall. She'd slept most of the flight from Toronto and was glad they'd had little turbulence. She didn't enjoy flying and hated that they needed to switch planes three times, but it was the one drawback to living in the Yukon. Most flights entailed two or three stops. She was definitely glad to be on the ground again.

As they walked into the hall, she began to get a little excited. New York wasn't a city she'd been dying to visit, but after Jada's continuous chatter about where they would go and what they'd see, she'd started getting almost giddy over it. Ever since they arrived, she couldn't stop smiling.

They walked side by side as they followed the others from their flight. Charley flexed her hand a little once they found the end of the queue. Her right hand kept a tight grip on her carryon bag as they were shuffled through the crowd. Even with her height, Charley couldn't see where the line ended. The mass of people had her unnerved. She didn't enjoy spaces with obscured exits.

"Welcome to New York." Jada's smile beamed extra bright as she spun in a little circle.

Charley wanted to be grumpy because of the horde of shoving people, but she had to smile in return. "Thanks. Is this a holiday weekend or something? There must be a thousand people in here."

Jada didn't seem bothered. "It's New York City. They're always busy." She moved along with the crowd. Charley followed for what seemed like hours but turned out to be forty-five minutes. They came to a row of kiosks. A pleasant-looking older woman in a blue uniform with a Transportation Security Administration patch on her arm and TSA on her epaulets pointed them to one.

Jada inserted her passport, answered a series of questions, then retrieved a printout with her picture on it. "Your turn," she said.

Charley stepped up, followed all the directions, got her photo taken, and received a paper with a big black X across her photo. "What's this about?" she asked.

"Oh, you've been a bad girl. I think there's a Black Notice on you from Interpol."

"Funny. Does it actually mean something?"

Jada pointed to a line branching off from the one they were now in. "You have to go over there. See the sign that says, 'If you have an X, use this lane'?"

"Yes. But what's it for?"

"You have to go through more checks. Make sure you're legit to enter the US. Get your passport ready to show them. I'll meet you at the baggage claim area." The moving throng of people swept Jada away.

Charley stepped into the queue. It seemed like an awful lot to go through to get into a country. Was it like this in Canada? It'd been years since she was out of the country and wondered if their immigration lines were this harried.

Another TSA person directed her to a new line, and in a few minutes, she was talking to a very bored officer. As they exchanged a few pleasantries, he gave her passport a stamp and she was legally in America. She headed right for the baggage claim area, but she didn't see Jada anywhere.

Hundreds of bags streamed along the conveyor belts. Charley smiled when her bright-orange suitcase came toward her. Such a wonderful gift from her mom. She sent her a quick text to let her know the plane landed, she was safe, and the orange suitcase was a superb idea.

A few moments later, Charley spotted Jada's black suitcase with a rainbow ribbon tied to the handle. She plucked it from the belt and found a spot along the wall to wait for Jada.

An hour later, Jada came into the baggage area, her face

flushed and her jovial demeanor dampened. "Wow. I mean, I've never been in a queue that long in my entire life. And the woman in front of me cussed the entire time. I think she lives here and was complaining about the foreigners clogging the lines." Jada's eyes sparkled with mischief. "I made sure to tell her I was a foreigner as we finished going through the process."

"I bet she enjoyed that," Charley said.

"Yeah. She said, 'Oh. Canada doesn't count.' I'm not sure if it was a dis or a compliment."

"Best not to ask." Charley pointed to the luggage. "I got your bag for you. Want to head to the hotel now?"

"Totally. How long have you been waiting? I'm surprised you were here first."

"An hour or so. The whole process was about ten minutes long."

"Seriously? Last time I got an X I was in the queue for two hours." Jada narrowed her gaze at Charley. "You suck."

Charley didn't try to hide her smile. "You wish." She laughed at Jada's shocked expression and led the way to the hotel shuttle area.

****

Charley stepped into their hotel room and smiled. Jada had indeed gotten them a king-size bed. The thought of holding her at night sent a thrill through Charley that was impossible to describe. She placed her luggage near the closet and sat on the bed. It wasn't too hard or soft, and the duvet smelled freshly cleaned.

"You like?"

Charley caught Jada's gaze before Jada turned to the window. "I do. Pretty spacious with a nice big bed."

"Not going to spend a week with you and not get some kind of cuddle time. But we've got a nice view of the Manhattan skyline from here. Come look."

Charley stood behind her to look out the window. Night greeted them outside, and the lighted skyline was beautiful. She spotted the Freedom Tower easily. "Can we go to the 9/11 Memorial?" she asked softly.

"Sure. I'd love to see it. Pay my respects, as it were. I

watched it happen during my biology class. I wanted to go help so badly; it's part of why I'm a Mounty now. Did you know they had to stage all the extra volunteer emergency folks in a baseball stadium?"

"No, but it's amazing what people will do when they know someone needs their help. I'd hope Canadians would do the same."

"I'm sure we would." Jada leaned back a bit. Charley wrapped her arms around her and held her close. "We'll do that tomorrow, okay? We show our IDs and we get in free. We'll get the sad part of the trip over quickly. Then I want to take you on a real touristy tour."

"Whatever you want. I'm up for it."

Jada turned in Charley's embrace so they faced each other. "I get the impression there's at least one thing you're not up for."

Charley knew her face shone with a blush. Again. How was it Jada made her do that so much? "No. Not that. But it doesn't mean I don't want to enjoy our time together." To prove her point, Charley kissed Jada softly, letting their lips brush lightly against each other. "Want dinner?"

Jada laughed and rested her head on Charley's shoulder. "You sure are romantic." She pulled away from Charley and went to the desk, where she found a large, leather-bound notebook. "Let's do room service. I'm kinda tired and I think it'll be fun to eat here and watch a movie or something."

"Sounds romantic. Can I pick the movie?"

"You can, but there's got to be at least a hint of romance in it. This is our week. Let's see where this is going, huh? Maybe try to do a few romantic things while we're here."

"Sure." Charley said the word, but she wasn't sure at all. She swallowed the lump in her throat and unpacked her tablet. "I'll find us a movie on Netflix. You order dinner. We'll work on the romance stuff. Okay?"

"Fair enough." Jada moved to her side and kissed her lightly on the cheek. "I'm going to keep working on it, Sarge. Promise."

****

"I can't believe you talked me into this," Charley groused as they got on the ferry to Liberty Island on their second day in the city. "Why do I want to see a gigantic, green, bronze statue?"

"You're being an ass." Jada bumped shoulders with her. "The smile on your face tells me you're full of shit. You're having fun. Admit it."

Charley tried very hard to hide her smile, but the adorable expression on Jada's face was too much. She had a strong urge to kiss her, and as she leaned forward, the boat rocked and nearly sent her to the floor. She grabbed the railing and moved her gaze to the Statue of Liberty as it came into view. Much safer than gawking at the woman she couldn't keep her hands off of.

"You okay?" Jada asked.

"Yeah, fine. And you're right. I'm having a great time." She moved a bit to the left so they were touching sides. Charley pointed to the statue. "I bet the view from up there is amazing."

"It is. I can't wait for you to see it. The stairs are a bitch, but it's worth it. Trust me."

"I do trust you." Charley put a lot of emphasis on *trust*. This whole romantic week Jada planned was getting to her in a very pleasant way. Her chest swelled when Jada was near, and all she wanted to do was hold her hand, hug her, kiss her—never let her out of sight.

"I'm glad, baby. Very glad." Jada smiled, pointed to Liberty Island, and spouted some random facts about it.

Charley mostly listened to hear Jada speak, so she didn't entirely pay attention to what she said. Her nerdiness was sexy. *Dammit,* Charley thought. *I can't even listen to boring tourist facts without my brain acting like I'm a horny teenager.* Well, she might not be a teenager, but the horny part was certainly in full bloom. She squirmed a little and danced from foot to foot as she tried to calm her body down. Everything was on fire, and if she could get Jada into a room with only the two of them it would be mind blowing.

But it wasn't going to happen, and while Charley normally took care of things on her own, she wouldn't have time tonight. They had dinner reservations, then tickets to *Hamilton*. Jada was so excited about their big night, Charley didn't want to do anything to disturb her enthusiasm. Even if it meant keeping her legs crossed all day when what she needed was a cold shower.

Jada stopped speaking and took pictures with her phone. She turned to Charley and grinned. "Smile." She took a quick photo. She showed it to Charley, proud of herself for getting the statue behind Charley. "I think I'll use this one on my phone so when you call me, I'll see it."

"We've not even been here two whole days, and already you've taken a million pictures of me. How many does that thing hold?"

"Don't know. As many as I can take." Jada held it up for Charley. "The kid who sold it to me said it held a ton of pictures. That's what he said. A ton."

"Well, a ton's a lot. You plan to take a ton then?"

"Oh yes. One ton it is. All of it New York City and the most handsome Mountie in Canada."

"Does the handsome Mountie have to be in all the pictures? What if she wants pictures of the adorable flight medic? Is that allowed?"

Jada exaggerated contemplation and nodded after a moment. "I believe I can accommodate the handsome Mountie."

"Good." Charley took a quick photo and smiled at the goofy expression on Jada's face. "Though I think it's going to be hard to get a shot of you being straight."

Jada's hearty laugh brought a smile to Charley's face. "Honey, I haven't done straight since, well, ever."

"This I have noticed about you." Charley leaned closer and smelled the flowery scent of Jada's soap. "I've not been able to stop thinking about it." She was so close they nearly touched noses. "Keep it in mind. Okay?"

"Okay," Jada said, her voice wavering. "Are you going to stare at me all day or kiss me?"

"You want me to kiss you?"

Jada closed her eyes and sighed. "I want it so bad—"

Charley pressed her lips to Jada's and savored the moment their tongues met and their bodies touched along their lengths. Jada wrapped her hand around Charley's neck. She pulled her closer, and her other hand gripped the belt of Charley's shorts. Her body was on fire as the kiss deepened and they became impossibly close.

An airhorn sounded and broke the spell between them. Both of them were breathing heavy and staring into each other's eyes. Charley didn't know what to say, but that kiss was magical. Nothing like the others they'd shared. It was crazy sexy and said more than let's go have some fun. Like they were promising each other something very special

"Wow," Jada said, lightly touching her lips. "I don't think I've ever been kissed like that before. Certainly not in public." She glanced at the people around them. Most of them were more interested in the statue. Of course there had to be one person who saw them—an elderly lady who gave them a knowing smile.

Charley ran her fingers through her hair and tried to get her thoughts in order. "I can guarantee you I've never done that in public before. Ever." She took Jada's hand as the ferry maneuvered to the docking platform. "You mean a lot to me, Jada. Let's be sensible about this okay? Let's not rush into anything."

"Be sensible. No rushing. I think I got it." She looked at their joined hands. "Does this mean no more kissing? Because I liked it just now, and I wouldn't mind a repeat performance."

"I think more kissing is required. I mean, I need to know what you like."

"What I like?" Jada asked as they joined the line to get onto the island.

"Yeah." Charley had stepped into line behind her, and she leaned forward to whisper, "Do you enjoy it when I nibble your lip, or suck it into my mouth? Maybe you'd like me to suckle your tongue."

Jada shook her body and the glare on her face didn't quite work out. "You're mean. Now it's all I'm going to think about for the rest of the day."

"Consider it my way of giving you something to look forward to." Charley kissed her cheek and moved to her side as they walked onto the dock and up the stairs to the park area. "I like teasing you. You're cute when you try to be mad."

"I'm not mad." Jada pulled Charley to the side of the crowd they'd been on the ferry with. "I'm now a little frustrated and excited and dammit I want to throw you on the ground right now and make love to you for hours."

"All that from one kiss?"

Jada's eyes fairly shined in the late morning sun. She held Charley's gaze for a few seconds and said, "All it takes is one kiss with the right person to make the world fall off its axis. One person can change everything. And I'm a little scared that for me, you're that one person."

"I'm right there with you." Charley gently kissed Jada's lips. "Remember, you're the one who wanted romance."

"I did and you sure as hell know how to be sly about giving it to me." She held out her hand to Charley. "Let's go explore."

Charley took the offered hand and realized she'd follow this woman anywhere.

****

Charley and Jada rode down an escalator that was placed parallel to a set of concrete stairs. Jada stared at the damaged steps, and once on the floor, turned to look at a display in front of them. The "Survivor' Stairs." Beside this was a photo of a group of people covered in dust as they descended those concrete steps.

Jada looked up at Charley, who was also reading the plaque. "Hundreds of people had to escape falling debris as they crossed the plaza to get to these steps to escape. Amazing."

Charley nodded, her attention already on another display. Jada followed her to the only fire apparatus in the museum. At the rear of FDNY Ladder 3 was a piece of the vehicle's side. It contained the truck's designation number and a handwritten note that read, "Jeff we will not forget you!"

Jada was unable to pull her gaze from the twisted metal. She blinked back sudden tears. Cabinet doors hung by the thinnest bits of steel. No equipment was to be found, no sign of the brave souls who once rode it into danger, but the specter of this vehicle spoke volumes to her.

The horror of the day. The lives of the men and women— it was almost too much.

A hand on her shoulder startled her until she realized it was Charley. She leaned into her touch. "It's—there're no words."

"I know. I keep imagining myself in their shoes. Wondering if I'd have run into the tower like they did or—"

"We'd both have run into the tower. It's who we are." She gently squeezed Charley's hand. "Let's keep going. Lots to see and absorb."

Charley swiped her hand across her face and sniffled. "Yep."

"You okay?"

"No. But I feel like the only way we can honor these people is to keep going through the museum, you know? Like we need to see this place. Does that make sense?"

"Completely."

Jada and Charley moved away from the ladder truck to another display. Jada said, "When I volunteered to come here they called us off as we were leaving. This was the morning of September twelfth, and New York was being inundated with volunteers. We were on standby for a few days, but we never got called in. It's a shame in a way. I wanted so badly to come here and help out. We kept a TV in the break room turned on and watched the news every day for probably a month after."

Charley said, "I was in Vancouver then. We were on high alert, because if someone was coming after the Americans, they'd probably come north. We weren't even sure who the hell we needed to watch out for, but I can tell you that we didn't have any calls to respond to for about three hours after the last plane crashed. There were so many hysterical reports of seeing planes in trouble, rumors of car bombs in front of government offices. We got called to investigate a plane crash north of the city. Total waste of our time, but we were scared that day."

"So were we. I think most of the world was. I mean, who the hell comes after America, right?"

"Right."

Jada turned to the elevators. "C'mon. Let's head up to the next level."

Charley and Jada continued their tour of the 9/11 Museum until sometime around one in the afternoon. They'd seen every inch of the place, neither willing to miss anything. When they stepped out of the building, Charley headed for the waterfall pools marking where the foundations of the twin towers had been. She leaned against the black marble and absently traced some of the names engraved in the shiny material.

Jada put a hand on the small of Charley's back and placed a hand on hers. "It's beautiful."

"It is." Her gaze was somewhere in the distance, and Jada

kept silent beside her, to give Charley time for reflection.

The water along all four sides of the monument flowed continuously into the square pool. The late afternoon sun sparkled off it and cast tiny diamonds into the air. Jada took a couple of pictures with her phone then slid it into her pocket. She leaned her shoulder against Charley. "I'm glad the parade's tomorrow. We're going to need something fun to do."

"We should do something now," Charley said, her gaze never leaving the water. "Like maybe go see a show. I heard there are kiosks all over the theater district where you can get tickets. I don't care what we see as long as it's something fun."

Jada smiled and kissed Charley's temple. "Then off we go. Let's head over there now, get tickets to something awesome, and find food."

"More food?" That got Charley to face her. "You just had lunch."

"I know, but the theater district is pretty far from here, and I know I'm going to be hot and sweaty and in need of nourishment when we get there. Besides, it's time you take me to a nice place for dinner. Part of the romantic stuff you're supposed to be doing while we're here."

Charley laughed softly and pulled Jada closer. "That so? Then I guess we better get moving, because I might actually be hungry soon, too."

"Perfect." Jada had more bounce in her step as they left the somber memorial in search of fun, adventure, and food.

****

Saturday was the NYC Pride parade, and Jada was super excited. Since she wanted to experience the full feeling of NYC Pride, she bought rainbow-striped gym shoes, hot pink shorts, and a T-shirt with the Star of Life and Caduceus in the center, in rainbow colors. Underneath it was the slogan Medic Pride.

She swept her hair away from her face and used a rainbow hairband to hold it in back. She fluffed it up a bit before knocking on the bathroom door. "We gotta get down there early. I want to get breakfast first. You about done?"

"I'm working on it. Hang on. I need time."

"Okay, Princess. I'll wait." Jada sat on the bed and tried

to be patient. She was more excited about spending this day with Charley than she ever remembered being. It seemed so right when they were together. Jada felt as though she'd found the other half of her soul. Whoa. What a crazy thought to have. But the idea made her belly flutter and her heartbeat quicken. Was it weird they'd not even had sex yet? That she was falling in love with a woman who stopped at heavy petting?

She wondered if she should tell Charley about this revelation. Would it spook her? She seemed skittish anytime Jada brought up their relationship. Her answer always was let it go where it goes. Well Jada, for one, had a feeling where it was going for her. She needed to figure out how the hell to tell Charley.

As if on cue, Charley walked out of the bathroom. She had a baseball hat with the RCMP logo on the front of it, but the rest of the hat was rainbow colors. Her orange T-shirt said "Rainbow Mountie" and showed a unicorn between the words. The unicorn was decked out like a real RCMP horse would be. She wore her standard cargo shorts and a very big grin on her face.

She said, "You like?"

Jada couldn't stop the smile on her face if she wanted to. And she didn't. Charley was adorable. "I love it. We'll be the hit of the parade. Let's get some breakfast before the car gets here."

"Car? I thought we'd take a taxi again."

"We might not be able to get one, so last week I booked us a car. The guy is going to drive us to the nearest train station, and we'll go right to Grand Central. He'll pick us back up around midnight tonight. If we think it might be later, I can call and tell him."

"You'd make a good travel agent," Charley said.

"I did some research, and I met a nurse recently who's been to the city before. She gave me some tips." Jada stood up and twined her fingers with Charley's and gave her a little tug toward the door. "C'mon. Food first. Fun next."

****

Jada kept a tight hold on Charley's hand as they navigated the gigantic throng of people along 5th Avenue. She felt the nervousness in Charley's body like it was her own and did her best to move quickly. She'd chosen a spot for them to see the parade and was determined to get there. It was at a corner where the parade would turn onto West 8th Street. She figured it'd have to slow to make the turn, and this would be a great spot to see everything.

They reached the area around nine in the morning, and not many people were there yet to stake out a place. "Awesome. We'll have a good view, I think."

"I think so, too. What time does the parade start?"

"Couple of hours yet. Bored already?" Jada teased.

Charley planted a delicious kiss on her lips and grinned. "Not really. I can think of stuff to do."

They heard some cat calls and whistles, and Jada ducked her head in embarrassment, though she didn't know why. It wasn't like she'd never kissed a woman in public before. "I like how you think."

"I'm sure you do."

Jada felt her cell phone vibrate and grabbed it out of her pocket. As soon as she read the text from Betty, she did a fist pump and said, "Yes!"

Charley wore an amused expression on her face. "Good news?"

"Hell, yes. Peter got fired."

"Good. We don't need nurses like him." Charley slipped her arm around Jada's waist. "So glad you won't have to deal with him anymore."

"I bet it's because of your uncle," Jada said.

"Maybe. Doesn't matter though. What he did was unacceptable. Period. That he got fired sends a strong message."

"Makes me feel better, too. I mean, it's not like I enjoy that the man lost his job, but I won't have to bear the brunt of his abuse anymore and neither will anyone else at the hospital. He can take his racist ass somewhere else." Jada leaned into Charley and enjoyed the feel of her strength surrounding her. "Thanks, baby."

"You're welcome." Charley kissed her and gave her a little squeeze. "Now, before I forget, where did you put your wallet?"

Jada pushed her sunglasses up in order to see Charley better, but Charley's eyes were hidden behind her reflective shades. "Why?"

"You need to put it in your front pocket for when the crowd starts getting bigger, and keep a close check on it. It's too easy for someone to get it out of your back pocket or a side pocket. Keep it where you can feel it." She looked over Jada's shoulder, and Jada realized Charley had subtly shifted into cop mode.

Jada looked around as well, comforted by the fact there were dozens of police officers around them, lined up along barriers to keep pedestrians out of the street. "Okay." She moved her small wallet to her front pocket.

"And keep a good grip on your phone when you take pictures," Charley whispered.

"You're going to make me paranoid. Besides, I'm not worried about anything. I've got you to protect me."

Charley flexed the fingers of her left hand, not quite able to make a fist. She frowned and continued to look around them. "That's not saying much. I'm not so good with my right hand."

Jada placed her hand on Charley's chest. She waited for her to stop scanning their surroundings and look at her. She gently removed Charley's sunglasses and said, "I feel safe when I'm with you. Doesn't matter if your hand isn't working fully yet. I'd take you over any one else any day of the week. You make me feel like the world is a good place. I like being with you. And I'm damn sure if something did happen, you'd be the first one to jump in and help. Far as I'm concerned, you're my Captain Marvel."

Charley's expression was hard to read. A mix of sadness and pride—maybe some amusement tossed in. Jada waited patiently for her to reply.

"I will always be here for you, Jada. And I promise to do what I can if you need me."

"Good." Jada put Charley's sunglasses back on her. "Stand here with your arms around me. Let everyone know I'm your girl."

"That I can do."

Jada leaned into her and enjoyed the feel of Charley's body against hers. "Sucks we have to go home tomorrow."

"It does, but you were right. New York Pride is amazing. I'm glad you dragged me here."

"I didn't have to drag you. You caved pretty fast when I

came up with the idea." Jada turned in Charley's arms and kissed her softly. "I'm glad you agreed to this."

"Me, too." Charley rested her cheek against Jada's and whispered in her ear, "I could get used to this. To us."

Jada nestled into Charley's embrace. "Ah, now you're getting the hang of it."

"I am?"

"Yep. All romantic and stuff. Saying things like that gets you huge points, baby."

Charley kissed her temple. "And I want points, right?"

"Oh yeah. You totally want points." Jada put her hands over Charley's, where they rested against her belly. Jada continued to fantasized about those soft, firm, strong hands. How they'd feel on her heated skin, sliding along her body. "Fuck," she muttered, trying to shake off the effects of her little daydream.

"What?" Charley asked, her lips still very close to Jada's ear.

"Nothing," she said. "I think I'm getting hungry."

"Hungry? You? Say it isn't so."

"Smart-ass." Jada pointed down the street at a hotdog cart. "I'm going to go over there and get a hotdog, fully loaded with sauerkraut, onions, mustard, and pickles. Want one?" She turned around to look at Charley's face.

"I don't know. I've never had all that on a hotdog."

Jada faked being shocked. "I will fix this right now. Be back in a few minutes."

"Can you get me a bottle of water?"

"Totally." Jada took off, very aware of Charley watching her every move. The crowd was thicker now, and it took forever to reach the cart. Another twenty minutes passed before Jada could get her order and head back to Charley.

When she arrived, Jada held out the hotdog like it was a trophy. "You're going to love this." She took a bite of hers and watched Charley do the same. The smile on her face said it all. "I knew it! Still glad you came here with me?"

"If you keep feeding me stuff like this"—Charley took another huge bite and spoke around the food in her mouth—"I'll follow you anywhere."

"Awesome." Jada handed Charley her water and glanced

at her watch. "Parade's going to be here soon." She finished her hotdog in record time and inched her way closer to the curb, tugging Charley along behind her. "This is going to be so freaking cool!"

"It certainly is." Charley wrapped her arms around Jada again. "Thanks, Jada. I really needed this."

Jada twisted her head around, smiled at Charley, and kissed her softly on the lips. "So did I."

****

The parade lasted two hours, and they spent the rest of the afternoon wandering around Times Square, weaving in and out of the throngs of people. Jada kept a tight grip on Charley's hand, determined to keep close to her. They stopped at a crosswalk, and as they waited on the light to turn, Charley looked at their clasped hands and grinned.

"Afraid I'm going to run away?"

"Nope." Jada gave her hand a squeeze. "I want to make sure no one comes along and tries to take you away." She kissed her cheek. "I've seen more than one person sizing you up. They need to know you're mine and I don't share."

Charley laughed and tugged Jada across the street when the light turned green. "You ready to get something to eat?"

"Totally." Jada noticed a crowd around a statue and maneuvered Charley until they were close enough to see it. The stone base read, "Rumors of War." Jada craned her neck to take in the life-sized vision of a young African American man atop a magnificent horse, ready for battle. The man wore modern clothes, Nike shoes, and his long hair was in a knot at the top of his head. He was twisted to look behind himself.

"Wow," Jada whispered the word reverently.

"Beautiful, isn't it?" A woman next to Jada spoke, and her accent made Jada think she was native to New York. "It won't be here long."

"Why not?" Jada asked.

The woman flipped her rainbow-colored dreads over her shoulder. "It's meant to be temporary. It's headed down to Virginia where it's going to sit among a bunch of Civil War statues."

Jada tried hard to dredge up notes from American history. "That's in the south, right?"

The woman gave her a comical look and turned her head to the side, making her dreads swish with the movements. Her deep brown eyes locked on Jada's. "Where you from?"

"Ottawa."

"That's in Canada, right?"

Jada laughed. "It is. So why Virginia?"

The woman grinned and a spark of mischief gleamed in her eyes. "So it can sit next to all those southern bastards and give 'em the finger. See, this statue is made to look like a famous one of General Robert E. Lee. The irony and the symbolism are amazing. And he's going to sit on Arthur Ashe Boulevard in Richmond. It'll be great."

Jada mirrored the woman's smile. "Now that sounds pretty damn cool." She glanced at Charley, who was getting jittery with the growing crowd. She needed to get her away from the people and find a nice spot to eat. "Thanks for the info, but I think I need to feed my girlfriend."

"Oh, you gotta try the West End Bar and Grill. Best spot in the city. It's on 8th between 50th and 48th." She leaned close enough to whisper to Jada, "Enjoy the rest of your day with your hottie." She gave Jada a little poke with her elbow and disappeared among the masses.

Jada muttered, "Hot indeed."

"What's hot?" Charley asked.

Jada kissed her solidly on the lips, lingering a bit longer than usual. "Duh. C'mon. I just got a tip on a great place to eat."

"Who needs food?" Charley returned her kiss and acquiesced to being led away.

More than an hour passed before they were seated and enjoying the most amazing, gigantic, Chorizo burger Jada'd ever had in her life. She had to cut it up to eat it because no way could she get her mouth open so far. She swallowed her mouthful of yumminess and looked across the table to find Charley laughing at her. "What?"

"Just having fun watching you gobble your food." She snatched a fry from Jada's dish. "I mean, where the hell do you put it?"

"In my ass." Jada gave her a saucy wink. "You wanna

check it out?"

"Hell, yes. Want do it here or in the hotel later?"

Jada nearly spit out the food from her next bite. "You're killin' me!"

"You started it." She went for another fry only to get her fingers smacked. "Hey!"

"My food. Eat your own."

"Meanie."

"You have no idea." Jada gently tapped Charley's leg with her foot. "I got lots to show you. Just you wait."

Charley kept grinning. Jada continued to enjoy her meal and the look of happiness on Charley's face.

****

Dinner was a nice, slow affair, and Jada almost wished it wouldn't end. But after two hours, they decided to go back to the hotel. They were well into the evening now, and traffic was horrible. Then again, Jada hadn't seen a moment when traffic wasn't horrible. But she didn't let that deter her excitement one bit. She didn't have to drive and could sit back and enjoy the ride.

She spent most of the trip talking about the parade and their journey through the center of New York City. She flipped through hundreds of photos on her phone and couldn't stop herself from recounting some of the floats they'd seen. The excitement bubbled up in her like it did when she was a little kid at Christmas time.

"I'm probably driving you nuts right now," she said, once they were inside the room.

"Nah. I love it when you rattle on and on about something you like." Charley caught Jada in her arms, which stopped her from looking at more photos. "You've had a smile on your face all day, and I love how happy you are right now." She gently traced the edges of Jada's mouth with her fingertips. "You're even more beautiful when you smile."

"I haven't had this much fun in years."

"Me either, to be honest." Charley's eyes held her with such deep emotion Jada could cry. Charley gently caressed Jada's cheek. "Thanks."

"Not necessary." Jada leaned closer, and her lips hovered

over Charley's. "Trust me, there's no one else I'd rather be with." She closed the distance between them and allowed this beautiful connection to come alive in her kiss.

Charley's fingers gently held Jada's face as their mouths melded together, tongues seeking each other as their passion heated up.

Jada's hands stroked the taut muscles of Charley's back. Charley's breathing increased as Jada guided her toward the bed. She pulled Charley's shirt up and over her head as they went. Charley's knees hit the mattress, and she fell onto it. Jada straddled her and they looked at each other so intensely it stole Jada's breath.

Jada'd had sex with several women in her life, but she'd never felt such a powerful connection as she did with Charley. It frightened her and for a moment she hesitated.

It was enough to slow the progress of their passion. Charley looked at her with an expression Jada wasn't able to decipher. She leaned closer to Charley and put a hand on either side of her head to support herself. "You are a beautiful woman." Jada kissed her sweetly and explored her mouth with tenderness meant to tell Charley how she felt. "The most amazing woman I've ever met."

"Jada, I—"

Jada quieted her with more kisses, then she leveraged herself so one hand explored the soft skin of Charley's breasts. She was in the process of removing the bra when Charley's hand stilled her own.

"We have to stop," Charley said, catching Jada's gaze. "Please."

"Sure." Jada reluctantly stood up and let Charley get up as well. They stood face-to-face for a few awkward moments, before Jada wrapped her arms around Charley's strong body. "I didn't mean to get carried away there. But you got to know I'm attracted to you in a big way. Right?"

Charley laughed. "I sort of figured it out. But thanks for stopping."

"I won't ever do anything you don't want to do." Jada rested her head on Charley's shoulder. "I promise. So why don't we get ready for bed? I'd like to curl up against you and go to sleep."

"Sounds like a great idea." Charley kissed Jada's forehead. "As long as I can watch a bit of TV while we cuddle. I'm still very awake."

Jada chuckled. "Same. Let's get ready for bed and find us a nice action movie to watch."

Charley joined her laughter. "Deal."

Chapter Fifteen

Three days later, Jada stepped into the CoffeeNut feeling better than she had in years. Like each step was lighter than the one before as she floated to the counter. Stefi greeted her with her amazing smile and began working on her order.

"Looks like a caramel macchiato kind of day," Stefi said. She reached into the display case and nabbed a cookie-flavored donut. "The kind of day you spend eating more sugar than you should. Am I right?"

"How the hell do you do it?" Jada laughed and took the offered donut. The place wasn't busy, and once Stefi served her coffee, she pointed to a nearby table, where they sat across from each other.

"I've always been good at reading people. As Charley puts it, it's my superpower."

"Yeah, she's more nuts about superheroes than I am, and that's saying something."

Jada sipped her drink, and her smile never faded. Stefi said, "She's something special."

"She is." Jada sighed and leaned back in the chair. "I sent her a text this morning. I'm off and feel like going for a drive. I thought she'd like to get out of the apartment for a bit."

"I bet she does. How's her hand? I haven't seen her in a while."

"Slowly improving, though not fast enough for her. She's worried she'll lose her job if she can't get it back to normal. I'm worried it might not happen, but she won't talk about it."

Stefi nodded slowly. "She shuts down when she doesn't want to talk about something bothering her."

Jada finished off her donut and asked, "Do you have any advice? How I can get her to talk to me? I get the sense something is going on in that handsome head of hers, but for the life of me, I can't get it out of her."

"Don't try. Let her come to you. Has she told you about

Raina?"

Jada narrowed her gaze at Stefi. "She said she died, but how she died wasn't important."

"Oh, it's important." Stefi's expression turned sad. "It was tragic, and I won't give you details because it's for Charley to do, but how she died matters more to Charley than losing her job as a Mountie."

The door chimed as someone came in and Stefi excused herself.

Jada stared after her. She let her drink go cold as she contemplated Stefi's words. What meant more to Charley than being a Mountie? Why did the cause of Raina's death hold so much power over her?

Was there a car crash Charley was responsible for?

Or a home accident Charley felt was her fault?

Did she have an illness neither of them saw the symptoms of before it was too late?

Or maybe Charley wasn't there when Raina died?

Stefi took her seat again. "You'll go nuts trying to figure it out. Charley will eventually have to tell you what happened. You might need to start asking hard questions to get her to do it." Stefi held Jada's gaze for a moment. "I think you two are perfect for each other. I haven't seen her smile so much in a long time. And in the short span I've known you, I can see a major difference. Your face glows when you talk about her, and your eyes light up."

"Should I push her about Raina though? If it hurts—"

"Don't push. Ask questions. Get her talking about Raina. Even if it's how did they meet or where they got married. She doesn't know how cathartic it will be."

The door chimed again, and more customers entered. Stefi slid off the chair. "Be gentle with her, Jada. Her heart is a fragile thing." Stefi went back to the counter and sported her most winning smile at her new customers.

Jada sent another text to Charley to ask her if she was available. Her first two texts had gone unanswered. She waited a few minutes then gave her a call. It went right to voicemail and her gut told her something was wrong. Jada tossed away her trash and headed directly to Charley's apartment.

****

Charley slammed the door of her truck closed. Anger mixed with despair fueled each footstep as she stomped up the stairs to her apartment. She opened the door and slammed it shut, too, shaking the walls when she did. She threw her keys in the general area of the kitchen, where they bounced off the table and landed somewhere on the floor.

She tried to flex her left hand and screamed her rage when it wouldn't work. She still couldn't get her fingers to close enough to make a fist. Zander thought she'd made progress. Her middle finger bent forty degrees now, up from thirty-five last week. Her other fingers ranged around sixty-five degrees, but there was still pain when she bent them.

Not good enough. She was terrified it would never be good enough. And what would happen then? What if she never returned to duty? Being a Mountie was all she knew—all she'd ever studied or trained for. All she had left. Charley spent a lot of time feeling useless, except when she was with Jada. Cooped up in her apartment and unable to do the one thing she knew best, the one thing that had always helped her cope with Raina's death. She would easily lose herself in her work and not have to think about the woman she still loved.

Not think about walking into the bathroom to find her lying in the middle of a pool of blood, a shotgun lying across her body with a string tied to the trigger—and the other end tied to the doorknob.

She would never shake the image of Raina's blood spattered all over the white tiles. Brain matter mixed with the blood. Her beautiful face no longer there, blown apart by the blast of the gun.

Charley started shaking and had to rush to the bathroom before she spewed her lunch all over the living room floor. She barely got to the toilet in time. Afterward, she sat down and leaned against the edge of the tub. She kept her eyes closed and willed herself to not revisit the horror of Raina's death. But the images were already there, jamming her mind with horror and pain.

She'd kept so busy with her work she never realized how

connected she was to it. How insulated she was from the one thing that could break her. Had nearly destroyed her.

The year she spent with her parents after Raina's death was a blur. She was like a zombie, moving around by rote without any purpose other than to survive. Which she did, but at what cost? Only her work had helped her survive.

Now she had no defense against the memories, and they were coming more frequently. Her only solace was in Jada's arms.

Charley stumbled to her feet and quickly cleaned herself up. She changed her clothes and went into the living room, where she paced the entirety of it. So many thoughts ran through her brain, and her head pounded with each heartbeat.

She considered calling Debra, but she didn't know what to say. Was she having a breakdown? A panic attack? What the hell was wrong with her?

One minute she was hurting over the prospect of losing her vocation, and the next—the next she was reliving a nightmare. How could she possibly explain it to anyone? Even her new psychologist.

Tears streamed down her cheeks, and she didn't try to stop them. Everything hurt and she didn't know what to do. She wondered if she ever would.

A knock at her door broke into her thoughts, and she balked at answering it. Whoever was there would certainly go away soon enough.

"I know you're in there." Jada's muffled voice reached her. "I saw your truck in the parking lot, and your mom hasn't heard from you all day. You haven't answered my texts or calls, so I'm here to find out what's going on." There was a long pause. Charley didn't budge from her place near the window. "Please, Sarge. Don't shut me out. I care about you. I want to help you."

Charley took a tentative step forward, but she wasn't able to make herself reach for the doorknob.

She imagined Jada leaning against the door as she continued to speak. "I know something's wrong. I can feel it. Please. Don't make me stand out here and beg you to open the door."

The urge to let Jada in was strong but not strong enough. Jada was special and beautiful and deserved so much more than

Charley was able to give her. She'd failed Raina and couldn't bear repeating her mistake. The best she could do for Jada was to walk away. No matter how much it tore at her heart.

There was a long pause, and Charley thought Jada must have left.

She hadn't.

"I don't know what to say to you to make you understand I'm here for you. I want to help you. You can tell me anything. You can trust me. I'll never judge you. You don't have to say a word. I want to come in there and put my arms around you and let you know how much you mean to me."

Charley made it to the door and peered out the peephole. Jada was leaning against the door, her posture slumped and her face turned toward the apartment, as if she could see Charley by doing so. Her hair was in a mass of curls on top of her head, held in place by the rainbow hairband. She was dressed in cutoff shorts and a white T-shirt. So beautiful.

The peephole gave a distorted view, but Charley thought she saw tears on Jada's cheeks.

Was she hurting Jada by pushing her away? Her chest clenched at the thought.

"I'm going to leave. Please call me or text me, okay? I'm worried about you. I'm sorry I can't do more for you," Jada said softly then pushed off the door and headed for the stairwell. She was gone from Charley's view, but Charley kept looking out there anyway, until her eye got tired and she had to step back.

Charley now realized her hand was on the doorknob. It would have taken so little effort to turn it and let Jada in. But letting her in was far bigger than a literal open door. Charley had remained closed off for so many years she wasn't sure she'd ever be able to open up to anyone again.

She released the knob and backed away. Her hand shook as she dialed the one person she trusted most in the world.

****

Jada sat in her car in the parking lot of Charley's apartment building for more than half an hour to stop crying and compose herself enough to go home. Only she didn't want to go home. She wanted to go back up those stairs and barge into

Charley's apartment. She wanted to make the woman confront whatever the hell was wrong. What kind of relationship would they have if they couldn't talk?

More tears came and she cussed at herself for being so damn emotional. If Charley didn't want to talk to her that was Charley's prerogative. Right? So why did it squeeze her heart to realize Charley literally locked her out?

Jada leaned her head against the driver's side window and let the tears flow. She couldn't stop them if she tried.

A tap on the window startled her. She sat up and saw Grace looking at her with deep concern. Jada opened the door and stepped out of the car. "Hey there," she said as she wiped her cheeks dry.

"I can probably guess what happened, but why don't you tell me instead? You look like you need a friend."

"I—I thought I was being a friend. I mean, I came here because she ignored my calls and texts. I knew something was wrong, but I have no clue what. She didn't even open the door, though I know she's in there. I heard her moving around inside."

"Yeah, she's in there. She called me to come over." Grace held up a hand when Jada started to speak. "She's angry and hurt, and I'm the one person she won't take it out on. If you go in there, she'll yell and scream and it won't be pretty. I've seen this side of her once before. Trust me, whatever happened today was huge. When she called me, she was crying."

"Gracie, I'm her girlfriend. If she can't talk to me about this, then what kind of future do we have? We need to trust each other. Be there for each other. It's not a one-way street." Jada tried not to let it, but anger welled inside her.

"I get it. I do. But right now she can't talk to you. I don't know what's going on with her, but I will find out." Grace shoved her hands into her jeans pockets and rocked back on her heels. "She hasn't been like this since Raina died. I'm worried about her."

"Me, too. But it's clear she doesn't need me, so I'll go." Jada started to get back into her car, but Grace stopped her. "No, don't try to placate me, Gracie. I came here to help her. She's rejecting me. It's going to be very hard to come back from that." Jada got in, started the car, and left before Grace said another word.

****

Grace steeled herself and knocked on Charley's door. She didn't answer right away. The expression on her dear friend's face almost made her cry. She looked lost, broken, and spent. Grace closed the door, and opened her arms, and enveloped Charley in a tender embrace.

Heartbreaking sobs wracked Charley's body as she clung to Grace.

Grace whispered soothing words to her and waited patiently for her to calm down. As the tears dried up, Grace led Charley to the kitchen table and got her to sit down. She found a box of tissues and handed them to her.

"You want some coffee?"

"Sure," Charley said between sniffles. "I'm a fucking mess, Gracie."

"I know." Grace got the coffee started. She leaned against the counter and faced Charley. "Want to tell me exactly what happened?"

Charley stared at her hands until Grace put the coffee cup in front of her. She wrapped her hands around it but never took a drink. Her injured hand didn't quite grip the cup. Grace sat down to wait her out.

"I'm having nightmares again, but only when I sleep alone. The week Jada and I spent in New York was magical, and I didn't think of Raina in a negative way. But we're back now, and reality is setting in again. I blew up at Zander today over the lack of progress with my hand, but I don't think it was the whole reason I got so pissed.

"If I can't go back to work, then I not only lose my vocation, but I have time to sit around and remember Raina. I need to be so busy I don't have time to think about her."

"No." Grace gentled her voice. "You need to call Debra and set up an immediate appointment." She lightly patted Charley's injured hand. "Trust me on this. You're going to call her right now. If you want, I'll go with you. You can't keep going on like this, Charley. You're going to open up and tell her everything."

Grace held her hand out, and Charley placed her cell

phone in it. She found the number for Debra and pressed Call.

Within ten minutes, Charley had an appointment with Debra later in the evening. Charley slouched in her chair and shook her head as she put her phone away. "You're a bossy woman, Gracie Lee. You know?"

Grace laughed. "Liv has mentioned it once or twice. But I think you need a bossy woman in your life. Someone like Jada maybe?"

"Are we back to her now?"

"We are. She was in the parking lot when I got here." Grace paused and watched a slew of emotions cross Charley's face. "She was crying."

"I couldn't open the door, Gracie. Literally. I had my hand on the doorknob and couldn't turn it to let her in. I couldn't handle her seeing me like this—I was shaking and crying. So I called you."

"How much does she know about Raina?"

Charley didn't answer for a moment. "Only that she died."

"How do you feel about Jada?" Grace watched a tiny smile find its way to Charley's face. "Ah. I don't think I need you to answer. You've been talking nonstop about her and New York since you got back. You're in love with her, aren't you?"

Charley nodded. "The thing is, I don't think I'm good enough for her." Grace started to protest, but Charley held her hand up to stop her. "I'm broken, Gracie. I just didn't realize how broken until today. I mean, the thought of never working again sent me into a meltdown. I had flashbacks of finding Raina. I ended up puking my guts up."

"You need to tell Jada what's going on."

"No way. I don't want to have her go screaming for the hills. I'd rather let her walk away now. I've hurt her enough as it is."

"It's not a decision you should be making for her, Charley. Don't you think Jada deserves to know what's going on? Let her choose for herself?"

"I—I don't know. Maybe."

"Maybe?" Grace almost laughed. "Honey, *maybe* is progress. But let's see if we can't get you to *definitely*. Why don't you call her? See if she'll come back over. I'll wait until she gets here and go home so you can talk in private."

"I don't know if I can."

"I don't think you can avoid it. If you do, you'll regret it."

Charley picked up her phone and hesitated. "Gracie—"

"Don't stall. Do it."

"Fine." Charley pulled up Jada's number and hit the Phone icon. After five rings, it went to voicemail. She left a brief message asking Jada to call her and hit the End icon. "Now what?"

"She might still be in her car," Grace said. "Give her time."

Charley put the phone down and spun it around on the table. "What do I do in the meantime?"

"You talk to your best friend."

"Have I told you how much I love you, Gracie Lee?"

"Like a sister, I know." She blew Charley a kiss. "How about I feed you?"

"I don't know if I can eat."

"Well, your belly's empty, so you should eat. Did your mom stock the fridge again?" Grace stood and opened the refrigerator.

"She did. There's lots in there to pick from."

"Excellent." Grace choose a couple of plastic containers and set them on the table. "After dinner you can try calling Jada again. If she doesn't answer, don't worry about it. She might need some time."

"I hope you're right."

"Me, too."

****

The phone rang again and Jada ignored it. She'd been home all of five minutes and assumed Charley called her at Grace's prodding. It's not what Jada wanted. She wanted Charley to do it on her own.

On the next set of rings, Jada grabbed the phone and hit Answer. "I don't want to talk to you right now." She almost hung up before she realized it was her sister's face staring at her, not Charley's.

After the debacle with the tablet, she'd set up her cell phone with Skype, and because she paid no attention to what she was doing, Jada now found herself staring at her sister. Tears streamed down her face, and from the looks of her surroundings, Celeste was in a hospital.

"Oh shit, Celeste. I'm sorry. I didn't realize it was you. What's wrong? Did something happen with the baby?"

"Maybe, I'm not sure. I felt a sharp pain and started bleeding. Anton called an ambulance, and I just now got to the labor and delivery ward. I'm waiting for my ob-gyn to get here."

"Bleeding? How much? Are we talking placental abruption here?" The idea the placenta may have separated from the uterus terrified Jada. Celeste must be feeling the same, or worse.

"Maybe. The ER doctor suspects I have preeclampsia, so I'm going to have another ultrasound in a few minutes." She sniffled and someone handed her a tissue.

"Is Anton with you?"

"Yes. He's right here, but—" Celeste's face scrunched up in pain for a few seconds. The phone's camera view went lower, and Jada saw Anton was holding Celeste's hand. Her sister was so lucky to have such a loving husband.

"Hey, you get some rest, okay? You need to take it easy. You know this. Keep your blood pressure low. Even if it means staying in bed."

"I don't want to ask you," Celeste said through clenched teeth as more pain must have hit her.

"Give Anton the phone, honey."

Celeste whimpered as she passed the phone to Anton. His chubby face was soon there, his eyes wide with fear. "Hey."

"Hey," Jada said. "Tell me what else is going on."

Anton's gaze was still on Celeste as he spoke. "She's afraid to ask you to come home. She needs you."

Jada was moved by the tears in his eyes. She didn't think she could cry anymore today, but the tears came all the same.

Anton said, "Please. Can you come over? Even for a few days?"

"Of course I can. Let me get work taken care of, and I'll be on the first flight there. I'll call you when I get to Ottawa. You text me or call me if anything changes, okay?"

"I will. Thanks, Jada."

"I'll see you soon. Give her a hug and a kiss from me."

"Will do." He disconnected and Jada immediately dialed work. She hadn't been there long enough to log any vacation time, and taking off like this would seriously dent her savings, but she simply had to go. She saw no other choice. Her sister needed her. It may be selfish, but she was glad someone did.

Chapter Sixteen

The ride to Ottawa General was excruciating. Traffic was horrible. Jada arrived at the airport at the start of rush hour, and every second it took to get to the hospital felt like hours. Jada's knee bounced in frustration, her energy high despite being exhausted.

She'd not slept at all last night, worry and fear keeping her up. Several times she started to call Charley. Charley wouldn't talk to her about her own problems. Why would she listen to Jada now?

She checked her phone. No new texts from Anton. Twenty minutes ago, he'd said Liselle was there and was taking charge of Celeste's care.

Which would not help Celeste's stress level one bit. Probably why she hadn't heard from Anton, because he had his hands full buffering Celeste from their mother.

Jada glanced out the window as the city so familiar to her crept by. Excitement at being back gave her a tiny thrill, but the knowledge she wouldn't be welcome clouded it. She'd never feel at home here again.

It also occurred to her she may know some of the staff taking care of Celeste. She used to know so many people—knew her way around the hospital like she did her own home. Except she didn't feel comfortable there any longer. The entire situation was untenable, and were it not for Celeste, Jada would be quite happy to stay in Whitehorse.

But her happiness didn't matter. She was there to hold Celeste's hand and help her through whatever lay ahead. Her own past be damned.

An hour later they were at the hospital. Jada paid the driver, grabbed her backpack and carry-on bag, and got out. She'd not bothered to pack a lot of clothes. She and Celeste were the same size, and whatever she needed, she could borrow or buy.

She rushed through the front doors and directly to the

elevator to the labor and delivery ward. The friendly volunteer looked at her curiously as she hurried by, giving her a little wave. Jada hoped the woman hadn't recognized her.

The elevator came and she was on the third floor in no time. She had Celeste's room number and navigated past nurses, doctors, and technicians to her destination. The sight gave her pause.

Anton sat on the edge of the bed, cradling Celeste in his arms. She looked like she was asleep. Her husband quietly wiped tears from his eyes. He looked up at Jada and tried to smile, but it didn't quite reach his eyes.

Jada waved, entered the room, and put her backpack and carry-on near the door.

Celeste was pale, dark spots underlined her eyes, and her usually full face was drawn. Her lips were pulled down, even though she slept peacefully. Jada's eyes followed the IV line to the bag, and she assessed the medication Celeste was getting. Then her gaze flicked to the heart monitor and fetal heart monitor and took in that information as well. At the moment, her sister was stable.

She sank into the chair beside the bed and gently touched the back of Celeste's hand. Her gaze finally met Anton's, and she saw relief there. At least now he'd have someone else there. She sometimes wondered if he missed his family in Vancouver.

Celeste stirred a little, and when her eyes fluttered open, they landed on Jada. She smiled weakly, and Anton took the opportunity to settle her against the pillows. "Hey," she said, her voice weak. "How long you been here?"

"Few minutes. Came right from the airport." Jada took a firm hold on Celeste's hand and brought it to her lips. "How you feeling?"

"Tired. Like I've worked a twenty-four hour shift. It's all taking a toll on me and the baby." Her free hand rubbed her extended belly. "But I felt a lot of kicking this morning. Maybe the baby's mad at all the fuss going on."

"Or maybe the little one's saying, 'Hey, I'm good. No worries here.'" Jada smiled at her and placed a hand on Celeste's belly. "I'm sure the baby's fine, sis. Seriously. You know you're in good hands here."

"I do, but try telling Mom. Oh God, Jada. She's been like

a madwoman around here. She gave my doctor hell for not catching this sooner, like the woman should have ESP or something."

"She knows damn well you can't predict an abruption. You have to deal with it."

"Exactly."

Anton kissed Celeste on the forehead. "I'm going to take a minute to get something to drink. Either of you want anything?"

Celeste declined, but Jada asked for anything resembling coffee. Anton agreed and quietly left. She had the feeling he was giving them some alone time. Jada returned her attention to Celeste. "Is it an abruption?"

"Yes, but it's not critical. I'm stuck here until the baby comes. Doctor Lisa doesn't want to take any chances. So for the next five to ten weeks I'm here, waiting for this little person to make themselves known."

Jada examined the static, white room around them. "If you're going to be here awhile, then I'm going to have to liven the place up. This is boring as hell."

Celeste snorted. "Anton said the same thing, but Mom told him no. He doesn't want to cause trouble, so he backed down. I did like his ideas though. I wouldn't mind some color and a few things from home. Doctor Lisa says it's a great idea. Lots of expectant moms do it when they're going to be here awhile. It's restful and what I need."

"I got this," Jada said with confidence. "And I'm going to stay here with you. I'll camp on your couch, since you were mean enough to turn the guest room into a nursery."

"We got a blowup bed. More comfy than the couch." Celeste looked down at their connected hands. "Thanks for coming. I don't think I can do this without you."

"Of course you can, but you don't have to. It's what sisters do, right?"

"What about your new job? How long can you stay?"

"I took emergency leave, and I'm here until your baby is born and you're good on your own. If it means ten weeks, fine. If longer, also fine. Besides, I can always get a job somewhere else if I need to. Not like I don't have amazing skills."

Celeste looked skeptical. "I don't want to mess things up for you."

"You aren't. I promise." Jada's phone announced a text, and she took a moment to check it out. Charley. She didn't bother to read it and tucked her phone away.

"Who was that?" Celeste asked.

"No one I need to talk to right now."

"Oh no." Celeste squeezed Jada's hand. "Tell me you didn't have a fight with Charley. Was it because you left so suddenly? Please tell me I didn't get between you two."

"No. On all counts. We never had a fight, and that's part of the issue. Look, you don't need to be worrying about me right now. Charley and I—we'll either work it out or we won't. Nothing I can do about it right now."

"You should read her text."

"I will." Jada kissed Celeste's hand again. "Later. I'm here with you right now."

Celeste opened her mouth to respond but closed it abruptly. Jada didn't have to look behind her to know their mother had walked in.

"I was wondering if you'd show up," Liselle said. She came around the bed so she was on the opposite side from Jada.

"Of course I came."

"You didn't need to. I've got things under control."

"I'm sure you think you do," Jada said. She felt Celeste's hand tremble and pulled back on her anger. The person always most affected by their arguing was Celeste. "We should let Celeste get some sleep. Why don't you and I go to the cafeteria for some lunch? I haven't eaten since I left last night."

"You aren't any good to anyone if you get sick." Liselle patted Celeste's hand and said, "Sleep. We'll talk later today after I've seen your doctor. I saw Anton and sent him home. He needs to get some rest as well, and he can't do anything right now. Besides, I'm here."

"Mom—" Celeste stopped herself and nodded.

Liselle and Jada quietly left the room. Neither woman spoke on the elevator ride to the cafeteria. They strode down the hallway together in perfect precision, side by side through the double doors of the cafeteria, each grabbing a salad and bottled water. Liselle insisted on paying for the food, which Jada let her do without question, then followed her to a table in the back section where hospital staff normally ate.

Liselle spoke to a few people as they passed, before she sat down with her back to the entrance. Her steely gaze was directed at Jada, and no matter how much she hated to admit it, those eyes affected Jada. Like she was a teenager again and about to get told off.

"I wish your sister had said something sooner. She's been having pains for a few days. She didn't think it worth mentioning until she started bleeding and needed an ambulance." Liselle practically ripped off the lid to her water, cracking the seal like it was a nut. "I tried to get Doctor Van Dyne assigned to her care, but he refused to push Doctor Klein out of the way. He's much more qualified to deal with this. I did get him to agree to consult."

"What's wrong with Doctor Lisa?" Jada preferred the more familiar moniker. Celeste spoke highly of Doctor Lisa, and from what Jada knew, she was well regarded among her peers.

"She's not as good as Doctor Van Dyne."

"Van Dyne has been around forever, but it doesn't mean he's better than Doctor Lisa. She's good, Mom. She's taking excellent care of Celeste."

"Did you read her chart?"

"No. I got here half an hour ago. I checked out the monitors. Everything's stable right now. She hasn't had any more pain other than the few times the baby kicked. As long as she stays in bed and rests, she'll be fine. Besides, even if the baby has to come out, she's twenty-five weeks along. They'll be okay."

"There's too much risk at twenty-five weeks, and you know it. Premature babies are at risk for any number of complications. She needs to get as close to full term as she can."

"Duh." Jada almost grinned at the look her mother gave her. The remark was childish but she felt better for saying it. "You do realize the neonatal unit here is one of the best in the country."

"You do realize I work here."

Jada rolled her eyes. "Of course. I think you slammed me more times over the years with your great accomplishments at this place than I can count. I have them all memorized. Probably what you want so I can give an accurate eulogy at your funeral." She didn't detect any hurt in Liselle's expression, only annoyance.

"You should be working here as well. Running off to the wilderness didn't change a thing. It made you look bad."

"No, it made me get a good night's sleep. I was being hounded relentlessly by reporters and online trolls to the point where I had to change my telephone number. Hell, I even got a new phone to wipe it clean of social media and pictures of Francine. That shit broke me, Mom."

"You should have come to me for help. Do you think I wouldn't have done something to set it right?"

"Honestly, no." Jada forgot her food and leaned back in the chair, arms crossed over her chest. "When was the last time you helped me do anything? Before the incident with Nancy, the last thing you said to me was I should break it off with Francine. You were more worried about me dating a surgeon you didn't like than you were about anything else. What any woman I date has to do with you is beyond me."

Liselle pinned her with a gaze that told Jada instantly she was in for another scathing lecture. Liselle didn't disappoint. "That woman was bad news, and I told you so from the start. You were a conquest, nothing more. She makes a game of going after every available man or woman in this hospital to see how many she can get. The entire time you were together, she was out there having sex with anyone available. I always thought you were smart, Jada. But clearly you had no idea she was being unfaithful to you. For four of the five years you were together."

Jada couldn't form a reply. She'd suspected Francine was unfaithful, but with their crazy schedules, it was often hard to get together. She never blinked an eye when Francine had to leave in the middle of the night. She was a trauma surgeon, and they get called in at all kinds of crazy hours.

Yet the look on her mother's face confirmed she was telling the truth. Liselle was a real bitch, but she wasn't a liar.

The news should have crushed her. Jada should be angry or hurt or both. She should want to go confront Francine and tell her off. Except she felt nothing and realized Francine no longer meant anything to her. Her heart belonged to Charley, even if it was breaking.

"It's in the past, Mom. And she has nothing to do with why I left. I was upset and hurt she broke up with me when the fake news story got out there, because I needed her. My sister, as always, came through for me, so I'm good. It's over. I'm here for Celeste. I don't plan to see anyone or do anything that isn't for or about her."

"You can't possibly be happy up there."

Jada took a deep breath and slowly let it out to calm herself before she replied, "You don't know me, Mom. It's nice up there. A slower pace for sure, but I like it. I've made friends. I've got a good job. I'm fine."

"Be that as it may, you belong here with your family."

"I belong wherever I decide to belong. Period."

Liselle stared at her for a few moments before getting started on her food. "Eat your lunch. We need to get back to Celeste's room so we can work out a schedule."

Jada was shocked she'd won the round with Liselle, as evidenced by the change in topic. She asked, "What schedule?"

"For who will sit with Celeste and when. She shouldn't be alone."

"Already done." Jada slowly started eating. "Anton and I will take turns. When I'm at their house, I can keep it clean and make sure there's food in the fridge so neither of us starves. He's going to work at the hospital sometimes, and we'll take turns sleeping there. Your schedule is too busy, so you can come when you have time. We got this."

Liselle didn't say anything for the longest time, and Jada got ready for another fight. She was shocked when Liselle nodded. "Fine. But I'm still going to have Doctor Van Dyne examine her. She needs a second opinion."

And that was it.

Jada's brain worked furiously to wrap itself around the fact she'd had a mostly civilized conversation with her mother. They finished lunch in silence and walked back to Celeste's room. As they walked, Jada's mind went to Charley and how much she wanted to tell her about this breakthrough with Liselle. But it would have to wait. Their wounds were still very raw.

Best she concentrate on Celeste.

Chapter Seventeen

Paperwork, Charley decided, was a wholly unnecessary part of police work. They had computers. Every car had an MDT, Mobile Data Terminal, and a tablet. All of it was backed up in triplicate, mostly in real time, to avoid losing anything. So why the hell did so much paperwork even exist? As she shuffled through it, she wondered how many trees sacrificed their lives to the cause.

Then she spotted Neil Burns. The only millennial in the world who was a complete techno idiot. He barely understood how to use his smart phone. The MDT was like a foreign language to him, instead of the amazing helper it was meant to be. There wasn't much to it. You press a button to let dispatch know you got a call, press a button when you got there, and press a button when you were done. Type in notes about the call, and everything uploaded to a server for you.

But Burns tried to do most of it while driving, and last week he crashed his cruiser into a parked car. Charley was glad he wasn't on her shift, because she'd have to worry about him using a weapon. In fifteen years, she'd never pulled her weapon from the holster while on a call. Burns however, had done it twice in three years. Once was to show off to a rookie. He was a menace, and so inept with computers, he was part of the reason they still printed things out.

She glanced down at her hands, her left one cramped a little from the workout, and wished like hell it was Burns doing this so she could get out on the road again. Burns gave her a limp salute and wandered off to do damage somewhere else.

"See they've got you hard at work," a female voice spoke behind her. As one of only two women in the department, Charley knew exactly who it was.

"Well, someone's got to make sure things are organized around here. Not like the shift corporal is doing her job."

"The shift corporal is a busy woman. It's nice to have a

lackey to do the work." Charley didn't look up when she heard the distinct creak of leather as Elle sat in the chair beside her, leaned back, and put her feet on the counter. "So, lackey, how goes it?"

"Eh. I'm wondering what the hell I was thinking when I asked for light duty. This sucks. I see everyone coming and going and end up dealing with nonsense callers all day. I'm glad I can type one-handed because I've filled out more reports in the last week than I did the last month I was on the road. I had no idea how many people call here every day. Hell, I think I've talked to everyone in the city."

"You probably have, my friend." Elle had a smile that lit up a room when she walked in. She dazzled Charley with that smile now. "How long is your desk duty sentence?"

Charley flexed her left hand a little. She still couldn't get her middle finger to bend properly, but the other fingers were stronger. "Zander, my physio guy, says another couple of months. Surgeon doesn't think I need any more surgery, but I have to get another nerve test at the end of this month. Make sure things are still connected right, I guess."

Elle tilted her head a bit, as if assessing Charley. That particular look always unnerved Charley. Like Elle knew what she was thinking. "You doing okay? I heard through the grapevine you broke up with your girlfriend."

"Does the grapevine serve drinks at the Pot O'Gold?"

"It does."

"It's wrong. Tell Izzy Jada left town on a family emergency. We didn't break up." Charley looked down at the report she needed to fill out. Technically, this was true. They hadn't broken up. But they also hadn't spoken in a couple of weeks.

"There's more to it, I can tell." Elle dropped her feet to the ground and kept her gaze on Charley. "Have you talked to her?"

Charley lowered her voice and, for the first time ever, decided to share something of herself with her longtime colleague. "No. She's ghosted me. I've texted and called every day, keeping it short of stalking. Or maybe I am stalking. Hell, she might have a new phone number by now."

"You'd know if she had a new number because you'd get

a message the call didn't go through or the text wasn't sent. Look, if she's not responding, maybe it has to do with the family emergency."

"If there is one."

"Would she have a reason to lie? I heard from Betty at the ER yesterday. Jada had to leave in a hurry. Sounded legit to me."

"You talked to Betty?"

"Yes." Elle chuckled and gave her a puzzled expression. "I know her, too. We used to date, remember? Besides, she's the best source of info at the hospital."

"So you went there to find out about Jada?" Charley realized she sounded stupid, but that was all she did at the moment. Sound stupid.

"You're making this out to be like I'm investigating your love life. While it might be interesting, since I've never known you to have one, that's not why I was there. I had to take a prisoner in to get some stitches. Betty and I got to talking, and she offered up the information." Elle leaned closer, her voice almost a whisper. "You may not realize it, but you have a lot of friends in this town. Betty happens to be worried about you and asked me to check in on you. So I'm checking in. How are you really?"

Charley pushed away the paperwork and considered what Elle said. She was aware she had a lot of friends, but none of them knew her well. She never let them get that close. But apparently they'd gotten close enough to know something was wrong. Stefi once told Charley her face telegraphed her feelings quite clearly. Did she look as brokenhearted as she felt?

"Not good," Charley eventually said. "I hurt her right before she took off to parts unknown. I've been wanting to apologize since then, but she's ghosted me. I don't know what I should do."

"Easy," Elle said. "Send another text. But this time don't just ask her to call you. Tell her how you're feeling. What you're thinking. What you'd like to do going forward. Nothing else."

"That's a lot," Charley said. "I could write a novel putting all of it into words."

Elle's laugh was easy, and the sound soothed Charley. "Honey, I'm sure you can use few enough words to get the idea across. I've read your reports. You know how to be succinct."

Charley reached for her phone and stared at it, like it held all the answers she needed. "You're sure? Tell her what I'm feeling in a text?"

"She's not answering your calls. How else can you tell her?" Elle stood and stretched a bit. "I got to get moving. I want to run a speed check on Highway 1 for a while. Some kids have been hill hopping out there last couple of days."

"Okay," Charley said as she pulled up the Messaging app. "Thanks, Elle."

"Anytime." Elle patted her shoulder and left.

Charley started to type immediately. She took her time to make sure the text was worded right. Jada needed to understand what was going on in Charley's head. And in her heart.

****

Jada lounged in the easy chair beside Celeste's bed and absent-mindedly watched TV. Celeste was asleep and Anton had gone home to get some work done. Liselle was God knows where, and it was blissfully peaceful.

Jada took the time that morning to put up some yellow roses beside Celeste's bed. In addition to the flowers, she found some colorful pillowcases and a patchwork quilt, which resembled one made of materials from the early nineteenth century. Celeste loved antique things, and it was perfect for her. A couple of bright-blue throw pillows and a green lap desk rounded out the scheme for the moment.

If she'd had more time, Jada would have gotten some things to hang on the wall. That was her plan for tomorrow. She also wanted to do some work in Celeste's garden, because the flowers were beginning to wilt.

Her cell phone vibrated for the umpteenth time. She could probably use it as a real vibrator as often as the damn thing was going off today. Most of the messages or calls were from Charley. She'd given each text a cursory glance but dismissed them all. Right now her anger was in full bloom where Charley Townsend was concerned. And yet she'd kept every text.

But the most recent one got her attention immediately. Jada stared at it for a long while and reread it four times. She had to scroll a lot to get the full message. And it hit her right in the heart.

Don't ignore this one. It's the most important thing I can say to you right now. I love you. I need you. And I'm sorry. I'm scared I've lost you, and the funny thing is, I was scared of losing you so I shut you out. I'm not proud of what I did. I had my hand on the doorknob when you came by, but I couldn't make myself turn it. I heard everything you said. I saw your tears, even though I was crying, too. I hurt you and saying I'm sorry isn't enough to make it better. I will come to you. Tell me where you are. I'll be there as soon as humanly possible. I love you.

Tears flowed down Jada's cheeks as she continued to stare at the message. Crazy way to tell someone you were in love with them. She'd heard of breakups via text message, but admitting your love for someone for the first time by text? But what other choice had she left Charley? She wouldn't talk to her. Wouldn't call her back. Hadn't had the courage to actually listen to any of her voice messages.

Now she had to do something. The ball was, as they say, in Jada's court.

"Hey, tell me what's going on," Celeste said, her voice a little hoarse from sleeping.

"Not much to tell. Still angry at Charley."

"Yeah, I got that part, weirdo. You need to fill me in." Celeste looked around the room. "I'm bored out of my mind, and I don't think I can get much rest knowing you're hurting. You can't hide your feelings from me. You never could. Now give me all the details."

Jada smiled at her and told Celeste everything she needed to know. "You called me and I snapped at you thinking you were Charley. I left without telling anyone but work where I was going. She's been trying to call and texting like mad since I got here."

"And you've ghosted her. Is that what you're telling me?"

"Yes." Jada cradled her phone in one hand and pulled up the last text. "She's consistent. She's sent no less than six messages daily along with one voicemail."

"You've been here two weeks."

"I have."

"You can't stay mad at her, Jada. You have to let her tell you what's going on, and you totally have to tell her where you are and why. You can't let her think you up and left her."

"I know." Jada stared at the words again. *I love you.*

"Remember how you felt when Francine did this to you."

Jada flinched at the reminder. She was doing the exact same thing to Charley. Only Charley had no idea why she wouldn't return her messages. At least Francine was very clear on why she broke up with Jada.

"Let me see it," Celeste said, reaching for her phone.

Jada handed it to her and waited.

"Oh wow." Celeste scrolled through more texts now, and Jada cringed as she read them. "This woman is such a sweetheart, and I've never met her. But her texts are heartfelt and make me want to cry."

"You're pregnant. You always cry."

"True, but I'd cry even if I wasn't pregnant. And she loves you. She told you in a text she loves you, because you won't let her say it in person. I want to find her and give her a hug."

"She gives great hugs." Jada took back her phone. "I always feel so protected when I'm with her. Like we can take on the world together." She leaned closer and whispered, "But she's got a lot of stuff going on. Her wife died ten years ago, and she hasn't had a girlfriend since."

"Poor woman."

"She's skittish about us, I think. I can see in her eyes sometimes that she's not sure if being with anyone is a good idea. Though it might be my imagination, I guess."

"I doubt that. You seem to know her really well. Which is why you need to take your phone and call her. Tell her where you are and why. Maybe she can come down here."

"I don't think it's a good idea. You don't need a bunch of people in and out of here."

"It's not a bunch of people, and I totally need new visitors. I love you guys, but having the three of you fuss over me constantly is driving me nuts. She'd be a welcome distraction."

"You're sure?" Jada was suddenly excited by the idea of seeing Charley. There was so much she needed to say to her, but what she needed most of all was to hold Charley in her arms and feel her love.

"Positive. Go. Call her. Now."

Jada grinned and popped out of the room. Before she made the call, a very familiar woman stopped a few meters from her. Deep brown eyes assessed her as the woman came closer.

Jada felt an old familiar thrill at the sight of her. Her jet black hair lay softly across her shoulders, permed to perfection. Deep purple lipstick covered full, soft lips. The click-clack of her heels fell in time with Jada's heartbeat.

Jada tried hard to lift her eyes above the light-brown cleavage taunting her at the neckline of the knee-length green dress. She remembered the feel of silk against her thighs.

"Jada." Francine fairly purred her name once she was much closer to her. "I never thought I'd see you again. I heard you moved up north. Looking for gold maybe?" Her teasing smile caused Jada to hitch her breath.

She hadn't expected to see Francine. She'd made it a point to steer clear of any areas of the hospital she thought Francine might go to. The OB ward wasn't a place one usually found a trauma surgeon. When she found her voice, Jada said, "Why are you here?"

Francine's head tilted slightly to one side as she looked Jada over. "Damn but you look hot when you're dressed down. That look always got my motor going." She leaned closer and whispered, "I could take you right here and now."

"Not a chance in hell," Jada whispered back.

"Fiery as always. To answer your question, there's a patient here I need to follow up on. She's seven months pregnant so I transferred her here. Though I never expected to see you on this floor. Someone get you pregnant?"

"Hardly." Jada glanced into Celeste's room, though she couldn't see her. "My sister's here. Complications."

"Pity. I like Celeste."

"Pity. She doesn't like you."

Francine laughed. "You haven't changed much."

"You wouldn't know. Probably because you had so many other fuck buddies you lost track."

"No. You're not one I'd ever forget. We were too good together."

"Not good enough for you to help me when I needed you most."

"Oh that," Francine said. "It was your mess, baby. I didn't need any of that. I don't do complications."

"Clearly."

"I miss you, baby. But I got to finish my rounds. Meet me later?"

"Fuck off, Francine." Jada got closer and raised her voice. "I wouldn't fuck you if you were the last lesbian on earth."

"Too bad," Francine said, unfazed by Jada's outburst. "You know what you're missing." She sauntered away.

Jada leaned against the wall and closed her eyes. She needed Charley to give her a cuddle. She looked at her phone and didn't hesitate to give the most important person in her life a call.

Charley answered on the first ring. "Hey, it's me. Can you talk?" Jada asked.

"Sure."

"Good, so sit there and listen, okay? I'm sorry. I shouldn't have ignored your texts and calls. It was childish of me."

"I understand why you did it. I hurt you. I can't take it back."

"No, but we can move on from it."

"I love you, Jada."

Jada closed her eyes. She took a slow, deep breath and exhaled softly. "I know. How about I call you when I get to Celeste's house later? We can have a Skype chat in private."

"Sure. Talk to you then."

"Okay. Bye, Sarge," she said and pressed the End icon. "I love you, too."

Chapter Eighteen

Grace stepped out of her car and felt every muscle in her body. When she agreed to help Liv in the shop today, she hadn't realized how much lifting it would involve. Not that she wasn't strong, but they'd spent the entire morning rebuilding half the engine of a D11 dozer. She'd rather have been driving the dozer and decided being a mechanic wasn't something she'd ever enjoy.

Five hours later, she left Liv and Dave to finish up so she could get dinner ready. After she'd had a shower, of course. They planned a nice, family dinner to share their news with everyone at once. Hence the reason Grace spent all day hefting engine parts around.

A smile crossed her face as she stepped onto the porch.

"It's nice to see you happy, Gracie."

The voice startled her and Grace whirled toward it. Seated on the swing at the end of the porch was Carly. She was dressed in white Capri's and her sunny-yellow golf shirt accented her tanned skin. She had crossed her legs at the knee, and she looked perfectly at home as she combed her fingers through her short hair.

Grace was frozen again. She tried hard to force her body to react and move. She couldn't take her eyes off Carly who now stood and sauntered toward her. Her left arm throbbed at the memory of Carly slamming a baseball bat into it.

She flexed her arm and rubbed along one of the many surgical scars with her fingers. Was it odd she felt pain in her arm? Her left eye twitched as a light ache began in her temple, and she touched the scar there as well, where the blow from the bat nearly killed her.

"You left me for dead," Grace said, her voice sounding hoarse. Time she got it all out in the open with Carly. "You hit me so many times with that fucking bat I should have died. You almost crippled me."

"I was so angry." Carly stopped less than a foot from Grace. She reached out and touched the scar she'd caused, sighed, and dropped her hand to her side. "I didn't mean to hurt you, baby. I love you."

"No you don't. You never did." Grace's heart beat so fast she thought it would jump out of her chest. Her entire body shook, and she clenched her hands into fists. "I tried to love you. I did everything you ever asked of me. I never did anything to hurt you. Ever. And you repaid me by trying to kill me. I don't remember much after you started swinging the bat, just waking up in the hospital broken and in more pain than I ever thought possible."

"I'm sorry," Carly said, though there wasn't much emotion behind the words. "I didn't mean to do it, but you've always known how to push my buttons. I never meant to hurt you."

"So you say. So you said every time you beat me bad enough I ended up in the emergency room or urgent care. But it's over now, Carly. You can't touch me ever again. And right now, I'm going to call the cops."

"I don't care," Carly said with a shrug.

"How did you find me?"

"Doesn't take a genius to find someone if you know the right people."

Grace stared at her, waiting her out.

Carly crossed her arms over her chest and sighed. "The Internet is a useful place if you know someone who can unlock its secrets. And if you pay someone enough money, those secrets are easy to find. Baby, everything is online these days. You had to register that you live here and to change your name, which I think was a big mistake." She reached out to touch Grace again and this time, Grace reacted.

She had tempered pure instinct all those years with Carly. But after being with Liv and feeling safe and free for the first time in a decade, Grace also felt free to defend herself.

She wasn't sure what Carly was intending to do, but it didn't matter. The moment Carly's hand reached toward her, Grace snatched hold of her wrist and twisted it until Carly was on her knees in pain, begging her to let go. Grace didn't inflict any real harm. She released her when she was sure Carly had gotten the message.

No words were necessary. They were written across Carly's face.

She rubbed her wrist and started down the porch steps but paused to look back at Grace. "I'm not finished here."

"I think you are. I won't let you hurt me again, Carly."

"I never hurt you without a reason, Gracie. But it doesn't mean I don't love you, because I still do. We were good together."

"You poisoned my soul, Carly."

Grace watched as something shifted in Carly's expression. She turned around and was suddenly in Grace's personal space again, nearly touching noses with her. "You listen to me, bitch. I'm not going to take this shit from you, and you know it. Maybe I need to try again to teach you a lesson."

"Are you threatening me?"

"It's not a threat. It's a promise." Carly glared at her, but Grace never flinched. Not this time. Not ever again.

"Touch me and you'll be sorry. I'll defend myself, Carly. What I did is only a taste of what I'm capable of. I was always afraid to defend myself against you when we were married. But not now. I've gotten my confidence back, and I know I'm not some piece of shit you can trounce on when you've had a bad day. I'm so much better than you'll ever be. I've got a great life here and an amazing woman who loves me the way I should be loved. With kindness and compassion. Words you simply don't know the meaning of. I want you gone, Carly. Off my porch, off my property, and out of my life for good."

Carly cocked her arm back to hit Grace, but Grace was expecting it. She blocked the strike and responded with one of her own. Her punch caught Carly on the edge of her chin. Her head snapped back, and she stumbled backward.

Grace kept her center of balance and waited to see if Carly was going to respond. When she did, Grace ducked her punch and landed one in Carly's abdomen and a second to her face right on her nose. Carly stumbled and fell down the two steps of the porch. She held a hand over her face as blood poured through her fingers.

"You're going to regret this," she said, her voice muffled. "I'll be back and you won't see me coming."

"No. You'll be in jail. I'm sure *Ojiichan* has already called the police."

"What?"

Grace nodded to the window, where Harry looked out at them, a hint of a smile on his face as he spoke into the phone.

"They'll be here soon enough. Even if you leave, they'll find you. Eventually. You can't hide forever. Whitehorse isn't very big."

"I should have killed you."

"Yeah, maybe you should have. But you didn't. I used to want to know why you did that to me. What I did to make you hate me so much. Now you no longer matter to me. I don't care what happens to you. I don't care if you end up in jail or have to run away and hide forever. I don't care. You don't matter to me anymore. You lost your power over me a long time ago. I'm glad I finally realized it."

****

Charley was incredibly happy to be leaving the station. Her conversation with Jada was short, but the connection was made. They'd talk more in a few hours, when Jada was at her sister's home. A simple text had done the trick. She wished she'd spoken to Elle weeks ago.

"Well, don't you look happy," Elle said as Charley approached the parking lot. She was just getting out of her cruiser. "The text was well received?"

"It was. I can't thank you enough."

"Of course, you can. I get off shift at 1800. Meet me at the pub and buy me a beer."

Charley grinned. "I'm expecting to be on the phone a few hours from now. But if I'm available, it's a date. I'll have to text you though."

"Oh, I see." Elle winked at her. "It could be a very interesting phone call. You know phone sex is highly underrated."

"Elle, you're awful!" Charley laughed. "I don't think that's going to happen, but I have a feeling we'll have a lot to discuss."

"Excellent. We can go to the pub on Friday."

"Perfect."

Elle closed the door of her vehicle as the dispatcher called her unit number. Elle muttered, "Dammit. She always senses when I'm about to take a break." She rolled her eyes and answered the dispatcher.

A quick conversation ensued, and Charley's heart rate sped up. The address was Gracie and Liv's house, and the call was a domestic disturbance. Before Elle stopped her, Charley was in the passenger seat.

Elle started to protest, but Charley stared her down. Elle eventually put the vehicle in gear and sped off, lights and sirens blaring.

****

"I meant what I said. I'm going to kill you, Gracie. You won't see me coming."

Grace almost stepped off the porch, but the front door opened and Harry came out, the phone still in his hand. She turned her attention back to Carly. "They're going to lock you up again, Carly. Maybe this time for longer. You might even end up in a Canadian prison. I'm going to file assault charges as soon as the police arrive."

"I'm sure you are." Carly reacted to the distant sound of sirens by backing up to her car.

This one was a brown Buick with no front license plates, parked along the street. Grace tried to memorize everything. She remembered her cell phone was in her pocket and removed it to take a few quick photos.

Carly drove off, spinning tires in the gravel on the edge of the road.

Harry put his arm around Grace's waist, and his strength kept her knees from buckling. "She meant what she said." Grace's voice sounded distant to her own ears.

"I know. She will try, but not succeed." He kissed her on the cheek and went to the first police car to pull into the driveway.

He pointed in the direction Carly left and stepped out of the officer's way. A few moments later, Charley practically leaped from another, still moving, patrol car. Her long legs quickly brought her to Grace's side.

She took note of the blood on Grace's hands. "You hurt?"

"No. It's all hers." She met Charley's concerned gaze with a small smile. "I think I broke her nose."

Charley returned her smile. "Good for you. Where's Liv?"

"Olivia is coming home now," Harry said. "I did not tell her what kind of car Carly is driving right now, so she could not go looking for her." His eyes connected with Charley's. "Go find that woman. Keep her from my granddaughters."

"I'll do my best," Charley said.

Grace held up her cell phone and sent a quick text to Charley. "I sent you pictures of the car she's driving. No front license plates, and I didn't see the one on the back."

"This is great. Good job, Gracie." Charley ran back to the waiting cruiser and got in. After a few seconds, they were gone.

Harry opened the front door. "Come inside. I'll fix you some tea."

"Sure." Grace's mind was on what Carly said. It felt so good to smash her nose, but the clear threat still terrified her. She could defend herself against Carly. But what if she was able to surprise them while they slept? What if she managed to get her hands on a gun? It wasn't as easy as in the States, but still a possibility. They suspected Carly had a fake ID. Was it enough to get a weapon?

"Gracie Lee." Harry spoke to her again. "Come inside, please."

Grace followed him to the kitchen table where she sat down. He gave her a wet towel to clean the blood off. Underneath the filth, the knuckles of her right hand were bruised.

Harry started the water for tea then gathered some ice cubes into a tea towel. He placed the towel over her hand. "This will hurt a lot tomorrow."

"It was worth it," Grace said. "I stood up to her, *Ojiichan*. For the first time ever, I told her off. She tried to hit me, but I kept her from doing so. She wouldn't stop, so I had to strike her. The look of shock on her face was priceless. I'm not proud of what I did—"

"You should be," he said, surprising her. "You should be very proud, Gracie Lee. You stood up to a bully, and that is never a bad thing. I'm sorry it was so physical, but I watched it all. I knew you could handle yourself, and ultimately, you got your message across. Never again, you told her. She'd never hurt you again. I'm proud of you,"

"Thanks," Grace muttered.

"Gracie!" Liv rushed into the kitchen, out of breath. "You okay? I got a call—where's Carly? Is that your blood? Where are the police? What happened?"

Grace used her left hand to guide Liv into the chair beside her. "I'm fine. Carly took off. The blood is hers and the police are looking for her." Grace removed the ice from her hand. "I'm pretty sure I broke her nose."

Liv's eyes flicked from Grace's hand to the bloody towel and back again. A slow grin formed, and she leaned forward to kiss Grace thoroughly. "I'm so proud of you, baby. I wish I'd been here to see it."

"I kind of am, too, but if you'd been here it would have been me keeping you from going after Carly again. As it was, she did try to hit me, but I kicked her ass. Oh, and I took a picture of the car she's driving to help the police locate her. They were a couple minutes behind her. Charley was with them."

Harry said, "Charley is determined. I think they'll find her this time." He picked up the ice pack and put it on Grace's hand again. "Keep it on there for fifteen minutes." He then placed a steaming cup of tea in front of her. "Drink and relax. We'll talk more later."

Liv put an arm around Grace's shoulders and kissed her temple. "I was worried when I got the call. I almost ran here from the office. Of all the days for you to come home by yourself."

"It's okay now, Olivia." Grace gently rubbed Liv's abdomen. "Besides, we don't want anything to disrupt our work in progress, right?"

"We don't, but it doesn't mean I can't still want to protect you. I've heard of women fighting up until they gave birth."

"Where in the world did you hear that?" Grace turned in her seat to face Liv. "Seriously? Where?"

"TV," Liv said, as if TV were the gospel and couldn't be disputed.

"TV? What show?"

Liv spoke, but made a coughing noise as she did, and Grace didn't understand her. She wouldn't look Grace in the eyes now, and Grace suspected she knew what TV show Liv referred to.

"This show—it wouldn't happen to have a lot of women in leather, would it?"

"Well, one very hot woman in leather. The other one's really cute but doesn't do the leather so much. Too blonde."

Grace laughed softly and touched foreheads with Liv. "I love you, Olivia. No matter how weird you are. And if you'd been here, I'd have gotten between the two of you. I'm still stronger than you are."

Liv leaned into her a bit. "Tough guy, huh?"

"Today I was. Still a little freaked out about it, though."

Liv pulled Grace into a tight embrace. "You're allowed to be, baby. But I'm here now, so it's all okay. This time they'll catch the bitch."

"I sure hope so." Grace closed her eyes and let Liv's warmth soothe her.

Chapter Nineteen

Charley sent a picture of the brown Buick to both officers on patrol. Since no other calls were pending, all three units were able to concentrate on finding Carly. She and Elle currently headed out of the city toward Blue River. Charley had a hunch Carly would hole up there. Blue River had an inn with three rooms and was far enough away from the city that Carly could come and go unnoticed. Probably why they hadn't caught her yet.

"You know we're both going to get our asses chewed by the inspector, right?" Elle said.

"I do. You should have left me at Gracie's."

"And have you go off on your own? Inspector Pike would probably fire me for it."

"Sorry, but I guess you're sorta screwed."

Elle said, "Shit happens. Besides, I get why you want this chick found so badly. The pub gossip told me all about her and Gracie and their past."

Charley rolled her eyes. "Izzy doesn't know that much about it."

"She knows Carly abused Gracie and nearly killed her. I think that's the basic part most everyone knows." Elle glanced briefly at Charley. "But you need to promise me something."

"What?"

"If we find her, you either stay in the vehicle, or stay out of my way. You don't touch her. I'll arrest her and you'll be an observer. Nothing else, or I will stop this car and shove your ass out. Got me?"

Charley narrowed her gaze at Elle, even though Elle couldn't see her. Her friend was right, though. She had to be an observer. Nothing could go wrong if they arrested Carly. She wasn't going to chance the bitch finding a way to be freed on a technicality.

"Deal. But if she stumbles or hits her head getting into the cruiser, I won't see it."

"You're terrible, Charley. Probably why I like you."

"Probably." Charley adjusted herself in the seat and tried hard to be a little more comfortable in the small space. She rarely rode in the passenger seat and hated it. The MDT didn't leave much room. "I'm thinking we should check the inn first."

"Me, too," Elle said. The vehicle lurched forward a bit as Elle sped up on a straight stretch of road.

Blue River was on the horizon, and Elle slowed down as they reached the town limits. The streets were deserted, which wasn't unusual in the late afternoon. It was close to three and the only real activity in Blue River would be the dinner rush at Marge's.

Charley fixed her attention on the inn and the parking area behind it. It held only one vehicle—an older model Chevy pickup missing a tailgate. "Dammit."

The other units checked in, and neither of them had spotted the brown Buick. Charley wanted to slam her fist into the window, but it certainly wouldn't help her any.

She grunted. "I can't believe the bitch managed to get into our country. What the hell are they doing at border control? Sleeping?"

"We discussed this," Elle said with a calm Charley certainly didn't feel. "Besides, right now it doesn't matter. She's here and we need to deal with her." Elle gave Charley a sideways glance. "You sure you're up for this?"

"I'll just observe. I promise."

"You better."

The radio crackled to life again. A report came in from one of the patrol units. A brown Buick was spotted near Whitehorse General Hospital. Elle turned their vehicle around and sped back toward Whitehorse. Charley was glad Jada was nowhere near the hospital. There was no telling what Carly might do.

****

Liv paced between the front door and the back door, while Grace looked on. Harry was in his bedroom resting. The strain of all the excitement took a toll on him. Grace was stuck between worrying about him and worrying about Liv. She hadn't stopped pacing for the last twenty minutes.

Finally, Grace had enough. She stood in front of Liv and placed her hands on Liv's shoulders. "Stop. This isn't going to help."

"I can't. I've got all this nervous energy. I know they're out there looking for her, and I should be glad about it. They know the car she's in, and everything should be fine. But it's not. Gracie, she came after you. Physically. I was scared when I saw all that blood on your hands…fuck. I want her out of our lives for good."

"And she will be. They'll find her. At least now she knows I won't back down from her. Olivia, you know how important this is? *She* backed away from *me*. That's never happened before."

"I get that and I'm so proud of you, baby. But it's like she's escalating, and the longer I'm not doing anything about it, the more worried I get."

"And what would you do?" Grace asked, though she was afraid of the answer she'd get.

"I think you know," Liv said. "I'd go looking for her and probably end up in a fight with her. I can't begin to tell you all the emotions running through me right now. I feel more and more out of control the longer I know she's out there."

"For all we know, they've found her already," Grace said, trying for reason. But the look on Liv's face told her reason was no longer an option. And if Carly was found, Charley would have told them by now.

"You know they haven't found her yet," Liv said, as if she read Grace's mind. She kissed Grace on the forehead and resumed her pacing. She paused by the front window for a few seconds longer than usual, and immediately, Grace's heart rate increased. She barely had time to make sure she had her cell phone before Liv was flying out the door and leaping off the porch.

Grace came out to find Liv tussling with someone along the edge of the house, near the bushes. Arms and legs were everywhere, and Grace had a hard time discerning who was who. At least she had the presence of mind to call 9-1-1 before jumping into the melee. She grabbed Liv by the back of her shirt and pulled her to her feet.

Liv's arms flailed as she tried to balance herself. Carly lay in a heap half in-half out of the bushes. She moved slowly and got to her feet, albeit unsteadily. She glared at Liv and felt the cut on her lip. "I should kill you," she growled to Liv. "I ought to fucking kill you right now! Maybe then I can get Gracie to realize it's time she came home with me."

"She's already home, you twisted bitch!" Liv lunged forward and knocked Carly to the ground again.

Grace tried her best to pry them loose, but Liv wasn't about to give up the fight. She continued to pummel Carly until an RCMP cruiser slid into their driveway. Two young, male officers rushed forward and separated them.

Liv kept herself between Carly and Grace, while holding a hand over a cut on her forehead.

Carly continued to rant and scream as the officers handcuffed her and placed her in their car.

One of them wrote down statements from Liv and Grace before joining his partner.

Minutes later, Charley and Elle arrived. Charley raced to Gracie's side. "You two okay?"

Grace put an arm around Liv's waist. "Fine. I don't think Carly managed to land any hits worth mentioning. She, on the other hand, is heading for a stop at the hospital before jail."

Charley examined the cut on Liv's forehead.

"I'm fine, Charley," Liv grumbled and swiped blood from her mouth. "I gave worse than I got. Promise me she'll never get close to Gracie again."

"I can't, but I can promise she's going to jail, and from there, she'll be deported back to America. Once in the US, she's their problem. Tell me what happened."

"I protected my property. Simple." Liv shrugged. "And I protected my wife, even if she doesn't need it."

"And your wife is furious with you." At Liv's surprised expression, Grace continued. "You might be pregnant. Remember? What if you'd gotten hurt? What if she'd hit you in the abdomen? Then what? Would it have been worth it then?"

"I—I'm sorry, Gracie. I reacted. If I was nine months pregnant, I'd probably do the same thing."

"You can't, Liv. You've got to think before you react. You scared the hell out of me today. I know you hurt her far worse than she hurt you. Not the point." Grace placed her hand over Liv's stomach. "What might be happening here—it's far more important than anything else right now. You're trying to make a new life, Olivia. You might have a child inside you, and you can't take a chance on hurting them. Please. You have to think about them from now on. You're carrying precious cargo."

Liv ducked her head and looked thoroughly chastised.

Grace spoke quickly. "I love you unconditionally. And I don't want you hurt any more than you want me hurt." She gently wiped a spot of blood off Liv's cheek. "All we had to do was lock the door and call the cops."

"I know." Liv had the decency to sound repentant. "Is it okay if I feel better now? Knowing she got what she deserved?"

Grace realized she fought a losing battle. "Let's just say I'm not surprised. But from now on, you think of the baby first. Got it?"

Liv sported a crooked grin then winced from pain. She cradled her hand against her chest. "I am kinda injured though."

Elle joined them and also gave Liv a once-over for her injuries. "Get to the hospital and get checked over, Liv. You need me to take you?"

"No, I'll take her," Grace said. "Thanks. We'll catch up to you guys there. C'mon slugger." She pointed Liv toward the car. "You get settled in, and I'll let *Ojiichan* know where we're going."

"No need," Harry said from the porch as he stepped out of the house. "I'll go with you."

Grace knew not to argue. She went inside for her purse and car keys and they were off to the hospital.

Chapter Twenty

Two days after Carly was safely secured in jail, Charley was off to Ottawa. She was excited to be seeing Jada, even though she'd not slept much since the incident with Carly. She and Elle got quite the ass-chewing from Inspector Pike, but Charley didn't mind. She'd have done the same thing in his position. At least neither she nor Elle was being disciplined.

The first flight out of Whitehorse was horrific, and Charley doubted she could hate flying more than she did right now. Not only was she shoved into the first flight like a sardine, pressed between two other people of equal height, but she had to run across the airport to catch her second flight. She got there seconds before the door was about to close. And of course, her seat was in the middle, and she had to wait for the very grumpy man in a wrinkled suit to get up so she could sit down. He hit her twice with his elbow as he got comfortable again. Charley glared at him until he tucked his arm close to his side and well away from her.

At least the third flight was uneventful.

Until the end.

They had a rough landing due to high winds, but once she was out of that tin box and on the ground in Ottawa, she felt able to breathe again.

Her phone lit up with text messages as soon as she landed. She skimmed through a few of them from her mother, asking her to call, and zeroed in on the ones from Grace. Carly was officially charged with six counts of assault, which included on the officers who arrested her, resisting arrest, stalking, violation of a protection order, and illegal entry into Canada. She was going to be in jail until her trial date, which was set for the end of August.

Charley felt some of her stress melt away. Carly wasn't going to be able to bother Grace again. She was sure to be sentenced to several years in prison, and once out, would be immediately deported to America. Charley could rest easy, as they all would, because Grace was safe.

The plane came to a stop, and the madness of dozens of passengers scrambling for their carry-on baggage began. Charley frowned at the man beside her when he dared to try to push past her. She stood to her full height and glared at him. He chose to sit back down.

She pulled out her duffel bag, slung it over her shoulder, and followed the crowd out of the plane. Once in the airport, she headed directly for the taxi pickup area. When she saw the crowd headed for baggage claim, she was glad to only have her duffel bag.

At the taxi stand, she sent Jada a text and let her know she was about to get a ride. Charley's phone rang in response.

"Don't. I'm almost to the gate," Jada said. "I'm in a dark-green Ford minivan."

Charley stepped outside into the fresh, warm air. "Okay. I'm in front now."

"Me, too. Can you see me?"

Charley spotted the van, disconnected, and shoved her phone into a pocket of her cargo shorts. She jogged into the pickup area and waved as she got to the car. She tossed her duffel bag into the backseat and got in. She kissed her on the cheek and smiled at Jada once she was settled and they were on their way.

"How come you decided to pick me up?"

"Taxis are expensive." Jada glanced at her. "Besides, it means I get to spend an extra few minutes with you."

"I like that," Charley said. "How's your sister?"

"Stable. Her doctor is confident if she has to deliver early, the baby'll be okay. They've got a great neonatal ward here. Top notch."

"Excellent. Is she up for visitors?"

"Tomorrow. We'll get you settled at her house first. I want you rested before you meet my mom."

"Sounds ominous." Charley tried to joke, but it didn't quite work. "Is your mom that bad?"

"She can be. We sort of came to an understanding right after I got here." Jada's grip on the steering wheel tightened enough her knuckles were lighter. "She almost apologized to me for not supporting me after the mess with Nancy spreading rumors about me."

"That's a positive thing, I think. By the way, I heard back from Facebook. The posts have been removed."

"Wow, that's great. I can't thank you enough."

"No need." Charley kept her eyes on Jada, uninterested in the scenery around them as they sped along. Jada hadn't slept well, as evidenced by the dark smudges under her eyes. Her hair wasn't quite as full as it normally was, and Charley wondered how much time Jada'd managed to get for herself. She wanted to ask, but she sensed this was a conversation for later.

For now, Charley wondered if it were possible to take more time off work. She'd have to discuss it with Jada later. Assuming it's something she'd even want Charley to do.

They pulled into the driveway of a two-story brick home, in the middle of a subdivision. Most of the homes looked new and nearly identical in style. It wasn't a bad place, but the uniformity of it made Charley want to laugh because she immediately thought of *The Stepford Wives*.

Jada got out first, and Charley followed and grabbed her duffel bag. They stepped into the house, and it looked much the way Charley expected it to: neutral colors on the walls; shiny, woodgrain flooring; open-plan living room; kitchen/dinette.

Along one wall was a blow-up mattress Charley suspected served as Jada's bed. The mattress was about the size of a double bed and half a meter thick. It looked quite comfortable.

Jada steered her into the living room and took the duffel bag from her. "I'll tuck this near the door. I hope you don't mind that we'll have to share the blow-up bed, or you can have the couch. They have three bedrooms. One is the nursery and the third is Anton's office."

"Is he home?"

"No, at the hospital. We take turns being with Celeste. Even though Mom is there, Anton and I like to make sure one of us is there, too. Keeps Celeste from getting too upset when Mom does her mother thing."

"Gotcha." Charley took a seat on the sofa and waited for Jada to return. Once she did, Jada sat on the opposite end, tucked her feet under her, and faced Charley.

"I guess now's as a good a time as any," she said without preamble. "I don't think it'll do either of us any good to put it off."

"No, it won't." Charley tucked herself into the corner of the couch and faced Jada. For some reason, the meter between them felt like a kilometers-wide chasm. While they'd returned to their easy banter on the phone, it seemed all they managed face-to-face was being exceedingly polite. Charley knew she had to get this going and struggled with where to start.

"I'd say I'm sorry, but I already did over the phone," Charley said.

"You did."

"It's not enough. It probably sounds lame, and I guess in hindsight it wasn't like I'd been given a life sentence, but—" She looked at her hand, still not close enough to making a fist. "I don't have the words I need to describe what it felt like. The only thing I ever wanted to do with my life, since the age of six, was be a Mountie. Not just a cop, but an RCMP Mountie. I learned to ride a horse when I was ten and did athletics to get fit. I entered the academy the day after I turned nineteen.

"I knew the qualifications, and when I was in school, I studied French to the point where I'm fluent in it now. That's a bonus qualification. I even had Dad teach me to use a shotgun, so I'd have some skills with a weapon. I didn't just pass the weapons exam, I passed it well enough that within two years I was an instructor. Still am." She looked at her hand again and felt the sadness welling up. "Well, I don't know."

Jada scooted closer. She took Charley's injured hand carefully into her own and cupped it gently. "You're a strong woman, Charlene Townsend. You'll get back to it."

"I hope so," Charley said, comforted by Jada's touch. "I can't imagine doing anything else with my life. I've saved people. I've seen where I can make a difference, and I know I've done a lot of good in the years I've been a Mountie. It's not my job. It's my calling and I can't let it go." Tears pricked her eyes, and Charley swiped at them with her right hand. "It's so stupid to cry over this, but it's important to me. I wish I could explain it better."

"Shh. You don't have to." Jada placed soft kisses along Charley's left hand and held it close to her heart. "You're a special woman. You're strong, beautiful, brave, and amazing. And you will get through this. I'll help you. You have to open up to me. Don't shut me out again, okay? I can't help if you don't talk to me."

"I'm terrified I'll lose my career, and if I let you in, I'll lose myself. I love you. It's the best and worst part of all this. I'm at my lowest point since Raina died. And here you are, holding my heart in your hands and I'm scared you're going to rip it apart. I don't think I can go through that again."

Jada got close enough their knees touched. She placed the palm of her left hand against Charley's cheek and wiped at the tears with her thumb. "I love you, too. But why—why do you think I'll break your heart? Is it because we had a miscommunication? Or because I ghosted you?"

"No. None of that." Charley's vision was blurred from her tears, but Jada leaned close enough Charley saw the tiny flecks of gold in her eyes. "I'm afraid you'll leave me. Like Raina did."

"Raina died. You can't always control that."

"You don't understand." Charley pulled back. She got up and moved away from the couch to put space between her and Jada.

"Clearly not. Why don't you tell me?" Jada asked.

"I can't."

Jada was quiet for an impossibly long time. "Can't or won't. There's a huge difference."

"Won't." Charley avoided her gaze and kept her eyes on the decorations in the room, the framed family photos, knickknacks from vacations.

"Can I ask why not?"

"You can, but I don't have an answer. It's part of the problem."

Jada remained on the couch and curled her feet underneath herself. She grabbed a pillow and held it against her belly like a shield. "If we can't talk to each other, then we're right back where we started. Francine never talked to me about anything until too late, and she blew up over it. Big, small, didn't matter. It always ended in a fight. And she had this way of making me feel like I was the most insignificant person one minute and the most precious the next."

"I'm not Francine," Charley said.

"I know, but she shut me out. I don't want that from you. I need you to trust me. If you can't—there's nothing more I can do." She rested her chin on the pillow, and Charley noticed she was crying. "I love you, but I'd rather we break things off now instead of later. We'll end up not talking about other things, and it won't make for a good relationship. It's best we protect ourselves up front, while we have a chance of still being friends."

The pain in Charley's chest was so sharp, she felt like her heart exploded. She stared at Jada, who had her eyes closed. "You're breaking up with me?"

"I guess I am."

Her voice was so soft Charley barely heard it. She wished like hell she hadn't.

"I can't do this, Charley. I'm sorry."

"No—wait. I don't get it. You're breaking up with me because I'm scared?"

"No." Jada wiped the moisture from her cheeks and shook her head. "No. I'm breaking up with you because you won't talk to me about Raina. If you can't tell me this one very vital thing, then our relationship can't work. I can't do that again. I already got my heart stomped on by Francine."

"Please stop comparing me to her," Charley said, trying hard to keep the anger from her voice. "I'm not hiding something from you. It's difficult to talk about, and I don't know if I'm ready for that."

Jada tightened her grip on the pillow. "Let me know when you are. Until then, let's just be friends."

"Friends?"

"Yeah. Look, I'm so glad you came down here to help me out, and you can still stay if you want."

Charley was nearly beyond words. Hot tears streamed down her face, but she swiped them away in anger. What the hell had she done to deserve this? "I can't believe you. You're willing to throw away any chance at a relationship because I'm not ready to tell you what's worrying me. Am I right?"

Jada nodded but didn't look at her. Her gaze was fixed on the floor. "You say it like it's easy, but trust me, this is hard for me, too."

"Kinda like it's hard for me to talk to you about Raina?"

"Maybe."

Charley felt like her guts were on fire. The pain in her chest was so overwhelming, she was afraid a panic attack would start. She stared at Jada, trying hard to understand what was happening. How could she be so callous about this? Did she think it was easy for Charley to stand there and remember the worst day of her life and yet be unable to talk about it?

Flashes of Raina's face crashed in on her.

The spatters of red covering the bathroom from ceiling to floor.

The shotgun that lay across Raina's chest.

The gore obliterating her once beautiful face...

"She fucking killed herself," Charley blurted out. She walked away from Jada, picked up her duffel bag, and opened the door. "She gave up on me, too. Like you are right now." She pulled her coat on and took hold of the front door handle. She wanted to say more, so much more, but nothing came out of her mouth.

Jada sat on the couch with her mouth agape. She didn't utter a single sound. She also didn't make a move to stop Charley as she left the house and slammed the door behind her.

****

Jada sat unmoving on the couch for several minutes. She expected Charley to come back inside after she calmed down. But the sound of a car pulling into the driveway sent her to her feet and to the door. She opened it as Charley climbed into a taxi. Jada bolted outside, but the taxi pulled away before she reached it.

For the next two hours, she tried to call Charley. Each one went to voicemail. She texted her as well, but they also went unanswered. Charley was ghosting her.

Jada sat on her sister's couch wondering where it all went wrong. Charley's inability to share something so clearly important upset Jada in a way she couldn't articulate. Only she had, and she'd done such a horrid job of it. Had she meant to break up with her? She loved Charley, that was not in doubt. She wanted to be with her, to make her believe she loved her. And she wanted Charley's love in return.

But how would she get past the bombshell Charley dropped on her?

Raina killed herself? Why hadn't Charley said so before?

Jada seriously misjudged the situation and spoke out of a knee-jerk reaction. In some twisted way, she was protecting herself, but at the same time, she managed to break her own heart by letting the woman she loved walk out the door.

How the hell was she supposed to get in touch with her now?

She looked at her cell phone for a long time before she realized there was one person she could call who would answer her. She hit the Dial icon and waited.

Grace picked up on the third ring.

Before she'd so much as said hello, Jada asked, "Did Raina kill herself?"

There was a brief silence on the line. "Is this Jada?"

"Yes. Did Raina kill herself? I need to know."

"That's something Charley needs to tell you. Not me."

"Please don't be evasive. Charley said, 'she fucking killed herself' and then walked out. I need to know what's going on, Gracie. She won't talk to me. I love her, and it's tearing me up she won't open up to me. Give me a chance here. Help me make this right."

Grace was silent and Jada worried she wouldn't respond. "Yes, Raina killed herself. And Charley found her. No note, no life-changing event we know of to make her choose to take her own life. She literally did it while Charley was at work. I'm not going to give you details. Those are for Charley to share, or not. But understand this. She's more fragile than you think. She may seem vulnerable to you right now, but it's more like she's breakable. It's why she hasn't had a relationship in the last ten years. Not a single date. Not even someone she was interested in. Absolutely nothing. There's a solid reason for it—in her mind. If she keeps everyone at a distance, she can avoid any kind of intimacy, which would open her up for more heartache."

"She's protecting herself."

"Exactly. And if she stormed off, it's because she's gone into overdrive to keep her shield up. You have to give her time."

Jada dropped onto the couch as fresh tears pooled in her eyes. "I told her we couldn't continue to be together if she wouldn't talk to me. Right before she left, she said something about me giving up on her like Raina did. Oh God, Gracie. What have I done?"

"I'm going to call her. Don't do anything until you hear from me, okay?"

"Sure." Jada stared at the phone and wondered how she could have been so damn stupid.

****

Charley tossed her duffel bag onto one of the hotel's double beds and scrolled through five texts and ten missed calls. All from Jada. She wanted to talk more, but what else was there to say? But maybe that was the point.

She was probably right in breaking up with Charley. Being unwilling to talk about Raina had caused Charley to be cut off from more than one relationship. Certainly not of a romantic nature, as Jada was genuinely the first woman Charley took interest in over the last decade. So many people had consoled Charley about Raina's death, nearly all of them asking how she died. Each time, at first, Charley gave some details as to what happened.

Those details became more and more graphic as people asked the same macabre questions, until finally, the only thing Charley could do was stop talking about it. The details gave her more and more vivid nightmares, and the one thing that stopped them was not talking about it. Now she only had the nightmares on the eighteenth of April. She supposed that was progress.

As the afternoon ticked by, she knew there'd be one helluva nightmare tonight. Probably involving Jada somehow. Her hands clenched and unclenched, and nervous energy surged through her.

When her phone rang again, she was tempted to ignore it, but she recognized the ring tone for Grace and answered on the second ring. "Everything okay?" Charley asked.

"I was going to ask you the same thing," Grace replied.

"Why? I sent you a text when I got here."

"You did, but you didn't send me a text saying Jada broke up with you. Or how you stormed out of her sister's house." Grace waited, but when Charley didn't speak, she continued, "You dropped a bomb on her, Charley. You should have stayed and talked it out with her."

"Why? She's already called it quits. What's the point? Gracie, I shouldn't have to explain myself. Maybe I'm being selfish, but why do I always have to explain things to people? I'm scared of commitment. I told her that, but she kept pressing to know why.”

“You have to tell her why. That’s one major thing she needs to understand, and she can’t if you hold back from her. You can’t have a healthy relationship if you keep secrets from each other.”

“She knows Raina died. Why isn’t it enough?”

“Because Raina didn’t just die. She committed suicide, and you’ve been tearing yourself up over it for years. If anyone was selfish, it was her.”

Charley nearly dropped the phone. She’d never heard an accusatory tone in Grace’s voice before, and it startled her. “How can you say that?”

“Because it’s true. Raina did what was best for Raina and to hell with the rest of us. I get that she had problems—problems she kept very well hidden from everyone, but dammit, Charley, it wasn’t your fault. Raina made her decision without your input. She took her own life and fuck the rest of us. I’m sorry if it sounds cruel, but it’s how I feel. I’ve always felt this way, and I think it’s time you realize, no matter what, you probably never could have stopped her. She was clearly determined. It was not your fault. Are you listening to me? Not. Your. Fault.”

“I—I, uh, yeah. I hear you.” Grace’s words were hard to take in, and it all sounded very cruel, but was she right? Was Raina being selfish? Or was she so despondent she couldn’t possibly think of the consequences other than she would be free from whatever was too hard to cope with. Something Charley never thought of. She’d been angry, sad, hurt, but never did the idea Raina was selfish come into her head.

“I’m sorry,” Grace said into the gaping silence. “I shouldn’t have gone off on you. I guess I’m frustrated. I blame Raina and I probably shouldn’t. I’m sure she never meant for you to be stuck in the past. I honestly have a hard time believing that.”

“Me, too. What do I do now, Gracie? I don’t want to lose Jada. I love her.”

“I know you do, my friend. Go back to her. Talk to her about Raina. Make her understand where you’re coming from and why this is so hard for you. If you don’t open up and let her in, there’s no point. You’ll have to accept the relationship is over

     For the Love of Charley

and probably come back home. But I'd hate that a lot. I've not seen you this happy in so long, I would feel heartbroken if you didn't give Jada another chance. Stop running from her and run to her instead. If you love each other, you'll find a way to make it work. Okay?"

"Okay. Thanks, Gracie."

"You're welcome. Call me if you need anything."

"I will. Love you." Charley disconnected and left the hotel room. She strode purposefully to the lobby and got another cab. She thought of nothing else but what she would say to Jada when she got to the house.

The details she'd have to give.

The feelings she'd have to reveal.

The fear living inside her.

The inability to move forward.

In the span of twenty minutes, Charley nearly had herself talked out of going back. But the driver pulled up to Jada's sister's house, and Charley got out. She steeled herself, stepped up to the door, and knocked.

Jada opened it and Charley barreled inside. She held up a hand to stop Jada from speaking. She whirled around to face her, momentarily stopped by the tears on Jada's face. It nearly caused her resolve to crumble.

"Hear me out. Then we can talk." When Jada nodded, Charley continued. The words came out in a jumbled rush...

The house was weirdly quiet when Charley stepped inside. She locked up her gun belt and headed into the kitchen. She smelled lasagna, but the kitchen was empty. A pan rested on the stove, still warm from being in the oven.

"Raina! Honey, I'm home," Charley called out. She ducked into the living room but found it empty. The stereo was on, but whatever was playing had ended. Raina never left the stereo on if she wasn't close by to hear it.

Charley decided to look upstairs and continued to call out as she climbed the steps. A feeling of dread settled in the pit of her stomach when she heard no reply. The bedroom was empty. So was the spare room Raina converted into a reading nook. The bathroom was the only room left, and Charley slowed her steps.

The sight of blood seeping into the hallway jolted her

forward, and she tried to shove open the door, but it only went partway. Something blocked it, and she screamed in frustration. "Raina!"

She froze when a hand came into view.

Blood covered the pale skin. Charley felt a renewed urgency. She managed to squeeze through the small opening and nearly crumpled at the sight before her.

Raina's naked body covered in blood from her waist up.

Her beautiful face blown away by the shotgun that lay across her chest.

Blood everywhere.

Charley couldn't breathe. Couldn't think.

She fell to her knees and stretched out a trembling hand to her wife.

The hand fell short of touching the body so very familiar to her.

Charley's stomach roiled. She turned from Raina and vomited.

She struggled to her feet.

Her eyes locked on Raina's body.

Her chest tightened. Her pulse raced. Her life crashed around her.

"I don't know how long it took me to call 9-1-1," Charley said. "While I waited for police to arrive, I searched the house for a note. Maybe she'd hidden it. Maybe it was under her body, and we'd find it later when she was moved. I didn't know, but I kept looking. For days I searched the house and found absolutely nothing. Not a note or email or text. Nothing on her computer.

"We lived in McAdam in Nova Scotia. It's a small town and our house was outside it on what used to be a large farm. No neighbors. We eventually found a receipt for the shotgun—she'd bought it the same day. She went out, bought the gun, came home, fixed dinner, and killed herself.

"My life was thrown into chaos. I couldn't function, and my mom flew out as soon as she was able to be with me. No matter what she did, she couldn't reach me. Like my brain was locked up.

"Gracie showed up a few days later with my dad. Mom got us adjoining rooms at a hotel. We couldn't stay at the house."

Charley looked down at her left hand as she clenched and unclenched her fist. "Our house was a crime scene. I never went back there. After the funeral, Gracie and Mom gathered some of my clothes, and we flew to Whitehorse. I took a leave of absence for a year.

"Jada, it took so long for me to function again. To feel like I could move on with my life. Raina—I loved her so much. We'd talked about starting a family together. She'd recently asked me to request a posting in Vancouver, because she'd never been there. I did, of course. I'd have done anything for her."

"I'm sure you would. You're a special person."

Charley didn't look up. She didn't want to see Jada's expression. She'd break down if she did. "Raina was thrown out of her house when she was fifteen. Her parents didn't want a gay child, and after a lot of yelling and screaming, they tossed her onto the street. She got lucky because she found an organization that helped homeless kids, especially LGBT kids. We met at a fundraiser for the group years later. By then Raina was volunteering for them as a peer counselor. She worked for a local fast-food chain. Didn't much care for more than that. She said working with those kids was enough for her."

Charley took a deep, steadying breath, released it, and waited for Jada to react.

Jada's mouth opened and closed a couple of times before she replied, "I love you." She put her arms around Charley, held her close, and rested her head on Charley's shoulder. "I wish you'd have told me sooner. I never would have said the things I did if I'd had any inkling about what happened."

"It's okay. You didn't know."

"It's not okay." Jada brushed her lips across Charley's. "You're a brave woman. I'm sorry I made you go through all this because of my own petty nonsense."

"I would have told you eventually. Gracie said I needed to do it now, though."

"Thank God for Gracie then. I'm glad I called her."

"So am I. And I'm also sorry, again. It wasn't fair to let you go without knowing why. I'm afraid I'll repeat whatever made Raina kill herself. I don't want to do that to you."

"I'll never take my own life. Never." Jada spoke emphatically, her gaze locked with Charley's. "I will never hurt you intentionally. I will never hurt myself. Raina had an illness that went undetected. There was nothing you could have done to stop her. Nothing. Do you hear me?"

"I do."

"But you don't believe me?"

"It's my worst fear." Charley took a shaky breath. "I feel completely out of control. Just like when I planned this quick trip. When I was travelling, I felt better because I was doing something useful. I was coming here to help you. To be with you in case you needed me. But once I got here, and we started talking, it all came tumbling down on me."

"I'm here. I'm right here. And I love you, too. Are you listening to me?" Charley gave a tiny nod and Jada continued. "You don't have to be scared with me. Together, you and me, we can take on the world. We're a couple of kick-ass women. No one can go up against us and win."

Charley smiled, accepting the humor and the sincerity of her words. "Like a pair of superheroes."

"Heroines. You and me, kid. Against the world."

"You suck at movie quotes."

Jada rolled her eyes. "Whatever. I'm still cooler than you. That's an established fact. But right now, I'm going to use my superpower and do something for the greater good."

"Oh? Can I ask what it is?"

Jada opened her arms. "I'm going to hold you until you're not scared anymore."

Charley gave her a small grin. "It might take awhile."

"I've got enough time. In fact, I've got all the time in the world. But my superpower is pretty strong. I imagine you'll feel better right away."

Charley leaned forward, and the moment Jada's arms surrounded her, she felt the fear subside. "Your superpower is awesome."

"Totally."

****

The next morning, Jada slipped her hand into Charley's as they got off the hospital elevator. She'd arranged to have Charley meet the whole family at once and get it out of the way. They'd had something close to breakfast, but Charley was too nervous to finish it. Jada felt bad she was about to shove her family onto Charley.

She squeezed Charley's hand and knocked softly on the door frame as they entered Celeste's room.

Anton, as usual, was seated closest to Celeste. He leaned on the bed, laughing at something on Celeste's tablet. Their mother was currently MIA. Celeste looked up first, and her face beamed as her eyes rested on Charley. She held her arms out, and said, "Get over here and greet me with a hug, Charley. That's how we do it in our family."

Charley's face glowed with embarrassment, and it was adorable. Jada stood back to watch her hug Celeste and shake hands with Anton. "It's nice to meet you both. How are you feeling today?" she asked Celeste in her most polite voice.

Celeste quirked an eyebrow at her. "I'm good. Don't be so formal. What's she told you about us? Did she say I'm a snob or something? You've seen my house, right? Normal suburban people. K?"

"Normal. Suburban. No snobs. Got it." Charley laughed. "Anything else I need to know?"

"Mmm. Probably not. Oh, wait. I should tell you my husband is a nerd."

"Hey," Anton said by way of a half-hearted protest. "Am not."

"Totally are," Celeste and Jada chorused.

Charley laughed harder. "I think you lost that one, dude."

"I always do," Anton said. "I work in IT and speak a language neither of them can figure out. So I'm the family nerd, to be ridiculed until some piece of expensive electronic equipment malfunctions and my services are required."

"Wow. You said it out loud," Jada said. "Did you rehearse that?"

Celeste said, "I think he saw it in a movie." She ruffled Anton's thick, tight curls and smiled. "But hey, you're my nerd." She then put her hand over her belly. "And this is our little nerd. Or doctor. Or whatever. I don't care."

Anton kissed Celeste's belly. "Me either. Stay in there until you're all done. Then I promise to be the best daddy in the world." He had his head on her belly and suddenly sported a big grin. "The baby kicked!"

"Yeah," Celeste said. "Every time he talks to the baby, the baby kicks. I can't decide if that's a 'Hey, hi, Dad' kick or a 'Leave me alone' kick."

"It's a 'hi, Dad' kick," Liselle said as she entered the room. "You did the same with your father."

"I did?" Celeste asked, a sweet smile forming on her face. "You never told me."

"You never asked." Liselle turned to Charley. She held out her hand and shook Charley's with her strong grip. "You're Charley?"

"Yes, ma'am."

"I see." Liselle's gaze went to Charley's left hand. "How long are you here for?"

"Just the weekend. I'm on light duty and have to be back Monday afternoon."

Liselle turned her attention to Celeste. "I need to see a patient. I'll be back in an hour. Text me if anything changes. I want to be here when Doctor Van Dyne shows up."

"Sure, Mom." Celeste watched her leave. "Who the hell was that?" Celeste asked when Liselle was gone. "Anton, you're the nerd. You need to find the pod with the real Liselle in it."

"No way. The nerd always dies. Make Jada do it."

"Nope. Not happening. I don't care if there is a pod. Mom's not in super bitch mode."

Celeste smiled and grimaced at the same time. "I think the baby agrees. But I do wish they'd stop kicking."

Jada stepped closer and put her face against Celeste's belly. "Calm down in there. If you do, I promise to spoil you, love you, and give you a ton of sugar, then hand you back to your parents. But we won't tell them until it's too late. Deal?" Jada felt the baby move around and kissed Celeste's belly.

"There. Auntie Jada fixed everything," Jada said.

"No sugar," Celeste said.

"No sugar. That's all you got out of that?"

"That's enough. You'll be a very bad influence."

"Or a damn good one." Jada plopped down on the chair beside Celeste's bed. She motioned Charley to sit in the chair beside her. "So, let's start the influence now, shall we?" She grabbed the TV remote and started searching the grid. "Find some amazing sci-fi, superhero, ass-kicking movie. Teach you to grow up to be awesome."

Celeste sighed and settled against the pillows at her head. "You suck."

"You'll never know," Jada muttered and smiled at the way Anton tried very hard to ignore them. He had his computer up and going and was probably trying to work, but she knew he was totally listening to them. "I'm going to be the best auntie ever."

"Anton, honey," Celeste said, her voice fairly dripping with sweetness. "Is it too late to sell the house and move?"

"Move where?"

"Wherever Jada isn't."

"We already live where Jada isn't," he said. "She's going home soon. The baby'll be safe."

"Oh good."

Jada laughed. "C'mon over here, Sarge. Let's settle in and watch a movie. You up for it?"

"You bet," Charley said, taking Jada's hand into hers. "What are we watching?"

"*Star Wars*," Jada and Celeste chorused then burst into giggles. "It's our favorite movie. We used to stay up all night and watch the original trilogy. Mom would get so mad when she found out Dad let us do it."

"How many times have you seen them all?" Charley asked.

"Is it too many if the number is over one hundred?"

Charley shook her head. "No way. It's one more thing to love about you."

Jada couldn't contain the huge smile on her face. She kissed Charley and then chuckled when Celeste started making kissing noises.

"Get a room!"

Jada raised an eyebrow at her. "Um, you done took my room, remember? All I got is a blow-up bed."

"I can tell you where to find a cheap hotel," Anton said, not looking up from his computer.

Celeste faked her shock. "And how do you know where there's a cheap hotel?"

"Um, I just did a search on Google."

"I love you, nerd," Celeste said.

Chapter Twenty-One

Jada dropped Charley off at the airport late Sunday night. Their visit was short but incredibly productive. Jada felt lighter and the kiss they shared before Charley headed into security was—memorable. She could still feel Charley's lips capture hers, Charley's hands cupping her face, and Charley's body pressed up against hers. Charley's grin was downright evil as she strolled away.

It took the entire ride back to Celeste's for Jada's body to calm down.

Now it was Monday morning, and she stood in Celeste's room while Doctor Lisa finished her exam, wrote a few notes in Celeste's chart, then addressed Jada and her sister. Anton was at home, hopefully asleep, but Jada had a bad feeling she'd need to wake him up.

"I want to schedule a C-section. Your blood pressure is up, and the abruption is worsening. You're at thirty-five weeks tomorrow, so I'm sure the baby will be fine. It's a bit underweight, but we can deal with that. I don't want to wait any longer."

Doctor Lisa was compassionate and it showed in her sharp, blue eyes as she waited for Celeste to respond. Jada took hold of her sister's cold and trembling hand. "Hey," she said, getting Celeste to focus on her. "It's going to be fine. I'll call Anton if you want."

"No. Let him sleep," Celeste said, her voice soft and shaky. "When do you want to do this?" she asked Doctor Lisa.

"Tomorrow. I'll get my schedule adjusted and secure the OR." She came around to the other side of Celeste's bed, now opposite where Jada stood. Doctor Lisa's focus was completely on Celeste. "You know the risks with a premature birth, so I won't go into it. But you also know I wouldn't do this if I thought you could wait."

"I know. Thanks. It's—I should have expected it might be

sooner rather than later. I'm kinda shocked right now."

"I understand. Call whomever you wish to. If you need me, have the nurse page me and I'll get here soon as I can. We got this. Deal?"

"Deal." Celeste gave her a smile. She waited until Doctor Lisa was gone before she turned to Jada with teary eyes. "This sucks."

"Hey, she said we got this. And we do, little sister. I'll get myself into the OR if you want me there. Anton will be there, and I'd bet you a million dollars Mom finds a way to scrub up and assist."

"No way I'd take that bet. You'd win." Celeste sniffled. "I want babies so bad, Jay. What if this is the only one I can have? What if something goes wrong and—"

"Nope. No way in hell are you allowed to talk like that. This is the first of those babies you want. Just the first. You're going to have as many as you guys want. You hear me?"

Celeste nodded. Her hand covered her mouth as a sob escaped.

Jada sat beside her on the bed and embraced her as she cried.

When the flood of tears abated, Jada released Celeste and handed over a box of tissues. "I'll call Mom first. You know Anton's going to be pissed we didn't call him right away, but you're right, he needs some sleep." She kissed Celeste on the cheek. "It's going to be okay."

"You don't know that."

"You don't know it isn't." Jada left the bed to dig her cell phone out of her backpack. "And I refuse to think it won't. I might not want babies of my own, yet, but I sure want to have yours in my life."

"Is your life always going to be in the wilderness?" Celeste asked. The question surprised Jada almost as much as her immediate answer.

"I don't know, but I'd like it to." She shoved the phone in her back pocket.

"I'm going to be selfish and say I don't want you to stay up there. I want you here so we can go to lunch or meet for coffee or hang out. I want you to see my babies born, play with them, spoil them." Celeste gave her a tremulous smile. "But if you and

Charley can make it work, really work, I'll be happy for you. You'd be a great mom, Jay. I mean it."

"I'd be a terrible mother."

"Nonsense." Both women turned to the doorway as their mother strode in. Liselle immediately went to the chart at the end of Celeste's bed and started reading it.

"Nonsense?" Jada asked.

Liselle muttered something then put the chart away. "Yes. Nonsense. You're a loving, caring woman. You're strong, independent, and wonderful with children. How could you not be a great mother?"

"I never thought I'd hear you say that," Jada said.

"I'm sure you didn't." Liselle walked to the opposite side of the bed and kissed Celeste on the forehead. "I didn't want to stop at two children, but it's all we got. Not for a lack of trying, mind you. I didn't think I wanted children when I married your father. We decided to let fate choose for us, and if I got pregnant, then fine. If not, also fine. Even though your father wanted a lot of children. He was, however, perfectly fine with two."

"I don't think you've told us this much about yourself in—ever," Jada said. She stared at her mother in awe, watching as the face that always looked so stern began to soften. What the hell was happening?

"You may not want children right now, Jada. But you'd be surprised how quickly it can all change. Don't discount the possibility."

"We'd probably adopt."

Liselle said, "Nothing wrong with that. Didn't you tell me Charley's adopted?"

"She is."

"There you go. Adopt and give some children a home who might not have one otherwise. Or find a sperm donor. Either way, I'll be happy to have more grandchildren. Even if they live in the wilderness."

"You're serious?" Jada had to sit down suddenly. Was her mother in menopause or something? Was all this because of Celeste's pregnancy? A few months ago, she was all pissed Celeste quit her job to be a mom. Now she couldn't wait for her first grandkid? And she wanted lots more? Jada felt like the world was tilting off its axis. She hadn't been listening and now caught part of her mother's conversation with Celeste.

"...I'm proud of you. You've done so well and you'll be fine tomorrow. I spoke to Doctor Klein in the hallway before I came in here. She is going to allow me to be there as long as I promise to not interfere." Liselle glanced at Jada. "You can be there, too, but we have to keep out of the way. If that's what Celeste wants." She looked back to Celeste, who had an expression Jada figured must mirror her own. Confusion mixed with shock.

"Of course I want you there, Mom. I wanted the family with me from the start. I didn't think I could make it happen. Besides, someone needs to be there for Anton. He's going to freak out when he sees the blood."

"We'll take care of him. You take care of yourself. I need to go because I've got surgery in an hour. But I'll come back when I'm done to check on you." She kissed Celeste again and stopped beside Jada on her way out. "Call me if anything changes."

"I will, Mom. Thanks."

"I love you both," Liselle said and left.

Jada's mouth gaped open. She eyed Celeste doing the same. "I always heard being a mother changes you. But being a grandma? I honestly never expected her to be like this, but I'm not arguing."

"Me either. I need her and I'm glad she's trying so hard." Celeste started crying again, and Jada reached for the box of tissues. "I'm sorry I'm a blubbering idiot right now, but she said she's proud of me. Do you know how much I've wanted her to say that instead of things like 'why didn't you do a surgical residency?' or 'how could you possibly give up a career you've barely started?'"

"Right there with you," Jada said. Her phone vibrated and she grabbed it up, seeing a text from Charley. "Sarge finally made it back to Whitehorse." She sent off a quick text back.

"She's good for you, Jay."

"I know."

****

Josie gave Charley a fierce hug the moment she stepped

out of her car at the pickup point outside the airport. She took Charley's duffel bag, tossed it into the hatchback, and took off once they were both settled into the front seat of her Hyundai. "You look tired," Josie said.

"I am. The weekend wasn't restful. Jada and I—we had a tough time of it, Mom. It's a long story, but the important bit is we love each other."

"Whoa. You love each other?"

"Yes. Very much."

"I'm so very happy to hear you say it out loud. Your dad and I've been betting each other on who would get to hear it first." She grinned from ear to ear. "Heh. I win that one."

"So you do," Charley said. "I know it sounds sappy, but I'm ready for another try at being happy. With Jada, I feel like it'll be different. Like she's the real deal, and we're going to make it work."

Charley's phone rang. She grabbed it and answered before she realized it was a video call. Jada's smiling face filled her screen, and she had to return the gesture. "Hello there."

"Hey." She stopped speaking as if she didn't know or couldn't find the words to say next.

Charley asked, "Is Celeste all right?"

"Huh? Oh, yeah. I mean, no. I mean, she's going to have a C-section tomorrow. Doctor Lisa doesn't want to wait any longer, and she's confident the baby'll be okay. Celeste is thirty-five weeks as of tomorrow, and the baby'll be underweight, but they can deal with that."

"I wish I was still there. I can probably arrange for a flight on Tuesday or Wednesday, but I have to check in with Pike first."

"It's fine. No worries. The whole family is going to be there with her. If you can make it up here for the weekend, I won't complain." Jada looked around herself for a few seconds. "I love you. I needed to see you, and I needed to say it to your face. Technology is kinda cool sometimes."

Charley felt the flush in her cheeks and knew her mother was smirking, but she didn't dare look. Instead she put her full attention on the beautiful face in front of her. She longed to stroke Jada's cheek. Feel the soft curls of her hair. Wrap her arms around her and hold on forever. "I love you, too," she eventually said. The comment brought a smile to Jada's lips.

"I missed you the second you disappeared through security."

"Same," Charley said. "I'm almost home. How about we talk some more when I get there? Do you have time for that?"

"I'll make time. Besides, Celeste is asleep and Mom's at work."

"Perfect. I'll call you back soon."

"Bye."

Jada's face disappeared, and Charley put her phone away. She was pretty sure she heard a snicker come from her mother.

"Feel free to tease me, Mom. You know you want to."

"You're adorable. I'm your mother so I'm probably biased, but you two are adorable. She brings out the real you, Charlene."

"She does?"

"Totally. I haven't seen you smile or laugh this much in years. You're playful. You go out a few times a week. You've been hiking I don't know how many times this summer, and you just flew thousands of miles to spend a day and a half with her. I've never seen you this happy." Josie stole a glance at Charley and said, "Not even with Raina."

"I feel like a new person with her, Mom. I think she's the love of my life."

"Me, too."

Chapter Twenty-Two

"I'm a slob," Jada said in way of greeting when Charley called her later that day. They were doing another video chat, and Jada was lounging on the couch at Celeste's, exhausted from the day. At least her mother was being nicer to Celeste. Enough so, she decided to spend the night with Celeste, kicking both Jada and Anton out of the room. Anton was asleep upstairs, and Jada was unable to sleep yet.

"Hello, you, too," Charley said with a laugh. "What brought this on? The flights all sucked, by the way, but at least I'm home."

"I figured as much, goober. I was thinking about how very tidy your apartment is. My apartment is one giant room, and I'm pretty sure I left a pizza box on my kitchen table. With pizza still in it."

"Eww. That's got to be rank about now."

"Completely. See, I'm a slob. I thought you should know. We should know stuff like this about each other."

Charley nodded. "Okay. Well, I'm not OCD about being clean, but I've never been a slob, as you figured out. I like to watch movies, but I do most of it during the winter season when there's less stuff to do outside. I am kinda obsessed with going to the gym. If I can't get there, I get out my set of dumbbells and work out at home."

"I've never dated a woman who enjoyed going to the movies. It's one of my most favorite things to do. I love my action/adventure stuff, but romcoms are a personal fave."

"I can do romcoms, but I admit to fantasizing about being the male lead. Not like there are a ton of lesbian movies—or movies with aboriginal people."

"True that," Jada said. "At least we got black people on screen more now. But it sucks there's not so much diversity. I'd love to see lesbians of color up there some day."

"Me, too." Charley was apparently sitting in her kitchen

and got up for some coffee. Over her shoulder she said, "I want kids someday. Not a ton of them like Liv and Gracie, but maybe two or three."

"I think I could manage it eventually. I kinda got a little envious of Celeste the other day. She's getting exactly what she always dreamed of. A family. I can't wait to meet the little person inside her belly."

"I'd love to be there for that. I did get to help a woman deliver her baby once. She was stranded on the highway because her car ran out of gas. We didn't have time to get her to the hospital, and the baby came five minutes before the ambulance arrived. I was freaking out."

"I've helped ten babies into the world. One of them was stillborn, and it was the most heart-wrenching thing I've ever had to do." Jada paused while Charley got settled at the table again. "This job can suck your soul dry. You know what I mean?"

"Yes, but you won't let that happen. You're much too good a person, Jada. You'll never become hardened by it."

"How can you be so sure?"

"I can see it in your eyes," Charley said. "You've got this light—it's hard to explain, and if Stefi were here, she'd take over for me. You have to trust me. I can see it. It's one of the many things I love about you."

"Many things? How many things?"

Charley leaned a little closer to the camera and winked. "So many I could never name them all. But someday I hope to show you."

Jada swallowed hard. Damn. The woman had the ability to turn her on from thousands of miles away. With a look and a wink? "You're mean."

"Maybe." Charley moved back so she was sitting up straighter. "Tell me more things about yourself. Do you like to read?"

"No. Most of what I read are medical journals and course materials. I have to do a lot of classes to keep up my certification, and every year I'm in some kind of course. I'd like to be an instructor someday though."

"Instructor of what?"

"All things paramedic," Jada said. "I know I can do it. It was offered three times back in Ottawa, but it wasn't the right time for me. In Whitehorse, however, I think it might be a good fit. I'm not as busy with calls, and it'd give me something else to do."

"I like the sound of that. You making plans for a future in Whitehorse."

"I do, too." Jada gave a little laugh. "I never thought I'd stay there very long. When I first moved to Whitehorse, I hoped it was temporary. Like a few years temporary. Until the dust settled on the crap with Nancy. I know I could get my old job back the second there's an opening. Or maybe work for the fire department until then."

"And now?"

"You know the answer. Now I've got a reason to stick around." Jada closed her eyes, wishing Charley was right there beside her. "I want to kiss you."

"Ditto. We'll do plenty of that when you get back. I promise."

"Have you always been so upstanding? Did you ever do anything you got into trouble for? I mean, I was a hellion."

Charley's laugh was pleasant, and it made Jada miss her even more. It didn't sound as deep and resonant over the phone. "Never. I was a good kid. My parents set their watches by me. If they said be home at six, I was home at six. If I said I'd be at a place by four, I was there at four. It never once occurred to me to do something bad or make trouble. My cousin, Mike, on the other hand, wasn't so much a hellion as he was an idiot. Got into a lot of trouble because he had idiot friends. I got a lot of practice bailing him out."

"Was he the one you hung around with most?"

"No. I mean, we hung out sometimes, but he's like an annoying brother to me. I hung out with other kids who were also Tutchone, trying hard to feel like I fit in. They looked like me, except I'm weirdly taller than all of them. I never got treated badly, but I didn't ever feel like I had a place I belonged in. I had a few other, superficial, friends, but the only person I ever confided in was Gracie. I don't think I told Raina half the stuff I told Gracie.

"One time when we were in our teens, I was on the phone with Gracie so much and for so long my parents almost lost their telephone line. The bill was over four thousand dollars."

"Holy shit, Sarge!" Jada clapped a hand over her mouth, hoping she didn't wake Anton. "This was before the long distance stuff was free, I guess?"

"Yep. I had a crush on a straight girl who slapped me when I tried to kiss her. I was devastated. I cried so much over her. When my parents found out why the phone bill was so high, they forgave me, but I had to work off the money by doing a ton of jobs around the house. I was grounded for two months. I can't tell you how glad I was when they got a free long-distance plan so Gracie and I could talk as much as we wanted to."

"Didn't her parents freak about the phone bill?"

"No. It was free on her end." Charley laughed. "She's so good to me she offered to send me her savings. A hundred dollars I think. I wouldn't let her."

"I like her. It hurt when you wouldn't talk to me, but even though I was mad at you, a part of me was glad Gracie was there for you. You're lucky to have her."

"I am. Like you have Celeste."

"I love you."

A slow grin spread across Charley's face. "I love you, too."

"It's scary, though. This being in love stuff," Jada said. She kept her eyes on Charley, who managed to catch her gaze. They didn't move for a long time.

Charley said, "It is. But it's worth it. Every heartache, hurt feeling, misstep—it's all worth it when you've got the right person. You're my right person, Jada."

"Right back atcha." Jada stifled a yawn. "I think I need some sleep. I'll call you tomorrow."

"Rest well. G'nite Jada."

"Nite, Sarge." Jada disconnected and placed the phone on the floor. She closed her eyes and dreamed of snuggling up to Charley all night long.

****

Charley was awakened by the phone ringing. She wasn't expecting a call from Jada until tomorrow and instantly worried something went wrong with the C-section. Jada's smiling face filled the video chat screen. "Hey there. Everything okay?"

Charley asked.

"Spectacular," Jada said, sporting the biggest grin Charley'd ever seen. "I want you to meet someone." Jada's face disappeared as the phone was moved around, and Charley saw Celeste and Anton, their smiles equal to Jada's. Celeste held a tiny baby close to her chest and cradled it gently.

Her eyes were watery, and Charley felt her own well up. "Hello there."

"This is Noah," Jada said. "He's six pounds three ounces of adorableness."

"Nice to meet you, Noah," Charley said, not feeling the least bit silly to be greeting a baby via a video chat. "I take it everything went well?"

Celeste nodded. She looked pale and tired, but happy. "No problems at all. He came out with a little yell, like he wasn't ready yet. Check-up went great, and we'll be going home in a couple of days."

"Congratulations."

"Thanks," Anton said as he kissed his son's forehead.

Jada was quiet while she moved away from her family, though Charley noticed she was still in Celeste's room.

"Your sister looks great. I'm so glad everything is okay now."

"Me, too. There were a few issues during the C-section, but Doctor Lisa handled them. I can't believe I got to see such a beautiful little man come into this world."

"You look as exhausted as Celeste."

"I am. Well, maybe not as much as her, but I'm dead on my feet. If I sit down, I'll collapse and wake up two days from now," she said with a humorless laugh. "So much is going on, Sarge. I hardly know where to begin."

"Why don't we start tomorrow? After I talk to Pike. I have a feeling I'll be able to make arrangements to get to Ottawa this weekend."

"You don't have to," Jada said, her gaze on someone in the room. Probably Celeste. "I'm being kicked out and sent back to Whitehorse. By order of my family. All three of them. Mom is going to stay with Anton and Celeste for a few weeks while they get Noah settled in."

Jada paused and again Charley sensed she wasn't telling

her something.

"Mom thinks it's best I get back home and back to my normal routine. Apparently, I've been a little stressed."

"Well, you've not been sleeping. It's obvious."

"You really know how to charm a girl," Jada said.

"Just telling it like it is. But if you'd rather stay there, I'll come to you. Doesn't matter to me one bit. I need to be with you."

"Same. I'll be home next week. Let's wait until then, okay? I promise to call you every night before I go to sleep. There's so much we need to talk about, but it's still better if we do it in person. Ya know?"

"I do. I love you."

Jada smiled, and this time it reached her eyes. "I love you, too. Bye."

Chapter Twenty-Three

One week turned into two because Jada's mom wasn't able to get all her surgeries covered. That was fine with Jada as it meant more time with Noah. She'd seen a dozen or more babies brought into the world and not always in the most desirable circumstances or locations. But holding Noah, smelling him, feeling his soft skin on hers—was indescribable.

She'd actually laughed when people said babies smelled good. But they did! Or maybe she was biased. Didn't matter. It was hard enough to let Celeste hold Noah to feed him. Jada had an urge to keep the boy in her arms forever. Like he belonged there. What the hell was she going to do when she had to go back home tomorrow?

"Hey," Celeste said quietly, putting Noah down for his nap.

Jada'd been watching her feed him and hadn't realized Celeste was done. Celeste nodded toward the door. They quietly left the nursery and walked into Celeste's bedroom. Jada said, "He's so beautiful, sis. I can't believe he's here. I can't believe I can touch him and cuddle him and that he's real."

"Of course he's real, Jay. Did you think I was fake pregnant?" Celeste asked with a chuckle.

"Ha-ha. You know what I mean. I guess I'm still super excited he's here."

"Me, too. I wake up and come in here to sit by him and stare. So much drama for such a tiny human, but he's here and he's healthy and I'm a mom. It's overwhelming and amazing and scary all at once."

"But you're ready for it, right?"

"I have to be. Doesn't matter if I am. And now that it's happened, I can see why people say you're never actually ready to be a parent. Not until you're holding your child for the very first time does it all seem real. You're responsible for creating this tiny human and taking care of him. It's huge."

"It is, but you got this." Jada hugged Celeste. "I know I'm attached to the little guy in the other room and don't want to leave him yet."

"But?"

"But I have to go back to Whitehorse. It's where my life is now. I'm so in love with her. I thought I was in love before, but I wasn't. Not even close. It's like I can't breathe if she's not in the same room as me. How crazy is that?"

"It's how it is with me and Anton. Have you told her?"

"That I love her? Sure."

"That you feel incomplete without her?"

Jada narrowed her gaze at Celeste. "Overly dramatic much?"

"In love much?" Celeste bumped shoulders with her. "Jay, look her in the eyes and tell her. She'll get it. All she has to do is see you when you talk. You light up and get all glowy. She'll believe you."

"I hope so." Jada stumbled over her next words, knowing how they would sound to Celeste. "I want to marry her."

"Whoa. You lesbians move fast."

"I know and I've made so many mistakes before, but this is different. I know it is. Okay, so this is TMI, but we haven't even had sex."

"Huh?" Celeste opened her mouth, but nothing came out for a few seconds. "I'm serious, now. Did you have a head injury I don't know about? I mean, I don't know of any woman you've ever dated who you didn't have wild monkey sex with like on the first date. And Charley, I mean, whoa. If I was gay, I'd be all over that. So what's up?"

Jada couldn't look Celeste in the eyes and turned her gaze to the doorway of the nursery. "She doesn't want to have sex until she's married. She was married once before, and they waited until their honeymoon. She was the only woman Charley ever slept with."

"You're for real?"

"Yep." Jada looked up at her. "She's serious. It's very important to her. I don't get it. Not at all, but I have to honor her wishes, right?"

"At the risk of sounding like an asshole, what happens if you're not compatible? What if sex with Charley is awful, and you have no chemistry?”

“Oh, there’s no problem there. We’ve got plenty of chemistry. Trust me. She can rev me up with a look, and I can’t tell you how much time I’ve spent with myself since we started dating.”

“Um, okay, we just landed in the overshare department.”

“We’re talking about sex. I think we passed the TMI line a long time ago.”

Celeste shook her head vigorously. “Fine. You’ve not had sex with Charley, just yourself. Does she know?”

“I’m sure she can guess it all by herself. Besides, does it matter if we’re not so great in the sex department?”

“Do you want me to answer that seriously?” Celeste asked.

“I think it’s rhetorical. Let me put it this way—sex with Charley is not a priority for me. I know how batshit crazy it sounds. But it doesn’t bother me one way or the other. I want to be with her all the time. I want to make a life with her. Sex is sex. If we finally get to that point, I don’t doubt it will be amazing. I don’t mind waiting to find out, either.”

“Wow. You’ve changed. It’s like I’m just now getting to know you.”

“Maybe I’m just getting to know myself.”

“As long as this is the right choice for you, I’m behind you 100%. But if she breaks your heart, I will fly up there and kick her ass.”

Jada laughed. “That’d be something to see. I think she’s half a meter taller than you.”

“Height doesn’t matter if you know where to place your punches.” Celeste smirked and Jada laughed harder.

“I love you, sis.”

“I know.”

Jada hugged her tightly. “I need to get packed. You take a nap and yell if you need me.”

“I will, and Jay,” Celeste said as Jada was leaving, “I meant what I said the other day. She’s good for you.”

“I know.”

****

Nervous energy kept Charley pacing her living room. Jada would arrive at any minute. While they'd done several video chats and at least one phone call per day, it wasn't even close to being together in person. And it would happen very soon. Charley looked at her watch, not surprised Jada was late.

Why was she so nervous? Their relationship was better, stronger, than it'd ever been. Even though she knew Jada kept something from her, Charley didn't get the sense it was a bad thing. They loved each other, and those three little words came out every time they talked. Like neither of them could say it enough.

The waiting stressed her out. The pacing increased until she heard a timid knock on her door. Charley was there in an instant, and the moment she opened the door, her arms were full of Jada. Charley nuzzled her neck, breathing in the sweet scent of her skin, holding her close and reluctant to let her go. Though she had to in order for Jada to come into the apartment.

"Hi," Charley said, once the door was closed. They stood in front of each other, gazes locked for a long time. "Flight home okay?"

"Yeah." Jada licked her lips, and the action stirred something deep in Charley.

Charley took a step forward, meeting Jada halfway in a crushing kiss, that nearly sent Jada off balance. Charley grabbed her upper arms and kept her upright as the kiss became something more. Something so heartfelt and emotional tears trailed down Charley's cheeks.

The kiss stole her breath, and when they stopped, they held each other's gaze again and Charley saw the love in her heart reflected back. Words couldn't describe what she felt right then.

Jada gently pried herself from Charley's grip. She reached out, cupped Charley's face, and wiped a tear away with her thumb. "I love you, Charlene Townsend."

"I love you, too."

"Good, because I want you to know the last two weeks were miserable without you. I can't tell you how many times I wanted to ask you to come to Ottawa. It was selfish really, because Celeste needed me and it wouldn't have been practical for you to come, but it didn't stop me from considering asking you to come over."

"I'd have been there in a heartbeat."

"I know. It's one of a thousand reasons I love you."

"A thousand?" Charley raised one eyebrow, and it brought a smile to Jada's kiss-swollen lips. "Tell me what's on your mind, baby. Whatever it is, we'll deal with it together."

"I know we will." Jada's hand left Charley's face and rested over Charley's heart. "You've got the biggest heart of any person I've ever met. For a while there, I didn't think I'd be able to convince you how much I love you. I mean, you can say the words, but people don't always mean them. And there's levels of love, right? I love my sister and my friends. I love Noah and Anton and my mom, but that love doesn't compare to what I feel for you."

Charley opened her mouth to speak, but Jada placed a slim finger against her lips. Charley got the hint and waited, even though she trembled with the anticipation.

"I've thought about this more than I should have, but I've always either been completely impulsive or put too much thought into something. I killed the idea before it could happen. But not this time. I'm not being impulsive, and I've thought enough about this to know it's the most important thing I'll ever do."

Jada reached into the pocket of her jeans and pulled out a shiny, silver band with a single, tiny, diamond, which she slipped onto Charley's left ring finger. "Sarge, will you marry me? Will you accept my offer to give you the family you deserve? To love you for the rest of our lives? To cherish you the way you were meant to be cherished?"

Charley, for the first time in her life, was shocked speechless. She looked down at the ring on her finger, which fit perfectly, then her eyes went back to Jada's. She was biting her bottom lip and holding Charley's hand gently in her own. It was a dream, right? Charley would wake up any second and find she'd fallen asleep waiting on Jada.

But in her dreams, she'd never kissed like they just did. Nor did she ever remember feeling tears on her cheeks. Tears ran like a river along the contours of her face. Jada's eyes watered as well.

How could she answer this beautiful woman's question? She was everything Charley had ever dreamed of. And even though she'd been considering asking Jada this same question, she was having trouble responding.

Images of Raina flooded her mind. She had to close her eyes to get rid of them.

Raina was a long time ago. She was nothing like Jada. What Charley felt for Jada was stronger than her bond with Raina. She loved Raina—had been in love with her—but with Jada things were different. Jada was stronger, livelier, and spontaneous in ways Raina never was.

It felt wrong to be comparing the two women right then, but Charley couldn't help it. She'd been the one to pop the question with Raina, so she'd been ready to take the next step with Jada. She wanted to marry Jada, but her brain didn't want to process the information.

After what must have felt like hours, Charley opened her eyes to find Jada's fearful gaze meeting hers. Charley resolved to never break this beautiful woman's heart again. No matter what, she'd offer her the world. Or at least her corner of it.

Charley lifted their connected hands and kissed Jada's fingers. "You are the love of my life. I don't want to imagine a moment without you in it. Forever. Yes, I'll marry you, Jada Deveraux. I love you." Charley leaned forward and placed a sweet, gentle kiss on Jada's lips, feeling her smile as she did.

"You had me there for a minute."

"You surprised me is all. My brain had to catch up on what was going on." She kissed Jada again, this time languidly, taking all the time in the world to explore her lips, tongue, allowing her hands to roam to Jada's perfect ass. When they parted again, Charley said, "Besides, I was going to ask you to marry me anyway. But I don't have a ring yet."

"Cool. I like how I beat you to the punch."

Charley wiggled the fingers of her left hand. "How'd you know what size ring to get?"

"I might have called a certain red-haired lady." Jada laughed softly. "She was so accommodating she went with me to pick it out. That's why I was late. You like it?"

"I do. It could have been anything, and I'd have liked it."

"There's an inscription on the inside," Jada said. "Have a look."

Charley removed the ring and held it up to the light. It read, "I love you." Charley smiled and put it back on her finger. "Cute."

"I thought so." Jada snuggled against her and rested her head on Charley's shoulder. "So, what's next?"

"I'm sure my mom has already started planning the wedding."

"She'll have to get in line behind my mom," Jada said. "She started planning the wedding when I called her from the airport. I thought she'd freak out since we haven't been together very long, but she was all for it. She's been civil to me since Noah was born, and I don't know what to do with that. When I called to tell her I was planning to ask you to marry me, I was expecting to have to explain why. She didn't seem surprised and started in on where we'll have it and who to invite."

"Maybe we should go to the courthouse, make it legal, and be done."

Jada laughed and hugged Charley a little tighter. "The idea has its merits, but let's not. It's the first time in years my mother has been this nice. I don't want to piss her off right now."

"Okay. They can plan it, and we'll show up," Charley said.

"Perfect. Why don't we spend the rest of the day celebrating in private? I'm sure by the time we're done there won't be a person left in the territory who doesn't know our good news."

Jada gave Charley a kiss that told her exactly how happy she was.

****

Grace held Liv's hand as they walked into the house. The news had her reeling, and as soon as they were inside, she plopped down on the couch. Liv settled next to her and wrapped her arms around Grace. Liv said, "I can't believe it. It's so surreal."

"I know. I didn't expect it to happen so soon. And now it is—and it's real and we're doing this." Grace turned to Liv. "We're really doing this!"

"May I ask what we're doing?" Harry ambled in and settled on the recliner.

"We're pregnant," they chorused and broke into a mix of tears and laughter.

Grace said, "I didn't expect it to happen so soon. This is our second try, and the doctor told us it might not happen, but it did. *Ojiichan*, we're going to have a baby!"

Harry looked at them each in turn and broke out a smile that didn't fit his face. "I'm so proud of you two. And very happy for you. Congratulations. Do your parents know?"

Grace shook her head. She left Liv and knelt beside Harry's chair. She took his gnarled hand in her own. "We wanted to tell you first. It really hit us when we got home. Liv's pregnant. We're going to have a family together. I can hardly believe this is happening."

Harry softly stroked her cheek. "You will make wonderful mothers. I'm very proud of you both, but especially you, Gracie Lee. You've come so far in the last year."

"Thank you." Grace kissed him on the cheek. "*Ashitimas*."

"I love you, too. But you're going to have to sit down for what I need to tell you next."

Concern took over as Grace carefully watched him pick up an envelope on the table next to his chair. "Is everything okay?"

"You tell me." Harry opened the letter and handed it to her. "You can read all the details there, but the short version is Carly pled guilty to get a lesser sentence. She'll be in jail here for twenty-four months and then deported. Once she's in the US, she'll face charges for using a false ID and a few other things. Point is, she will be going to jail once more. With any luck, you will never see her again."

Grace fell back on her butt and nearly passed out. The air left her and she looked up at Harry's smiling face and reminded herself to breathe. Liv was by her side and took the paper from her to read it herself. "It's over?"

"It's over," Harry said. "So now you have one more thing to celebrate. Why don't we have a party? We can invite Olivia's parents over, Charley and her parents, and her fiancée, Jada. It would be fun."

Liv gave Harry a big kiss and said, "Hell yes! We'll get all our friends over here and have a massive party." She touched her stomach, and Grace swore she was glowing. "Dammit, life is good right now."

Grace pulled Liv on top of her and wrapped her in a tight embrace. "It most certainly is."

****

Charley made her rounds of the party, showing off her engagement ring. She wasn't into jewelry at all, but this was one thing she had to show off. Her mother found it adorable; Jada found it sweet. Charley didn't care either way. She was too happy.

Eventually the number of guests dwindled, and Charley took a moment to get some fresh air. She stood in Grace's backyard, staring out at the sunset. Orange and yellow painted the horizon, slipping out of sight as darkness descended. In her busy life, Charley rarely had a chance to enjoy the simplicity of nature. Even her hikes had gotten fewer and fewer through the years.

She flexed the fingers of her left hand, satisfied she was indeed making progress. But when she did return to work it would be with a new outlook on things. Gone were the days she worked until exhaustion took over. She would do her shift and leave on time as often as possible. No more extra shifts. No more hiding away where she didn't have to face the world or its harsh realities.

The ring caught the last vestiges of the sunlight as she turned her hand over. She had reason to enjoy life again, and she planned to do so to the best of her ability. Forever.

Charley heard someone step outside and was pleasantly surprised when Jada's arms snaked around her waist. Jada leaned her chin on Charley's shoulder. In Charley's ear, she whispered, "It's a beautiful night. Want to go for a walk with me?"

"I'd love that." She turned around to face Jada. "I'm ready to do more than take a walk with you." Charley held up her hand and wiggled her ring finger. "I'm ready to build a life with you."

"And we're going to. I promise you. We'll have a house, kids, picket fence, minivan, the works. As long as I got you, I'm good. And our life is going to be fucking amazing."

Charley had to laugh. "Are you sure we can't elope?"

"Positive." Jada leaned closer and softly, sweetly, kissed Charley's lips. "In the meantime, I'll be here making sure you know how much I love you. Every day of your life. I'm doing this for me, but I'm also doing it for you."

"For me?"

"Of course for you. Why else would I give you a ring? You have a big heart, Sarge, and I will take care of this precious gift for as long as I live."

"I don't know what to say."

Jada kissed her softly, sweetly on the lips. "You don't say anything. Take me home and hold me tonight."

"Forever."

About the Author

Patty is the Goldie Award-winning co-editor of *Blue Collar Lesbian Erotica* with Verda Foster. She and Verda also coedited *Women in Uniform: Medics and Soldiers and Cops, Oh My!* and *Women In Sports*. Her first novel, *Souls' Rescue* was a finalist for the Ann Bannon Popular Choice Award. Patty is a retired paramedic and currently resides in The Netherlands with her wife, Sandra, and their kitties. Visit her website at www.pattyschramm.com

Books by Patty Schramm

Sara's Choice
Book Two In the Romance In the Yukon Series

Sara Hyatt knows what it is to be in love. She's been there, done that twice in her life. The second time she was sure would be the last. She'd found the woman that owned her heart; except that woman chose to stomp on it instead.

Now Sara's single again and attracting interest. Problem is, neither woman is Terry.

Terry Alexander moved herself and her daughter to Whitehorse, Canada to live with her mom, after realizing she couldn't continue on her own in Quebec. She never expected she'd ever date again, much less fall in love. She never expected to meet Sara Hyatt. When she did, she fell hard. Until she was forced to break up with her. Now she sees her on every street corner and she aches to talk to her. But Sara isn't exactly inviting her over for coffee.

Can she find a way to convince Sara that she still loves her and they should be together, or end up spending the rest of her life alone.

Ultimately, it's Sara's choice. Will she choose her true love? Or will she settle for the love of someone else?

A lesbian romance about forgiveness and learning to find your way home.

ISBN 978-1-949096-18-7
eISBN 978-1-949096-19-4

Finding Gracie's Glory
__Book One In the Romance In the Yukon Series__

Gracie Kato survived years of abuse at the hands of her wife. While her body has healed, her heart and soul remain damaged. Gracie seeks solace at her grandfather's home in the Yukon Territory of Canada. There she'll be able to work at his gold mine, named for her grandmother, Gracie's Glory. It's the perfect place for her to start over again.

Liv Templeton's heart was crushed years ago and she doesn't see any chance of recovery. She's never alone unless she wants to be, but never seeks any commitments. Instead she puts all her energy and time into running the family mining business.

From the moment they meet, Gracie and Liv's connection, physical and emotional, is obvious to them both. Is Liv ready for a serious relationship? Even if she is, will she be able to convince Gracie to trust again? To let her soul heal? Will Gracie open herself up to Liv? Or will she close her heart forever?

ISBN: 978-1-949096-15-6
eISBN: 978-1-949096-16-3

Reflections of Fate

Leoni Wolf lived and worked on the Qualla Boundry in Cherokee, North Carolina her entire life. It was her home and the place she belonged. Leoni once believed in fate and that everything happened for a reason. Until her wife, Tayanita, was killed in a tragic accident. What possible reason could there be for her death? The event shattered Leoni's world.

Each day Leoni awoke, gazed at her reflection in the old free-standing mirror and convinced herself she could get through one more day.

Nicola Daelis was tired of fate intervening in her life and wanted to throttle her. Before Nicola could act on the event that could change it all, fate landed a beautiful, dark-eyed woman in her lap and turned Nicola's world upside down.

Fighting for their lives, and often against each other, Nicola and Leoni must embark upon an adventure that could be the beginning of something new. Or the end of them both.

ISBN: 978-1-949096-12-5
eISBN: 978-1-949096-13-2

Better Together

Mac Bradenton has never been south of the Mason Dixon Line or across a body of water wider than the Ohio River. But her best friend is sick and on a quest to complete her bucket list. First stop is Paris, France. Mac goes along expecting to enjoy the time with Kristy, never anticipating just how much her life will change.

They meet up with Kristy's friend, Lenie, who has promised to give them a guided tour of Paris and while there, romance blossoms between Mac and Lenie.

Once home, life takes some major turns for Mac. As she struggles to deal with the challenges thrown at her, will everything fall apart? Or will she be able to lean on Lenie knowing that, no matter what happens, they are better together?

ISBN: 978-1-949096-09-5
eISBN: 978-1-949096-10-1

Souls' Rescue

Kelly McCoy is a firefighter and paramedic who's lived most of her adult life in New York. After 9-11, she relocates to Cincinnati, nursing a broken heart and looking for a new start. She takes one day at a time, trying not to let her losses overwhelm her.

Talia Stoddard is an insurance wiz who's always been smart on the job, but unlucky in love. After years of being told that she's too big, too tall, too black, too lesbian, and not a very snappy dresser, Talia has resigned herself to a life alone with only her dear gay friend Jacob for a diversion.

When Kelly and Talia's lives crash into one another, it's under the most stressful and threatening circumstances. Talia is in terrible danger, and it's up to Kelly to rescue her. In the horrendous situation they end up in, neither expects to find a friend, much less a soul mate.

Will they rescue one another and heal the wounds of their pasts? Or will they both continue to believe that they're not worthy of the kind of love the other might offer?

Souls' Rescue is the story of opening up to love, taking chances, and building a life that everyone dreams about, but few people ever find.

ISBN: 978-1-949096-06-4
eISBN: 978-1-949096-07-1

Because of Katie

Siobhan Landry's granddad had one wish before he died. That she would travel from their small town in Indiana to the place of his birth in southern Ireland and become the artist he knew her to be. She never expected how much her life would change when she got there.

Katie O'Briain nearly lost her life, but that couldn't stop her from doing what she's always loved—being a marathon runner. However, no matter how much she pushes herself, or convinces herself life is good, there's something very obviously missing.

But Katie has a lot of scars and even though her attraction to Siobhan is immediate, can she bare those scars to the lovely American?

Siobhan also feels that attraction. Will she be able to move beyond her broken past and let Katie heal her heart?

Or will the scars they both hide keep them apart forever?

ISBN: 978-1-61929-380-9
eISBN: 978-1-61929-381-6

Love Is In the Air — w/Nann Dunne

Love Is in the Air is a collection of romantic short stories about   love that comes to us in different ways, different forms, and in ways we   might never suspect. Whether we feel worthy or not, love is there. And   it will find us all.

ISBN: 978-1-61929-278-9
eISBN: 978-1-61929-362-5

Women In Sports: Sweaty, Sexy and Hot, Oh My! — w/Verda Foster

Women in Sports: A collection of romantic and erotic tales.

Hot. Sweaty. Tight shorts. Sports bras. Six-pack abs. What sparks your imagination? Muscular legs? Hands that are strong and sure? Baseball, soccer, hockey, track and field...does it really matter? She's sexy, she's incredible and she's all yours. Sit back, relax and enjoy some wonderful tales from this group of talented authors. Women in sports—does it get any better than that?

This amazing collection of romance and erotica includes stories from: Lee Lynch, Jessie Chandler, Mary Griggs, MB Panichi, Tonie Chacon, Kate McLachlan, A.L. Duncan, Jeanine Hoffman, Erica Lawson, Sharon G. Clark, Nann Dunne, Pat Cronin and Verda Foster.

ISBN: 978-1-61929-278-9
eISBN: 978-1-61929-279-6

Blue Collar Lesbian Erotica — w/ Verda Foster

Blue Collar Lesbian Erotica is a collection of stories about the average lesbian in hot, steamy encounters in not-so-average places. Santa and her elf, a tryst in an oil mechanics pit, or what nuns really do in the convent, this anthology goes outside the norm.

Several talented authors have joined together for this collection of erotica including Karin Kallmaker, Radclyffe, Ali Vali, Kate Sweeney, Verda Foster, Vada Foster, Trish Sheilds, Nann Dunne, Sammo, Cheri Crystal, Pat Cronin, Georgia Beers, Anne J. Kingsley, MJ Williamz, Kathy Smith, and Victoria Oldham.

ISBN: 978-1935053019
eISBN: 978-1-61929-045-7

* 9 7 8 1 9 4 9 0 9 6 2 8 6 *